ALL DRESSED IN WHITE

D1255578

By Charis Michaels

The Brides of Belgravia
Any Groom Will Do
All Dressed in White

Coming Soon
You May Kiss the Duke

The Bachelor Lords of London
The Earl Next Door
The Virgin and the Viscount
One for the Rogue

ALL DRESSED
IN WHITE

A Brides of Belgravia Novel

CHARIS MICHAELS

GLOUCESTER COUNTY LIBRARY
389 WOLFERT STATION ROAD
MULLICA HILL, NJ 08062

AVONIMPULSE
An Imprint of HarperCollinsPublishers

This is a work of fiction. Names, characters, places, and incidents are products of the author's imagination or are used fictitiously and are not to be construed as real. Any resemblance to actual events, locales, organizations, or persons, living or dead, is entirely coincidental.

ALL DRESSED IN WHITE. Copyright © 2018 by Charis Michaels. All rights reserved. Printed in the United States of America. No part of this book may be used or reproduced in any manner whatsoever without written permission except in the case of brief quotations embodied in critical articles and reviews. For information, address HarperCollins Publishers, 195 Broadway, New York, NY 10007.

Print Edition ISBN: 978-0-06-268584-1
Digital Edition ISBN: 978-0-06-268581-0

Cover design by Amy Halperin
Cover art by Fredericka Ribes

Avon Impulse and the Avon Impulse logo are registered trademarks of HarperCollins Publishers in the United States of America.
Avon and HarperCollins are registered trademarks of HarperCollins Publishers in the United States of America and other countries.

FIRST EDITION

18 19 20 21 22   HDC   10 9 8 7 6 5 4 3 2 1

If you purchased this book without a cover, you should be aware that this book is stolen property. It was reported as "unsold and destroyed" to the publisher, and neither the author nor the publisher has received any payment for this "stripped book."

For Amy Hughes Thompson, who really was all dressed in white once upon a time but now wears every color. Big love for you, my dear friend.

ALL DRESSED IN WHITE

Tessa St. Croix was not a natural-born liar.

She was a charmer, perhaps. A flirt. A minx-y, chattery coquette. A reckless taker of risks. But a liar? A natural liar?

Not particularly. Not smoothly or boldly or effectively. Not without feeling as if the acid of the lie was burning a hole through the underside of her heart and her spirit was slowly leaking out.

Lying was a challenge for Tessa, perhaps because of her parents, who had always given her everything her heart desired, and her four brothers, who had doted on her since birth. Hers was a charmed existence, simple and expected and fun. On what occasion did she have to lie, considering all this?

The lies (or rather, the failed lies) began in October of 1830, when a trio of marriages swept the village of Pixham in Surrey like a crisp autumn wind. Tessa was one of three local girls, all friends, all with dowries well over £10,000, who sprinted down the aisle in less than six weeks' time.

"And married to who?" the gossips had asked. Because the men rode into Pixham, bold as you please, made the acquaintance of Tessa and her friends, and before anyone could say, "And from where do you hail, sir?" they were betrothed to the girls, then married, then . . . *gone*.

The girls' immediate removal from Surrey was perhaps the most alarming bit. The brides were uprooted after their weddings and installed in a townhome in London, in the posh new neighborhood of Belgravia, while the three grooms sailed out of the country. The friends made a life for themselves together in London, the so-called Brides of Belgravia, while the men pursued a foreign venture that promised to make them richer than their wildest dreams.

The first girl to marry and leave Surrey was Miss Sabine Noble, Pixham's great beauty. Sabine had always been sharp-tongued and proud, and in the scheme of things, her hasty marriage caused the least alarm. It was said that she had not been the same since her father died, and when a domineering uncle moved in to look after Sabine and her mother, no one expected her to remain in Surrey for long.

The next friend to marry was Lady Wilhelmina Hunnicut, the daughter of Pixham's highest-ranking peer. As such, Lady Willow married the only titled gentleman of the lot, an earl from Yorkshire, with a castle and ancient ruins and mines of coal. Despite the speed of their union, a young earl marrying the daughter of a peer was not so very odd, after all.

But the last of the friends to marry was our own failed liar, Miss Tessa St. Croix, and the gossips of Surrey struggled with the whys and hows of this marriage for years to come.

Some said Tessa had grown weary of courting country gentlemen, of their hunting and horses and dogs. Some said she cast one glance on her handsome groom-to-be and fell in love at first sight. Others said her father influenced the match, because the young man she married was a London shipping merchant with grand plans, and Tessa's father was a lucrative shareholder in the West India Docks.

But the real reason Tessa St. Croix married a man she barely knew (and the reason the gossips would never learn) was that she was ten weeks pregnant on the day she walked down the aisle.

Or, perhaps it would be more accurate to say Tessa *assumed* she was ten weeks pregnant. Ten weeks was her most prudent guess. In truth, she was vague about the date. Vagueness was, in fact, the pervading view of her pregnancy overall. She could no more understand the schedule of her changing body than she could explain how the pregnancy came about. One moment she had been up against a tree, kissing Captain Neil Marking, handsome and charming and newly garrisoned in Surrey; and in the next, her skirts were hitched up and the kiss had gone sloppy and toothy and she was trying to find the breath to cry out.

By the time she found her voice, it had been altogether too late. The captain was beyond hearing. Her attempts to push him away were as futile as pushing away the tree. Five minutes later, he had whispered what a good girl she had been and how happy she had made him.

The irony of those affirmations had been Tessa's clearest memory. Because six weeks later, when she sought him out to inform him of the baby, he had said the opposite.

"You're a very bad girl, aren't you?" he said. "And I'm very disappointed. Why, you're just like all the other very bad, very disappointing girls, Miss St. Croix."

After that, he had bowed briskly, backed away carelessly, and softly closed the door in her face. Three days later, his regiment left Surrey for the Isle of Wight.

In Tessa's estimation, the conception of the child plus Captain Marking's rejection had taken, all told, ten minutes. In the months that followed, as Tessa's petite body had swelled into pregnancy, she could not really say what had happened—not during that strange mix of fear and shame against the tree, and not in the cold, breathless shock of the garrison stoop.

The only thing she knew for sure was that the man she married two months later was not the father of the baby, and that he knew nothing of her condition.

And that had felt like a very great shame—a larger shame, perhaps, than the troubling predicament of the captain and the tree and the baby. It was a shame because she had ended up liking her new husband, Mr. Joseph Chance, very much.

The notion that Mr. Chance might *want* Tessa and another man's baby had not even crossed her mind. In this, Captain Marking had taught her the lesson she would never forget. No one, Tessa thought, could know of her pregnancy.

Not Joseph Chance, not her parents, not the doctor who had been summoned to treat the unexplained nausea that plagued the early days. And so she endeavored to lie. And if Tessa had been able to sustain the lie of her unborn baby—if she were a natural-born liar—her new husband never would have known.

But Tessa St. Croix was not a natural-born liar.

CHAPTER ONE

Before . . .

The first time Joseph Chance saw Tessa St. Croix, he was leaning against the fence post across from Gibson's Mercantile, trying to guess which young woman coming and going was his future potential wife.

His business partner Cassin had provided her name, and his other partner Jon Stoker had learned her schedule for the day. This included delivering flowers to sick villagers, some errand to do with a church piano, and ribbon procurement in Gibson's shop. It was an innocuous list, virtuous even, but Joseph elected to view it as matronly and boring and expected to see a short, spotted spinster with flat feet and a limp.

He missed her arrival to the mercantile by ten minutes, and now he had no choice but to wait. The delay grated, as his trip to Surrey had amounted to little more than awkward failure, and there was so much real work to be done in London.

They'd come to Surrey at the prompting of an advertisement that promised "a modest fortune" in finance capital for their next import venture.

"Wealthy investor seeks suitable candidates for dispersal of modest fortune," the advert, posted on the docks in Blackwall, had read.

But when they sought out the "wealthy investor" in Surrey, they had discovered it was not one man—not a man at all—but three young women. And the "modest fortune" was their dowries.

Joseph had no interest in marrying for money—hell, he had no interest in marrying at all, not at the moment—but after traveling all this way, he'd grown curious. Before they returned to London, Joseph would have one quick look. His partners, Cassin and Stoker, had done the same.

It was impossible, of course, to watch a young woman emerge from a shop and know whether or not he might marry her, but certainly he could know whether he could absolutely not marry her. That is, he could quickly rule her out, which he absolutely intended to do. Just one quick look, that's all it would take.

"Pray do not punish her, Mr. Gibson. She is only doing her job."

Joseph looked up. A woman's voice spilled from the open shop door, followed by musical laughter. Not the polite tinkling of mild amusement, but an honest-to-God laugh, full-bodied, surprise and delight spun together. Joseph shoved off the fence post.

The shop door was vacant except for a large cat. The animal marched into the sunlight with a rodent in her mouth. Behind the cat came a corpulent shopkeeper, light on his feet despite his size, with a broom held high. The laughter persisted from inside the shop, more of a giggle now, and then Tessa St. Croix stepped into the bright light of the Autumn sun.

She wore a pink dress and red bonnet, and her arms were laden with parcels. Joseph stepped toward her as if someone had called his name. He stared. The sunshine was suddenly too bright and he shielded his eyes.

Her laughter had stopped but her face was lit with a relaxed smile. She watched the cat disappear around a corner. The shopkeeper grumbled and waved his broom. She made some comment, laughing again. The older man turned away and applied the broom to his stoop.

Joseph forgot his position of anonymity and walked to the edge of the road. All thoughts of boredom and matrons fled. He was . . . riveted. This girl was like an actress, bathed in light, standing on a stage. The combination of the bright dress and the easy smile and the stack of parcels cast her in the role of Village Beauty. No, Gentleman's Daughter. Damsel. Fair Maiden.

She had creamy, fair skin, carefully protected by the brim of her bonnet and high gloves. Her eyes were light—summer blue—with blond hair, two smooth braids looping like thick yellow ropes.

The pink of her dress was almost too sweet, and the crimson ribbons were a garish contrast, and yet somehow it was the prettiest dress and bonnet Joseph had ever seen. She looked like a confection. A birthday present. She looked like something Joseph had not expected but that he suddenly wanted very much.

Joseph glanced down at his own rumpled suit and dusty boots. He'd brought a change of clothes, of course, a fine suit—they'd planned to meet a proper investor in Surrey—but when the investment came to nothing, he had not bothered. He swore in his head. Of all the times to look like a plowman. Cassin and Stoker teased him about his Italian barber and expensive tailor, and yet look at him now.

The bell on the shop door jingled again, and the shopkeeper retreated inside. He and the girl were alone with only the road between them. Joseph swallowed hard. He swiped his hat from his head and ran a hand through his sweaty hair. He considered and rejected ten different greetings. He wondered if she might greet him. Could anyone so radiant on the outside, he wondered, be tedious or petty or simple within? The answer, of course, was *absolutely*.

The likelihood of radiant beauty and tedium or pettiness or simplicity was quite high.

Even so, Joseph's heart raced. He said nothing, he watched her look up and down the street. Finally, she turned her head, and their eyes locked.

Her smile was instantaneous, an open, guileless, authentically happy smile. The smile of someone who had just found something she'd been looking for.

"Hello!" she called cheerfully. Her voice was confident but casual. She sounded very much at home, comfortable in the sunny street, in her bright dress, in the role as greeter of the mute man who gawked at her from the center of the street.

"Hello," Joseph finally said.

He should also say *how do you do?* he thought. Gallantry was as important to him as fine clothes and good boots. He should introduce himself. He should take her parcels. Instead, he stared silently, barely breathing, waiting to see what she would do next.

"I seem to have misplaced my brothers," she called and she laughed again. "They were meant to drive me home in our carriage. Clearly I spent too much time in Mr. Gibson's shop." She shrugged and the ribbons on her bonnet fluttered.

"May I assist you with your parcels?" he called. His plan to observe her from afar now seemed irrelevant.

"Oh, but I could not trouble you." Her smile grew brighter. He began walking to her, crunching on the gravel of the road in long, sure strides. She watched him with what felt like anticipation. She watched him like someone waiting in line to meet the king. Joseph had experienced many reactions from women in his life, but no one had ever stared at him like that.

When he reached her, she said, "But I've not had the privilege of making your acquaintance, sir."

Her face was even lovelier at close range. And she smelled like a flower. Every flower. She smelled like every flower and the very best flower.

"Are you, by chance, Miss Tessa St. Croix?" he said.

"But I am the very one," she laughed, looking up at him. Joseph's heart stopped.

He began to unburden her of her parcels, and she relinquished them easily, no suspicion or faux protest.

"But you'll forgive me because I cannot say I know your name," she said. "Or have we met?"

"No," he said. He shook his head gravely. He felt suddenly, deeply serious. He shuffled the boxes. All at once, the weight of the moment seemed too important and life-changing to be cheerful.

"My name is Joseph Chance," he said. "My partners and I have just arrived in Surrey from London. We are . . . responding to an advert."

Her smile dissolved and she made a little gasp.

Yes, he thought. *Gasp*. That reaction seemed exactly, perfectly right. *Whatever you do, please do not go.*

He said, "My partner, the Earl of Cassin, has already spoken to your friend, I believe. Likewise, I could not resist seeking you out. Forgive me. There was meant to be a formal introduction, but . . ."

Slowly, her smile changed. She looked . . . delighted. His name was familiar to her. She knew why he'd come. And her reaction was delight. His heart surged.

She said, "Mr. Joseph Chance. I'm pleased to make your acquaintance. But are you . . . ?" She let the sentence trail off.

The next words were out of his mouth before he'd fully thought. "Your future husband," he said.

"Are you, indeed?" she laughed. Her voice was a frothy combination of a gasp and smile and something else.

Falling back on years of practiced charm and manners, Joseph winked. He smiled down at her with what he knew to be a very popular smile. "Shall we discuss the advertisement while I help you locate these brothers?"

Chapter Two

The potential of Joseph Chance-Future Husband hinged on whether he would call to Berymede the next day. If he called, Tessa would allow herself to hope. If he did not, the momentum would be lost, the attraction they felt in Pixham would dissolve, and Tessa would . . .

Well, Tessa was not sure what she would do. The worst thing about Tessa St. Croix's condition was the persistent, terrifying question, *What am I to do?*

She lay awake at night, heart pounding, and tried to predict what would happen if she did nothing at all, if the pregnancy became obvious and her family discovered what she had done.

Banishment immediately. Disinherited completely. Turned out with no way to provide for her baby or herself.

Such specific threats had never been made—who could have ever guessed she'd find herself in this situation—but Tessa *knew*. She knew in the same way she knew she would not survive a fall from a high cliff. She'd had a girlhood of stumbles to prove her mortality.

Only a harlot would find herself in this situation.

We would never recover from the shame.

A condition worse than death.

Not in this family.

She'd heard years of comments about village girls, cautionary tales of distant shamed cousins, reactions to certain young women brought around by her brothers. No one had to say the words; Tessa was well aware.

Purity had always been her parents' highest goal for their only daughter, followed closely (and ironically) by allure. Tessa was meant to be a paragon of chastity *and* beauty, with no partial credit for beauty alone. What was beauty if she could not hold at bay the men she attracted? Beauty used in service to baser instincts was not beauty, it was craven. It was ruined.

Considering this, perhaps Tessa was more desperate than confident that Joseph Chance would call the morning after they met. Perhaps she willed it to happen. Really, she had few other choices.

And anyway, he'd said he would. Calling had been *his* idea. Even so, they had only spoken for twenty breathless moments as they walked the high street of Pixham, looking for her brothers.

Although twenty minutes had been long enough.

On the walk from Gibson's store to Alabaster's Tea Emporium and back, they had established two very promising things: a mutual interest and a loose plan.

The plan was for Joseph to call on her and seek permission from her father for a courtship. Tessa had objected at first, insisting that she be the one to smooth the way with her parents, to make the introductions, to do the talking, but he refused. He would not be managed. He would approach her father formally and ask permission properly.

As to mutual interest, Tessa was so far and away more interested than ever she planned to be. Joseph Chance was a stranger who answered her friend's advertisement, and she had long since reconciled herself to the certainty that any stranger elicited by the advert would be terrible. Old, tedious, and petty were three of the better assumptions held for any man solicited by the advertisement.

Instead, Joseph was clever but not silly, masculine but not arrogant, attentive but not oppressive or clingy. And he was so very handsome. The opposite of old and tedious. Young, golden, tall, with broad shoulders and long legs. He smiled and his eyes wrinkled at the edges. His hand swallowed hers, but not aggressively, not clinging. Gently, carefully. From a crowd of fifty men, even a hundred, she would have chosen him every time.

Joseph Chance was so superlative, she struggled to trust her good fortune. The advert needed only elicit a man desperate enough to marry her and then detached enough to sail away from her.

And yet this was the man who came to call? A strong, gentle Adonis who was not intimidated by her vibrant personality and whom she did not want to go?

As for *his* attraction to *her*, Joseph Chance stared at her like she was a pin on the globe, like the world spun around her.

As if handsome and clever and confident had not been enough.

When he turned up on Berymede's front stoop by eleven o'clock the next morning, she thought only this: *As if handsome and clever and confident had not been enough.*

From her vantage point on the stairwell landing, Tessa found it difficult to separate gratitude from delight.

He swept inside, the consummate gentleman, greeting her parents with bows and handshakes. His attire and bearing were as fine as any of them had ever seen, even her mother, who made a study of the finery, and her brother Lucas, whose own meticulous tailoring and grooming was second to none. As promised, Joseph requested time alone with her father.

The door to the library closed, and Tessa shrank back, counting to ten. She listened, she said a quick prayer, she waited. Nothing. Silence. After five minutes, she slunk away.

In her room, the maid tried to distract her with various accessories—ribbons for her hair, a broach, a fan—but Tessa refused. She'd worn a pale dress, fawn-colored, with the barest hint of a golden thread. If yesterday's pink dress had turned Joseph's head, the gold dress of today was designed to make him unable to look away.

She'd held her breath while her maid buttoned her up, praying the gown still fit. Her middle thickened a little more each week. If the girl had noticed, she made no comment, thank God. Tessa and her friends had virtually no way to discover what to expect from the early stages of pregnancy. Sabine was an only child, and Willow had only older brothers. No one among their neighbors or families had welcomed a new baby for years. Pointed questions felt risky, like a suspicious level of interest, and so the three friends had simply guessed. Their best calculation put the baby's arrival in late spring. The sooner Tessa found a husband, the better.

"Miss St. Croix?" Ten minutes after Joseph's arrival, the Berymede butler knocked gently on her open door. "Your parents have summoned you to the garden, if you please. They are with the gentleman caller."

"The garden?" Tessa repeated. The garden was her mother's sanctuary, used almost exclusively for family gatherings or entertaining her closet friends. First-time callers were never invited to the garden.

And yet, Joseph Chance had been. He was seated beside her father and across from her mother in the autumn sunshine. He rose smoothly when he saw her.

"Miss St. Croix," he said. His smile was mild, but he shot her a knowing look. She felt a somersault in her chest.

"Mr. Chance," she said.

Her mother would expect Tessa to be poised and aloof, a little unattainable. But she struggled not to stare.

If she'd found him handsome the day before, with dusty hat, rumpled hair, and wrinkled suit, today he really did look like a prince from a book. He wore snug-fitting buckskins and a blue coat of the finest wool. The pattern on his waistcoat brought out the blue in his eyes; his cravat looked as if it had been sculpted in marble.

Tessa blinked, recovered, and then smiled demurely. It was no secret how he'd earned his mother's invitation to the garden. Appearances meant everything to Isobel St. Croix, and Joseph Chance's appearance said two things: *I matter*, and *You want me*.

Yes, Tessa thought, *I do want you*.

"Ah, yes, here she is now," her father called. "Tessa, you've finally stumbled upon a young man with some actual mettle and ambition. It's about time, I daresay." To Joseph he said, "No father should suffer the procession of worthless dandies who have paraded through my house."

Tessa blushed. Had it really been a *procession*?

Her father asked her, "I understand you are in the acquaintance of this gentleman?"

"Indeed, I am, Papa," she said, leaning down to kiss her mother's proffered cheek. "We met yesterday. In the village. He has business with Lady Willow's family."

Joseph nodded smoothly, endorsing the fiction. Her first earnest lie, and she'd made him complicit. She told herself it was for the baby. Everything was for the baby.

"I do value fine horseflesh," Joseph improvised, "but my primary business is importation of goods to England from around the world. This is the partnership I mentioned earlier. My associates and I are working on a new venture—in Barbadoes, no less—about which I am very hopeful."

"The devil you say?" said Tessa's father. "But did Tessa's

brothers tell you that we are shareholders in the West India Docks in London? I sit on the board, in fact. We see vessels from Barbadoes every week. But will you reveal the details of your venture?"

And then they were off, discussing ships and levies and imports. Joseph spoke confidently, his experience and intellect plainly clear, while her father asked pointed questions and nodded along. When her mother asked about imported silks, Joseph recited the names of fabrics and dyes and sellers from the Orient and then guessed at the source of the silk of Isobel St. Croix's morning dress. While Tessa's mother enthused her delight, Tessa smiled down into her cooling cup of tea.

You will never tell him.

The thought, previously hovering somewhere in the back of Tessa's consciousness, now loomed fully formed in the front of her mind. The second lie.

Or was it less of a lie, and more an . . . omission?

For the baby.

He came, she reminded herself. *And Maman and Papa like him, and I like him. If he will consent to marry me, I will give my body to him, and there is no reason to tell him that the baby does not belong to him.*

She repeated again, *You will never tell him.* Her palms began to itch, but she ignored them. *Never, not ever.*

She could do this. She would do it.

"But would you two like to take a turn around the garden?" her mother trilled. Tessa looked up, nearly spilling her tea.

"A turn?" she asked.

Her mother narrowed her eyes. It was neither charming nor blithe to repeat questions like a parrot, and she knew better. From the earliest age, her mother had taught her the art of sparkling conversation, and Tessa was expected to use it. So very much had been expected of Tessa. So much.

"That is, I should be delighted," she corrected. "If Mr. Chance is so inclined?"

"It would be a pleasure," said Joseph. He rose and affected a small bow. While her parents smiled on, he collected her from her chair and asked her to choose a pathway. The Berymede gardens were a web of walks and hedges, the envy of the county. Tessa chose a winding path secluded by a wall of junipers, and they walked in silence until they were a safe distance on.

"Thank you for coming," she said finally. She slid her hand to his and scooped it up. "Truly."

He looked down at their joined hands and then up at her. "I hope there was no doubt," he said.

She shook her head. He was steadfast, she'd seen that immediately. She'd known he would come. She thought about telling him how much his steadiness impressed her, but it was imprudent to gush. She must not do anything too much or too little. She must do everything exactly right.

She said, "Does it shock you that you answered an advert from a strange girl and yet we . . . seem to get on so well?"

"Define shock," he teased.

"Oh, you know . . . speechless, wide-eyed, frozen. Shocked." She lifted her eyes from the path to his profile.

She wanted desperately to stare openly, to take inventory of each detail on his face.

"If I am those things, it is my reaction to you—not the random luck of a random advert."

Another somersault in her chest.

"I am keenly susceptible to beautiful, charming women," he said, "and you, Miss St. Croix, may just be the most beautiful and most charming girl I have ever had the unearned fortune of meeting. If anything, I am surprised that a girl as lovely as you should be forced to advertise for a husband." He looked down at her with raised eyebrows. He waited.

Tessa nodded quickly. She and her friends had expected this. Her friends, however, assumed she would simply tell him the truth. He would receive her £15,000 dowry in exchange for accepting her pregnancy. It was meant to be a fair and open trade. She and Joseph would part ways after the wedding and rarely, if ever, see each other again. This had been the arrangement struck by her friends and their convenient grooms.

But her friends had not been paired with Joseph Chance.

Joseph had the potential to be so much more than one half of an open trade; he had the potential to be a real husband. In every way. She wasn't prepared to put that unbelievably lucky potential at risk, and talk of a baby could only scare him away. It had scared away Captain Marking. If her parents knew, it would horrify them—they would disown her. How much more ruthless would a near-stranger be?

"Oh, that," she said. "Well, my friends are determined to move to London, you see; and I cannot bear to be left behind. My parents would never allow me to go alone. The three of us have been planning to make our lives in London together since we were girls. And now Willow has the opportunity for an apprenticeship and Sabine must escape her terrible uncle, so they will go for certain. I cannot be abandoned in the countryside while they . . . while they have all the fun."

He considered this silently, and she added, "My family is lovely, but they stifle me. With four older brothers, I shall always be viewed as a child. I've waited many years for an opportunity to be an adult person with a life beyond Surrey. Even so, the advert was . . . sort of . . . a lark for me honestly. And then you came along . . ."

There, she thought. *I've said it.*

And none of it was a lie, not really. If it was, it would be her third. Three lies. Tessa shut out the growing number.

Joseph continued to study her and she pressed, "So we are in . . . agreement?"

"In agreement . . ." he repeated. "Is that what we shall term our . . . ?"

He smiled in a way that caused Tessa's insides to expand and resettle. She wanted to laugh and tease, to draw the moment out. She wanted a real courtship that allowed them to become truly acquainted. She wanted to fall in love. But her future was at stake, the future of her child. She stayed the course. She wanted to hear him say it.

"Our *arrangement?*" she provided. "My dowry goes to your venture. And your, er, proposal comes in exchange?"

He stopped walking and looked down at her.

"I'll be honest with you, Miss St. Croix," he began. "May I call you Tessa?"

"Absolutely," she blurted. She cleared her throat. "That is, yes, please."

"Tessa," he repeated. "If I'm being truthful, I sought you out yesterday also on a lark . . ."

Tessa sighed. "Yes, we placed the advert on a lark, you answered on a lark, you sought me out on a lark. It's all a great lark—"

"Until it's no lark at all," he cut in. Tessa held her breath.

He said, "That is, until I saw you. From that moment, I've scarcely been able to believe my incredibly good fortune. Was it a lark or was it . . . fate?"

She opened her mouth to speak but he cut her off. "I've not stopped thinking of you since the moment we parted in the village," he said. "I am beguiled and dazzled by you." He narrowed his eyes. "Does it alarm you to hear me say this?"

Slowly, as if in a daze, Tessa shook her head.

He continued, "Unless I am sorely mistaken, unless I cannot trust my unerring instincts—which are always right, by the way—yes, we are in agreement."

Tessa closed her eyes and said a silent prayer of thanks.

"Should I take your closed eyes and tense expression to mean that you are quietly reconciling yourself to me?" he teased.

She laughed and blinked up at him. "No, no. Take them to mean that you have made me very happy."

He nodded and turned again down the path, leading her along. The silence was charged with a playful, uncertain anticipation. Tessa cleared her throat and said, "Were you aware that practically no one outside the family is invited to my mother's garden for tea? No one. Clearly my parents are impressed."

"Is that so?" he said and whistled. "Honestly, I cannot believe I was admitted to the front door. Your home is lovely, by the way."

Tessa glanced at the green, stately beauty of her mother's gardens. She'd never cared less about Berymede. "Thank you," she said, and she snuggled more tightly to him.

Joseph licked his lips. "I'm in trouble."

"Why?" A shy smile.

"The expression on your face."

"And what expression is that?"

He hesitated for a moment, and then he leaned in, so close Tessa could smell the musky scent of his soap. He whispered, "The suggestion that you would like to see more of me than my face."

Tessa knew she should gasp, she should go rigid or pull away. Instead, she swayed closer. Her face hovered just inches from his; she looked up from beneath lowered lashes.

"Perhaps I do," she whispered.

He swore then, a soft frustrated oath, and then swiped his lips across her mouth. Once, twice.

Tessa closed her eyes, allowing the feeling of what she wanted and what she needed to intertwine and wrap around her. She felt safe for the first time since the tree. Perhaps she had never felt so safe.

A bird called in the distance, and Joseph cleared his

throat. He swore again. Before she had even opened her eyes, he was tugging her down the path.

"Miss St. Croix," he began.

"Tessa," she corrected.

"Tessa. There is one essential thing that I did not fully explain to your parents, but I will. First, I should like you to know."

Oh, let us not reveal bald truths, Tessa thought, but she nodded.

"It was my intention to present myself as a gentleman today. To dress and speak like an educated man of means and breeding."

Tessa nodded again. No description could be more accurate.

He went on, "In many ways—my house in London, my carriage, other trappings of dress and comportment—these all suggest that I am, indeed, a gentleman. But be aware . . ." and now he stopped walking and looked down at her ". . . that none of these are *inherited* possessions. They have been earned. By me. By my own hands—hard work, wits, and ambition."

He paused, watching for some reaction. Tessa was confused. She shook her head.

He went on, "In fact I have very little family to speak of, and my start in life was very humble. Please . . ." he faltered again ". . . be aware. I alluded to your father that I was a self-made man, but I did not tell him just how far I have made myself."

"How far is that?" And now she was really intrigued—but also worried. Her parents would struggle with the notion of *humble*.

He stared out at the field beyond the garden. "I began life as a servant, Tessa." He looked back, his blue eyes fast on hers. "I was . . . a serving boy, a footman, a groom, and valet all rolled into one. I served a man who would become an earl. My mother had been a lady's maid to this man's mother."

"A servant," Tessa repeated.

She was endeavoring to arrange her own marriage to a former servant.

My parents will never consent if they know, she thought.

If they know.

The heap of half truths continued to grow. Three? Four? Tessa felt herself begin to sweat. She looked again at the smooth wool of his jacket, the fine leather of his boots. His face was like that of an angel. He was as handsome as any man she'd ever met, and yet now she noticed a handful of marked distinctions. The strength of his build—the physicality in his movements, powerful and deliberate. There was no loll or lazy graze to his touch. When he brought her hand to his arm, he took it firmly, placed it securely. When he walked, he strode. When he looked, he stared.

He was not a blithe observer of life, he was an achiever. He came across as capable most of all, and she was shocked by how much this thrilled her.

It would not, however, thrill her parents.

"Are you alarmed?" he asked. "Does it put you off?"

She shook her head, not trusting her voice. "No. Not put off. I am impressed." This was the truth, she was impressed. But her parents? Dear God.

She said, "But how did you . . . ?"

"How did I come up in the world? The story is not so riveting, I'm afraid. The earl for whom I worked saw some potential in me beyond servitude and hired tutors to educate me."

"Of course he did," she laughed. "What else would an earl do when faced with such potential?"

"Well, it was a sacrifice, because I was a valuable servant. You should see the polish I put on a pair of boots."

His tone was light and teasing. He was so very confident, even about this. Especially about this.

She said, "Not only a servant but a skilled one."

"I am nothing if not skilled." Another wink.

Tessa felt her cheeks go hot. She'd known she would flirt with him today, but she had not anticipated how effectively he would reciprocate. She put a hand to her throat. He was . . . irresistible. Irresistible and totally unsuitable for her parents' expectations.

"But the earl spared you as valet?" she prompted. She would hear it all and determine some way to frame it for her parents. Or conceal it.

"Before I was educated, one of my roles was as the earl's . . . sort of . . . arms bearer, I suppose you'd call it."

"His what?"

"He was a bit of an adventurer, and I worked in his service when he traveled abroad. While I was an excellent valet,

I believe I was even handier in a fight. There were years in Greece when our lives were rougher than . . . well, than life in his London townhouse."

Tessa was fascinated. A fighter in Greece? Yet another detail her parents need never know, but she herself would squirrel it away to savor when she was alone.

"In any event," he went on, "when the earl insisted that I begin daily lessons, it became clear that my brain was the asset to pursue. One tutor turned to two, then three. The older I got, the more my household duties fell away. Eventually, the earl sacked me as servant and sent me to university instead."

"Unbelievable," Tessa whispered. "And then he sponsored you in your shipping venture."

"Ah, no. Then I refused his financial support and became wholly self-sufficient. The shipping company I've built with my partners is the result of hard work, ambition, and instinct."

"And my dowry," she added. She couldn't resist.

He laughed. "Yes, and your dowry."

"From a servant to a gentleman," she marveled.

"Well, from a servant to a man of means. We'll leave it at that. You understand that I cannot conceal this from your parents, Tessa?"

"Actually . . ." she began. "Would you consider hedging this bit of your history? Holding back? Just until they become better acquainted with you? They are quite wrapped up in appearances and social expectations, I'm afraid."

"Holding back until when?"

"Oh . . . until after we are safely married, to be sure."

"You mean conceal it?"

"Well, I mean perhaps don't raise it? That is, if no one asks."

He stopped walking. "The parents of my wife-to-be can hardly be considered, 'no one.'"

"Yes, but some pieces of our potential union are too complicated to share, aren't they? My parents shouldn't know about the advert, for example. They shouldn't know that my friends are marrying your partners. Excluding these fine details simply helps to ease the way. If we mean to succeed. If you want my dowry, and I want to get to London with my friends. If we want these things to happen post haste."

Joseph considered this, his expression pained. He shook his head, struggling to reconcile himself to masking his history.

Tessa forged ahead, determined to convince him. "I am very taken by you, Joseph Chance. So very taken. I want you very much. I should be devastated if something as inconsequential as my parents' obsession with rank got in the way of—well, if it got in the way." In a day of half truths and outright lies, this was, perhaps, the boldest truth of all.

He smiled again and bent his head. Not taking his eyes from hers, he brushed another faint whisper of a kiss across her lips. "We won't tell them yet," he whispered.

Tessa's eyes closed and she tipped forward for another kiss.

Can this happen? she marveled. *So easily? With a man I enjoy? Nay—a man by whom I am captivated? Can I have a father for this baby and a loving husband, just for me?*

This kiss went deeper, and Tessa made a sighing noise. Joseph growled and gathered her up, kissing her in earnest. Tessa felt swept away.

I will not risk any part of it, she thought idly, swimming in the kiss. *Not his disdain. Or his outrage. Or his leaving. I need only not tell him to make it work.*

He will love me, he will love us both.

I shall not tell him, and the child will be his. And I will be his. A family.

We. Are. Saved.

Chapter Three

Joseph called on Tessa at Berymede every morning for the next five days. On the sixth day, their discussion of marriage turned from conjecture (*Do we dare?*) to reality (*How soon can it happen?*).

On the seventh day, Joseph asked Wallace St. Croix for his daughter's hand in marriage.

If there had been more time, Joseph would have happily stretched their courtship by weeks, if not months, but the guano expedition was already underway, buyers were expecting delivery on the fertilizer, and Tessa herself seemed urgently motivated to pass over an extended betrothal and proceed immediately to the altar. He would be lying if he said her urgency did not thrill him.

Despite their shared rush, Tessa's parents imposed a two-day consideration period during which they would weigh Joseph's proposal.

Joseph had expected this—in all honesty, Joseph was

shocked that they'd welcomed his escalating devotion from the start—but Tessa had been angry and indignant about the delay. Joseph assured her, imploring her to remain patient and respectful. Meanwhile, he kissed her good-bye and forced himself to stay away until some summons—yea or nay—came from the St. Croixs. He holed up at the Pixham Inn in the meantime, enduring the skepticism of his partners, Jon Stoker and Brent Caulder.

Brent, the Earl of Cassin, had his own complicated proposal to sort out. He had managed to shackle himself to the leader of this unlikely trio of "dowry investors," Tessa's girlhood friend Willow. Cassin was back and forth to London as he reconciled himself to a marriage of convenience.

Unbelievably, it appeared Jon Stoker would marry before either of them, as his Convenient Bride was under the dominion of a violent uncle, and few things motivated Stoker more than abuse. Stoker was sorting out a special license and skulking about, alternately complaining about the marriages of convenience and not being able to wed his bride sooner.

If Joseph thought his friends would congratulate and encourage his own rushed marriage (the only affectionate and authentic marriage of the lot), he was mistaken. The men riddled him with questions and cautions instead, heaping on doubts and dire speculations. By the second drink-fueled night of scrutiny, Joseph had had enough. The three men sat before a blazing fire in the common room of the inn, drinking ale and eating roasted chestnuts.

"I refuse to answer another accusation about her," he told

his friends, wiping his mouth with his sleeve. "I've enough to answer for from her parents."

"And what is it that her parents accuse her of?" asked Jon Stoker.

Joseph glared. "Tessa is blameless in this. Her parents will accuse *me*, which I'm sure you realize."

"Accuse you of what?" asked the Earl of Cassin. "You're a rich shipping merchant with an even richer future. Your manners are above reproach, you dress like a courtier, and aspire to run for bloody Parliament. I'd marry you myself if I could."

Joseph made a face but Cassin continued, "Best of all, you've made no secret of falling madly, adoringly in love with their daughter. In record time, no less. And let's not forget that you've saved her from any other rotter who might answer the advert."

"First of all," sighed Joseph, "I don't dress like a courtier, I dress like a gentleman. If you'd begun life polishing someone's boots instead of wearing them, perhaps you would value the pleasure of your own fine pair."

"But don't you mean *pairs*?" Stoker cut in. "How many in your collection at the moment? Three? Four?"

"*Second*," continued Joseph, "her parents are blissfully unaware of the advert, as you well know. And there's no credit for being the best of the worst, if that's what you mean."

"What I *mean*," said Cassin, "is Tessa St. Croix and her esteemed parents should be grateful to have you." He raised his glass. "And I've no doubt that their joyful permission will come down from on high any hour. My concern was always that Miss St. Croix and her lot deserve you."

"Deserve me?" said Joseph. "A man who could be laying her supper instead of eating it beside her?"

Cassin said, "You're preoccupied with your past life in service."

"Says the man in possession of an ancient earldom," Joseph shot back.

"What did her parents say when you explained about your previous life *below stairs*?" Cassin took a drink.

"She's asked me not to elaborate on it."

Cassin's tankard froze, halfway to his mouth. "Define elaborate?"

Joseph sighed. "It would take too much time to convince them to endorse the marriage if they knew I was not . . ."

". . . A rich shipping merchant who may one day be prime minister?" provided Cassin.

". . . if they know we are not of the same class," Joseph finished.

"You know what I think?" said Stoker. "I think you *like* it that she is so very haute and modish, and she has set her cap for you."

"You're full of shite."

"Stoker makes an excellent point," said Cassin. "Are you certain the mad love into which you've fallen is tied to the girl and not her place in society?

"Wealthy gentlemen's daughters abound," Cassin went on. "Despite your so-called 'humble beginnings,' you could have your pick of fine ladies . . . assuming fine ladies are what you want."

"And you've borne witness to my long history pursuing society misses, have you?" Joseph asked.

His friends considered this, sharing a look. He'd won the point, and they knew it. He'd never courted anyone as wealthy or esteemed as Tessa St. Croix.

"All we're asking," said Stoker, "is why *this* girl? You've only known her for a bloody week."

"And yet I knew the first day," said Joseph carefully. He pushed up from his chair and threw a handful of chestnut shells into the fire. His friends were merely trying to protect him, he knew this, but their suspicions grated. He was a grown man, well in touch with reality. He was familiar with the notion of class envy. He was not shallow—*or* envious for that matter. It was Tessa he wanted, not her place in the haute ton.

"You knew *what* the first day?" asked Stoker.

Joseph turned away from the fire. "That I was changed."

"That you were randy, more like," guessed Stoker.

"Careful, Stoker," Joseph warned, shoving off the mantel. A brawl in the stable yard would bring a satisfying end to this conversation, and Joseph suddenly wanted that very much. Stoker merely rolled his eyes.

"Was I drawn to her at first sight?" asked Joseph. "Yes. Do I desire her? More than any woman I've known. But it is more than desire. And it's more than her bloody family and their bloody money. She is . . . buoyant in a way that holds me up. She is so clever. Her wit makes mine funnier. She is wholly confident and capable, and yet I find myself wanting to provide for her. She is alive in a way that makes my own life seem a little less livable without her in it."

There was a pause, and Cassin raised his glass again.

Stoker said, "And she would say the same of you, no doubt?"

"She does not hide her enthusiasm for me," Joseph said, biting back a smile. "From the beginning, she has wanted me. She has made that very clear."

The dining table of Berymede seated twenty-four, but when her brothers were away and there were no guests to dinner, Tessa and her parents took their evening meal in a small windowed alcove that overlooked her mother's roses.

Joseph had joined the family there on Wednesday, the day before he proposed. He had laughed with her father and described tropical flowers to her mother. He had winked at Tessa across the table and asked her to tell them about her antique German piano.

Until that meal, Tessa had never realized how rare it was for anyone to ask her to contribute to dinner conversation. Oh, she had always made herself heard at mealtimes. In a family of four brothers, she'd learned early to interject and tease and speak loud enough to be heard over the din, but she couldn't remember ever being *asked*.

What are you reading, Tessa?

What piece are you working on at the pianoforte?

What new music would you like us to collect for you when we are in Town?

But Joseph had asked. He'd asked this and more.

And no matter what she said, he appeared captivated. His attention thrilled her in a way that no male attention ever had, after years of earning the attention of so many men. He truly wished to know—and not simply the *what*, he wanted to know *why*.

If Tessa waited for a certain question—*Why a rushed convenient marriage, why me?*—she did not prompt him, and he did not ask. *Thank God.*

If he *had* asked her, would she have told him about the baby?

Possibly.

Maybe.

Hopefully.

Hopefully she would have blurted out the truth and begged him to understand her desperation—and also her burgeoning love.

Because she was falling so very much in love with Joseph Chance. And not simply because he was saving her and not simply because he was handsome and charming.

She loved him because he seemed to truly *see* her, to decipher her.

He understood that she was pretty and silly and gay, but also that she was curious and empathetic and felt happiest when she encouraged other people. Had anyone at Berymede ever seen her as more than entertaining or cute? To Joseph, she felt entertaining *and* interesting; she was pretty but also so very clever.

And despite the secret about the baby and the manipulation

of her parents, she believed she understood him too. She understood what he had overcome, the brilliance and hard work that had hastened that triumph. She saw the humility, the strength, the desire—desire to achieve all of his wild aspirations and desire for her.

Her parents, of course, were oblivious to all of it. Her parents, as always, were concerned with only one thing: the appearance of the St. Croix family in the eyes of the world—or rather, in the eyes of *their* world, which was lofty London society. What would their friends and peers think? How would the gossip papers depict their union? What level of envy was painted by the picture of Joseph Chance and Tessa St. Croix?

"I had held out hope for a title," said her father, Wallace St. Croix, a day after Joseph's proposal. He was seated with his back to the alcove window, sawing into the bony side of fish. "You could have been a countess or even a duchess, I daresay."

Although the St. Croix family boasted wealth and refinement, their bloodline was more French than English, with nary an aristocratic relation in sight. It was no secret that Tessa's beauty and dowry might one day see her married into this previously unattained rung of society.

And perhaps at one time, Tessa had dreamed of marrying a lord. But only vaguely, only in as much as she dreamed of having curly hair instead of straight, or of seeing Venice instead of the canals of any other place in the world. It sounded nice, but so did so many things.

Her more defined, more authentic dream had been far

purer—simple, really. She had dreamed of falling in love. Real love, like in a play, like Orpheus and Eurydice. She dreamed of falling in love the way Berymede's head groom, Virgil, loved his wife, Susan, the kitchen maid. She wished to be in love like her friend Sabine's mother and father, before her father had died.

In contrast, the marriage of Tessa's parents was a partnership. Wallace St. Croix was wealthy and well connected, and Isobel St. Croix was beautiful, stylish, and exacting. Together, they shared one goal, which was to be revered in society. They worked in tandem to achieve this, they reveled in their strides, they cursed their setbacks.

Her mother had brought her up to marry the most eligible man she could possibly ensnare, but Tessa's own intent had been to use her considerable allure to marry for love.

She would be lying if she said she had not enjoyed four seasons of auditioning one potential True Love after another. There had been many men, yes, but was True Love special if it was easy to find? If she stumbled upon it with the first man or the second . . . or any number of *wrong* men? Mostly, she told her friends, who teased her about her many beaux, she would meet the wrong man. But she would not find the correct man if she did not weed through all the others.

In the end, she cared less about eligibility and more about finding her one, perfect match. What good, she'd thought, were the dresses and the dance cards if the end result was not True Love? She wanted the fairy-tale union with a handsome, dashing man and a passionate wedding night that swept them both away.

The life after the wedding night? She had perhaps given this less thought. More of the same, she thought, more dash and more passion?

The great irony was of course that "what came after" actually seized Tessa first. Within one month of Captain Marking and the tree.

Just like that, Tessa's long idealized romantic love was set aside in favor of survival. In favor of "what came after."

And then Joseph Chance magically appeared, and she wondered if fate might have actually sent her a savior and a happily-ever-after all in the same man.

The possibility made her doubly determined to extract her parents' speedy blessing, and for every challenge issued by her parents, she had an answer.

"Mr. Chance is not a titled gentleman, no," Tessa told her father at dinner, "but his dearest friend, a man he loves like a brother, is an earl of considerable means. The Earl of Falcondale. Many of his friends are highly esteemed, I believe. One of his partners is also an earl. The Earl of Cassin."

Tessa idly set a copy of *Burke's Guide to Peerage* beside her mother's plate. Isobel St. Croix raised her eyebrow and picked it up, thumbing to the *F*s.

"And perhaps I have known my share of young lords through the years," Tessa went on, "but the titled men who have called on me have been rather . . . *impoverished*, if I'm being honest. Debt-ridden or otherwise sniffing around for my dowry. I abhor the notion that I should be married only for your money, Papa. How much more confident we will appear when I marry for actual affection. Joseph is successful in his own right. His interest in me *is* me. And me alone."

"Is he successful?" challenged her father. "I hardly see him refusing the dowry, do I?"

"Oh, quite successful, Papa, as you well know. The boys told me they've looked in on his company in London. He's taking the dowry only to finance his next expedition without dipping into his own fortune. He is a shrewd businessman. All of London will marvel at his wealth when he returns from Barbadoes."

"But this is another concern," said her mother. "Why marry a man set to leave the country within days of your wedding? A young couple should devote their first year to establishing themselves in London. You should be seen out, you should start a family. How will society acknowledge his business acumen if he is on the other side of the world? Out of sight, out of mind, as you know."

"Oh, but this way," said Tessa, scrambling, "we shall have two opportunities to make an impression. This year, we'll have a grand wedding in high style, and all of your friends will attend. Next year, Joseph will return with his new riches, and that is when we will make the rounds to parties and society functions. Don't you see? His travels will forestall the usual slide into matronly obscurity after the wedding. We will wait a year and then burst onto the scene anew."

Tessa forced her most dazzling expressions, gesturing with her hands to paint the picture of acclaim her mother's vanity could see. Inside, she was trembling, praying she was convincing them.

"Well, he has impressed us more than any other man you've trotted out," her father finally said.

Tessa cringed at the thought of her old life and "trotting out" men. *This*, she thought, *must end*. The men, obviously. But also the flirtation, the coquettishness.

If she managed to marry Joseph, she vowed to become a new woman.

"He *is* very handsome and successful," conceded her mother. "I should relish the looks on people's faces, I daresay, when he returns and you may bask in your new wealth. One would never wish to boast, of course, but what is boasting and what is a triumphant homecoming? Can you imagine the ball we might give in London, Wallace?" Isobel St. Croix looked into the distance, fantasizing. "And afterward, you would likely move across town . . . to Mayfair, perhaps? Or Knightsbridge? New vehicles, of course. And who's not to say—maybe even a country house?"

"Perhaps," said Tessa, trying not to think of the reality of Joseph's *triumphant homecoming*.

"Very well," said her father, sharing a look with her mother. "Your Maman has taught you nothing if not distinction, Tess. To sparkle. To be special. To be *envied*. What could be more distinctive than a marriage to an upstart who is poised to shower you with riches? But you must give us time to plan a proper wedding. We will send you off in high style. There will be no doubt in anyone's minds that this is a union that *matters*."

Tessa's heart caught in her throat. "How much time?"

"Four months?" said her mother.

And now Tessa did stomp her foot. She pushed up from the table. "We shall do it in three weeks," she said.

"*Three weeks?*" said her mother, strangled.

Tessa nodded with finality. "Joseph cannot enjoy his triumphant return if he postpones his opportunity to go. His partners are already sailing without him. The wedding must be in three weeks or . . . or we elope."

Isobel's face went white and Wallace's glass froze halfway to his mouth.

An elopement, of course, would be the ultimate embarrassment. Well, perhaps not the *ultimate* embarrassment, but she dare not threaten that.

Tessa crossed her arms over her chest.

"No elopement," conceded her father, and her mother said, "We shall see what we can manage in three weeks."

CHAPTER FOUR

"But will you be gone so long as a full year, Joseph?"

One week later, with the days of their hasty betrothal well underway, Tessa sat at the pianoforte in the Berymede music room while Joseph leaned against the instrument and watched her play.

Despite being a skilled musician, she barely acknowledged her talent and seemed to play only to entertain herself. The nonchalance intrigued him, because she was so very aware of all her other gifts. She flaunted her beauty and her cleverness with an ironic, flirtatious sort of vanity that, God save him, Joseph found charming. She was well aware that her dresses were expensive and beautiful and never grew tired of praise or second glances.

The music, however, she simply played.

Even now, she departed the memorized notes and improvised skillfully, timing the tempo and notes to the ups and downs of their conversation. His heart pounded as he watched her. The focused sort of . . . determination (there was no better word for it) that she brought to their early days seemed to dissolve when the wedding date had been set. After that, a playful vivacity took over, and the change took his breath away.

"But will you be gone a year?" Tessa sang, repeating her question. She clinked out dark notes of sadness and dread. She hunched dramatically over the keys, her blonde hair spilling forward, and pounded out a mournful refrain.

Joseph smiled and looked away. Everything she did delighted him.

"We cannot say how long we will be away," he said, speaking over the music, "because we are learning as we go."

"We are learning as we go . . ." Tessa sang lightly, switching to a lively march.

He made no effort to hide his amusement. Even this conversation was to be a performance. He could watch her, he thought, indefinitely. It required real restraint not to scoop her from the bench and pull her into his arms.

Still, he warned, "It would not hurt you to understand more about the expedition. Your dowry has underwritten it, after all. And it will take me away from you—"

"Yes, but not so long as a full year," Tessa cut in, pounding out a series of ominous chords.

Joseph chuckled. He had never met anyone like Tessa St. Croix.

"Tell me," she sighed, switching the music again, now a rolling melody, slowly building, the soft beginning of a great opus. "Tell me about the venture . . . underwritten by my dowry . . . that will take you away from me for nearly a year . . ."

"Will you stop playing?" He raised an eyebrow.

"Will you provide some incentive for me to stop?"

A flash of heat shot through him, and he glanced at the open door of the music room. He cleared his throat.

"Tessa . . ." he warned. She loved nothing more than to goad him.

She did not answer and he watched her play, allowing the music to wrap around him. He opened and closed his hands.

Their betrothal had brought him no end of delight and hope. Her parents wished to host a large wedding and elaborate breakfast feast, and he'd delayed his departure for Barbadoes to accommodate the grand affair. His partners had sailed ahead of him. He was grateful for the additional time with Tessa but also anxious to get underway. The sooner he reached Barbadoes, the sooner he could come back to her.

But before he went, he would have her comprehend what he was doing and why. His expedition had been oddly difficult to explain to her. She was loath to be serious, even for a moment, to speak of business and logistics. He, too, would like to be always in jest, to tease and flirt and nearly succumb to their considerable attraction, but he was determined. She must understand where he was going and how very long he would be away.

She glanced up from the pianoforte and flashed him a pout. He was pierced with another shot of lust.

She returned her attention to the keys with renewed volume.

"Your parents assign a great deal of trust in me, allowing us to spend time alone together," he said. "I am meant to be listening to you play, not compelling you to leave the instrument."

"Yes, but you're the one who asked me to stop playing."

"I want your attention, not your—" Joseph stopped talking. Of course he could not describe what he really wanted.

Tessa slid her left hand from the keyboard and picked out a few notes with her right, a spare little melody, just the tinkling of a few keys. "Will you come sit beside me, Joseph?"

He narrowed his eyes. She pushed the bounds of his self-control. It was as thrilling as it was frustrating.

"I promise to be a very good girl," she vowed, alternating two notes together in a fluttery little trill.

"That remains to be seen. But will you listen to what I'm trying to tell you about the expedition?"

Another trill. "I will listen so very carefully."

Joseph glanced again at the door and then slid onto the piano seat beside her. If he expected her to move to create ample room for them both, he was mistaken. She snuggled closer. Her skirts lapped over his lap. Her foot worked the pedal of the pianoforte and their legs rubbed together. He felt the heat of her body up and down his side. He was swamped with the scent of her.

He swallowed hard. "Now will you stop playing?"

"Playing helps me to listen, don't you see? It occupies my hands." She glanced at him. "How else am I to occupy my hands, Joseph, while I listen to the long details of your long expedition?"

Joseph made a growling noise and shifted on the seat. She slid closer. She was playing with both hands again, a rhythmic succession of chords that seemed to mimic the accelerated thud of his heart.

"How about this?" she suggested. "For every detail to which I listen and acknowledge, you will give me one kiss."

Joseph laughed. He'd never met anyone as bold or diverting. "You want me to kiss you here, now, in the midst of the servants? With your mother somewhere in the house?"

"No one pays any mind if they can hear the pianoforte. What trouble can we get up to if I am still playing?"

Joseph growled again. His mind spun with the very great potential for trouble. Tessa made no secret of her desire for him; in fact, she had made it clear that he could make love to her even now, before they were married, if he so desired.

He did desire, very much, but he was also an honorable man, and he had been granted the respect and blessing of her parents. The wedding, however elaborate, was being thrown together in a matter of weeks. Although his need for her was colossal, he assured her they could wait.

"And what if these kisses cause you to stop playing?" he asked.

"They won't," she promised, leaning over him, pressing the lush curve of her breast against his arm to reach the highest note on the keyboard. She pinged it twice and scaled back down with renewed volume. Joseph grinned at the opposite wall.

"It might," he said, watching her profile as she bent over the keys.

"I suppose we'll never know. . . ." she sighed, and he was undone. He bent his head and brushed his mouth across her ear once, twice, breathing against the soft whirl of skin.

"I know a challenge when I hear one, Miss St. Croix," he whispered, "and you give me little choice but to accept." He kissed her ear lightly, nipped her earlobe, and breathed deeply against her skin once more.

The music came to an awkward pause and the room filled with the sound of her hitched breathing. After that, two flat notes. *Clink-plink.*

Next, a sigh, a laugh, and she resumed her playing. The recovery took only five notes. She'd reverted back to the memorized piece from before. She sat bolt upright, tossing her hair over her shoulders. "Go on, then," she said, smiling down at her hands. "You have my full attention."

He watched for a moment more, wondering if he would ever recover from the delight of her, marveling that a spirited, beautiful, irresistible gentleman's daughter seemed to want little more than to delight him.

He cleared his throat. "The shortest conceivable time I will be away is eight months," he told her. "We will sail for Barbadoes, buy supplies and hire workers, and then decamp to the island to begin work."

The past June, Joseph and his partners had won a small, seemingly worthless tropical island in a game of cards. They assumed the island had no value, until new scientific research revealed an unexpected resource with the potential to make them all very rich. Their scabby little island was heaped with it. They needed only to determine how to extract it from the island and sell it back in England.

Tessa nodded and proffered her cheek.

Joseph bit back a smile, checked the doorway, and then

nuzzled her skin. He refused to be led and bypassed her cheek for the sensitive spot on her neck, just below her jaw. He breathed deeply, reveling in the scent of her, and then laid a line of kisses from her neck to her lips, sucking gently. His left hand slid across her back and around her waist, pressing her more tightly against him. Her playing slowed but did not stop. He heard her slight intake of breath and she swayed a little on the bench.

"And what is it . . ." she began, but her voice was a squeak. She cleared her throat and tried again. "And what is it that you are mining from the island? Dead birds?"

"No. Not dead birds. It's a naturally occurring resource called *guano*. It is dried bird excrement."

She crinkled her nose, and he was overwhelmed with the urge to pull her from the keyboard and draw her into his lap.

She glanced at him. Deftly, she lifted one hand from the keys. With her other hand, she maintained the steady drum of a throbbing chord. With the raised hand, she proffered her wrist, flipping it so he could kiss the sensitive underside.

Joseph blinked at the creamy skin beneath her sleeve and the soft palm of her hand. Slowly, he raised the hand to his face and settled it on his cheek. She made the tiniest gasp. Her fingers formed gently around the curve of his face, warm and delicate. Slowly, he tugged, sliding her palm downward, scraping it against the stubble of his emerging beard. When her open palm was centered directly over his mouth, he kissed it. One gentle kiss in the center of her palm. She gasped again.

Joseph himself felt a little like gasping. He fought arousal endlessly when he was near her, but when he touched her?

When he touched her, he surged with need. What would it be like to make love to her, if kissing her palm ignited such lust? He counted the days—the hours—until he knew.

In the meantime, he employed extreme restraint, kissing her wrist and then wrapping his own hand around her arm and tugging, pulling her to him. She listed in his direction, and he kissed the very corner of her mouth.

Tessa went still again, her extended hand hovering above the keys. Disjointed chords rose faintly from the other hand.

Another kiss to her mouth, and the chords grew slower and flatter and—

"Tessa?" he said softly. "Keep playing."

She rolled her shoulders and returned both hands to the keyboard. She cleared her throat softly. "Bird excrement, yes," she said, formally. "And it's meant to make us all rich?"

He watched her, dazzled by her recovery. "If all goes well, it should be quite profitable. The scientists claim guano is the most potent fertilizer known to man. When we grind it up and sell it to farmers, English crops could increase a hundredfold. They say that guano fertilizer will change agriculture forever."

"And you have found quite a lot of it? On your island?"

"The entire island is caked with it in fact. A veritable mountain of dried bird droppings, sixty feet to the sky. We need only chip away at it, put it in barrels, and bring it back to England to sell it."

She nodded, playing more strenuously now, but she glanced at him. An invitation. She wanted the next kiss.

He swore under his breath. He glanced at the open door

and then leaned in to do what they both wanted. This time, he kissed her square on the mouth. Long and firm and open. His free arm went around her. The notes of the pianoforte were reduced to a disconnected smattering of keys. He kissed her until neither of them could breathe.

"You will drive us both mad," he whispered against her skin. She was breathing hard and leaning against him. Joseph whispered, "Play . . ."

She made a whimpering noise but her hand found the keys. She plucked out a few notes, then a cord. She rallied herself and added the other hand. She played on.

Joseph released her and gripped the bench with his hands.

"And this will take eight months?" Tessa said. Her voice shook. "You will be away for eight months to harvest the miracle fertilizer. While I . . . while I play the pianoforte alone?"

"It is my very great hope," Joseph said, scooting the bench back from the instrument, "that you'll be playing it alone."

Tessa made a small yelp and tipped forward, but he caught her around the waist in the same deft movement. In the next second, she was on his lap, pivoted to face him. He plunked down his right arm on the keyboard, unleashing a garish tangle of notes.

Propping his forehead against hers, he rasped, "It will kill me to leave you for that long, Tessa, but the very soonest I may return is July. Possibly longer. Can you bear it?"

She shook her head violently. "No, I cannot," she breathed. The movement rocked his arm against the keys, eliciting another terrible jumble of notes.

He kissed her then, hard and thorough, wrapping his

arms around her and propping her on the keyboard with an un-musical plunk.

Tessa fell against him, kissing him back, winding her fingers into his hair and down his shoulders, clinging to him. Their mouths collided in a ravenous frenzy of lips and tongue and breath and heat.

"Come back to me," she whimpered, turning her head to breathe.

"You could not keep me away," he panted, seeking her mouth again.

They lost all notion of time, they lost all notion of everything but the sensation and the closeness and each other.

By some miracle, they heard footsteps when a footman strode down the corridor, and Tessa's head shot up. Joseph stole one final kiss and then slid her back onto the bench and spun her to face the keys. He was standing behind her in the next moment, sliding the bench in place.

He gave her a gentle nudge on the lower back. "Play . . ." he reminded.

By the time the footman found his way into the music room with a tray of tea and cakes, Tessa was well into the second stanza of "The May Queen's Farewell" and Joseph was calculating the days until his wedding and the night that would follow.

CHAPTER FIVE

"Come in," Tessa called when Joseph knocked softly on the bedroom door.

"Tessa?" Joseph's voice was gentle through the thick wood.

"Come in," she repeated. She rose from the dressing table, hairbrush still in hand. Her heart began to drum.

The day of their wedding had come at last. The ceremony, a music-and-flower-filled two-hour affair, with clergy and a boys' choir brought in from London, had been a testament to her mother's speedy planning and her father's money. The wedding feast that followed boasted enough food to nourish all of Surrey for a week.

But now the food and guests had come and gone. Darkness crept across the garden outside the cottage window in long, cold shadows. Tessa sat alone, waiting for her new husband.

She called his name, and there he was. The door creaked open and he filled the doorway. Her heart squeezed like a fist.

"My God, Tessa," he whispered hoarsely. She looked down at her nightgown, the matching peignoir, the fur slippers. A long, straight lock of blonde hair fell over her shoulder, and she pushed it back. Joseph took it all in and slowly swiped his tongue across his upper lip.

Tessa's heart squeezed again. No reaction could be more thrilling, not in her wildest dreams, but Joseph had never made a secret of his desire for her. He'd wanted her. That he'd refused to avail himself, despite her frequent offers, only made his desire seem more thrilling. He was exactly, precisely the opposite of Captain Marking.

She'd told herself that when he took her body, this too would be exactly, precisely the opposite of what Captain Marking had done. If they made it that far . . .

For days, Tessa's resolve had been slipping—and not just because she was afraid of the violence involved in sex. She was afraid of the lie she was living by passing her baby off as Joseph's. She squeezed her eyes shut and looked away.

"What's this?" he teased. "Modesty—no. I'm in disbelief." He stepped inside and shut the door.

Her parents had spruced up a vine-swathed cottage on the edge of Berymede's expansive parkland for the newlyweds' use after the wedding. Their plan had been to spend a few days in Surrey before they departed for London. When Joseph saw her safely settled in Belgravia, he would embark on the guano expedition.

"Or is this shyness?" Joseph went on, his voice still teasing. "Not my Tess . . ."

He ambled toward her, taking in the room in a slow, lazy

glance. The high, canopied bed, the roaring fire, the cart of food and wine.

Now it was Tess's turn to stare. He'd removed the jacket he'd worn for the wedding and party, revealing a snug-fitting waistcoat, billowy shirt, and beautifully styled cravat. He was always impeccably turned out, and today was no different. He unspooled the cravat with a yank, pulling it roughly from his neck. Locking eyes with her, he began to unfasten the top buttons of his shirt.

This, she thought, swallowing, *is new.*

Despite their weeks-long courtship, she'd never seen him without his coat and certainly not with his chest bared. The first thing she noticed was muscled torso and broad shoulders. These had not been an illusion of tailoring. With every flick of a button, she saw more of his throat and pectorals. She let out a miserable half whimper.

He stopped and cocked his head. "Tessa? Darling? What is it?"

She almost said it.

I have lied to you, Joseph. All along.

There is a baby.

You are not the first man.

When you return from sea next year, we will be—I will be . . .

When you return, I will have had a child.

I will have had another man's child.

But she wondered for the hundredth time if these statements were strictly accurate. *Had* she lied all along? Was it more accurate to say she had made . . . omissions? *Significant* omissions.

She would have a baby, this was true, but Joseph was the first man in her heart and in her mind. To her, he would be the first. No man before him had ever taken her breath away, captivated her, thrilled her. Any man before him was but a faint, dull memory, insufficient and forgotten. The memory of Captain Marking in particular was a dark blot that obscured a full season of her life.

"Tessa?" Joseph said again. His boyish features quirked into a confused grin.

"Perhaps I am a bit . . . nervous," Tessa said faintly. She could not remember having been more nervous.

"Come," he said, winking at her, taking her hand. "Let us discover what the servants have left. Are you hungry?" He made a low whistle. "Wine? Lovely. Let's eat something, shall we? And drink something. We'll indulge in a . . ." he took a deep, amused breath, winking at her again ". . . chat."

Tessa swallowed hard and allowed him to lead her. From the beginning, he had approached her with a teasing mix of confidence and gentleness. She would follow him anywhere.

He added, "The ceremony and party were such a to-do, we've hardly spoken all day." He took up the bottle of wine and inspected the label and then tucked it under his arm.

Tell him, she thought. *Either tell him or compel him to bed you and never look back.*

He dropped into the leather armchair before the fire and tugged her hand, pulling her down on his lap. She fell across him with a little yelp. She still clutched the hairbrush in her right hand. He caught her around the waist and tucked her against him. The possession thrilled her despite her nerves, but it was fleeting. She hadn't the luxury of being thrilled by sitting in his lap. She looked down at her nightgown and peignoir. The silk settled over the two of them like a ruffled, teal mist.

"Hold still," he chuckled, "easy. There you are." He set the bottle aside and tossed away the brush. "No more preening. You are beautiful, as I'm sure you are aware. Far too beautiful for me to be expected to spend any length of time . . . *chatting.*" He raised an eyebrow. "Luckily, I enjoy talking to you nearly as much as I will enjoy . . . not talking to you. It won't be a hardship. At the moment." He dipped his head and swiped a swift, soft kiss on the skin of her neck, nuzzling her with his nose.

Tessa squeezed her eyes shut. This was the bit she'd always loved, the kissing and embraces. The experience of . . . coupling had been very painful with Captain Marking. A piercing, confining intrusion that had caused her to go speechless with fear. But the kissing, especially with Joseph, she adored. She could easily steel herself to be bedded if there was kissing.

It also helped that she'd fallen in love with Joseph Chance in these last weeks, a condition she had begun to admit to herself and she wanted, very badly, to admit to him. But it was a qualified love. It was a love mingled with selfishness for her own situation, with fear, with desperation. Why, she wondered for the thousandth time, couldn't she have met Joseph before Captain Marking, when the two of them could have fallen in love without secrets or lies or omissions?

Why, indeed? She wasn't sure what to do with this burgeoning love except use it to find the words to reveal the baby—because, when it came down to it, the real reason she would now tell him had little to do with lying generally and everything to do with lying to a man with whom she'd fallen in love. Considering this love, could she continue with the deception, even for the baby? Was the strength of her love worth the risk of . . . of . . .

Well, the real risk now was annulment.

If she told him (*when* she told him), he might very well undo the marriage. An annulment would leave her not only heartbroken, but truly destitute as well. Her parents would discover the ruse and refuse all manner of aid; and it would be impossible to marry someone else.

Her best estimation was that he would *not* annul their new union. First and foremost, he needed the dowry money. Second, he was a principled man, but he was not cruel. She'd seen this from the very beginning. She'd been drawn to it, like a warm fire on a cold day. It was one of the things about him she loved the most.

Finally, impossibly, was there a chance his affection for her would make him sympathetic to her plight? Could he possibly love her enough to overlook her deception?

She would only know if she spoke the words.

But . . . not yet. Please, she begged herself. *Just a few more moments.*

She allowed herself to ask, "What should we talk about?"

His hand had found its way inside the peignoir to the thin silk of her gown. It settled on her waist. Tessa could feel the outline of each strong finger against her hip. It was not horrible, she thought. In fact, it was quite nice. It was more of the same, like kissing and embracing. Oh, how she wanted more kissing and embracing and his hand on her hip.

"Hmmm, I've an idea," he said, reaching for the pocket on his waistcoat. He removed a tattered piece of folded parchment. "A little gift for you, if you'll have it. For the two of us, I suppose."

Tessa recognized the paper even before she reached out to take it. The advertisement her friends had posted on the docks in London in order to solicit husbands. Had that been only a month ago?

With shaking hands, she unfolded the parchment. "The advertisement," she whispered, blinking to keep her eyes dry. "You've kept it?"

"Of course I kept it. I wouldn't have any other 'gentleman sailors' sniffing around, asking about your particular brand of 'investment.'"

She fingered the crumbling edge of the parchment. She wondered if he would allow her to have it as a keepsake—after he knew.

Without thinking, she folded herself against his chest and buried her face in his neck. He gathered her to him, cradling her. He tugged the rumpled parchment from her hand.

"Careful, darling," he said softly, "what is it?"

She soaked in the gentle pressure of his large hand against her back. She listened to the steady thud of his heart. He pressed a line of small kisses to her temple and she sucked in a breath, as if she could breathe his kisses in. She felt the roughness of his whiskers against her eyelids and cheek and mouth. His fingers flexed gently, in and out, in and out.

How blissful this scene would be on a different night, under different circumstances. But it wasn't a different night. And the circumstances grew inside her, more every day. She squeezed her eyes shut.

Suddenly, limb by limb, her body began to lock up; stomach clenched, shoulders seizing. She was a tight knot of dread and regret. "Joseph . . . ?" she began, speaking against the skin of his neck.

Her voice was higher pitched than usual. She paused, trying to find the courage. He waited.

There was a good chance he might drop her when she said it—simply roll her off his lap and onto the rug. The deceit would outrage him, there was no doubt about that. But it was an outrage she deserved. She squeezed her eyes more tightly shut. She deserved all of it.

But not yet, she thought. Five more moments. Five more.

"You weren't displeased by the wedding, I hope?" he asked. Gently, he tipped her back. "It was what you wanted?"

She swallowed. "Well, the wedding was what my parents wanted."

"Come now. You cannot say that the bunting and pine boughs and candles and . . . How many distinguished guests were there? Three hundred? You cannot say this was not exactly as your heart desired? I looked out at the scale of the wedding feast and thought, what a lifetime of grand affairs I am in for." He kissed her on the ear. "Lucky for you, I am up to the task. I should like nothing more than hosting ridiculously large parties with you beside me."

Tessa nodded, unable to speak. How did he know her so well? Already? When she'd managed to conceal such a large part of herself?

"Yes, it was very . . . grand," she finally said. "But was it too grand?"

"For me?" he chuckled. "No. Grand is one of my chief pursuits. When you begin life as a servant and rise to become a man of means, 'grand' holds a certain appeal. Within reason." He gave her a squeeze.

"Was the Earl of Falcondale impressed, do you think?" Tessa asked, speaking of his old friend and sponsor. The earl, Tessa thought, was another reason Joseph would not annul the wedding. If she had to guess, she believed Joseph would rather die than admit to the earl that he had been deceived by his wife.

"Oh, it never really occurs to Trevor to be impressed by large crowds or ceremonial claptrap. But I do believe his wife, Lady Piety, admired it greatly," Joseph said. The pride was clear in his voice. "She likes you very much. No one can believe I've done quite so well for myself." Joseph gave her a squeeze. "Least of all, me."

Before she could stop herself, Tessa sucked in another breath and said, "Joseph?"

"Are you aware that you have not kissed me once this night?" he said lazily, staring at her mouth.

"I've something that I must tell you," she pressed. The impulse to tell him increased suddenly, jumping from dull hum to a whip-snapping urgency. If she did not say the words, she would bolt from the room, running away as fast as her legs could take her.

With jerky movements, she picked her way out of his lap and stood before him. Her peignoir sagged, and she yanked it on her shoulders.

Joseph's arms slid away and he held them out, like he couldn't believe she'd left him. For the first time, he looked truly alarmed.

"What is it?" He leaned forward in the chair. He waited.

Tessa closed her eyes and took a deep breath. She crossed one arm low over her belly, reminding herself that the pain she would inflict was for the baby. Everything she did now was for the baby.

"In about seven months' time," she said, "I'm going to have a baby."

"You're what?" Joseph's voice came out in a kind of airy, soundless rasp. He mouthed the word more than said it.

Tessa forced herself to hold his gaze. She watched all trace of affection and indulgence drain from his face. The blue of his eyes went icy with shock.

She nodded, endorsing the thing he thought he had heard. "I . . . I am ashamed to admit that I have not been entirely honest with you." She looked down at her hands, squeezing them together. "I—the baby will come in May. We think."

Joseph shoved from the chair. "'We?' Who is 'we?' Surely not the father?"

"Oh, no." She winced. "I mean, we—my friends. Sabine and Willow."

She wanted to tell him about Captain Marking then, to explain what happened—but she had scarcely found the words to reveal the truth of her condition. Who would believe that Tessa, a girl who loved nothing more than flirting and dancing and handsome men had not meant . . . had not wanted . . . had been . . .

She could not even articulate what she had not meant or wanted. She could not say what happened.

Joseph made a low, guttural sound of frustration and hurt and moved around her, careful to keep distance between them. For a horrified second, she thought he would storm from the room, but he pivoted and began to pace. His movements were terse and clipped, his hands on his hips. He looked at the floor.

"Of course you all knew," he said, speaking to himself. "The advertisement and the marriages were part of a master plan, were they not?" He stopped pacing and stared at her. "Are the other girls pregnant, as well? Is this why the three of you were all so desperate to marry and leave home?"

"Oh, no," said Tess, holding up her hands in horror. "We . . ." She swallowed hard and started again. "Willow has always wanted to move to London; it's been a dream since she was a girl. And Sabine, well, you've seen how Sabine and her uncle . . ." When Sabine met Jon Stoker, her prospective groom, her right eye had been freshly blackened from her uncle's fist.

Joseph considered this, nodded, and then resumed pacing. "Of course. 'Tis only you. How ironic." He laughed bitterly. "I was warned of something like this, you know. Cassin and Stoker said all along that your sudden affection was too good to be true. 'But why should your girl fall so quickly in love, Joe?' they said. They hounded me about it—especially Cassin. 'Her parents are rich,' he said, 'she lives on a sprawling estate, and has beaux aplenty. Why leave it all to be with you, Joseph?' "

He stopped pacing again and looked at her. His face was tight and his eyes burned bright, cold blue. "Well, I suppose now we know."

Tessa dropped her head again, nodding to the floor. The tears had begun to spill over, running down her cheeks, and she made no effort to stop them. She'd told herself she could endure his anger and his disgust, that only his heartbreak would affect her. What a stupidly noble ideal. She was loath to endure any of it. She wanted to be loved. She wanted Joseph to love her.

"Who is he?" Joseph asked now, barking out the words. He paused at the window, bracing his hands on either side of the frame.

"Who is who?" For a suspended moment, she was confused.

"The father of the unborn child."

"Oh," she said, her stomach turning, "right." It was ridiculous how little she thought of Capitan Marking. "He . . . he is no one. A . . . an officer who was garrisoned in Pixham for a time. He's gone now. Forever gone."

Joseph turned. "Clearly." He smiled—actually smiled—a mean, heartless expression, pure in its contempt, and Tessa raised her chin just a notch. She might have done a horrible thing and lied about it, but some unknown store of self-respect refused to allow her to be fully condemned. She narrowed her eyes.

"Does he know?" Joseph asked. "About the baby?"

And now she did feel condemned, and she ducked her head. Marking's door-slamming rejection would shame her forever. She nodded to the floor.

"He wouldn't have you?" Joseph asked. His voice was flat, not a question.

"Yes," she agreed, her throat painfully tight. "He would not have me."

"And so you married me, because you thought that I would?"

Tessa squeezed her eyes shut, wringing out the last of the tears. She swiped her cheeks with her hands. She looked up. "My affection for you was not an act, Joseph, despite what you may think. I wanted to tell you but I . . . I could not."

It was agony to say the words, but she would not play the victim, not now. She would not implore him. She would not beg.

Joseph blew out an exhausted breath and ran a hand through his hair. He swore loudly. "So why tell me now, Tessa?" He spun on her. "Why not simply allow me to take you to bed and pass the baby off as mine? I can only assume that was the original plan."

"I . . . I had reached my limit," she said. "With the deception." She squeezed her hands into a double fist, one outside of the other. "I couldn't lie anymore. I could not." Silently, in her head, she added, *I could not love you and lie to you.* He was too angry to reveal that love now. She knew he would be angry, but it had been impossible to predict how truly livid. He stalked the room like a different man.

He said, "How lucky that your limit was reached after we said I do." His voice was so bitter, Tessa took a step back.

We will never reconcile, she thought, watching him pace. Had that been the thing for which she'd held out hope all along? If she had, that hope was now destroyed.

"Will you annul the marriage?" Tessa heard herself ask. Her voice was a whisper. This was all that mattered, really.

Joseph stopped pacing and turned to her, his hands on his hips. His blue eyes pierced her very soul. "And what do you think?"

Chapter Six

Joseph glared at the woman to whom he'd been married for one afternoon. He was behaving like an arse. Tessa—his Tessa—stood before him, terrified, beseeching, openly weeping, and he simply . . . allowed it. Nay, he was the source of it.

But the lies.

No, not mere lies. She hadn't simply *lied* about being pregnant with another man's child, she lied *and* manipulated. She had made him fall into some sort of flying infatuation with her. All the while she was merrily, strategically, trapping him.

He should be the one weeping, and he cursed himself for the blind fool he had been.

Meanwhile, the entire life of this young woman hung in the balance—her baby's too. And yet, it satisfied his deeply wounded pride and extreme hurt to draw out the question. To make her wait. Even better, to make her bloody guess.

Cruel? Yes. Did it solve anything? Not particularly, but

what of the cruel lack of solutions for the entire rest of his bloody life? He had gotten married—married, for God's sake—and the woman to whom he was forever bound hadn't cared enough for him to be honest about why she'd done it.

"Surely you would not have selected me to ensnare if you believed I was the sort of man who would end the marriage when I learned the truth," he said.

Tessa blinked, her blue eyes shiny with tears. Ten minutes ago, he would have done anything to prevent even one tear from dropping down the perfect curve of her perfect cheek. Ten minutes ago, he would have . . .

Joseph cursed the difference ten minutes could make.

How had he not seen her duplicity? Of course, she had laughed at his jokes, but when had he ever struggled to amuse women? She had stared into his eyes, but he knew women found him handsome.

But she had felt special, hadn't she? Different. *More.* She was wealthy and proper and well-bred and yet—she wanted him, she couldn't seem to get enough of him. And not simply his face; she seemed to revel in his very life as a scrappy, half-refined upstart, plucked from servitude and sent to university and success on the high seas.

He'd had dalliances with other society women, of course. Rich women, titled women. Desirability to any woman had never been a challenge for him. But Tessa's desire had felt deeper, more rooted in her soul than his face. Her regard for him had a breathless sort of "at last" nature to it. She made him feel as if scores of wealthy, proper, well-bred gents had left her wanting, waiting, just for him.

And all the while she shopped for a legitimate papa to solve the result of . . . of . . . the loss of some other bloke.

Joseph made a growling noise and spun on his heel, striding to the window and back.

"I know how very much you require the £15,000," she said, "from my dowry."

Joseph growled again. "Oh, of course. I'll commit to any life-changing thing for £15,000. Don't flatter yourself, sweetheart. We require financing for the expedition, but I'm not destitute. There are other investors to be had. That's not why I married you, and you know it."

He glanced up, desperate for some reaction and saw her flinch. He swore and spun away.

"Honor," he heard himself say. "Honor, *Mrs. Chance*, is the reason that I would not annul the marriage. Although I would not fault your uncertainty, considering whoever left you in this condi . . ." He lost heart and repeated, "Considering whoever left you."

He looked again, another flinch. Truly, she could not appear more vulnerable. Her night rail and peignoir, a profusion of blue-green ruffles and silk, sagged limply, like the feathers of a wounded bird. Even now, the impulse to go to her was great. He clenched his fists and stalked to the other side of the bed.

"Your honor has never been in question," she said. "Even a man of honor would not be faulted for leaving our . . ." She blinked three times. "For leaving a woman who has been as dishonest as I have been. I hoped you would remain for the money."

Joseph ground his teeth together. He wanted to snatch

the frilly white pillows from the bed, rip them to feathers, and hurl them into the fire.

"The spoiled life of relative splendor in which you have existed until now prohibits you from seeing the insult of the money," he said. "I'm not a pauper, Tessa, regardless of what you may think."

"I did not mean to diminish your fortune," she said. "I merely meant. . . ." She faltered. He felt her struggle in his own throat, in his own heart. It tortured him to see her anything less than confident and laughing and proud.

But he was so bloody angry, and anger had a way of blotting out sympathy. He pounced on it. "Careful not to count your chickens before they hatch, darling. If I don't need your father's money, and honor does not require me to stay, then why do you think I'll remain?"

She shook her head.

"No, really," he pressed bitterly, "I want to know."

She blinked, her misery gave way to shock, if only for a minute. "You wish me to beg you?"

No, he thought miserably. "I want to know. Honestly. You've piqued my curiosity."

She narrowed her eyes and took a step back. She collided with the chair and reached for balance. Joseph fought the urge to steady her.

"Well," she began, "I thought you would not annul the marriage because an annulment would tarnish your reputation."

Joseph dropped his head back and stared at the ceiling. "The noose tightens. I require your money *and* your reputation.

I might reconsider the second one, darling, under the circumstances."

She made a little gasp. "Not *my* reputation, you cretin," she said, and Joseph looked at her, surprised at the bite in her voice.

Good, he thought, feeling a modicum of relief. Perhaps it was easier to behave like an arse in the face of someone who fought back.

She went on, "And I thought you would not wish to admit to your mentor, the Earl of Falcondale, that your new wife is . . . unfit."

"Trevor trusts my judgment, whatever I do," Joseph said. "Although I failed to spot this particular calamity before it jumped up and bit me on the arse, so perhaps that trust is misplaced."

"I beg your pardon, sir," she said, standing up straighter. "My child is not a calamity. No matter what you may think of me. And . . . and I'll seek annulment myself if you make the suggestion again."

Joseph stared, watching her chin go higher. *Yes*, he thought again, desperate for her to challenge his terrible behavior.

But now she seemed to lose heart. She dropped her face in her hands. He wanted to vault across the bed to reach her. He wanted to . . .

"Fine, Joseph," she said, raising her head. "You don't need the money. And your friends don't care who you marry. But you've said you intend to run for Parliament one day. Surely life in politics will call your reputation into question. How is that? Do you feel properly begged?"

"You believe gossip would prevent me from annulment?"

"I would expect you to avoid gossip when you can," she replied softly. "And I would expect you to want a loyal partner by your side."

He laughed. "Loyal partner? Do you hear your own words? You've just lied to me for a month, Tessa! Where's the loyalty in that?"

"I meant that a loyal *wife*, even a wife with a shameful secret, is preferred to chatter and gossip. If you annul the marriage, you will always have a hint of scandal, you will have this botched marriage in your past."

He nodded, barely listening. "Parliament is a dream—yes—but even without political office, I should like to have the companionship of an *honest* wife at my side. Above all. Honesty, Tessa. But not because of political aspirations, because life, in general, requires it. I always said that when I married, it would be to navigate life together, with a partner."

She made a sound that was half laugh, half sob. "Then why agree to marry a woman through an advertisement for money? This is hardly a scenario brimming with the potential for trust and partnership."

He spun around. "Because it never felt like advertising or money to me! I thought I was marrying a girl for whom I had genuine affection!"

"But I am that same girl." Her voice was small, so small he barely heard it. She spoke to her shoes. She did not lack conviction so much as . . . enthusiasm.

Joseph forged ahead. "Call me foolish, but I . . ." He laughed bitterly. "I was a believer in instant attraction, in Cupid's bloody arrow. Ridiculously, I assumed that when I saw the girl meant to be my wife, I would know her. On sight. And when I looked at you . . ." The pain in his throat and heart increased, and he coughed. He thumped a fist against his chest. For a terrible moment, he worried that he would retch. He left the bed and shoved open the window, breathing in great gulps of cold December air.

"I am the same girl," she repeated.

He looked over his shoulder. She'd followed him a handful of steps and hovered in the center of the room. Her arms where wrapped protectively around her body, embracing her own self. He wanted to hold her. He wanted to dry her cheeks of tears.

Tonight was meant to be the night when finally he could touch her, all of her. Tonight was meant to be the first of thousands of such nights. Now? Now he could not say what tomorrow night or any of a thousand future nights meant for either of them. A fresh wave of vengeful words rose in his mind, and he seized them.

"I've no idea *who* you are," he said and turned back to the window.

The night was damp, and he saw his breath in billowy puffs. He closed his eyes, trying to determine what in the bloody hell he was supposed to do now.

Their original plan had been for him to settle her in London next week and then sail to the Caribbean to join his partners for ten months, perhaps a year, making a go of an expedition that had the potential to make them all very rich.

For weeks, he and Tessa had bemoaned the impending separation—how they would miss each other—but she had been playacting all along. A ten-month absence was ideal for a woman with a nine-month secret—yet another reason, he realized, seeing it all so clearly now, she'd set her sights on him. She could swell into pregnancy, have the baby, and present it to him as his own when he returned. The passing of months and exact dates of their wedding would be vague and unimportant by the time the baby was born. Her plan was brilliant, really.

"Would you mind closing the window?" she asked quietly behind him. "Joseph? I'm cold."

Yes, he thought, *you are cold*. He rolled his eyes at his own dramatics. His new wife had revealed herself to be a great many things, but was she truly "cold"? In calculation or demeanor? She was a pregnant woman, desperate, and she'd done what she had to do for her own future and the future of her unborn child. She'd lied as long as she could, and then she had stopped lying. Now, she looked to him to sort out what they would do and how they would carry on. These were hardly the conditions he envisioned for the beginning of his marriage (in general) or his wedding night (in particular), but hadn't his entire life been one, long, un-ending heap of obstacles to be sorted? Why should his marriage be any different?

He locked the window and turned to her, leaning against the sill. "Tell me one thing. Do you still love him?"

"Who?" she asked, and she looked genuinely confused.

"The father of this baby," he ground out.

The look of horror on her face came on so quickly and was so distinctly repulsed, he thought for a moment she might be sick.

"No," she said, spitting out the word like poison. "No. Nor did I ever." She put a dainty hand to her slim throat, as if she choked on the man's very memory.

A dalliance then, Joseph thought, feeling the burn of jealousy, but he did not press her. Obviously, the topic distressed her. He was behaving like an arse, but he was not a masochist.

He dropped his head in his hands. "Why did you not simply tell me from the start, Tessa?" He looked up at her. "Say to me, 'I'm in a bad way. Will you help?' Why pretend to be so . . . taken with me?"

She nodded to this, whether to indicate she understood the question or to agree, he did not know. After a moment, she said, "My experience with revealing the pregnancy has not been . . . agreeable."

Joseph swore. "Who did you endeavor to marry before me?"

"No one! I told only the father of the baby, and his reaction was . . ." She trailed off.

"But *me*, Tessa?" He crossed to her. "Did I seem so horrible that you could not tell *me*? For the days and weeks we have been together?"

"You have been horrible tonight," she whispered. "Tonight you have proved my point."

He chuckled. "Yes, I suppose I have."

He ambled away from the window and came to a stop in front of her. She took two steps back. Joseph swore again.

Just this morning, they'd used any excuse to reach out and touch. Fingertips, shoulders, the rare and precious embrace. And now . . .

"Not that your reaction isn't . . . warranted," she said. "And you have been far less horrible than . . . than the other."

"Never let it be said that I am equal in horribleness to a man who would destitute a pregnant woman."

To this, she had no answer. She stared up at him. Her eyes were huge and solemn, a dark blue he'd never seen. The authentic blue of the authentic woman. Finally.

After a moment, she repeated her urgent question in a whisper. "Will you annul the marriage?"

The most important thing. She would debate motive all night long. She would apologize. She would endure his outrage. But what she really wanted was to know *this*.

"Am I horrible enough to annul the marriage to a woman who I do not know? At all?"

"I am not so unknown to you as you think," she whispered, closing her eyes.

"You are entirely unknown to me," he said.

She flinched, and Joseph shook his head, marveling at her. This particular barb did not even seem so cruel. Merely true. *You are entirely unknown to me.* He did not know her. He could not believe she would deny it.

"Will you do it?" she whispered, drawing a deep breath. When she looked up, tears spilled down her cheeks.

He sighed heavily. "No, Tessa, I will not annul the

marriage. I'm not sure what sort of man that you believe me to be, but clearly he's as far from reality as the person I believed you to be."

She raised her chin at this, scraping the tears from her cheeks with a careless flick of her hand. "I am not proud of this night, Joseph, or these last months or of my situation, but I . . . I cannot believe that I am rotten to the core because I found myself pregnant and alone, I cannot."

"Oh, no," he said, pointing his finger at her. "Don't make me the bastard who cried harlot or tried to shame you. Do not. Let us be very clear. I am not angry about this baby. I am angry because you misled me. For weeks!"

"I was terrified of you."

"In no way am I terrifying, Tessa, ask anyone."

"I am terrified now," she said in a small voice.

"No, you are not, you are relieved."

"You've no idea how I feel."

"That, madam, has been perfectly well established. I have no idea. None. You are a mystery to me in every way."

She dropped her face in her hands then, and he finally heard a wrenching sob, then another, and another.

He swore violently and spun away. "It is impossible to articulate the very great ambition I had for our marriage, Tessa. I loved everything about you—or the you that I believed you to be. I loved your playful spirit, your provocativeness, your curiosity, your *joie de vivre*. Your beauty took my breath away. You made me feel clever and capable. You made me feel as if you believed that I, a former servant, could rise to the occasion and deign to marry a wealthy gentleman's daughter.

It was the perfect combination of enchantment and vanity. And I believed all of it."

"I never . . ." Tessa began, but Joseph cut her off.

"You never what?" he demanded. "Lied to me? You've just admitted to lying, daily, for weeks. And surely you can see how I may no longer trust your . . . your wiles? That perfect spell of beauty and charm and scintillation? What confidence I felt about our . . . our union, how proud I was to provide for you? Now that I've learned that these were the expertly calculated desired results . . ."

Tessa blinked at him three times, shook her head slightly, and then put her hands to her hair, grabbing long, blonde handfuls. She made a shrill noise of frustration and turned away from him, stalking across the room.

"There is no winning," she said. It was the loudest she'd yet spoken. "But what did I expect?" She dropped her hands and her hair slid down her back. "Honestly, what did I expect?" Now she laughed, a sad, deflated sound. "Actually, I expected far worse. Or rather, I expected far different, but in a worse way. Although . . . I'm not sure how it could be worse than this. I'm sorry, Joseph." Tears cracked her voice, but she forged ahead. "I'm so incredibly sorry. Likely there are twenty different ways I could have handled the situation from the moment we met. Each time I chose what I could manage or what I could not resist. The indulgent life I have led up until this moment is no excuse, but still, I hold it up. To say I was unprepared to deal with the ramifications of an unexpected baby is such an extreme understatement. If my friend Willow had not placed the advert that brought you to me"—now she pointed to the advert laying half folded beside the chair—"God knows what I would have done."

Joseph listened, coming to terms with the reality of her authentic self, making an appearance for the very first time.

"And what if you had simply told your parents?" he asked. "Tessa, what if you had simply asked for their help? They indulge you in most things. They've just thrown you the wedding of the century. Why not appeal to them?"

Tessa shook her head. "Impossible. Indiscretion is something they would never tolerate. Their priorities for me revolve around the family's reputation and place in society. I am to be beautiful but also above reproach. My mother plays the grand lady but her beginnings are nearly as humble as yours. She craves acceptance and esteem among the other women in her circle. She would not recover from the shame if she knew. My father could not look me in the eye if he felt I had succumbed to something so base as . . . as to conceive a child outside of wedlock. It is unthinkable to view me in this way. I asked you to conceal your history for the same reason. They would never have allowed the union if they'd known. They are . . ." She stopped and swallowed. "Things are either right or wrong to them. Proper or improper. Allowed or . . . banished. They have indulged me, yes. But conditionally. Their indulgence would not . . . extend to this situation. I had so few choices. So, I ruined your life instead."

"My life has not been ruined," he said, an impulse. He narrowed his eyes to think this over. Had his life been ruined? His life had been given a detonating shock that rocked him to the very core.

He heard himself extrapolate. "My life has changed course. I only intend to be married once. And now I find myself married, but . . . under entirely different auspices. So far from what I thought of my once-in-a-lifetime union."

"I had different intentions as well," she said, turning away. "Of course my new path should not affect your path, but it does. For this, I am so sorry, Joseph."

"Yes," he said. "How very sorry we both are."

There was a pause. He allowed himself to look at her, to take in her beauty.

After a long moment, she said, "But what of our plans for your departure and your return? Will I . . . ?" She paused, watching him, waiting.

He could feel her uncertainty. He almost broke under the pressure of the . . . was that regret in her eyes? But the phrase *our plans* echoed in his ears, as if the future they had so carefully planned together still applied, now that she had trapped him. He raised an eyebrow, forcing her say the words.

She cleared her throat and began again, raising her chin. She was not accustomed to ungracious behavior. "Will I see you when you return from Barbadoes?"

He'd not thought of this, of course. He'd only just learned his life was not as he believed, he'd thought of nothing.

"I will deliver you to your friends in Belgravia tomorrow," he said, a snap decision. "I can hop a steamship bound for the Caribbean tomorrow night. I . . . I cannot say what will happen when I return."

She began shaking her head. Her eyes shone. He gritted his teeth, hating that he had caused her to cry again.

She said, "But are you certain this is what you want? Perhaps we should talk about—"

"No," he cut her off. "I've . . ." he exhaled heavily ". . . grown weary of talking. Enough has been said for one night. I'm exhausted. You are exhausted. I will leave you. There is another bedroom. I will sleep there."

She took a step toward him, and he froze, holding his breath. He honestly had no idea what he would do if she asked him to stay. His anger had cooled, but his hurt glowed like an ember. And still, the pounding desire he'd felt from the first was an urgent, underlying thud. He was shocked by the persistence of his desire.

"The servants," she said weakly. "My parents must not learn that we have not . . ."

"Tangle the bedsheets," he said, grimly satisfied to feel himself walk away. His pride had not left him entirely. He turned. "I've work that will see me up before sunrise— provisioning and ledgers. I will rise before the staff. They will not know the difference." He sighed and stalked from the room. "We will leave before luncheon. No one need ever know."

CHAPTER SEVEN

After . . .

Ten months later, Joseph Chance returned to England with a plan to salvage his future. The plan had five tenets (six, if you counted the research he'd already done on Parliamentary districts).

"Six tenets," Joseph told Stoker as they strode down Upper Belgrave Street, autumn leaves swirling at their feet, "and not one of them includes hunting down my wife."

Stoker grunted, clearly disinterested, and Joseph amended, "Forgive me, my *estranged* wife."

"You could hardly return to London and not see her at all," sighed Stoker. "You were always going to call on her eventually."

"Yes," agreed Joseph, "*eventually*. In a fortnight. Or two months. The date was not important because it was never meant to be today, our first morning back. We've scarcely been on dry land for two hours. I've not even had a proper English breakfast or a bath."

After five weeks on rough seas, the partners had sailed

into the Thames Estuary just after midnight. Stoker's brig sat low in the water, weighted down by 150 barrels of guano squeezed into the hold. The haul represented nearly a million pounds in profit from anxious buyers, pending delivery.

Pending being the pivotal word.

"This does not happen to me," Joseph grumbled. "It happens to other shipping merchants. To careless amateurs. Reckless, lazy men with no foresight."

"It happens to everyone," said Stoker.

"Not to me," said Joseph emphatically. "By design, it has never happened to me."

Joseph and his partners were, at the moment, adrift. Their heavy-laden brig and sea-weary crew had coasted just outside of London and dropped anchor. Joseph and Stoker and two crew members had rowed a small tender boat to shore and checked in at the West India Docks to claim their docking rights for the brig. Joseph had reserved a slip, their spot in docks, more than a year before. But, when they presented themselves to the mooring officer, they learned their long-reserved slip had been *canceled*. Given over to another ship. Let go.

By one Tessa Chance.

"Is it a ploy?" Joseph asked Stoker angrily. "A joke?"

"Honestly," Stoker sighed, "this is the least of what I might expect. Considering."

Joseph continued, "This is a woman who could not have shown less interest in the brig or the island or the guano when she and I met. Her previous interests were fashion and dancing and kittens. And now she's canceled my docking privileges and made off with hundreds of pounds?"

"Things rarely carry out exactly as you plan them, Joe. Especially when you've been out of the country for the better part of a year. You know this."

Joseph ignored him. "What I *don't* know is why. Why would she begin to meddle *now*? Is she trying to drive me out? Is that it? Did she believe that barring us from her father's precious dock would actually keep us from reaching London at all?"

Joseph had reserved a slip at the West India Docks in Blackwall, the most established dockyard and warehouse space in London. Their sail date had been unknown, and he'd paid the highest price to guarantee a slip whenever they returned. It was true, Tessa's father sat on the board of the West India Docks, but the slip had been bought and paid for before he'd even *met* the St. Croixs.

"You believe her father is behind the canceled slip?" asked Stoker.

"That's not what the mooring officer said, was it?" Joseph ground his teeth together, remembering the scene in the dock house just hours before.

"'Tis all been canceled, sir," the jolly man had informed Joseph and Stoker. "More than four months ago."

"Canceled?" Joseph had repeated stupidly. "Canceled by *whom*?"

"Well, by your wife, of course, Mr. Chance. She saw to it all."

"I beg your pardon?" Joseph had been certain he'd misheard.

"It's all been taken care of, never you fear. Your wife was very thorough and *emphatic*."

The conversation had revealed little more than this revised reality: the spot he had reserved to dock their brig upon return from Barbadoes had been *let go* by his wife.

The River Thames was the busiest shipping port in the world. Without the guaranteed slip, he and his partners would have no place to dock their brig on the crowded river, a circumstance that could extend for weeks, if not months.

"This might mean finding a dock outside of London," Joseph said. "Imagine the losses. And that says nothing of the warehouse space."

"Before you convict her, *ask her*," said Stoker. "She may have some surprise solution."

"Oh, she's full of surprises," scoffed Joseph.

They rounded the corner at Chesham Place, bound for Wilton Crescent. Joseph scowled at the shiny new sign that marked the street. He'd left Tessa at the last townhome on this street some ten months ago.

"If she's bolted from that house, I swear," Joseph said, "I cannot be held accountable for my actions."

"I'm on the brink of bolting myself," said Stoker. "I only agreed to come as far as Hyde Park. You're on your own when we reach the house, Joe. I've no wish to see Sabine."

"And I've no wish to see Tessa," said Joseph.

"That remains to be seen."

They walked half a block in silence, looking up and down the street. Belgravia was a hive of activity; lurching wagons, crews of masons and carpenters, and lines of men digging to contain the endless mud. The neighborhood held the promise of great majesty and aplomb, but at the moment, it was still being built, block by block.

Joseph had visited the neighborhood only twice. Once before his wife's confession of her pregnancy, and once after. On the first visit, he had regarded their forthcoming union as an unexpected love match—and how lucky they were. He'd gone to Belgravia to ensure that the house in which his new bride would live was safe and comfortable, and to make the introduction of the aunt with whom she and the other brides would live.

On the second visit, he'd known the truth, and his heart and pride were in tatters. He came only to deposit Mrs. Tessa Chance with her friends and go.

And now the third visit: an unscheduled call for which he did not have time, to ascertain why a cancella—

A bell jingled across the street and Joseph looked up. They had just made the corner at West Halkin. The bell rang again, a shop door opened and closed.

Directly in front of him, not three yards away, stood a petite young woman in a drab beige dress and a bonnet the color of mud. Her arms were loaded with parcels. A lock of pale hair, bright against the dark silk, dropped from her hat and fell across her face. She blew it away. The September sun was bright and she paused on the sidewalk and turned her face up to the warm light.

Joseph stopped walking. Stoker continued and Joseph held out a hand to stop him. And now, *everything* stopped, the whole rest of the world.

Her dress and hat were different, but she looked almost exactly as she had the very first time he had ever seen her.

Tessa.

Joseph grabbed a handful of Stoker's shirt in his fist. Stoker swore and shoved him off, but Joseph didn't notice. The only sound was blood rushing in his ears. He was shot through with a jolt of anticipation, like the snap of a mandolin string.

But what did he anticipate? Confronting her? Demanding answers? Boasting about what a great success the expedition had been?

His throat began to close. He drew a ragged breath. He was sweating.

And then he felt the soft, buoyant feeling of his heart, rising in his chest. He felt . . . delight.

And desire. Hot, hungry desire.

His outrage took on a new shape, its true shape, and it had nothing to do with the cock-up with the docks or the lost money.

The true outrage was that he wanted her still. Mind. Soul. Body. All of her. Even now, even after all these many months, after all the deceit and subterfuge.

Joseph gritted his teeth, furious with himself for his reaction. He'd only glanced at her for a split second, for God's sake, and from the width of the road.

This, he thought, was why he had planned to stay away as long as he could.

This was why her interference infuriated him.

"Go, Stoker," Joseph said, not looking away from her.

"Gladly. But Joe—"

"*Go,*" Joseph repeated.

Stoker eyed him for a second, glanced at Tessa, whistled low under his breath, and was gone.

CHAPTER EIGHT

Mrs. Tessa Chance had embarked upon her new life in London by devising two lists. The first list outlined all the ways she would no longer behave. It covered affectations such as eyelash batting, pouting, playful, lingering taps with her fan, and the long, slow controlled fall she affected when a gentleman lifted her from a horse.

The second list comprised all the things she *would* do. She would be serious, she would be reserved, she would be discreet and detached. She would be all the things that would never invite a man to attack her against a tree. Or marry her because she was tricking him into doing it.

In short, the lists were meant to repel men who might betray her and keep her away from men that she, herself, might betray.

She had worked many days devising the lists and even more days, weeks, and months adhering to them. She had made such progress.

Until.

Until her estranged husband stepped before her in West Halkin Street and called her name, setting off a jolt of reactions that were the *opposite* of progress.

"Tessa?" Joseph Chance said, Tessa looked up, and there he was.

Or rather, there was an (unbelievably) more rugged and handsome version of him. His skin was as tan as the pelt of a buck. His shoulders were broader—work-muscled shoulders—his waist leaner. His hair was streaked with shades of white-blond. He must not have shaved for a week.

The sight of him set off the cold tingle of shock, as if all the blood had been drained from her veins. She stopped breathing. She somehow managed to stop her beating heart.

Joseph is home.

Home, standing before her, tanned skin and dusty clothes and all the rest. After ten months.

She struggled to catch her breath. Blood and heat rushed quickly back in a rolling wave. She clung to her packages like buoys in the surf.

"You've returned," she heard herself say. Her voice was an airy little gasp, winded, absolutely nothing like she had planned.

"Well, I'm *endeavoring* to return." He raised his eyebrows. He waited. He sounded . . . sardonic? His voice was as flat and cool as the surface of a brick.

Tessa was confused. She'd prepared herself for him to return when she least expected it, and she'd prepared for his residual anger. But she did not expect him to stand in the road, raise his eyebrows, and speak to her as if he was throwing down a gauntlet.

A small wagon pulled between them, and she held her breath, waiting for it to pass. She tried to think of what reserved, measured thing she would say next. She took a step toward him.

"But have you all come?" she asked. "Cassin and Stoker, too? You've sailed the brig back to England?"

"Yes," Joseph said, "*back to England.*" He frowned as the tail of the wagon rumbled past. He moved around it and stepped closer, but not close. It was a cautious distance, an uncivil, suspicious distance. She stared at the four feet of gravel between them. It seemed as wide as the Atlantic.

"Look," he said, crossing his arms, "you'll have to forgive my directness, but what the bloody hell have you done to the slip I arranged at the West India Docks?"

She blinked. She had anticipated a great many things, but she had not prepared for him to *accuse* her. If she was being honest, she had not been prepared for him to fail to say hello.

He went on, "The mooring officer has turned me away, naming *my wife* as the reason. We've dropped anchor in the estuary, but we can hardly remain there. I hope you can tell me why I have sailed for five weeks across the bloody Atlantic, carrying a fortune in cargo, only to reach London and have nowhere to dock the brig?"

"But did the steam tug not give you my letter?" she said, trying to catch up.

He sucked in a breath and held it, an exaggerated gesture of irritation. "*What. Letter?* I would be a rich man if I had a shilling for each time I've been forced to repeat something about this day that makes no sense."

I thought you were already a rich man, she thought, but she did not say it. The last thing she wished to appear was greedy. He would not cooperate with her plan for a house and modest income if she came off as greedy. And besides— she was not greedy. She did not want his money, she wanted only to survive.

Her second instinct was to laugh. He'd made a joke and it was marginally clever. But she had worked very hard to purge herself from laughing at the jokes of men. She was a serious woman of business now, not to mention someone's mother. There was no place in this conversation for laughter.

Ultimately, a passing gentleman saved her from any reaction at all.

"I beg your pardon, miss," said a tall, fashionably dressed man drawing up beside her. "May I offer my assistance with your parcels?"

Tessa smiled immediately (smiling at polite gentlemen was one habit she could not break), and she said, "How very kind you are, sir, but that won't be necessary. I—"

Suddenly the distance between herself and Joseph was not so great. He was beside her, his hand on her lower back. Tessa blinked at the warm pressure of his palm.

Joseph told the man, "I've got them, thank you very much."

"I've *asked* the young lady," said the gentleman.

"Bugger off," Joseph growled, jerking his chin in the direction of the street. He took Tessa by the elbow and began to hustle her along. "What letter?" he repeated.

"I can walk unassisted, thank you very much," she said, jerking her arm free.

He grumbled an apology, but he was glaring at the other man over his shoulder.

Tessa stopped walking. Joseph tried to unburden her of the boxes, but she clutched them to her. She took a deep breath. Even before the lists, she could not tolerate being rushed or bullied. When she explained what she'd done, she'd wanted the tone to be exactly, perfectly right. She'd wanted to be proficient and useful. She'd not planned to be defending herself.

She shuffled her parcels and said, "You've been misinformed, Joseph. And I'm sorry. There has been no effective way to communicate with you in Barbadoes, as you well know. I've written you several times and left word at both the West India dock office and Waterman's Steam Packet Company, which, as you know, operates the steam tug. The cancellations at the West India Docks could not be avoided. I've made new arrangements to salvage what I could of an efficient return to London."

He blinked down at her, almost as if he was seeing her, really seeing her, for the first time.

Good, she thought, *he is seeing me for the first time. And I am changed.*

She cleared her throat and imbued her voice with a rehearsed businesslike clip. "But I refuse to hash it out in the street. You will have to accompany me home to discuss it."

The old Tessa would have turned her nose in the air, spun on her heel, and marched away. The old Tessa would have expected him to rush after her. Now she simply waited.

Joseph hesitated, and for a moment she thought he might refuse.

"Right," he finally said. His voice came out in a huff. "Home. To discuss it."

The exchange sounded like a concession, a concession between very formal, very irritated strangers, and Tessa supposed that was exactly what it was. Unfortunately, there were so many more formalities and irritations and concessions to come. But she had new priorities now, her infant son chief among them. If it had been only her, she would have joined a convent and retreated from society forever, carved out some safe place of solitude. But it had not been only herself. Christian was the center of her world now, and his future was all that mattered.

They reached No. 22, the house in which she, her friends, and now her son lived with Mr. and Mrs. Arthur Boyd. The Boyds were the aunt and uncle of her friend Willow, and they had generously taken them in when all three girls came to London, newly married with husbands sailing across the Atlantic.

The townhome was small but fashionable, one of the very first built in Belgravia. Tessa was nearly as grateful to Mary and Arthur for taking her in as she was to Joseph for marrying her. But despite the Boyds' seemingly endless generosity, she could not impose forever. Her friend Willow had already moved to Yorkshire to be with her husband's family. Willow's aunt and uncle were dear, generous souls, but Tessa arrived on their doorstep as one person, and now she was a mother with a baby and a nursemaid. By springtime at latest, she and the baby must move on.

"Mary and Arthur are calling on clients at the moment," Tessa told Joseph, clipping up the steps and knocking for the butler to admit them. *And the baby is napping*, she added silently in her head. Joseph would eventually have to meet the child who bore his name, but good lord, one thing at a time.

The butler admitted them and signaled for a footman to relieve her of her shopping. She unpinned her hat. Her hands shook, the movement appearing tense and jerky. Her heart raced like she'd sprinted home from the shops.

She said, "Sabine is out—she's always out—so we should be able to sit alone in the parlor, ring for tea, and discuss what's happened."

"*Forget* tea," Joseph sighed impatiently. "I prefer to get right to it, if you don't mind."

Or, she thought, *we will get right to it*.

The butler hovered discreetly, and she handed him her hat and pelisse and dismissed him. She turned back to Joseph. He looked prepared to shout, *You did what?* regardless of how she explained the new situation. She would not be intimidated by him, but she was a little saddened. She never meant for his return to be combative. She took a deep breath and resigned herself.

"My parents traveled to London in late spring to call on me," she said. It felt strange to tell this story while they hovered in the entryway, but she couldn't force him to sit down. She'd forced him enough already.

She continued, "By that time—this would have been May, I suppose—the baby had just arrived. Their visit took me completely by surprise."

She glanced up, hoping for reaction. Of course he had not yet inquired about the baby, about her lying or her life as a mother. He hadn't asked anything about her except how he might dock his brig.

She went on, "My parents were . . . shocked to discover a grandchild so soon after my marriage. As you know, you left the country within days of the wedding. It took very little time for them to count the months and conclude that there was no way that you could be the baby's father."

And now he gave some reaction. It was not a generous reaction, no concern revealed, but at least the blank stoicism fell away. He had the look of a horseman who had come upon a dead tree in the road. *Jump over it or rein in?* Panic mingled with indecision. Finally, he said hoarsely, "What happened?"

"I've been disowned," she said. "That's what happened. I've been evicted from the family."

"I beg your pardon?"

She shook her head. "I wish there was a more pleasant way to say it, but 'disowned' seems to sum things up nicely. They will not receive me, support me, or acknowledge me. Or my son." She took a deep breath. "Now will you sit down?"

CHAPTER NINE

Tessa's parents' rejection drained Joseph's righteous indignation. It was the very last thing he expected her to say. She was meant to be cool and calculating. She was meant to be happily carrying on with her life, using his name. She was meant to be . . . if nothing else . . . well. Happy.

Fine.

He took a step back, trying to reconcile this news. Tessa's face tightened.

She said, "You've made it clear that you are a busy man, but I believe this conversation warrants at least five minutes of your time."

"Of course," he said. "I didn't mean to retreat, merely—" He paused, searching for what he meant. "I don't know what to say, Tessa. I'm stunned."

He was also angry, confused, and . . . sorry. So terribly sorry.

However, he wasn't prepared to say those things yet.

"I endeavored to put it all down in a letter," she told him.

"I even managed to get some version of it off, but obviously the note has missed you."

"Obviously," he repeated, and then he winced. He didn't care about the damned letter. He also cared far less about the brig and the cargo and the missing slip, but it was all he could think to say at the moment. Before he'd fully considered his words, he said, "So, your *father* canceled the slip?"

"No, I did it," she said. "A preventative measure. When my parents disowned me, they vowed to separate themselves from you, too."

"They believe the child is—" He stopped himself and frowned. It wasn't important what they thought of him.

Her voice was sharp. "I told them you were not the father. I've sworn off dishonesty, if you can believe it."

"I do," he said. They hovered in the doorway, half in the corridor, half in the parlor. His world shrank to her. "I believe you," he repeated, and he realized that this was true.

Tessa turned away and began to pace the parlor. "After my parents discovered the truth, they looked more closely into your life and business. They had been wholly won over by you, and they couldn't understand why a man of your accomplishments would help me and my fatherless baby." She turned back to him.

"You didn't ask for my help, did you?" he asked. "You simply pushed things through."

She nodded and looked at the floor. "Regardless, they soon turned up the details of your boyhood in service, and they had their answer. After that, they wanted nothing to do with you."

"The feeling is mutual," Joseph scoffed.

Tessa finished, "I am truly sorry, as I know you valued my father's mentorship. It is another casualty of my . . . situation, I'm afraid."

"I've no further need of your father," he said, and he meant it.

Tessa stared at him. Her expression was confused and cautious and something else he could not name.

Finally, she took a deep breath and said, "And *that* is the reason I canceled your slip at the West India Docks. My father's position on the West India board gives him the power to block you from the docks forever, and I assure you, he harbors quite enough outrage and ill will to do it. In order to salvage what I could of your Barbadoes venture, I saw no choice but to seek out the dock house myself, learn the system in the mooring office, and cancel your previous contract. I'm sorry you arrived with no warning about the change. It was done only to prevent him from taking some other action. He can be very rash and destructive when he feels betrayed. I felt it would be best that all trace of your business had been removed from the records."

"Forgive me," he said, following her into the parlor, "my mind has not moved on from this treatment by your parents, I cannot think about the dock. I don't understand why you cannot . . . ? That is—"

He shook his head and began again, "Your parents seemed like reasonable people. Granted, I did not know them well. I was at Berymede only a matter of weeks." He frowned. "A little adherent to propriety, I suppose." Another frown. "But to disown you?"

"It was always ambitious to think they would not discover my . . . secret."

"Alright, fine, they learned about the baby. But to separate from you entirely?"

Tessa threw up her hands, fingers spread. "Joseph? Why do you think I kept the baby secret and scrambled to find a husband? For what reason did I marry you?"

Not because you loved me, he thought. *Not because you trusted me to help you.*

Joseph shook his head. "Because you made some solitary plan and were determined to see it through?"

She raised her hands again. "Because I knew this would be their reaction." She turned away and stalked the length of the room. When she spoke again, her voice was controlled. "To them, reputation is paramount. Even if they had managed some compassion or understanding, their shame would have been very great. I would have been secreted away, my baby taken from me, some fabrication would have been spun about my absence."

She shrugged. "But they are not compassionate or understanding. As I knew they would not be." She circled a yellow chair and then dropped into it. "At least they've been quiet about it. A public shunning would only have compounded their humiliation. To the world, we married for love and had a baby right away. So, please do not think our marriage was in vain."

"I do not believe we married in vain," he said.

To his surprise, she blushed at his statement. Her color was already high, she'd had so much to convey. She looked, he thought, so beautiful. Despite her terrible dress and the tight, unyielding way she'd styled her hair. Despite the look of distress on her face.

But beauty had never been the problem. He had spent sleepless nights on the island, dreaming about her beauty. He wanted to stare. To take in what he remembered and account for the changes. To admire. To lo—

Instead, he cleared his throat and looked around the room.

The decor of the townhome was lovely. The walls and upholstery were coated in soft colors. There were potted ferns. A lush garden glowed autumn red and gold through the window.

"The Boyds' house is lovely," he said. From nowhere, he thought, *Tell me you hate it.*

Weep and tell me you hate it.

Beg me to take you away from it.

Ask me to take you anywhere.

Joseph blinked, reeling from this radical new line of thought.

Tessa told him, "Willow's aunt and uncle have been so very generous. And it is a fine house. This townhome will always be the envy of the neighborhood, even with mansions going up around it. It has been very comfortable."

Joseph nodded and looked around again. It was not an unfit house. Certainly, it was more modern and tastefully arranged than his own London home. He'd bought a house in Blackheath the year before, sparing no expense. Blackheath was a respectable neighborhood (the *only* respectable neighborhood) near the London docks, but the house sat empty while he was at sea. He furnished it in fits and starts, a work in progress.

Is it fit for a wife and baby? he wondered, surprising himself again—shocking himself. He'd not come here to relocate Tessa and her baby to his own home. He'd not planned to come here at all.

Tessa finished, "It's been lovely, but I have a mind to move us in the near future. In the spring, I hope."

Joseph's heart stopped.

He realized with stunning clarity that, somewhere deep inside the hard knot of his heart, he *had* fantasized about taking her and the baby away. He'd fantasized so many scenarios for her.

As for the baby?

Honestly, Joseph had expected to encounter the child immediately upon entering the house. When he had thought of Tessa from Barbadoes (which had been frequent), he thought of her always with the child. In his mind's eye, the infant would be crying, or she would be preoccupied, or both.

And yet now here he was, his first day back in England, sitting down with Tessa, and there was no baby to be seen. And now Tessa was telling him she would relocate, and Joseph's throat felt like it was closing up.

His brain screamed, *I've not even seen the boy—*

Tessa interjected, "The baby and I cannot impose on Mary and Arthur forever. I am accustomed to caring for him now." She looked up and gave him a weak smile. "This took some . . . time. Also, Willow's former lady's maid, Perry, has agreed to stay on as our nurse for a while longer. But the baby and I must eventually settle somewhere in . . . in earnest. This was always temporary, wasn't it?"

As revelations went (and it felt very much like a revelation), it was calmly stated and oddly devoid of specifics. She hardly sounded happy, but he could not name the other flat emotion in her words or her expression.

Was she hopeful about relocating or regretful? He couldn't say, but he wanted to know. Even more, he wished to know what role she envisioned for him in this move.

Her vague calmness unnerved him. *Unnerved* was a mild word for what he felt. She was calm, direct, and controlled; so very different from the chatty, flouncy, reactionary girl he had met last autumn.

Is this the authentic Tessa? he wondered.

Would the spiritedness and colorful dramatics that so intrigued him when they first met not be seen again? The Tessa of their courtship had veritably bubbled with conversation. He'd listened to countless stories about shopping trips or her vexation with her brothers or some funny trick she'd seen from the cat. She'd discussed her love for the piano, for her friends, her hatred of the grey and hopeless month of March.

Of course, she had been playacting all those months ago. What he'd taken as spirit had been feminine wiles meant to distract him. And what need had she for wiles now? He'd married her, hadn't he? She could not care less whether he was attracted to her or not.

Joseph studied her face, her bright blue eyes and pink

mouth. If she'd been playacting when they first met, she had been deuced good at it. In all honesty, this new calmness seemed just as natural.

"Before I detain you any longer," Tessa said, "let me explain to you what I have done about the brig. It was never my intention that you would reach London and be shut out."

Joseph stared at her. And now they would discuss docking rights? He opened his mouth to tell her he would sort it out himself, that he was sorry for his insistence and assumptions before, but she spoke over him.

"I'll skip to the most relevant bit that will, with any luck, put your mind at ease and allow you to dock the brig immediately—today, if we're lucky." From the pocket of her skirt, she pulled a small, leather-bound booklet. It fell open on the low table before them, revealing pages of handwritten notes.

"There are irrelevant bits?" Joseph asked. He squinted at the book.

"Well, no," Tessa said, "I simply meant we should get right to it. I made a promise to myself not to burden you with the details of my family."

"I am not burdened by the topic of your family, Tessa." His voice was defensive. He *felt* defensive. He'd never put off anything she'd wanted to discuss. *She* had been the one who chose to shut him out.

"No?" she challenged.

No, he wanted to shout. But he raised his eyebrows.

"But you've not asked about my son, have you?" she said quietly.

Oh, *that* part of her family. *You're entirely correct,* he thought. *I haven't asked about the baby because I don't want to know.*

And on the heels of that thought, he had another, more powerful, thought: *It's killing me that I do not know.*

Slowly, haltingly, he asked, "How have you and the baby . . ." He paused, considering which of a million questions to ask her, ". . . gotten on?"

"Oh, very well, thank you," she said, also halting. Their conversation sounded as if their primary language was some foreign tongue, and they were practicing at English. "He is called Christian. You may remember this from my letter. Thank you for the money, by the way." She looked up at him, a little abashed. It occurred to him that she felt beholden to him. Good lord, money had been the easiest sacrifice, it had been no sacrifice. His heart, his pride—these were a different story.

He tried again. "Are you . . . well? Is he healthy?"

"Quite well," she said briskly. The formal, businesslike smile was back. He frowned. Was this all she meant to say? Her tone forestalled further discussion, but now he wanted to hear more. He suddenly, *urgently,* wanted to hear everything about the boy and Tessa's journey into motherhood.

He ventured, "I should like to meet him, when you are ready."

She'd been looking down, studying her notes, but now her head came up. She searched his face. What she looked for, he could not say. She studied him like she was trying to identify an insect in a book.

Finally, she said, "He is napping at the moment, but I should like very much to introduce you. He is a lovely baby." She paused for a moment. "Motherhood is nothing like I expected. But I like it. And I love my son. Above all, I love him."

My son, Joseph repeated in his head. Her words held an unexpected fierceness and it heartened him. Fierceness had been one of the qualities he'd loved about her in the weeks before the wedding. It felt good to see some connection between the girl he'd thought he'd loved and the stranger who sat before him.

"But let me show you what I've done about the dock," Tessa said, pulling his attention back to her notes. "All is not lost, I hope."

Joseph sighed and looked down at her notes. "I hope not."

CHAPTER TEN

Tessa forced herself to push aside talk of the baby, though it had not been easy. She'd *wanted* to discuss the baby, to describe at length how happy and alert and *round* he was. She'd wavered half a second, debating whether to dart from the room, scoop Christian from his crib, and return to present him to Joseph, this little wonder with whom she had been entrusted by God. Proof that she had survived—nay, she had transformed—and that Christian was so very worth all the heartbreak.

But of course, Joseph might not agree that he was worth the heartbreak, and this she could not bear. She glanced at him, sprawled on the opposite chair in the parlor.

Her instinct was correct, she thought. An introduction now was wrong, odd and rushed and muddled with this other business. She had decided months ago that when she was finally reunited with Joseph, she would lead with her work on the docking rights and the brig.

Removing a pen and inkpot from what she considered her office kit, Tessa ran a hand over the crease in her notebook. She considered the serious, businesslike expressions she had rehearsed in her mirror. Her reflection had always looked as if she was trying to repress a sneeze.

Be direct, she reminded herself. All the progress she'd made since embarking on the new deal with the docks had been the result, in part, of directness.

She cleared her throat and looked to Joseph.

"Can you tell me where the brig is at the moment?" she asked, tapping her pen against the notebook. "You mentioned the Thames Estuary. But where exactly? Margate? Sheerness?"

Joseph scrunched up his face, looking at her as if she'd spoken in code. "What difference does that make?"

"Well, it will influence the steam tug company we use, won't it? I see my error now in leaving word for you only with two tug companies. Of course you'd use Waterman's if you've dropped anchor as far out as the Medway Estuary. But perhaps you made it to Canvey Island?"

"Forgive me," he said, speaking slowly. "I did not expect you to question me. When did *you* learn the difference between Margate and the bloody Medway Estuary?"

Tessa closed her little book. Of course he would be surprised. Every man with whom she had dealt since she'd begun to rearrange his docking rights had been surprised by her—and they hadn't even known the old Tessa, frivolous and featherheaded and coy. She was a young woman, and that had been surprise enough.

She laid her pen on the table between them. "Well, I

hope you did not expect me to cancel your existing docking reservation without learning how best to sort something else out."

"I did not expect you to cancel my docking plans at all." He ran a hand through his hair. "I understand that you've had this . . . falling-out with your family and that you were trying to make some concession. But this does not translate into you knowing anything about steam tugs or the ports along the River Thames, does it? You've not even set eyes on the brig. I'm shocked you're even aware of the existence of a steam tug."

And here was the second attitude Tessa met when she dealt with the men who ran the warehouses and docks. Condescension.

Before she realized it, she was on her feet. "I've not had a falling-out with my family—on this I wish to be perfectly clear. On *every* point," she clarified, "I want to be perfectly clear. I vowed to stop revising the truth on the night of our wedding."

She glanced at him. He stared at her as if she had grown a tail.

She went on. "My parents have *disowned* me. I will never see them again. I can carry on, thanks most of all to you, but I proceed knowing that the family meant to support and love and provide for me did so only conditionally. I failed at their conditions and they have . . . forgotten me. In no way was it a falling-out, so let us not call it what it is not."

He pushed from his chair. "Tessa, wait, I—"

"*And*," she continued, "I have not made some *concession* for your docking rights, I have spent months learning the system of importation, levies, warehouses, buyers, and yes, docks, and arranged an alternative. Your unannounced arrival has caught me off guard, but I am prepared, nonetheless."

He opened his mouth to say something and then closed it.

Tessa forged ahead. "Perhaps you will disagree with what I've done or perhaps you won't, but I've made a study of every dockyard in London, and I've been methodical about it. I may be a student of the importation, and I may not have gotten everything exactly right, but it has not been for a lack of effort."

She felt too jittery to pace the room, so she returned to her seat. "Now," she said, "I have every intention of explaining what I've done, but in order to do so properly, I should like to know where to start. So allow me to ask you again." She took up her notebook and pen. "Where is the brig anchored? At this moment?"

Joseph stared at her, blinking (in her opinion), far more frequently than strictly necessary.

"Canvay Island," he said finally. "I believe. We sailed as far as the Thames Estuary on the tide, and then a steam tug brought us to the West India Docks on the Isle of Dogs. A tender rowed Stoker and me—"

"General Steam Tug then?" she asked, interrupting.

The high volume of vessels on the River Thames made it impossible for large brigs to navigate the narrow stretch of the river in Blackwall. Instead, small, maneuverable steam tugs towed the large vessels from the Thames Estuary to the docks.

He blinked at her again. "Yes. In fact it was General Steam Company. When I was turned away at the dock office, I paid a boy to row out to the ship and convey the news that we were dock-less until I could sort out something else. And then I came to find you."

She shook her head and made a note in her book. Absently fingered the tight bun at the base of her neck, lifting it up to relieve the pressure.

"Your hair is different," Joseph said, and Tessa's hand froze. She glanced at him. He was watching her as if she was a puzzle to be solved. She dropped her hand.

The old Tessa had reveled in her long, blonde hair, styling it into different braids, chignons, or elaborate piles (really there was no other word). Tessa's new attitude about her hair had been the less attention it gained, the better. She slicked it tightly back and pinned it into a low bun. It was hardly pretty, but the opposite of prettiness had been the desired result of all the behaviors on her lists.

"Joseph," she said, "the end result of what I've done is this—before I canceled your reservation at West India Docks, I visited all the other docks to learn if I could get similar privileges elsewhere along the Thames—in Blackwall if possible, because I saw the value of warehousing there."

He laughed. He actually laughed. "You did, did you?"

Tessa frowned. "When I found a dock who would take you, and for nearly the same price, I transferred the booking."

"You . . . ?" he began. He paused. He appeared to be thinking over what she said. He continued slowly, "Forgive me if I struggle to comprehend how you knew *where* to go or *for what* to ask. You've no notion of the type of brig, the length or the height. You didn't even know the date we would return—"

"Yes, well, I suppose I asked, didn't I?" she said, watching his expression. How gratifying it was to watch his disbelief dissolve into shock. "I asked and asked and asked. I am still asking and still learning, but I am not the mindless girl you left ten months ago."

"I never thought you were mindless, Tessa," he said quietly, seriously.

"Yes, well." She was unsettled. She examined the nib of her pen. "Perhaps that was how I viewed myself then." She forced herself to return to the topic at hand. "Regardless, I've asked *you* a question, and I should like an answer." She returned to her notes. "Also, can you tell me how much poundage you carry?"

"No," Joseph said, "I *cannot*. Who has taught you the term *poundage*?"

She screwed up her face. "Have you been listening to a word I've said? I've taught myself. I do speak the language of English and can expand my vocabulary with negligible effort."

"And this—*this*—has been your preference? To bother yourself with learning jargon like *poundage*?"

"Well, if I wished to sort out the *levies* on imported goods—yes. And if you must know, I found it rather fascinating. Exciting, really, to learn the business of which my father and brothers have made such a study all these years. Perhaps their rejection only fueled my desire to learn."

He thought about this. Finally said, "Fine. What if I tell you the poundage is 121 tons?"

"You've squeezed 121 tons into a ninety-foot brig?" Tessa's

head snapped up. "Your previous booking called for only 118 tons."

He smiled then, a proud, handsome smile. "We've been very busy, Tessa."

"Well done," she enthused, and she meant it. "121 tons."

"Of course, I'm doubtful I'll find available warehouse space to store it at such short notice."

"I've arranged for 20,000 feet of additional space just in case," she told him. "But I believe we can broker more."

"You've *what?*" Now he shoved up. "Tessa—stop. Simply stop. I understand your motivation, that you wanted to help. I believe that you have been very diligent, although I still do not understand why. But this discussion is beyond the pale. For the love of God. I'll admit that you have learned a few new words, but you—a woman, alone, who has never lived in London and who has no notion of shipping or docks or even bloody commerce, and who *has a new baby*—could not have arranged a dock reservation, and certainly not warehousing."

Tessa crossed her arms over her chest. She had expected this. "I can, and I have," she said.

Joseph shook his head. "Look, I believe you have been rejected by your family, and for that, I am sorry—truly. I also know your regard for me is very low. I hardly think being disowned is reason enough for you to try to manage even a fraction of this on my behalf." He spread out his hands wide. He was almost shouting.

Tessa blinked once, twice, and then snapped. She bolted

up, standing nearly nose-to-nose with him. She began to rattle off the facts.

She told him the name of the new dock, which was St. Katharine.

She said the name of the dock master, Mr. Harold Blue.

She quoted the size of the slip, the contingencies for their unknown arrival, the cost, their time in port, the dimensions and security of the warehouse space, the levies on the poundage . . . The list went on and on, and she explained it all, one detail after the other, months of research and negotiation and diligence—and results. So many solutions to so many problems.

And she had loved every minute of it. She wondered if this came through in her litany of names and numbers. She wondered if he would care.

She was winded when she finished, her chest heaving up and down. He stared at her, not blinking, his expression beyond disbelief. He looked as if someone had sloshed a bucket of cold water on his handsome, golden face.

While she had his attention, she added, "And you have no idea of my regard for you, clearly, so please don't suggest that you do. I can appreciate that you are surprised, Joseph, but I refuse to hear that my work is not legitimate or does not count simply because you didn't expect it. I refuse."

CHAPTER ELEVEN

Joseph couldn't remember the last time his brain let him down. His brain had always been so very reliable and so *fast*. When his heart led him astray or his body gave out, his brain leapt adroitly forward, quick and smooth, with no confusion or fogginess or doubt.

Until now.

Until the spiel of facts and figures tossed out by his wife had literally ground all intellectual function to a dead stop. Once stopped, it hung there, flapping uselessly in the windy place inside his skull.

He felt himself drop into his seat. Everything she'd said—about the dock and the warehouses, the levies and the cargo—made perfectly reasonable sense. And not the kind of sense that compelled him to marry her for £15,000 and the potential of a pretty wife. It made literal sense. He understood everything she'd said. He saw the reasoning behind it. He would have done it the same bloody way himself.

He looked up to her. "Why didn't you lead with this?"

"I beg your pardon?" she said.

"Tessa, to say that I am stunned at your . . ." He shook his head and tried again. "I am stunned at what you claim to have accomplished. Forgive me. All I can think at the moment is why you did not tell me this first."

She turned away, dropping her pen back into its little box. "Yes, I suppose it was rather foolish of me to believe we would . . ." she cleared her throat ". . . have a proper meeting about it and . . . collaborate. In the manner of *colleagues*. That you would think of me as an associate with a derby and a moustache."

"I've hardly gotten used to your . . . brown dress, and now I'm to think of you with a moustache?"

To this, she had no answer. He pressed, "You want to be my *colleague*, Tessa—is that what you want?"

"I want . . ." she began, but then she moved to the window. He could no longer see her face. "It doesn't matter what I want. Certainly I am in no position to ask you for another thing."

He made a scoffing noise. "Asking for things might be an excellent start, where you are concerned."

She turned back. "What do you mean?"

"I mean, there was a time that I would have given you anything—you needed only but to ask. Instead of . . ." he trailed off.

"Instead of tricking you," she provided softly.

"Instead of concealing the depth and breadth of your situation."

She nodded. "In hindsight, perhaps I can see the error in that. Perhaps not. It is impossible to communicate how very afraid I was of driving you away."

He watched her, waiting for an elaboration.

Finally, she said, "The work I did on behalf of the docks was meant to be the opposite; it was meant to be clear and seamless."

"It was clear and seamless. I'm so very impressed." He made a gesture to her notes. She hadn't looked at them, not once. She knew the information by heart.

He asked, "You're certain you've arranged this all on your own?"

She closed her eyes. She had the look of someone who had just been given an undeserved shove. He swore in his head.

"'Tis me alone, Joseph," she said tiredly. "You cannot escape what I've done, I'm afraid. Sorry." She turned to face him, bright blue eyes sad and somehow older now, but no less beautiful.

His heart gave a lurch. "Don't apologize," he managed.

"I feel like I shall apologize to you forever, and it will not be enough."

Apologies were never what I wanted, he thought. *I wanted you.* Instead he said, "Please stop."

She brought an idle hand to the tight bun at the nape of her neck and patted it, wincing slightly. He had the impulse to go to her, to study the mystery of where she had bound all of her magnificent hair and to liberate it. To rub the place on her nape that caused her to wince.

"But how would you like to proceed?" she asked on a sigh, her hand still gently massaging her neck.

I should like to touch you, he thought. *I should like to ask you why you've hidden your hair and why you're wearing that terrible brown dress.*

I should like to meet the baby.

I should like to hear what you meant to say when you almost told me what you really wanted.

Now he knew his brain had shut off. These were his wishes for the *other* Tessa, the fraudulent one, the one who lived only in his memory. He had no notion of *this* Tessa, the Tessa that managed his business and slicked back her hair and wore brown.

"Obviously I cannot fully comprehend these arrangements without you present," he said. "You'll have to come to St. Katharine with me, to advise me."

She took a deep, steadying breath. Relief? Endurance? Mettle? He couldn't say.

"Yes—of course, yes," she said.

And now he was flooded with relief. He would see her again.

She continued, "Only I cannot come today, I'm afraid. My son will awaken very soon, and I've promised our nursemaid, Perry, the day off. But here." She returned to the lacquered box and removed an envelope. "I've a copy of the letter I mailed to you informing you of the new dock and the original dock warrant. The letter should explain enough for you and Stoker to safely bring the brig in to St. Katharine tonight. The customs office will not be open until tomorrow morning, and you cannot unload without their inspection. Perhaps you can give your crew shore leave until morning, and I will meet you by ten o'clock? Would that be suitable?" She extended the envelope.

Joseph stared at it, stared at her small hand and delicate wrist.

It occurred to him that he was being dismissed. Politely and quite justifiably. He did not live here with her. He had very little to do with her at all.

Now she would resume whatever it was that she did with her day. She was not his *real* wife. Never had she been his *real* wife.

Still. They were finally in the same city, but she would *meet him in the morning.*

You weren't even going to seek her out, he reminded himself. His inclination to linger, to discuss the docking—to discuss *anything*—burned at the edge of his consciousness, a low flame at the edge of a dry leaf.

"Alright," he heard himself say. He took the envelope. "Tomorrow, then. Ten o'clock."

She smiled then, her first smile in what felt like an hour, and he drank it in. He almost, almost reached for her.

Instead, she took up a bell and summoned the butler. The man appeared in the doorway, and Joseph followed him into the street.

Chapter Twelve

Tessa longed to wear any other dress than the grey wool. Or the taupe silk. Or the beige. Or the terrible green dress that reminded her of residue on a dry fountain. One by one, she ticked through the drab dresses in her wardrobe, frowning at each boring, matronly one.

It was the day after Joseph returned and she dressed with care, if not color, while Perry, the nursemaid, sat in a chair with baby Christian. "I wish you'd consider the blue, Miss Tessa," Perry offered. "Or any of the pinks. The red?" She rattled off an inventory of Tessa's former wardrobe, as if the problem was recalling the pieces. Remembering was not the problem. Tessa remembered them all too well.

"Today, of all days, it is imperative that I be taken seriously," Tessa recited, frowning at the grey silk. "No distractions or misconceptions—not for Joseph or any other man with whom I've dealt at St. Katharine Docks."

Tessa could not say for certain that the drab, unadorned

dresses had contributed to her newfound success as a novice businesswoman, but they could not have hurt. Certainly no man had pressed himself on her since she began donning the parade of muted plainness, and for whatever reason, wearing brown stifled Tess's natural tendency to tease and flirt. She'd pushed away these tendencies, just as she'd pushed her beloved dresses to the back of the wardrobe.

"Have you considered," said her friend Sabine, leaning against the doorjamb, "that you are taken seriously because you're conducting actual business with these men? This was bound to happen when you dealt in commerce rather than the relative smallness of your dainty little hands."

Tessa cringed, thinking of the vapid games she had once played. "If wearing grey will help distance me from any such nonsense, it is but a small price to pay."

It was also a small price for the damage that she had done to Joseph—and herself. She'd broken two hearts on her wedding night, and the truth was, the drab dresses matched her state of mind. Bright colors and silk flounces were difficult to stomach when she'd first moved to London. Meanwhile the world's most boring dresses seemed like exactly what she deserved.

Still, her hand hovered tensely over the grey gown, her fingers curled in a claw. For the first time in many months, she *wanted* to wear something light and cheerful. She wanted to appear pretty when she saw Joseph today.

Perhaps the new dresses had contributed to her success or were more appropriate for heartache, but she had never felt truly like herself when she wore them. They were so mournful and dour. Still, she'd made a commitment to the New Tessa, and the dresses and tight bun were the outward show of that commitment.

She sighed deeply and dragged the grey silk from the wardrobe.

Behind her, Sabine made a snickering noise. Sabine managed to wear any old color—today she'd worn scarlet— and still seemed to repel unwanted male attention as a matter of course. But Sabine regarded all men with sharp distrust, and she carried around an air of isolation like a shield. But Tessa could never seem to manage isolation.

Captain Marking aside, Tessa quite enjoyed men, and she harbored no wholesale distrust of the entire gender. She was quite certain that she could never *lie* with a man after what happened with the captain—Joseph had been her one and only go at that—but this particular fear hardly surfaced in day-to-day interactions.

Ironically, Sabine was the most classically beautiful of the two friends in Belgravia. Her large green eyes, small nose, and pink mouth were aligned with perfect symmetry. Her hair was so black, it shone almost blue in some light. And her skin was the color of fresh cream.

Meanwhile Tessa's beauty was more a trick of motion and light. Anyone with hair as blonde as Tessa's was bound to cause men to look twice. Add bright blue eyes and a ready smile? The Old Tessa had merely played up these features with beautiful dresses in bright colors, fluttering ribbons and lace trim. Oh, how she had adored lace trim.

Or she had, before she'd made a point to mute everything

about her appearance and bearing. Hence, the grey, which she donned now with due irritation, wincing at the stiff fabric.

"Where is the grey bonnet, Perry?" She turned around to allow Sabine to do up the back of her dress.

"Oh, but not the eel-colored bonnet, Miss Tessa?" said Perry innocently.

"Yes," sighed Tessa, "the eel-colored. Can I trouble you to get it?"

The maid cooed over Christian and laid him carefully on a blanket in the center of Tessa's bed. "If I owned ten bonnets," the maid said, "I can tell you that the eel is the very last one I'd wear." She trudged from the room.

"How will you go?" asked Sabine softly.

"Carriage," said Tessa, looking over her shoulder. "Won't you reconsider and come with me? Stoker is sure to be there." Sabine had been the first of the three brides to marry and move to Belgravia. Her union with the brooding and enigmatic Jon Stoker had rescued Sabine from an abusive uncle. But within hours of the wedding, Sabine had bidden Mr. Stoker to deliver her to Belgravia and leave her. According to Sabine, she'd left her new husband with little more than a formal thank-you and the suggestion that he should carry on with his life as if they were not married at all. It was exactly the way the brides' advertisement had been originally conceived, and yet . . .

Sabine shook her head without hesitation. "Oh no. Mr. Stoker will not expect to see me, nor I him. And you can very well manage the docks without me in the way. I would not dare attach myself to your crowning moment. That said," Sabine went on, "would you mind delivering this letter to Mr. Stoker? If you see him, that is. And it's not too much trouble." She produced a tidy envelope from her pocket and held it out.

Tessa barely stopped herself from whirling.

"Pleasure," she said simply, flashing a smile. She took the envelope and tucked it into her own pocket. She eyed her friend, so very anxious for details but she dare not ask. And now Christian was fussing on the bed.

Tessa scooped her son into her arms. "They've finally come home, Dollop." She kissed the top of his soft round head. The infant's chubby legs churned.

"I wonder if his father will endorse his nickname?" chuckled Sabine.

Tessa went still. "It's far more alarming to hear, 'Father' than, 'Dollop.'"

"But Mr. Chance *is* Christian's legal father. He remained married to you after all. And I might add that he sought you out literally within hours of his return. And now he will see you again today? If he does not threaten divorce or annulment now, he never will."

Tessa laughed. "*That* is hardly guaranteed. Yesterday proved nothing more than our future together is . . . undefined. But I can live with undefined—for the moment."

"You are afraid to press him," guessed Sabine.

"Yes." Tessa nodded. "It's no small thing, what I've done to him. Entrapment? Fatherhood? He has earned a bit of freedom from being pressed. When I saw him again, I promised myself that I would not allow emotion to spill over into our discussion. No heartbreak, no longing, not even regret. I will not manipulate him any longer, even unintentionally. I had only two goals yesterday: to reveal this split with my parents and to discuss what I've done with the docks. By some miracle, I achieved both."

"You've managed a new baby almost entirely alone," recited Sabine. "You've learned London's dockyards—also alone. Your behavior before the wedding was not ideal, I'll grant you, but you needn't present yourself as if made of stone."

"For my part, I'm committed to professionalism with Joseph—this is all I mean. Any overture must come entirely from him, with no leading agenda by me. I've led him too far already."

"Overture?" said Sabine.

Tessa shrugged. "Widest possible definition of the word, I mean. Warmth toward me, forgiveness. Overtures toward the baby. Although, surely no one is prepared to bandy about the word *papa* just yet. Honestly, I dare not speculate. I have forced myself not to speculate."

"But I thought you said he was receptive to the baby?" Sabine took up a rattle from the bed and handed it to Christian.

"He was many things, I suppose. Irate and adversarial in the beginning. After that, quiet and pensive and almost . . . contrite?" She shrugged and began to wrestle Christian into his tiny jacket. "In the end, his regard could best be described as shocked. Which was the most satisfying of all, I must admit. I wanted to appear . . . *changed* to him. To be proficient and business-minded rather than frivolous and wily. He was right to be shocked, considering the avalanche of information with which I inundated him."

"But he showed nothing more than this? Nothing of the affection or devotion from before your confession?" Sabine grabbed hold of one of Christian's swinging feet.

"Well, there were flashes, I suppose, of what one might call curiosity. He asked about the baby. *And* he asked about my hair." Absently, she touched the severe bun at the nape of her neck.

"Well, your hair is a mystery to us all," said Sabine.

Tessa smiled weakly. "It was hardly the sort of conversation to which one could pin her future. And besides . . ." she hoisted Christian on her hip ". . . I'm not even certain I want a future with Joseph Chance."

"Now that is perhaps the biggest lie of all," said Sabine.

Tessa crinkled up her face, running her nose along her son's sweet-smelling profile. "You're right." She let out a deep breath. "Of course I want a future with Joseph. I wanted him then, and I want him now." Tessa looked up. "But I want so much more now that I am a mother, now that I've . . . managed all of the business of the docks. Perhaps too much."

"Well, I'll not argue this point. You've never wanted enough for yourself in my opinion."

"Stop. Mine has always been the longest and most elaborate list of desires."

"Not bows and fripperies, Tessa. What do you truly want?"

Tessa opened her mouth to put her off again, but Christian kicked in her arms and affected one of his signature, long, determined coos. Tessa stopped. She kissed her son. The New Tessa was honest, even with herself.

"I want," she began, "a modest house that I can call my own. Nothing grand but tidy and safe and a place Christian may grow up. I want a means to support the two of us. I want to scrimp and economize and possibly save enough to send him to university when the time comes. I want to have a go at more work like the arrangements I've made with the brig and dock. Assuming I have not mucked it up, I have more ideas for how to do it better next time, more efficiently, faster, with a larger profit." Her voice had grown louder and more convicted. She squeezed her son to her chest.

"And I want Joseph as he was. In the weeks before the wedding. I can forgive his reaction when I confessed. The things he said, the cold, bitter manner in which he hauled me to London and left me? It was truly awful, but what I'd done was so very regrettable. I understand, and I deserved awfulness, I suppose. But if he means to always behave this way, if this is his *future* regard for me, I'm not sure I could abide him. I want him, but I will not feel forever resented, I cannot be merely *tolerated*."

"Well said," Sabine chuckled, smiling at her. "As you should not."

Tessa added, "I could not allow even a sliver of resentment toward my son. Not a sliver."

"No," Sabine agreed. "Look, Tessa, no one is more committed to a solitary life than myself—you know this—but Willow and I both feel that you should have Joseph Chance if you want him. On your own terms, that is."

Tessa nodded, putting her lips to Christian's soft, warm forehead and pressing another kiss. She turned away, bouncing the baby gently against her.

"Mama loves Christian," she whispered, squeezing him. "Be a good boy for Perry while I go out, alright?" The baby made the loud, shrill shriek, the contented squawk of a baby exploring the full capacity of his voice.

"Here, let me have him," said Sabine. "Go. Show them all you've accomplished. You've been waiting nearly a year for this."

Tessa kissed the baby again and handed him to Sabine with a grateful look. "Do you suppose Perry has located my eel-colored bonnet?"

Sabine danced the baby to the window. "Good lord, let us pray she has not."

CHAPTER THIRTEEN

Joseph Chance paced back and forth at the gates to St. Katharine Docks, casting shrewd glances at the morning hustle. A rank-smelling crowd of laborers loitered behind him, shiftless in the wake of being passed over by the foreman. Hired men grunted and swore just inside the gates, applying their muscle to the backbreaking work of unloading cargo. Everywhere, drunken sailors wove in and out, staggered to vessels after a night on leave. Swabbing crews sloshed pails of filthy water and shipwrights cursed their apprentices. Up and down the quay, messdecks were emptied into the Thames with an intermittent chorus of heavy, slurping *plops*.

"Absolutely no place for a woman," Joseph ground out. "No place. It's not safe. It's not decent. It smells like . . . like . . . rot."

"What did you expect?" drawled Stoker, leaning on the gatepost behind him. The smoke from his cheroot masked the other grime-and-gin-fueled odors that hung like a dead animal in the air.

"How could I have known she was dashing about the docks of London, trying to . . . trying to . . . ?" Joseph swore, unable to define all that his wife seemed to have achieved in the months since he sailed away. Behind him, a drunken sailor emptied the contents of his stomach into a boot.

Joseph swore again and spun away. Stoker was correct, of course. What *had* Joseph expected? That St. Katharine Docks was somehow different from any other port in any other corner of the bloody world? Clean and tidy and populated with respectful, gentlemanly men?

They'd managed to dock the brig by sundown, but only just, and a moonless night had precluded Joseph's opportunity to take a proper look around. It was a new dock after all, barely two years old, and known mostly for luxury goods. In the light of day, he could see that it was *exactly* like any other dock he'd known before, complete with vomiting sailors.

"Look sharp," mumbled Stoker, and Joseph turned back.

There was a commotion at the far end of East Smithfield Street. Sailors shouted and leapt from the path of a briskly moving carriage. The driver, smartly dressed but not livered, ignored them, navigating the busy road as if he knew it well.

Tessa. It could be no other. It occurred to him suddenly that he had sailed from England without arranging a vehicle for her. In truth, he'd left England without providing for her in any tangible way, except a bit of money. The fine carriage must belong to Willow.

My wife has made her way around London in a borrowed conveyance.

To arrange for my business.

Shame burned his face. He'd felt so betrayed when he left, he had not thought beyond his own anger to consider how her daily existence would play out. In his view, Tessa had overtaken his life, what more could he give? In hindsight, he might have given any number of simple things, things that were negligible to him but would lend convenience and status to her difficult months ahead.

Joseph made a mental note to write to Cassin and Willow and ask to buy Willow's carriage if Tessa liked it. Or perhaps he would have a new carriage built for the—

A footman leapt down from the bench and opened the door.

Joseph felt an unfamiliar gush of anticipation. He narrowed his eyes. There was movement inside carriage. He held his breath, he leaned in. He braced himself for—?

What?

The dock logistics she would now walk him through? Who anticipated *logistics*?

The balance of the money from the canceled slip? She could keep the money.

News of her move?

Her regret?

Her penance?

And then he realized. He braced himself simply for the sight of her. Those blue eyes. That infectious smile.

He'd always braced himself. The response of his body and heart threatened to overwhelm him.

Even now? he wondered, tightening his gloves.

Even now.

From the carriage door, he saw steel-grey silk. Next, black glove, black bonnet, black boot. More grey silk.

And then there she was, stepping lightly down, notebook clutched to her chest. She waved smoothly to him. She shaded her eyes with a gloved hand to stare at the tall ships in a line along the quay.

"Is it here? Have you docked?" she asked excitedly.

Joseph nodded, allowing the sight of her to wash over him. She seemed barely to notice him, staring up with enthusiasm at the boats. Her face was lit by the sunshine and unmasked anticipation. She'd worn another horrible dress—dark grey mottled fabric with brown-black trim. She looked like a pearl inside the hard grey shell of an oyster.

Oyster or not, he struggled to absorb the sight of Tessa Chance on a London dock. He was reminded of a sparrow in a church. He understood how she got in, but he had to stifle the urge not to whip off his coat and spirit her safely back the way she'd come.

"Which one is it?" she prodded, waving the carriage away. She stepped lightly around a trio of laborers who bickered over an open flask.

"There," said Stoker from the gatepost. "Third brig."

"Mr. Stoker?" Tessa gushed, turning her smile to him. "How lovely to see you! I apologize for this change of plan with the docks. I am gratified to see that you've found a place to rest your head after all."

"Thanks to you," he said, stomping out his cheroot.

"But where is Cassin?" she asked, speaking of their third partner.

Stoker made a hissing noise. "Halfway to Yorkshire by now." He drew a timepiece from his waistcoat pocket. "He set out on horseback from Canvey Island yesterday."

"Home to see Willow . . ." Tessa sighed, her smile softening. "Of course he did. It was so difficult for Willow to say good-bye to him again after she'd settled at Caldera."

Joseph watched her closely. There had been happiness all around when Cassin and Willow's marriage of convenience grew into earnest love; but now Willow and Cassin appeared to be the very last thing on her mind. She stared up at the brig with an expression of fascination. Joseph felt something squeeze in his gut. He had delighted in her enthusiasm over many things at Berymede. Enthusiasm from Tessa had been as reliable as the sunrise. But she had exclaimed over snowflakes, the ribbons on her shoes, the shine on his boots. He rolled his shoulders, admitting that this new enthusiasm was no less alluring.

"Tessa," he heard himself say, "we've given the crew an eighteen-hour furlough." He sounded as if he were reading a speech, and he cleared his throat. "They'll be back by sunset, and we'll need to know our length of time in port. I'm prepared to take over from here—with our deepest gratitude for all you have done—but you'll have to explain what they've told you about the warehouse space. And . . ." he hesitated ". . . I will need to know what's become of the money. From the canceled warehouses at your father's docks."

"Oh, yes." She swung her attention back to him. "But

there is no need to be cryptic about the money. Every shilling rests safely in an account in the long room of the dock house. Do you have the manifest? The searcher's office is just here." She pointed. "Hopefully Mr. Cosgrove won't be too behind for today. I arrived as early as I could. There's no point in coming before he's unlocked and taken his coffee. Oh, and I have my own copy of the dock warrant, in case you've mislaid the one I gave you yesterday."

"I have the warrant," Joseph said.

She isn't going, he thought, and he felt a rush of relief. He'd been afraid she'd give him an overview and disappear, return to her little townhouse and her new life. Without him.

She isn't going, he thought again. *There is more.*

He looked at the line of men filing into the stone outpost that bore the sign Customs and Levies.

"I have the manifest," said Stoker.

"Lovely," Tessa said, sidestepping two more laborers and an overturned barrel of chum. She strode to the customs office as if she'd done it every day for a month. Joseph and Stoker were given little choice but to follow.

Stoker shot Joseph a look. "Chin up, mate," he said.

The events that followed, first in Customs with the searcher and then with the auxiliary examiner, and after that with the cargo ledger clerk in the dock office, and finally with the indecipherable hierarchy of dock and warehouse workers, were nothing short of astounding.

Tessa presided over it all with a balance of studied authority and delight. He thought she might actually clap her hands as she watched each new development fall into place.

In Joseph's experience, making port and warehousing cargo was a slow, tedious process; to Tessa, it was like opening night of an operetta—with her in the director's chair.

"You'll be amazed at how quickly the ship will be unloaded," she told Joseph as they stood quayside and stared up the hull of the brig. Stoker had boarded to work with the auxiliary examiner to weigh their barrels.

"I'm told," she went on, "that docking at St. Katharine is five times faster than any other dock on the river. You see how the cranes remove the barrels from the hold and swing them directly into the warehouse? From Point A to Point C. So efficient."

"Indeed," said Joseph, watching cranes rise barrels of guano lightly into the air, fly them across the dockyard and lower them onto a warehouse ramp. He cast a sideline glance at Tessa. She watched the same machination with cheeks flushed and eyes that sparkled.

I thought you enjoyed roses, he thought. *And bunnies. And the sugar glaze on strawberry cake.*

The auxiliary examiner clomped down the gangplank, studying his bill for the tax they would owe on their cargo. When he reached them, he faltered. His eyes darted uncertainly back and forth between Mr. Chance and Mrs. Chance.

"Do you mind?" Joseph asked Tessa respectfully. If she wished to facilitate the levy payment, he would not usurp her.

"Please," she encouraged him. When the examiner handed the bill to Joseph, Tessa nodded to the man. "Thank you, Mr. Hammond. Is it what we expected?"

"Very nearly, Mrs. Chance," said the examiner, walking on.

Without thinking, Joseph held out the bill so his wife could see it.

"Can you pay that sum?" she asked, looking at him. She winced a little. The levy they owed was not small by any stretch, but of course he had planned for this.

"I can pay it," he said. The question did not irritate him so much as rile some unforeseen defensiveness. "Despite this being my first time at St. Katharine," he went on, "I *have* brought goods to port in the city of London before—hence my professional distinction as *importer*. The expertise you've collected in three months' quick study may seem like a lot of common sense to you, but—"

"Common sense?" she laughed. "Oh, Joseph. If only you knew the hours, the *days* I have spent at this dock, observing, taking notes, asking questions, making a nuisance of myself. Learning the very basics of what's happened this morning has been like . . . like, like learning to fly. Please be patient with me." She screwed up her face. "I'm still learning."

Joseph shook his head. "I don't mean to be impatient. I . . . I . . ." He blew out a breath. "My hesitation says it all, doesn't it? I find myself rather speechless."

She waited, and it occurred to him that he should find the words.

"It is astounding what you have accomplished," he said. "You should . . . you should be very proud."

It was a true statement, he was astounded. And she should be proud. Hell, he was proud and he had absolutely nothing to do with it.

Tessa beamed again, an expression that pierced his heart.

"And did you see? I've managed considerable savings compared to your previous arrangement. St. Katharine Docks is very keen to take business from West India, and the warehouse space was far less expensive." She began flipping through her notes.

Joseph had done the calculations in his head in the long room. She *had* saved them money. She had also negotiated more space and a longer time in port. This said nothing of the English-milled fabric she'd arranged for them to take under sail when they returned back to Barbadoes—also for a larger fee.

But the notion of returning to Barbadoes—a priority just one day ago—seemed suddenly wildly reckless, shortsighted, impossible. The loose plan had always been for Stoker and Joseph to return to the island. They had sailed with a full hold, but there was more guano to be had.

That said, it now felt precipitous for him to the Caribbean so soon. He'd achieved not one item from his Plan for the Future. He'd not called on the Earl of Falcondale, his mentor. His reunion with Tessa might have been accelerated, but had it been a proper *reunion*? They'd discussed levies and warehouses, for God's sake.

And what of her new manner and appearance and the way she bloody . . . passed her days? It was so far and away from what he had expected—literally nothing about her was as he had expected.

No, the script he'd anticipated for their discussion of His Future would have to be reconsidered. After more time spent together. Much more time.

He glanced at her. But did she wish to spend time with him

outside of docks and warehouses? His eyes darted surreptitiously to her lips, the delicate line of her jaw, her perfect ear.

She startled him by gasping, "Oh!" She held up a finger. "I've a letter from Sabine that I'm meant to give to Mr. Stoker." Her eyes widened conspiratorially. "Can you believe it?" she whispered.

I no longer know what to believe, he thought, but he simply shook his head.

It occurred to him that, more than anything, more than settling the warehouse space or contacting the buyers or making the rounds at all of his favorite London shops or calling on Falcondale, he wanted to solve the mystery of Tessa Chance. To finally, perhaps, truly understand her. Intimacy? Reconciliation? He would not yet allow himself to hope for those. He would begin with understanding.

It was a dangerous endeavor—she had already broken his heart once. Was it foolhardy to study the very qualities that had once enchanted him? Perhaps, but he struggled to see how she could rebreak an organ that had never fully healed. The resulting calluses would protect him, along with the bitter grudge he'd muscled on like a coat of armor for the past ten months.

She was, after all, his wife. Their futures, however impersonal, were forever linked. It was only fair to make some effort to understand her. And if he could also make peace with her, more's the better.

He watched her call to Stoker from the gangplank and hand him the letter. Stoker studied it for the briefest second, frowned, and then shoved it in the pocket of his waistcoat.

She gave a little wave and then returned to Joseph, her step light. She looked so very happy.

He considered various ways to ask her to meet him to discuss . . . something more. Despite his poetic regard for the calluses on his heart and the armor-like grudge, the thought of her rejecting his invitation made him sweat.

She was nearly to him before he lit on the perfect, undeniable request.

"Tessa," he said casually, staring indifferently out on the Thames, "if you would permit it, I should like to meet the baby. When you are ready."

Chapter Fourteen

Two days later, Tessa was situated on a blanket in Hyde Park, arranging a picnic basket. Her hands shook, despite the mundane task. She blew out a breath, irritated by her nerves. She and Christian had enjoyed the park from the vantage of this very blanket, beneath this very maple tree, all summer long. Today would be—

Well, today would be marginally different.

Today would steer the entire rest of their lives.

Tessa took three quick breaths, telling herself she had accommodated Joseph's request to meet the baby. She'd wanted to gush, *Oh, but let us rush home so you may meet him immediately!* But this was the Old Tessa's answer. The New Tessa did not gush or rush. The New Tessa knew the meeting should occur when Christian was happy and rested, where Joseph would feel the least overwhelmed or confined.

Christian tended to be happy on his blanket in the park, and they would not have the stuffy interruption of servants. Best of all, perhaps, Joseph could arrive (and then subsequently depart) in a manner that made him feel the least . . . trapped.

Trapped. It was a horrible term, and Tessa had danced around the risk of it. But she quite liked her new policy of simply calling things as they were. Joseph had been trapped. There were times when Tessa herself felt a little trapped. The potential for a negative reaction was very real—hence, the park. Who could feel trapped in a park?

"Oh, but you're not so demanding are you, Dollop?" Tessa asked the baby.

Christian lay on his stomach in the center of the blanket, gainfully lifting his chin and sucking on his fist.

"Well, perhaps just a bit," she corrected. "When you are hungry. Or wet. Or tired. Or stuck on your stomach when you would like to flip onto your back. But these are all significant frustrations, aren't they? Who doesn't become demanding when faced with challenges such as these?"

She chattered away, smiling down at her son as she unpacked a strawberry tart and ate the berry from the top. Purposefully, she did not scan the open green behind her nor the paths to the right and left.

She would not watch for him, she had told herself. She would not fidget or check the timepiece in her basket or, God forbid, stand up and pace. She would be calm and contained, the serene picture of experienced motherhood, just as she had been for every other outing to the park. A young mother and her baby, enjoying the sunshine. In no way should she appear to be rapidly unspooling inside because her beloved son was about to meet the man she herself once loved and wanted to love again. The man who he might refer to as Papa.

Christian made a signature squawking noise and lashed out a slobbering hand, rocking to his side. "Oh, you almost have it," encouraged Tessa, smiling at the baby's favorite new trick. Any day now, he would rock himself over from his stomach to his back. Christian squawked again and lashed out an erratic hand, grabbing a fistful of beige silk.

"Oh, but let us not eat Mama's dress?" She tugged, preventing the fist's unerring progress to Christian's mouth. "It's horrid, I know, but the dye may not be safe. Here, let us find Goose . . ." She dug in the bag for his toy.

Perry and Sabine had tried to persuade Tessa to wear one of her old dresses, but Tessa resisted. Not today, when the most important interaction with Joseph Chance would take place.

Joseph had been very stoic at the docks, but it had been obvious that he regarded her bland, suffocating new dresses with confusion, if not outright distaste. But her appearance had no bearing here; what mattered was how Joseph regarded her son.

With this in mind, Christian had been carefully dressed in a gown of bright white with blue embroidered dots around the collar and hem. He wore a white cap with the same blue embellishment, and if the day turned cold, there was a matching blue jacket.

Tessa's one concession to her own appearance had been her hair. When Perry had volunteered to braid it loosely and rope the yellow plait across the crown of her head, Tessa had complied. She did not think she could bear the tight bun or a dour bonnet today—not in the shade of the park. The last warm days of September would give way to autumn soon, and she would allow herself to enjoy a small straw hat while she could. Besides, the stiff bonnet brim got in the way when she lifted her son to her mouth for a kiss.

Perry had been delighted and pinned the straw hat and a whirl of ribbon to the left of the plait, a pretty little flourish, a bit of whimsy. Tessa almost wept at her reflection. She patted the braid now, delighting in the freedom from the bite of pins at her nape.

"Tessa?"

Her hand froze above her head.

She looked down at Christian, chewing on the beak of Goose. She looked at her half-eaten tart.

He is a decent man, she reminded herself. *He will not reject a baby.*

He hasn't even rejected me yet, not really.

Her heartbeat increased to an accelerated pound. She drew a shaky breath and then looked up, shading her eyes.

Joseph Chance sat mounted on a chestnut stallion, staring down at them from the path. He wore an emerald green coat, grey waistcoat, and ivory cravat. His breeches, molded to his muscled legs, were tan, and the sun glinted off black Hessians. His hat was rakishly low. The combination of elegance and easy confidence in the saddle was not lost on her, and she thought absently of how the Old Tessa would have appreciated that look. Now she only cared how he would or would not appreciate her son.

"So you have found us," she said lightly. She put a palm on her son's warm, soft back.

"So I have," he said, unmoving. His eyes did not leave hers.

The baby, she willed. *Look at the baby.*

Christian let out a shrill squawk and pitched the goose doll so that it fell just out of reach. His squawk turned into a fuss and Tessa quickly replaced the toy.

"I . . . I assumed you would be walking." Joseph nodded to the empty pram beside the tree.

"Oh," she said, looking at the pram, "no, anything but that, I'm afraid. If I push him, he will fall asleep. Better that he sleep at home, when I can be busy with other things. When we reach the park, we generally spread out on the ground. Won't you—that is," she tried again, "can you—?"

Before she could finish, he slung his leg over the horse and stepped down. "May I join you?"

"By all means." Tessa stared down at her son, who chewed willfully on the foot of his goose.

The horse's tack jingled as Joseph wordlessly secured him beside the maple.

"Your horse is well mannered, I hope," she said. She worried about the large animal so close to Christian lying prone on the ground. Worry was now a mainstay of her life.

"He is," Joseph said. He came to stand beside her. It occurred to her that the logistics of this meeting would be strange. Joseph was dressed to promenade, not sit on a blanket beneath a tree.

"I'm sorry there is no easy place to si—"

He dropped down beside her, spreading his legs in front

of him. He crossed his shiny black Hessians at the ankle. "It's impossible to overstate how much I value solid earth after five weeks at sea."

"You are gracious to say so." She wanted to look at him, to really look at him. Even in their brief courtship at Berymede, they had never sprawled out on a blanket. It had been winter, and he had been so very careful to resist situations that would tempt them before the wedding. Oh, the irony.

Now he sprawled just two feet away. She could smell his soapy, woodsy smell. He tugged off his gloves and laid them beside her on the blanket. Tessa watched this but then darted her eyes away, looking everywhere but at him. She unrolled the baby's damp collar from the chubby folds around his neck. Christian let out a long, indignant coo. If she had been alone with him, she would have scooped him up and repeated his babble, trying to make him speak again. Instead, she cleared her throat. Joseph said nothing.

But perhaps he was uncertain and wished only to *observe* the baby? Or the sight of him raised the awkward question of domestic logistical matters, none of which Joseph was prepared to discuss?

She felt herself begin to perspire. She'd foolishly put too much emphasis on getting the introduction exactly right but devoted no thought to the words she would use to make it.

"Tessa?" Joseph said, drawing her gaze back to his face. He took off his hat. "I'm afraid I must to admit something to you."

Tessa's stomach cinched into a tight knot. This was the moment he would reject everything—the baby, herself, the marriage. This was the moment he would walk away forever. "Yes?" she whispered, unable to meet his gaze.

"I find myself at quite a loss. I've no idea what to . . . do, er, next." He winced slightly. "Forgive me. But can you . . . ? That is—?"

Tears of relief sprang to her eyes.

Joseph cringed, watching his wife's face crumple into tears. He cursed under his breath and reached for his handkerchief.

"Here." He thrust the monogrammed linen at her. "Perhaps I should have concealed my ignorance. Although it's fairly obvious, I'm afraid."

Tessa shook her head, and tiny wisps of blonde flew out from her face. He blinked, enjoying the loose, relaxed beauty of her hair with no stiff bonnet. He tried and failed to think of something light and funny to say.

"You'll have to forgive me," she said. "I . . . I have looked so forward to this moment, and I was so afraid that you would be . . . that you would be—" She faltered.

"Competent?" he offered.

She laughed. "Resentful."

She said it lightly, but it felt like a punch to his gut. He picked up one glove and laid it down again. He settled the other glove on top of it, carefully aligning the edges, finger to finger. "Oh, Tessa," he sighed. "Resentful? I've been angry—yes. But is this how I have portrayed myself to you? So callous?" He laughed without humor and plucked at the gloves, tossing them into the air. "No, don't answer that."

She watched the leather fall into a heap. "You have every reason to resent us, Joseph. Few men could look at a child who was . . . not of his own flesh, yet thrust into his lifelong care, and not feel resentment. I have only the reaction of my own parents and brothers to compare. Please remember." She looked away and added softly, "And then there was the reaction of the man who fathered Christian."

As ever, Joseph's breath stopped at the mention of Tessa's former lover. "You have spoken to this man since the baby? You have made some introduction?" He could barely grit out the words.

Tessa shook her head wildly. "Oh, no. I shall never see him again. What I mean to say is, when I discovered my condition. I told him. He was cruelly indifferent." She gathered herself up on her knees. "Joseph, please understand. I, alone, am to blame for the circumstances of our marriage— this I know. But I kept the details of the pregnancy concealed because I had met such resentment from the man who fathered the child."

"I would implore you not to transfer *his* resentment to *me*."

"Oh," she said simply, chewing her bottom lip. "I suppose this is fair."

Was it fair? Joseph wondered. He knew himself to be justified in his outrage, his anger, his feelings of betrayal— even his bloody wounded pride. His friends understood— Cassin and Stoker claimed they would have reacted in precisely the same way. And yet—

Was he so blameless? The night of her confession, he had

heaped resentment on her. Soon after, he had fled England and scarcely looked back.

He cast an eye around the sunny park, thinking of those angry months after the wedding. His outrage had felt wholly justifiable at the time. Even now, his pulse quickened and his head ached, thinking about how foolish she had made him feel, how hurt he'd been.

But now? He glanced back to Tessa and her baby.

Nothing in London was as easy to justify as it had seemed in Barbadoes.

Joseph ran a hand through his hair, scrambling for a new topic. Tessa toyed idly with Christian's fat fists, watching Joseph from the corner of her eye. She seemed as uncertain as he was. He wondered for the hundredth time how involved she wished Joseph to be with the baby. The future was uncertain, obviously, and that uncertainty included today, this very moment. Was he meant to only observe the baby? Would it be intrusive to ask about his temperament or daily routine? Would he *hold* the baby?

There was a rather large chance that Tessa considered the baby to be hers alone, despite bearing Joseph's last name and, presumably, relying on Joseph for financial support.

The thought of this unsettled him in a way he could not really define, but he could not conceive of a way to assert himself. He wasn't even certain how to reach out and touch the child.

Rolling his shoulders and giving her a smile, Joseph elected to ask about the baby in terms of their newfound common ground. "When you are ready," he said, "I should like to hear about the summer you spent learning London's dockyards while also caring for a newborn babe. Stoker and I are still in a mild state of shock over how you managed it all."

She sat bolt upright. "I hope nothing is amiss?"

He shook his head. "On the contrary. I find myself in the position of defending my contribution to our partnership. Stoker now wishes to cut me loose and deal only with you. Thank God Cassin is in Yorkshire. I should never hear the end of it. I'm meant to be the brains of the operation, although you could not tell it yesterday."

She laughed and began to ask questions about the warehouse and the buyers, the distribution of the guano, and the fabric they would take under sail for the return to Barbadoes.

Joseph answered her questions but eventually their conversation drifted to London—how she enjoyed the city after a girlhood in the countryside; their friends Willow and Cassin and their unexpected love match; and the coronation of the new king, which had happened only weeks before.

He was just about to ask her if she ever found time to play the piano, when the baby suddenly caught their attention. He'd been cooing, making loud but happy baby sounds, and now he had begun to rock to his left, to and fro, enjoying the sound of his voice undulating with the effort. Tessa smiled down at him and Joseph paused in his questions, enjoying the sight of her enjoying her son. They both happened to be staring down at the baby in the moment he rocked, rocked, rocked, and then dug his left knee into the blanket and flipped over.

Tessa gave a gasp of delight and sat on her heels. "But did you see that? He turned himself over!"

Joseph looked at the baby, now lying on his back, blinking up at the maple leaves and bright September sky. His small round face was like a pink full moon, his blue eyes wide with shock.

Joseph leaned over him. "Is he . . . all right?"

"He's rolled over—and so early! He was on his stomach—you saw it—and now he has flipped! All of his own accord." She scooped the baby in her arms and squeezed him, kissing all available skin. "Good boy, Dollop!" She beamed at Joseph. "Perry told me he might flip himself as early as four months, but it might take longer. Some babies go until six or seven months without turning over."

She seized the baby against her again, hugging him so tightly he let out an impatient squawk. She laughed and tucked him under her chin. "Perry has six younger brothers and sisters," she explained, "and she's been an invaluable resource for what to expect. I knew nothing of infants, Mary Boyd does not have children, and my own mother is no longer a part of my life." She held the baby at arm's length. "Perry will be so proud, Dollop!"

Joseph sifted through the pieces of information she'd just given him. For all practical purposes, his wife was navigating motherhood entirely alone. On his very rare encounters with the maid Perry he found her to be sweet but also young, impulsive, and silly. She was Tessa's guide? He wondered for the hundredth time how her own family could abandon their only daughter.

How could you? he suddenly thought, and he felt color rise to his cheeks.

"Let us see if he will do it again," Tessa said, replacing the baby on his stomach on the blanket. The baby cried out, opposed to being returned to the position he had so recently conquered. But within moments, he dug his foot and knee into the blanket and flipped himself again.

Tessa clapped and laughed, smiling down. Joseph wanted to watch the infant, truly he did, but he struggled to look away from the delight on Tessa's face. He felt another prick in his heart. Another pinhole. He felt oddly light.

With considerable effort, he tore his eyes away from his wife to look down at the child.

"*Oh,*" sang the baby's mother, "how hard you worked to flop over, but you aren't quite sure what to do now that you've managed it. Poor Dollop."

I know the feeling, mate, Joseph thought, peering down. He felt his own smile form. Christian Chance had three distinguishing features: chubbiness, which gave him the look of a tiny, pink monarch; a shock of dark black hair, like down on a gosling's back; and crystal blue eyes.

Like his mother's.

Joseph said, "He is a beautiful baby." In his experience, this was never the wrong thing to say. It was also not a lie.

"Oh, thank you," said Tessa. "He has been beautiful to me from the first moment."

Joseph wanted to ask if he looked like the man who fathered him, but could not. With effort, Joseph fought off all thoughts of the man who fathered him. Instead, he watched the baby stare up, captivated by his mother. Joseph, too, knew what it felt like to look into her blue eyes.

He considered what to ask next. He was far more interested in the baby, and even more so in Tessa's new role as a mother, than he had expected. It was an understatement to say he had never given much thought to fatherhood. He had not known his own father, and the Earl of Falcondale, who had brought him up in many ways, was far more like an older brother.

Joseph wondered what, specifically, fathers *did* for or to newborn infants? His only thought was to provide for the child and for his mother. His mind leapt immediately to the money he'd left to sustain Tessa and Christian while he was away. Had it been enough? He wondered suddenly where the child slept. Was his crib sturdy and safe? Could there possibly be a proper nursery in the Boyds' small Belgravia townhome?

Christian wore a spotless white gown, but did Tessa have what she needed in the way of tiny garments for the child? What of this quilt on which they now sat? The picnic basket with leather-and-brass handles and the food inside it?

He was overwhelmed, suddenly, with the impulse to be some part of the small family before him, but he was so very uncertain about how. Were finances an appropriate way to start? Joseph cast around for some inroad.

"What do you enjoy most about being a mother?" he finally asked. It was one of a painfully short list of questions he'd stayed up half the night to compose.

Tessa blew out a breath, sending the wisps of hair fluttering around her face. "Oh, there is only one good thing about being a mother." She swept the baby off the blanket. "And that is this little dollop." She kissed the baby on the neck and Christian let out a happy shriek. He flailed his chubby arms like he was trying to fly.

"All the rest is quite a lot of hard work, I'm afraid," she said. She set the baby on her lap, facing Joseph. He settled in, entitled to the spot. He chewed on his fist, considering Joseph with half-lidded eyes.

Tessa went on, "Getting up in the night, washing and mending baby clothes, bathing him, feeding him, trying to fit my own meals and mending when he sleeps. And then of course fitting in my work at St. Katharine. I am lucky because I have Perry to help me, and she loves him like a sister. Our shared love for him drives it all." She looked away, staring out across the park. "I love him even when he is screaming at the top of his lungs, dirty, and it is the middle of the night."

She shook her head, as if dislodging a memory, and returned her gaze to Joseph. "I did not expect to love him quite so much, honestly. I cannot find words to do it justice. And he doesn't even really *do* much of anything—not yet. He does not speak, he does not show preferences for anything more than meals and a dry nappy and me. He is indifferent even to his toy goose, but Willow sent it, and I would love him to eventually attach himself to it. Even with all of that, he is—" She paused and kissed the top of his head. "I would endure any amount of sleepless drudgery for him. And my love for him is so . . . comprehensive, I know that I shall endure any hardship, for the rest of my life, to provide for him, even though I know nothing of the boy or man he will become."

She took a deep breath. "But it cannot be said enough, I

have Perry to help me, and in this I am so fortunate. Thank you for the money you left for her salary, by the way." She smiled gratefully as if the money had been remotely enough.

The baby began to croon, a low, gurgling noise that began comical and pleasant but soon dissolved into a cranky, dispirited fuss. Tessa bobbed her leg, gently bouncing him up and down, but his fussy croon began rising to a low cry, then a wail.

"Ah, are you tired, Dollop?" she asked, kissing him on the cheek. She smiled up at Joseph. "If I push him home in the pram, he will fall asleep. Will you—?" She paused and turned the baby over her shoulder, patting his back. "Do you have time to walk us home?"

"Of course," he said, shoving up.

"Oh, lovely, thank you," she said, sounding surprised and happy. He wondered if it was the only correct thing he'd said all afternoon.

"Will you hold him while I pack up the basket?"

"I—ah . . ."

Before Joseph could qualify his hesitation, Tessa thrust the fussing baby at him, and he was given little choice but to receive him. He wrapped his hands around his thick middle and held him out like a muddy dog. The baby's wail paused, mid-crescendo, and Joseph Chance stared at the boy, blue eyes to blue eyes. The baby blinked. He crinkled his nose and formed his mouth into a little O. He opened his wet eyes very wide. His expression seemed to say, *Who the devil are you?*

"Who, indeed, mate?" Joseph said lowly, and he felt something break off inside of his chest and fall into the pit of his stomach.

Tessa chuckled. "Tuck him into your arm," she said. "Here. Like this."

She came beside Joseph and spun the baby in his hands to pull Christian to the crook of his arm. "There you are. Now support him under his bum."

Joseph allowed her to guide him while Christian resumed his wail in honor of Joseph's obvious incompetence. Tessa ignored the infant's outrage, and Joseph felt himself relax. He watched her situate the baby in his arms, straighten his gown, and pat him on his head.

She'd not touched Joseph since he'd returned, not really, and now she eased him around with gentle pats and tugs. He could smell her soft, floral scent. His body pulsed at every point of contact. He fought the urge to step closer. The baby reached out to her, and he had the ridiculous urge to reach out for her, too.

She moved away, seemingly unaffected, to pack the basket. The baby's temper fit rose, but Joseph was transfixed by the sight of Tessa's fluid, unhurried ministrations. She crawled on her hands and knees, offering an eye-blinking view of her bottom as she tossed crockery into the basket. The quilt was not precisely folded so much as loosely halved and quartered. She held it to her nose to breathe deeply before she piled it beside the picnic basket.

"Sabine made this quilt for us," Tessa told him. "Isn't it

lovely? I thought it was too pretty to spread on the ground, but she insisted that we use it. Now it's taken on the smell of summer grass and soft earth, and I love it even more."

She held a half-eaten cake between her lips while she repacked sundry picnic items. Every few minutes she paused to take a bite, closing her eyes in simple pleasure.

"I've offered you nothing," she laughed, popping the last bite into her mouth. "How very rude of me. The Boyds' cook packed a full tea."

"I came to meet the baby," he said.

Tessa laughed again, climbing to a stand and reaching for her son. "Well, you've met him. Come here, Dollop. You've shouted quite enough at your papa—" She froze, her blue eyes huge on Joseph's face. "I'm sorry. I . . . That is, Perry and I have been referring to you as Papa when we talk to the baby."

"I've done so very little to earn that title, I'm afraid," he said. The words were out before he thought about them. A relief. The truth.

Tessa continued to stare. The baby cried louder, reaching for his mother.

"What is it that you feel you should have done, Joseph?" Her voice was a confused whisper. He could barely make out the words over the baby's cries.

"I . . . I cannot say," he lied. "My own father died before I was born." He shrugged and relinquished the baby. "More." He thought of a hundred things he could have done. *Anything.*

She gathered the baby close, kissed the top of his head,

and then settled him, wailing, in the pram. She stepped back and dusted her hands together. "Can I trouble you to carry the basket and the blanket? He will fall asleep within minutes if I begin to push."

Joseph tossed the blanket over his saddle and hooked the basket over the horn. He tugged the horse on a long lead behind him and fell in beside Tessa. As she predicted, the baby's cries turned into a long, low sort of gravelly song, and then dropped off altogether.

In silence, they walked along Barrack's Way, the spindly wheels of the pram popping over the gravel walk. After a moment, she said, "He is easier to become accustomed to when he is asleep." Two children ran past, giggling, holding fast to the straining leash of a dog. "It was ambitious, perhaps, to have introduced you during our time at the park."

"Is it your wish that I become accustomed to the baby?" Joseph asked. He was determined to discover what she really wanted.

Tessa glanced at him and then looked left, steering the pram toward High Row. He held his breath.

She nodded. "If you are so inclined."

"I would like that," he said. In his head, he thought, *I would like to become accustomed to you both.*

Suddenly, she stopped walking. Joseph was two steps ahead and turned around, nearly colliding with his horse. "What is it?" He peered into the pram at the sleeping baby.

"On Friday, Sabine and I have plans to visit Vauxhall Gardens. In Kensington."

Joseph paused. "I beg your pardon?"

"Vauxhall Gardens," she repeated. "Do you know it?"

"Yes, I know it." Vauxhall Gardens was a centuries-old outdoor public entertainment venue with music, food stalls, dancing, and fireworks. Men and women from every class frequented the Gardens for mischief and merriment—and trysts. So, so many trysts.

Joseph worked to keep his voice level. "Have the two of you visited Vauxhall before?"

She shook her head. "'Twill be our first time. Sabine, who has been exploring the city bit by bit, has begged me accompany her for an age, but I only now feel it is safe enough to leave Christian with Perry for an evening. We are looking forward to it, to be honest."

"Indeed," Joseph said. She was walking again, and Joseph was grateful to follow two steps behind. His sight narrowed to the vulnerable vision of Tessa and Sabine embarking on Vauxhall Gardens alone on Friday. Or any day. Ever.

"I mention it only," she went on, "to see if you might like to join us? Mr. Stoker, too, of course, as long as you don't reveal to Sabine that I mentioned it. She is strenuously opposed to any machination toward Mr. Stoker."

"We'll be there," Joseph said. He let out a trapped breath. The very thought of Tessa and Sabine venturing alone into Vauxhall stopped his heart. The gardens were festive and diverting, but every manner of rake, swindler, inebriate, and thief prowled the dark paths and secluded bowers. And these were the upstanding patrons. The fights and assignations that he and Stoker had enjoyed at Vauxhall through the years were too numerous to count.

But she was *not* going alone, he reminded himself; she had just smoothly invited him, despite his general ineptitude at anything resembling manners throughout this outing.

And of course he had no right to forbid her to go anywhere. She'd been making her way around London, including to two separate Blackwall docks, for months.

He took a deep breath. "Will you allow us to collect you? I've a phaeton that rides four, and if the night is not too chill—"

"Oh, no, an escorted journey would spook Sabine for certain. There are front gates, I understand. Let us simply convene there. Shall we say at six o'clock?"

Joseph bit the inside of his cheek, thinking of the rabble that loitered outside the gates of Vauxhall Gardens. "Six o'clock," he repeated tightly. "We will be there. I shall look forward to it."

"Lovely," she sighed, smiling up at him. "Sabine will be irritated that we've included Mr. Stoker, but she will survive."

Joseph smiled and nodded, his brain choked by the terrible vision of his wife and Vauxhall Gardens and survival.

Chapter Fifteen

Tessa and Perry had quarreled over the dress.

Tessa had prudently chosen the brown wool for the evening at Vauxhall and asked Perry to press it, but Perry had defiantly wadded that very dress into a ball and hidden it in the bottom of the mending basket. She had pressed a blue silk instead, a beautiful gown she'd found in one of Tessa's trunks. The maid had aired the dress and carefully repaired snags to the myriad tiny, rose-colored embroidered flowers that swirled up and down the bodice.

"Perry . . . no," Tessa had said when she emerged from a bath. She frowned at the bold blue dress splayed out across her bed.

"Yes, yes, yes, yes . . ." Perry had chanted, artfully arranging the matching hat on the pillows as if an imaginary woman lay prone across the bed.

In the end, there hadn't been time to rethink the blue dress, which had always been one of Tessa's favorites. On it went, and Tessa allowed Perry to dress her hair in two looped braids and pin a small blue hat at the back of her head. How nice it was to feel the kiss of braids on her shoulders each time she turned her head, even nicer to enjoy the unobstructed peripheral vision of no stiff bonnet brim. Looking at her reflection in the dress and the little hat, the braids and the matching leather gloves, was like catching sight of a long-lost friend.

An hour later, some combination of the New Tessa, who felt nervous and conspicuous, and the Old Tessa, who really did love this dress, stood beside Sabine in front of Vauxhall Garden's bustling gates.

"Tell me again why I must share my long-awaited outing to Vauxhall Gardens with Joseph Chance?" asked Sabine, peering through the gates at the garden beyond. Strains of lively music drifted above the hum of voices. They heard the unfamiliar squawk of an exotic bird. Someone out of sight hurled a torch, its fiery tip painting a glowing arc through the air.

"Joseph and I have so much to discuss. Chief among them my move from Belgravia," Tessa said. "His arrival caught me off guard, despite my planning, and then we had to contend with the new dock. I haven't quite gotten around to discussing the future yet."

"Naturally you chose a crowded pleasure garden as the most useful setting for this conversation."

Tessa laughed. "It was never going to be *one* discussion, I'm afraid. I must . . . ease into it. It's no small thing to ask him to buy a little house or to sort out a means for me to support myself."

"You cannot think he intends to leave you with the Boyds forever, Tessa," said Sabine. "He will have anticipated some change."

"If so, he has not mentioned it. And I have very specific plans for a fresh start."

"Yes, but they are not *greedy* plans. And you are his wife, for God's sake."

"Yes, and he had aspirations to run for Parliament. He must own property in a district that has the potential to elect him. There is much to be considered."

A small eruption popped and fizzled just beyond the gates. Whoops and gales of laughter followed. They turned to peer inside, but queuing revelers blocked their view.

"Again," sighed Sabine, "a pleasure garden? And what of your new vow? To innumerate exactly what you want, when you want it?"

"Yes, well." Tessa ran a flat hand against the corset stays beneath her gown. She had not worn a proper corset since before the pregnancy and strangely, it heartened her. She was likely the only female in England who relished the tight squeeze of a finely made corset, but it made her feel long and lithe and dressed up, it made her feel as if she was going somewhere important. "Determination and execution are two different things."

"You know what I believe?" asked Sabine. "I believe you wanted to pass a diverting night in a lovely park with your husband." She tapped her friend on the hand with her closed fan. "And why shouldn't you?"

Oh, because he cannot abide me, thought Tessa. *Because*

I've saddled him with Christian and me forever. Because I am
about to ask him to buy me a house in County Durham . . .

She said, "I did rather hope they would say yes for that
reason."

Sabine went stiff beside her. "*They? They, who?*"

Tessa made a repentant face. "Hmmm?"

"Tessa, you did not," said Sabine. "You did not arrange
for me to prowl around this park at dusk with Jon Stoker."

"I made no arrangements one way or the other," said Tessa
defensively. "I merely mentioned that you and I planned to
take in the gardens together. Given what I know of Joseph
and Mr. Stoker, I'd say there is a chance he will come. But
Sabine, what could be—"

"*Tessa!*" Sabine hissed. She wore a deep purple shawl and
she snatched it tightly around her shoulders. "If he is coming—if
there exists even *a chance* he is coming—I will go in alone."

"Sabine, no, wait. It won't be nearly as enjoyable if you set
out by yourself. You cannot go in alone."

"I've explored every other corner of London alone—I very
well can. And I shall." She tugged her gloves, tightening the
purple leather. "Good luck, Tessa. Give my regards to Mr.
Chance. And Mr. Stoker, if he turns up. I will meet you here
at nine o'clock."

"*Sabine,*" Tessa implored, but her friend was already
walking away. A moment later, she slipped through the gates,
joining the throngs of revelers streaming into the gardens.

Tessa shook her head and checked the timepiece in her
reticule. They'd made far better time than expected, arriving
a quarter hour before she and Joseph were meant to meet.

She was given little choice but to stand alone, feeling the strange balance of conspicuous and so very comfortable. She felt so much more like herself in the blue dress than ever she did in the brown or the grey, she wondered what could one night hurt?

She waited only five more minutes before she spotted Joseph. He appeared like she'd fantasized about his return from Barbadoes, striding up the hill from the Thames, confident, proud, handsome. Mr. Stoker was beside him. They were a head taller than most men, their skin tanned compared to the clammy, pale-faced, London throng.

Tessa's heart began to pound. She checked over her shoulder for Sabine—gone now—and looked back. Joseph was dressed for evening in head-to-toe black except for his shirt and snowy cravat. He was as finely turned out as any of the well-heeled men she'd seen gliding up to the ticket booths, their servants scrambling behind them with purses or umbrellas.

But how much more substantial Joseph seemed, more solid, broader chested, with big shoulders and large hands. He'd been tall and strong before Barbadoes, but he returned with the size and bearing of something akin to a conqueror.

Without thinking, Tessa looked down at the blue dress and gave the skirts a shake. She raised her hand to squeeze her cheeks but felt her own natural flush even through her gloves. She was just about to wave but Joseph turned his head, and their eyes locked. Tessa's hand froze. He quickened his pace and scanned her appearance as he walked. His eyes moved up and down her body like fingers on a pianoforte, from high C to low A, and her body responded as if he'd touched her. She heard the music in her head.

"I worried you might arrive before us, and now you have," he said when he reached her.

"We made excellent time," she told him. Such mundane conversation, when what she really wanted to do was launch herself at him. She wondered idly if they would discuss the weather. Or the crowd.

We've done it, she wanted to exclaim. *We've moved beyond. You know about Christian and I've docked your boat, and we're here, together, on a beautiful night.*

We've started again.

Joseph held out one large, gloved hand and Tessa's breath caught. She placed her fingers over his, and he bowed. She stared down at the tussle of sandy blond hair, thrilled by the propriety of the gesture. When his head came up, she tightened her fingers, unwilling to let him go. Joseph looked at her, a question in his blue eyes.

Yes, she wanted to say. *And why not?*

She was just about to slide her hand down his wrist and tuck it into the crook of his arm when Jon Stoker caught up.

"Stoker, mate," Joseph said, almost as if he'd forgotten he'd arrived with his friend. He looked at Tessa. "Sabine is . . . ?"

"Oh . . . she was very impatient to see inside, I'm afraid." Tessa glanced apologetically at Stoker. "She has bought a ticket and gone ahead."

Mr. Stoker said nothing, but his eyes went narrow and hard. He nodded slowly, once, twice, and began backing away.

"Stoke, no—don't go," implored Joseph. "Come inside with Tessa and me and have a look around. She's inside, Tessa has just said as much."

"This," said Stoker, still backing up, "was a bad idea. As I knew it would be."

Just then, a group of staggering young men broached the garden gate, their arm-and-arm progress heralded by whistles and two bars of a bawdy song in uneven harmony. An outlying man used his walking cane to lift the skirts of an unsuspecting young woman in his reach. The woman shrieked and skittered away while the men gave a cruel laugh.

Joseph mumbled a curse and stepped more closely to Tessa. Stoker paused in his retreat. He frowned at Joseph and closed his eyes. "How long?" he said.

"I beg your pardon?"

"How long has Sabine been alone inside?"

"Oh," said Tessa, "Not so long. No more than ten minutes."

Stoker nodded curtly and left them, crossing to the gates. He cut the queue, tossed a handful of coins at the ticket taker, and slipped inside.

"I implored her to wait," Tessa told Joseph. "But she is very . . . conflicted about seeing him again."

Joseph nodded. "He works hard to feign indifference, but he wanted to come."

"Have the two of you been to Vauxhall before?"

Joseph looked down at her with an odd expression, like

she'd ask him if he'd ever been to church or the market. "Many times. I don't suppose there's a chance you feel you've seen enough from here? That we might retire to a proper dinner—in Kensington, perhaps? With footmen to serve the talents of a French chef?"

She laughed. "No, I'm afraid not. I cannot wait to get inside."

CHAPTER SIXTEEN

Joseph devoted so much thought to what he would say and do in Vauxhall Gardens, he'd made no assumptions about what Tessa would say or do.

The result was his brain wiped clean. He spoke very little. He reconciled himself to simply observing her.

No, not *observe*. Observe was too passive and detached. Joseph was *relishing her*. How could he resist, when she twirled and laughed her way through wet flowers, torchlit pathways, dancers, pantomimes, and trained dogs.

How, he wondered, returning her dazzling smile with a thin, uncertain grin, had he not braced for Tessa's joyfulness? He'd felt something very akin to love with her at Berymede because of little more than her joy.

The combination of fair hair, blue eyes, and splashy silks had also played some part, of course—he'd loved those too. Like a sneak attack, she'd trotted these out tonight. Gone were her horrible dresses and severe hair.

The sight of her in this dress had quite literally stopped him where he stood. Stoker had nearly collided with his back and mocked him, which Joseph supposed he deserved. He'd been blindsided. Again.

But perhaps this had been his chief failing from the beginning. He'd never stopped to anticipate. Not in Belgravia, when he'd been on the attack, not at St. Katharine Docks, or in the park.

He wondered if it would always be this way. Would she always take him by surprise? And if so, was it so terrible?

Yes, he thought, watching her gasp at the antics of a diminutive juggler, *it is.* He was unsettled by surprises. Surprises meant he was unprepared. Surprises put him at a disadvantage.

You love the surprise of her, he thought, the notion as nonsensical as it was true.

"How talented he is," Tessa said of the small man, clapping breathlessly.

She turned to Joseph and put two gloved hands on his forearm. "Can you believe it? Five teacups and a pot of water? And all the while on one foot!"

Joseph stared at her hands on his arm, blinking down at the snug blue leather. It was unnecessary to look, of course. Her touch reverberated through him like the lash of a whip. The juggler's foot was the furthest from his mind. He saw only her hands, he lived and breathed her hands.

"Sorry," she said, snatching herself away.

It's nothing, he wanted to say. *Come back.* But she was already spinning, her attention caught by a five-person choir singing a ballad in a gazebo across the path. She took two steps toward their syrupy voices, and then rushed to the periphery of the assembling crowd. Joseph followed as if tied to her with a string.

"It's lovely," she whispered when he caught up. He glanced down. Her blue eyes were filled with wonder, her lips slightly apart.

Joseph squinted into the gazebo. Musicians at Vauxhall were a mix of spotlight-hungry hobbyists and seasoned professionals. The assemblage in the gazebo was clearly the former, but Tessa clapped enthusiastically as they garbled their final note.

"Shall we seek out supper?" he said, hoping to veer her away before the choir came to some consensus on their next song.

"You don't really enjoy Vauxhall, do you?" she said. "You wish you hadn't come."

Joseph frowned at the impossible thought of him not coming. "I don't *not* enjoy Vauxhall. I'm just a bit jaded, I suppose."

"*Oh*," she said. She gave an exaggerated, knowing nod. "You've sailed the world and seen sights far more fantastical, have you?"

"It's not so much that my travels have outpaced Vauxhall," he said, "more so the perception of what I enjoy."

She laughed. "What do you mean? Either you enjoy something or you do not."

I enjoy you, he thought, but he said, "When your earliest years are spent in service—literally cleaning mud from boots, emptying chamber pots—and you rise above it, those early trappings become a little warped in your view."

They came to a fork in the path, two smaller walkways branching around a great trellis, heavy with roses. Tessa admired the flowers, stepping forward to smell each blossom.

"Stoker and I came to Vauxhall often as boys," Joseph said. "Sometimes we had money to buy tickets, sometimes we navigated the river on a skiff and slipped over the wall. Now that I've the means to avail myself of any meal or entertainment in London, it's difficult for me to return."

"But is this the way you view every simple thing you enjoyed as a boy? Do you eschew sunrises, for example? Or puppies? These were available to you, then and now."

"No. Not sunrises or puppies. I'm happy Vauxhall rages on for the masses, and it is my pleasure to escort you, but I'm dubious of attractions that charge less than four shillings at the gate. That was my old life, you see, before I made myself over into . . ." He struggled to find the correct word.

"A rich man?" she provided.

"I was going to say *man of means*, but it's clear you take my meaning. Vauxhall was the purveyance of Joseph the servant. Joseph the—"

"Rich man," she cut in, laughing.

"*Man of means*," he emphasized, "prefers the opera."

She made a little noise of understanding, neither judgment or affirmation, and they crunched down the path, weaving around couples and families and a man with a large snake coiled around his outstretched arms.

"I've a question," she announced. But she said nothing for

another four or five steps. "At Berymede," she finally went on, "you spoke often about an ambition to run for Parliament. Is this still your plan?"

Joseph looked at her. *This, now?* he wondered. He said, "Yes, in fact. It is. But I admit it knowing full well that Parliament is an unlikely ambition. I may pass my entire life in pursuit of it. But it's not impossible, is it?"

They turned a corner and a food stall came into view. It was a rolling cart stacked with wheels of cheese, baskets of fresh bread, assorted fruit, and paper cones of warm chestnuts. Joseph raised his eyebrows, an invitation, and Tessa nodded with enthusiasm. He bought a block of cheese, two loaves of the aromatic bread, and a cone of nuts.

"Ale?" he asked the vendor, but the old man shook his head and pointed to a half barrel stacked with bottles of wine. Joseph held up a finger. "One bottle, if you please."

They carried the meal to a wooden bench, Tessa pulled off her gloves and carefully unfurled the cone of paper, nudging the chestnuts into a little pile and arranging the bread and cheese. Joseph used his knife to open the wine and then stabbed the point through the paper with a *whack*. Tessa gave a satisfying jump and then laughed.

"Now I wonder," she began, dislodging the knife and slicing the cheese, "can a man who is too lofty for Vauxhall Gardens properly advocate in Parliament for poor children? This was your goal in running for office, was it not? Resources for children without means?"

Joseph took up a loaf of bread and tore it in half. "Yes, well—for schools." He'd often wondered at Berymede if she'd been listening when he spoke about his Parliamentary dream.

Tessa nodded and selected a slice of cheese. Delicately, she sniffed it and nibbled a small sample. Her tongue darted out. She licked her bottom lip.

Joseph's own mouth watered. He reached for the bottle of wine and took a swig. "I believe I take offense to the notion that I am *too lofty* for Vauxhall. It's not loftiness. More like . . . unease."

"You are *afraid* of the Gardens?"

He choked on the wine. "*Ah*, no." He wiped his mouth with his sleeve. "Returning to the fixtures of my youth—Vauxhall, for example—feels a bit like going back in time. I have this feeling that the very space might reclaim me in some way. Swallow me up. As if all that I have accomplished has been a dream and here is where I really belong."

"But you are not uncertain of your station, Joseph, surely."

He shook his head. "Not uncertain, merely—forward-looking. No looking back."

"Except for the poor children."

He laughed again. Her wit was so very quick. He'd seen this at Berymede, although not applied in this way. Not insightful. She had gushed over his every comment in those weeks; now, she challenged. He had the thought that he could talk to her all night.

"I fell into the path of education out of chance. But it's so very rare for a serving boy to happen into the generous employ of an earl willing to hire tutors and cancel chores so he could learn calculus and French. I believe the education of children should not be left to a one-in-a-million chance. If primary school in England was standard—a school in every village—imagine what talent we could discover."

"But have you given thought to seeking out lower-class boys who show some potential? Boys you could sponsor, as the earl sponsored you?"

"I believe every child in Britain can be taught to read and write and do sums. No one should be singled out. Potential can be hidden, and even those without any particular potential should enjoy literacy. It's ambitious, I know. But if I could win a seat in the House of Commons, I might effect real change."

"So this is why you dress so finely and ride such an expensive horse. This is why your matchbox is silver and you never seem to wear the same boots twice?"

"If you're accusing me of loving the finer things in life, I've no defense. Conveniently, these finer things also fit into my larger plan of running for public office. So the answer is both yes and no. I both enjoy *and* require fine clothes and horses. A good meal and other luxuries."

"And a wealthy gentleman's daughter as your wife . . ." Tessa said.

Joseph went very still. He replaced the bottle on the bench. "No, Tessa." His tone was harsh and she flinched, but on this point, he could not be misunderstood. "That is not the reason I wanted a wealthy gentleman's daughter." *I lived and breathed you,* he thought.

But she had known this at the time. He'd never been vague about his affections for her. *He* had concealed nothing. *She* had been the concealer.

"Forgive me," she said, casting her eyes down. "I . . . I've consoled myself with the knowledge that my father's wealth and connections would be a boon to you. Marrying you saved two lives. I wanted you to gain from it as well. Of course, now—"

"My interest was solely in you," he said quietly. The truth. It made him angry that she would suggest otherwise.

She stared at the food. After a long moment, she said, "I understand your tenuous relationship with your old life— when you were a servant—and the way it is now, with your wealth and refinement. When I . . ." She paused and glanced up cautiously. Joseph refused to soften his gaze.

She swallowed and continued, "When I think of the idle, vapid, featherheaded girl I was before I moved to London, I cringe. I am loathe to ever slide back into that . . . that . . ." She picked up three chestnuts and then replaced them in a line, one by one.

She finished softly, "May I never entertain such a pointless existence ever again."

"Your existence was not pointless at Berymede," he said. Another true statement. *Your existence thrilled me.*

She shrugged and picked up a piece of bread. "My existence at Berymede is not like it is now."

Joseph's stomach dropped. "No," he said. "I suppose it is not."

Now, her life contained a baby, it contained a newfound interest in business. Now she was beginning to explore London.

Also now, Joseph was not part of her life.

Tessa took a deep breath and brushed the crumbs from her hand. She gestured to the wine bottle. "May I?"

She brought the bottle to her lips, laughing a little. He watched her struggle to drink and grin at the same time.

"I've compelled you to drink wine straight from the bottle," she said. "I would understand your wanting to leave this habit behind."

"Drinking from the bottle is one of the few habits I carry over from youth. There was precious little crockery in Barbadoes. Life at sea, and all of that."

"Stop," she teased. "I cannot imagine you drinking wine from a bottle as a matter of course. In fact, I can't imagine you drinking to excess at all. You were rather temperate at Berymede, I recall."

"I nearly drank myself to death," he said, "in Barbadoes." All pride seemed to have left him.

"Oh." She looked over her shoulder at a bed of moss and rock. "I'm glad you did not."

He watched her profile, soft and perfect in the waning light, and she felt his gaze and smiled. Something warm and soft flowed between them.

I'm glad you did not.

It was hardly a declaration, but it was better, he thought, than wishing him dead.

He stood, grabbing the bottle of wine by the neck. With his other hand, he gestured to the path. "Come on then. There is more to see."

He saw her eyes trace the tall, solid line of his body, saw awareness and playfulness and something more flit across her face. Her cheeks pinkened, but he didn't look away. Slowly, he cocked one suggestive eyebrow.

She rose as if in a trance. He had the overwhelmingly welcome thought that she would walk to him, walk right into his arms, but instead she reached for his outstretched hand. He'd only meant to point the way, but she closed her fingers and tugged.

Joseph allowed her to lead him, following her down the trail. By the next turn, she had coiled her hand around his bicep and leaned in. His heart went very still for two beats but he strode on, escorting her with a nonchalance borne of a thousand female encounters with a thousand women all over the world, and thank God. It would not do to stumble now.

"What would you like to see?" he asked.

"Everything."

Chapter Seventeen

The spectacle of Vauxhall Gardens was an entertaining diversion, but Tessa found it inconsequential compared to the conversation.

Ultimately, her talk with Joseph did very little to raise the topic of her departure from Belgravia, but it had been gratifying in a more intimate, personal way. She learned things about him that she'd not known. She'd been treated to the sight of him drinking wine, straight from a bottle. In all honesty, she'd been loath to leave their quiet bench for the next footpath, but his mood had shifted, and he held out his hand, and the only thing better than talking to him had suddenly seemed like touching him.

It was no mystery why his mood changed. She'd made the suggestion that he'd married her to enhance his collection of fine, expensive things—that she was one of these fine things—and he had objected. It was a ploy reminiscent of the Old Tessa, and she'd made the suggestion for the sole purpose of hearing him deny it—which he did, with an emphasis that sent a small shock down her spine. The heat of his denial made her realize how much she'd been waiting for him to make some . . . claim. To her. To offer his arm, or to rest his hand on the small of her back, or to *say something*.

But then the conversation had gone a little off, and she'd lost her nerve, and the New Tessa was out of her depth as how to salvage it. Never fear, the Old Tessa had danced back in and taken his hand, slid close, and leaned against him as he led them down the path.

In all honestly, the New Tessa did not hate walking down dark paths on his arm. The New Tessa wanted a night out at Vauxhall Gardens with Joseph Chance just as direly as the old one. But she had to be careful, so very careful. If Joseph rejected her, every incarnation of herself would be shattered.

"I've heard there will be fireworks," she said, glancing at him on the dim pathway.

"Indeed," he said. "There is also a small replica of a palace and formal grounds, with an orchestra and dancing. We've somehow managed to bypass it so far, but it is worth seeing."

They turned one corner and then another, less able to find their way in the dusk. He allowed her to choose the route, and she wandered with no real direction, enjoying the feel of his bicep beneath her hand, his warmth, the intimacy of tucking herself so closely beside him. They passed one food stall and then another, but when they came to a cart selling fragrant fruit tarts, Tessa paused.

"Will you take a sweet?" Joseph asked.

She was just about to point to a strawberry tart when

laughter burst from around the next bend. She raised her eyebrows at him and drifted to the sound.

The path opened to a clearing where a crowd had gathered around an informal theatrical performance. Actors in bright costumes had taken over an expanse of exposed rock and they portrayed some manner of domestic melodrama with exaggerated aplomb. A young mother and father fussed over a bundle of cloth meant to be an infant while a disapproving grandmother looked on.

Tessa grinned, immediately taken in. "Do you mind?" she whispered to Joseph, stopping at the edge of the crowd. "Surely I've not truly experienced Vauxhall without live theatre?"

"'Theatre' in the loosest sense of the word," he whispered back. She chuckled and moved closer, watching drama unfold.

The actress who portrayed the mother was squinting at the actor-father.

"Are you certain he likes that, dearest?" the mother said in flat, long-suffering tone. The actor swung the baby to and fro in a mad sort of rocking motion that bordered hysteria. Somewhere offstage, another actor mimicked the sound of a baby crying. The audience roared with laughter.

The next scene depicted the baby falling to sleep just as the sun rose; another showed the father heaping the baby with blankets before a stroll on a snowy day. Each scene played off the exaggerating drollness of the mother, the ineptitude of the father, and the reliably interfering advice of the grandmama.

"They've almost got it right," someone whispered in

Tessa's ear. She jerked her head to see a middle-aged woman sharing the edge of the crowd. She was flanked by a grinning companion, likely her husband, and the two nudged each other conspiratorially.

Tessa nodded. "Oh yes, they are quite good."

"You two young people know something of family life, I'll wager," said the woman. She pointed back and forth between Joseph and Tessa.

Tessa shifted uncomfortably. She smiled tightly, meaning to end the conversation.

The woman was not deterred. "Newlyweds?" she guessed. "I can spot them from a mile."

"She can spot them," confirmed the man.

Beside Tessa, Joseph went tense.

"We married in December," Tessa rushed to say.

"Oh, God bless you," the woman crooned. "Is there a happier pair than a couple just wed? Good for you . . ." she gestured to the lantern-lit park ". . . for taking in a bit of pleasure while you can. When the babes come . . ." She trailed off but gestured knowingly to the actors on the stage.

Tessa struggled to form a pleasant expression. Joseph took a step back.

"When the babies arrive," repeated the woman, "the two of you will fare better than this lot. My advice? Be honest in all things. And allow for mistakes, large and small." The old woman chuckled and gave Joseph a knowing wink.

Tessa glanced at him. He had the pained expression of a man waiting for a tooth extraction.

"Do you mind if I go back for the pasties?" he whispered to Tessa. "What would you like?"

Tessa searched his face. "Whatever smells good. Thank you."

He nodded once, glanced at the woman, and then disappeared down the path. Tessa stared at the shadowy spot where he stood. She was cold, suddenly. Darkness had fallen in earnest, the mild September day dissolved into a cool autumn night. She searched her reticule for her gloves and tugged them on, returning her attention to the stage.

Another domestic blunder unfolded, evoking peals of laughter from the crowd. The young wife reclined downstage with a fan and a tray of biscuits. She devoured the sweets with loud, sensual abandon. The husband, meanwhile, clutching the infant in his arms, darted round the stage, voicing his desire to find some place to safely rest the child so that he might steal a few amorous moments with his wife. As he clamored and tripped, and the actor off-stage wailed louder, affecting the sound of the crying baby.

The audience laughed, and Tessa supposed there was some humor to the stolen moments of the wife, stuffing herself with biscuits. The husband was particularly adept at looking hopeless with a crying baby. But something about the scene struck Tessa as distressing and sad rather than funny. Suddenly, she felt a little like crying herself. When the audience roared again, Tessa looked away, tears stinging her eyes.

Joseph had not returned, but she felt an urgent compulsion to get as far away from the fake crying as she could. She took two steps back, and then three, and then she spun and hurried to the path.

The noise of the crowd had attracted more onlookers, and she was forced to dodge left and right to weave her way through the stream of revelers. All the while, the droning cry of the pretend baby followed her. She was swamped with thoughts of Christian, left at home with Perry. The nursemaid was perfectly capable, and her son loved Perry, but suddenly Tessa wanted the baby in *her* arms, she wanted to feel the weight of his warm, pink body and smell his baby smell and see for herself that he wasn't crying like the baby on the stage.

Breathing over a painful lump in her throat, Tessa reached the main path and looked left and right. From which way had they come? She was jostled by a painted-cheeked woman who bumped her from the side. Tessa spun and staggered.

"Sorry, love," the woman called, and her friends snickered. Behind them, the audience erupted into another wave of laughter. Underlying it all, the persistent wail of the stage baby droned on and on.

Go, Tessa ordered in her head and she turned left on impulse. Her skirts tangled in her haste, and she stumbled and hitched them up to run. Her hat sagged and she reached up and yanked it from her head. The trail curved left and then right, eventually giving way to a small clearing dominated by a square pergola. The wooden structure formed a high grid that hung heavy with wisteria vine.

Tessa came up short, her attention caught by the thick

vine climbing each pillar like a serpent. The leafy canopy was a natural ceiling of green and autumn gold that obscured the night sky.

An outdoor room, Tessa marveled, spinning a little. A yew hedge surrounded the little square, with an opening for the pathway in and an opposite pathway out. Glowing lanterns hung at the corners of the pergola, four adjacent swinging orbs of yellow light. Best of all, the thick vines had a muffling effect on the mix of sounds of the park, and the wail of the infant could no longer be heard.

"Thank God," Tessa breathed, leaning against a vine-knotted pillar. She was being silly, she thought. How much more emotional she'd grown since Christian had come. Rampant sentimentality made her weep at sunsets and hymns in church.

Thinking of Christian, she pushed off the pillar and began to amble beneath the vines. She paced the length of the pergola twice and dropped on a bench at the far end. She had just begun to mentally retrace her steps back to Joseph, when she heard voices. A shout, a laugh, three bars of a song. She looked up.

A quartet of young men drifted into the pergola from the opposite path. They paused when they saw the wooden trellis and heavy vine but quickly fanned out, marveling at the leafy canopy climbing above their heads.

One man looped an arm around a vine-choked pillar, leaned with outswept hand, and began to sing. His friends joined in immediately, shouting more than singing, and one man chanted "for crown and country!" between stanzas.

The four of them laughed and sang and trudged with the staggering shuffle of men deep in their cups. They were young, Tessa thought, not older than her own twenty-three years, and dressed more or less like gentlemen.

Taken individually, they represented almost no threat. They were lads, cheerfully drunk, out for a ramble. But they had not come upon her individually. There was a scrum of them, and she was alone in the darkness.

Tessa shrank back, her mind racing for some comment that might calmly alert them to her presence. Silence made her feel like a fox hiding in a hole.

Without warning, the man who'd begun the song leaned his shoulder against the pillar and hung his head. After a pause, he let out a slow, loud belch. His companions burst into laughter. One man made a show of kicking him in the arse.

Harmless, Tessa told herself, but her eyes returned again and again to the trail, willing someone else to come along. No one came. Three minutes turned to five minutes. With each passing second, Tessa's unease grew. She sat very still, so still she thought she might snap in two. She waited, counting the beats of her drumming heart. After what felt like a quarter hour (but was likely far less), she decided a better course of action was to flee—to shove up and dart from the square, disappearing down the opposite path. She wouldn't speak, she wouldn't even look. They were preoccupied with their whistles and jibes. In theory, she could simply slip away.

Drawing a silent breath, she gathered her hat, her reticule, her skirts. The heavy silk rustled and Tessa cringed but kept moving. She darted right and—

"Ho there!" shouted one of the men. Four sets of bored, bleary eyes turned to the bench.

Now Tessa was the cornered fox. Vein by vein, fear spread through her body. She willed herself to animate, to look less like stricken and terrified. She released her skirts and grabbed hold of the bench. Her hat fell and she let it go.

She tried to affect the expression of inconsequence, of not being worth the hassle, but they advanced on her, winding their way through the pillars from four directions. They reminded her of boys descending on a fallen grouse.

Their faces became clearer with proximity, and she watched them take in her shape and dress and braids. Their talking and jests fell silent.

"Well, hello," boomed the first man, coming to a stop before her. He had ginger hair and freckles. His voice was too loud for the small space.

"Deafen her, Francis, while you're at it," joked the next man. He wore a tall hat pulled low over his eyes.

"Don't dignify them with a response, love," called a third man, the one who'd belched.

"Sage advice, coming from you, Nevil," said the ginger-headed one.

They formed a loose half circle around her bench and stared down. Tessa could smell their collective aroma of brandy and tobacco and hair tonic.

Harmless young men, she chanted in her head. She thought of the Old Tessa, the confident girl who had handily dispatched intoxicated males with a roll of her eyes and a wave. She thought of the girl raised with four brothers and their myriad of rowdy friends.

But this was not the same. She was isolated; she did not know these men. Worst of all, she was glaringly conspicuous in her vibrant dress with her head bare. The fabric of her indigo gown seemed to radiate in the lantern light. The yellow loops of her braids were heavy on her shoulders. She wanted her pelisse, her bonnet—she wanted to gather up her skirts and run. Fear rose in her chest like icy water in the hull of a sinking ship.

"What's your name, love?" called the ginger-headed man.

"My husband has just stepped away," Tessa answered. Her voice was breathy and high, fearful. She swore in her head and glanced to the right and left. Could she run without colliding with one of them? Could she squeeze through the thick branches of the hedge behind her?

"Husband?" cried the third man, the belcher. "Oh, you break my heart."

"As if she'd consider the likes of you," said the man in the tall hat. They laughed.

They were so close, their bodies cast long shadows like the bars of a jail. Their voices were slurred, and they spoke *at* Tessa more than to her.

Harmless, she repeated in her head. *Drunk, harmless boys.*

She edged up from the bench. "I implore you, please allow me to pass. I . . . I mean to locate my friends."

"Oh, thank God," one of them said, "there are *friends*.

But, are your friends also married, love?" He studied her like an old man considers a flight of stairs.

"But let us escort you to these friends," said another. "Not Francis, of course, but a real gentleman, like myself."

This was met with hoots of laughter. Knee slapping and shoulder leaning ensued. The belcher staggered forward and Tessa shrank back. Her skirts hit the bench and she lost her balance. She caught herself with one hand.

"*Careful,*" laughed the ginger-headed man, reaching to pull her upright. He made the simple gesture of reaching out to steady her—an open palm and long fingers wrapped around her wrist—but something about the tight, clamminess of his hand caused panic to set in. Tessa bit back a scream and breathed, "*No.*"

"Bloody hell, Francis," said the man in the hat, "you've terrorized her, and why I am not surprised. You are a bane to all women. Allow me." He swooped toward Tessa, his arms outstretched. "Come on, then, love. Up you go."

And now Tessa did scream.

She yanked from their hold and scrambled over the bench, backing into the sharp needles of the hedge. "Please," she gasped, "you are too close. I beg you."

"Familiar words, no doubt, Nevil," said one of the men. This was met by laughter and a round of whistles. One of them lost his balance and fell on the bench. Tessa pressed herself more tightly into the hedge.

She was just about to launch herself to the right, to skirt the corner of the pergola and make for the pathway, when she saw a flutter of movement inside the dim pergola. It was just a flash, an arc of blackness, blacker than the night. It came and went so quickly, she thought it was her own hysteria playing tricks.

But suddenly the laughing man called Nevil was jerked backward—one moment he reached for her, the next he was gone. The snorts and snickers came to a sudden hiccup-y stop.

One of the young men shouted, "What the bloo—"

His exclamation was cut off when a forearm lashed out from behind and clamped down across his throat. The young man went bug-eyed and scratched at the arm around his neck.

Joseph.

Tessa's husband had materialized from the night. First she saw his arm, which wrapped around the neck of the young man; next broad shoulders and chest. When Joseph's face came into the light, Tessa saw a mask of rage. She let out a sob of relief and dropped onto the bench.

"Tessa, are you harmed?" he called out.

She shook her head.

"Tessa?" he repeated, his voice urgent.

"No," she said, staring at her hands. "They've done nothing. I was frightened. It was silly. You should let him go."

"Let—merc—go . . ." said the man held by the neck.

Tessa slapped her hand on the bench, mortified by the scene she had caused. "Please." She looked up. "Let him go."

Joseph released the man and he dropped to the ground on a gasp. Joseph rounded on the others. When he spoke, it was in a voice she had never heard. Raw, loose, the dialect of a common man. "Take another step toward her, no, *look at her* again, and I'll sink a knife into your neck before your next breath."

"Careful, sir, no harm meant," said one of the men, edging away.

"Just trying to be of service," said the other man.

Joseph ignored them and moved to the bench. "Tessa?" He hovered above her but did not reach out. His posh voice had returned. "Tell me what happened?"

She shook her head. "They are harmless," she said hoarsely. "Let them go. They did nothing."

"Harmless, mate," repeated one man, working with the others to haul their gagging friend to his feet.

Joseph ignored him, staring at Tessa. "You're crying."

"It's nothing. Please . . ." She wanted the men gone. She wanted to be alone with Joseph. She saw her hat on the ground and she reached for it, but her hand shook. She grabbed the bench and closed her eyes.

Joseph eased beside her. "Tessa, what can I . . . ?" he whispered cautiously.

It was her undoing. She fell against him, burying her face into his neck, grabbing handfuls of his coat. His arms went around her and she sucked in a breath.

Over her head, he growled, "Bugger off."

Tessa heard scrambling, guttural *oofs*, and retreating footsteps. She clung to Joseph with a fierceness of a survivor on a raft, eyes squeezed shut, breath held. She listened, straining to hear the last crunch of gravel, a stray curse, a snicker. Joseph said nothing. He held her and rubbed circles on the small of her back.

When the pergola was quiet at last, Tessa allowed herself to breathe again. A torrent of relief and anger and fear came out in gasps and gulps. Next, tears. She wept against his chest.

"Shh," Joseph said softly against her hair. "I have you. Tessa, *shh*. I'm so sorry. This is my fault. It was stupid of me to leave you alone. Forgive me—please forgive me. But please tell me you are unharmed? What did they—?"

She shook her head, burrowing deeper into his cravat. "No, there was no danger. Drunk boys out for a lark."

"You're trembling. Did they touch you? My God, if they touched you—"

"No, no," she said against his shirt. "I'm being foolish. I simply can't—"

She stopped, uncertain of how to explain all the reasons she couldn't manage the men on her own. Giving voice to her fears seemed worse than riding out the moment. She repeated, "I simply can't."

"I don't understand," said Joseph. "Simply cannot—*what*?"

An easy answer formed in her brain and she seized upon it. "I simply cannot dress in this manner, ever again," she said.

"*You can't what?*"

She repeated it, louder this time, and it felt very much like the truth. "It was my fault. This dress, this stupid dress. The elaborate braids. I invite unwanted attention because of my own . . . vanity. *I* was the reckless one. Reckless and selfish and vain."

"Tessa—no. Stop." Gently he pulled her from his chest.

He took her by the shoulders and squared her to him. "These men were stupid with youth and drink and the sort of shared brain that boys acquire when they prowl around together in the night. They were harassing you for their own sport, despite the fact that they likely know better. *They* are at fault—and me, for leaving you alone. It's nothing to do with you." He pulled her hand from his lapel and kissed her knuckles.

She stared into the pergola. "It's not. . . ." She shook her head. She began again. "I told Perry I would wear the brown dress, that I would fade into the background and be unseen but safe. *Safe.*"

Joseph kissed her hand again. Tessa wanted to pull the spot to her lips.

She said, "But Perry *hid* the brown dress and convinced me to wear this gown, which I have always loved. I . . . I wanted to feel beautiful just once more. I wanted you to . . . to see . . . I wanted—"

Her explanation dissolved. How had she managed to lose both the cleverness of the Old Tessa and the placid good sense of the New? She was a weak, simpering, third version of herself. Steeped in regret and shaking in Joseph's arms. She squeezed her eyes shut.

Joseph craned his head, trying to see her downturned face. "Please tell me," he said, "that you do not believe your beautiful blue dress and your lovely braided hair are the source of this harassment. Please tell me you do not believe it to be your fault."

She blinked up into his blue eyes and tried to control

the fresh tears. He sounded . . . shocked. His voice held such emphasis, she could not press her rebuttal again. She despised playing the victim.

Joseph continued, "I cannot think who or what put the idea of blame in your head, but you are wrong. I've seen roving bands of young men in every corner of the globe and I assure you that no pretty dresses are required to encourage their interest. They are listless and bored and their chief concern is impressing each other. No young woman would have escaped their boorish attention, unfortunately—not in any manner of dress, brown or otherwise."

He paused, likely waiting for her to respond, but Tessa had used up her contribution to this discussion. To say more would only make the experience more horrible. She leaned into his chest and he closed his arms around her.

"Every man appreciates your beauty, Tessa," he said softly. "No one more than me. Only these cretins had the poor judgment to approach you. And that is their mistake, their crudeness and inebriation. And mine, because I left you alone. I was sick with worry, Tessa, when I couldn't find you—and now I see it was warranted. I returned to the clearing, but—"

"Oh, it was the play," Tessa cut in, sitting up. "The terrible little play. Something about the production upset me. And the old woman—she, she was so meddlesome. I couldn't remain. I know it was merely playacting, but—"

"Make no excuses, please. That production was the worst piece of amateur theatre I have ever had the misfortune of witnessing. And the woman? Our own friends struggle to characterize our relationship—even *I* struggle—so it's difficult to take counsel from a gossipy stranger. Even so, it was unconscionable for me to leave you alone. I shudder to think what would have happened if I hadn't found you."

Tessa's heart, already overworked from the night, clenched. What had he said? He struggled to characterize their marriage? It was hardly a declaration, but there was some . . . softness in the way he said it. Was it possible he felt more confusion than outrage? Tessa felt the same confusion. And hope. So much hope.

"I'm sorry I've dragged you to Vauxhall," she said. It was a classic Old-Tessa machination. Despite the young men and the play and the old woman, of course she was not sorry at all.

"Don't be silly. I've a mind to return tomorrow. Perhaps we should come every night until we get it right. I'd hate for your lasting impression to be drunken revelers and my threatening to stab them in the neck."

She laughed at his suggestion. A proper laugh, devoid of fear or alarm. She wanted suddenly to crawl back into Joseph's arms, and not because she was falling apart.

She thought of the way he fought back the young men. Of his confidence and strength. She thought about his different accent and the way he prowled the space. A small quiver of something unnamed but intriguing burned in her center. She wanted to kiss him. Desperately. To kiss like they had at Berymede. How had the Old Tessa accomplished this?

"Should we locate Sabine and Stoker?" Joseph was saying. He held out his hand. "You're meant to meet her at nine o'clock, I believe?"

"Yes, I suppose we should." She took his hand. "Thank you for coming to my rescue."

The Old Tessa would simply get it done. Reach up and pull his face down.

But the New Tessa smiled and took his arm and walked modestly beside him, waiting for *him* to reach up or pull down, waiting for him to make some show of affection for which he did not feel obligated or tricked or honor-bound to make.

CHAPTER EIGHTEEN

Joseph forced himself to wait a full day before initiating some future contact with his wife.

Not only was he uncertain that Tessa wanted to see him (and if so, in what vein), he needed a full day to recover from Vauxhall Gardens.

The twenty minutes that she was lost had taken years off his life. Icy fear thudded through his veins long after he'd followed her carriage home that night. For decades, Vauxhall Gardens had played dark, shadowy host to every manner of shady assignation. The moment he'd rushed into the pergola to find her ringed by a half circle of drunken louts made him want to rip the vine from the canopy and strangle each man. He thrummed with violence, but the situation wanted control and stealth, and every fight he'd ever fought had been brought to bear in those moments. He'd been outnumbered four to one and his first priority had been Tessa.

Looking back, he marveled that he'd allowed the men

to go, to simply fade into the darkness unaccounted for, but Tessa had required him more.

In that moment, he met yet another side of Tessa he'd not known. Terrified, guilt-ridden, nearly inconsolable. He couldn't stop thinking about her response. There was no question she'd been frightened, and this alone was enough to trouble him, but what bothered him more were her tearful ramblings. She seemed to believe that she'd somehow *invited* their attention, that vanity was to blame.

It made no sense. She'd looked beautiful that night, colorful and happy and *herself*—or at least more like the self she'd presented in Berymede. She'd seemed not just pretty but *comfortable*, he'd thought. *Natural.*

She'd eventually found some calm, but still she had clung to him, keeping close to his side far more than she had during the spirited, early hours that she'd enjoyed in the park.

Despite her distress, it was impossible to deny that he savored the feel of her in his arms. Like the selfish blackguard he was, he'd tried to memorize the fierce strength in her small hands, the softness of her head beneath his chin, the outline of her perfect ear pressed against his chest. He'd waited so many days to touch her. He'd worried for months that he would never touch her again. But that night, she'd clawed to get closer. His heart had been perforated with piercings, prick after prick after prick.

After the requisite day and night, Joseph had settled on a generic request: that he might spend some time in Belgravia with her and the baby and then, if possible, he might squire her around town in his phaeton.

As added incentive, he mentioned a potential stop in the offices of the buyer for the guano haul. Tessa had seen the cargo brought to port, but he wasn't sure if she learned how the fertilizer reached the buyers.

The invitation he sent her was brief and general, and he was careful to make no mention of what he really intended, which was to show her his house.

Six months before the guano scheme had been launched, Joseph had purchased a five-story, Georgian-style house in Blackheath, a borough of southeast London. He'd grown weary of his leased suite of rooms and Blackheath was not only respectable, it was convenient to the London docks and home to a growing number of shipping merchants and importers.

The house had figured centrally in Joseph's Plan for the Future. He would furnish it finely, staff it professionally, and live there when he was in town. A fine house was important, he knew, for entertaining political connections.

After Tessa's confession, Joseph assumed he would eventually give over the fourth floor to her and the baby. He'd not thought about whether she would like it, only that it would solve the question of his estranged wife and her baby.

Now, he was consumed with what she might think. He paced the empty house, glowering at how unfit it seemed. Large and cold and mostly empty, it held only a stray collection of mismatched pieces that had caught his eye around the world. Was it fit for a gentleman's daughter? Hardly. Would it be comfortable for a baby? Not at all. Was it too far from central London? Too cold and cavernous? Yes and yes.

And the illustrious fourth floor, which he had assumed she would quietly and gratefully inhabit? It now seemed like a banishment reserved for a mad relative or a pet that could not be trusted.

The whole notion of the house seemed awkward and impractical at best. At worst, gaudy, presumptive, and unfit.

But Joseph tried very hard not to get ahead of himself. First, he would take some measure of her plans for the future. If she seemed amenable, he would casually suggest she consider the house. Make no assumptions. Let her lead the way. He could sell the house and everything in it.

Or, he thought as he stood on her doorstep in Belgravia, he could live in it alone while she moved on, quietly go mad and lock himself on the fourth floor.

But first, he would see her again.

"We couldn't be sure how much time you meant to spend with the baby," Tessa told him as she led Joseph into the parlor.

The brown dress, he noted, had made a reappearance. Joseph could not care less what colors she wore, but he could not help but be troubled by the *way* in which she wore them. She trudged along in the brown wool as if the fabric weighed a stone. The bun at the back of her head looked like a painful knot.

"I shouldn't like to disrupt the baby's schedule," he said.

"He should go down for a nap in a half hour," she said. "If your day permits, perhaps we can sit with him until then."

"I'm at your disposal," he heard himself say. The nursemaid Perry, holding the child, leapt up from the sofa when they entered the parlor.

"*Welcome home*, Mr. Chance," the maid said brightly. "We have been waiting for you ever so long."

This sounded like a planned recitation, but Joseph smiled. If memory served, one tended to part company with Perry with a touch of stunned deafness. The less said to encourage the girl, the better.

Perry went on, "Your son, especially, has waited so long to make your acquaintance." She presented Christian to him like a platter of biscuits.

"Thank you, Perry," Tessa sang, sweeping past the maid to scoop up the baby. "Remember what we discussed? Mr. Chance has limited experience with infants. He may wish to learn how to comfortably hold a baby before we pitch Christian in his path."

"Oh, holding babies is as easy as holding a sack of potatoes," the maid lectured sagely. "The trick is never to *drop* them. Babies do not take kindly to being dropped."

"Perry—" began Tessa, but Joseph said, "An aversion I share."

Now the maid was encouraged. "You should have seen Miss Tessa the night the baby came. The doctor and Miss Sabine and I sat with her all night, it was a hard labor, really, almost twenty hours—"

"Perry . . ." said Tessa, her voice pained.

The maid ignored her. "We thought the little bloke would never come. He's such a round, fat baby and Miss Tessa is ever so slight."

"*Perry . . .*" Now Tessa pleaded.

"But then out he came, squalling to wake the dead. And

the doctor cut the cord and I wiped him down and brought him to Miss Tessa to have her first look. But she was so tired from laboring so many hours—all through the night and the day before—and she said to me, 'But Perry, I don't know how to hold him,' and I told her, same as I told you, 'You hold him just like a sack of potatoes, *just don't drop him.*' And I set him in her lap, and that was that. And she hasn't dropped him yet."

"Thank you, Perry, that will be enough," said Tessa. She shot the maid a pleading look. The baby chewed on his fist and stared at his nursemaid as if he would like to hear more.

Perry said wistfully, "He was a dear babe from the very first. Miss Sabine and Miss Tessa and I stared down at him that first night, and I said, 'You've done so well, Miss Tessa. You done so very well. He's a fine boy.'"

Tessa opened her mouth to interrupt, but Perry carried on. "And you know what she said? I'll never forget it. She said, 'I wish Joseph could see him.'"

"That will do, Perry!" Tessa said, and she took the maid by the arm and hauled her to the corner of the room, whispering harshly.

Joseph turned away, thinking of his wife, alone with an eighteen-year-old maid, her friend, and a strange doctor. He thought of her laboring for hours, and then meeting the baby without a husband nearby. His chest constricted, like he was being pinned by a great weight.

The baby began to cry in earnest, and Joseph took a step toward the sound. The two women continued to argue as if they did not hear him. Joseph looked at the crying infant, his son, and the sound plucked at something urgent and troubled inside him. His gut felt tied with a thread, and each sharp cry gave the thread a little jerk.

"May I?" he said.

Both women fell silent. Tessa looked down at the fussing baby. "He is peevish when he is ignored, I'm afraid," she said.

"Another shared sentiment," Joseph said, and he crossed to her and lifted the heavy, wailing baby from her arms. Christian went rigid. His round face weighed the possibly that Joseph might be better or worse than his distracted mother.

Joseph chuckled and turned away, bouncing the child slightly. Christian's cries dissolved into a disgruntled sort of song, long notes interspersed with voracious fist-sucking.

What must it have been like for Tessa to hear the baby's cry for the first time? Without thinking, he bent his head and kissed the ebony fluff of hair on the top of Christian's head.

When he turned back around, both Perry and Tessa were staring at him.

"May I offer you my gratitude, Perry?" Joseph said. "For your . . . expertise. And the tireless aid you've given Tessa while I was away. I realize that I've had no real stake in the baby's life—this has been a great deficit—but I still feel compelled to say thank you."

For once, the maid was speechless. She blushed and gathered her apron into a ball in her hands.

They stood in silence for a moment, even Christian seemed content to suck his fist and gaze at Joseph's profile.

Joseph glanced at Tessa. She stared back with tear-bright eyes.

After a moment, Perry said, "But would you like to help feed him?"

Joseph face went mortifyingly red hot and he nearly dropped the baby. He glanced again at Tessa. She opened her mouth as if to speak, but no words came out.

Reliably, Perry filled the silence. "Of course, Miss Tessa could not make milk, or not enough to keep this fat baby satisfied, so we feed him goat's milk, right from a spoon." She retrieved a basket near the door.

"Could not make . . ." repeated Joseph.

Tessa turned away and walked to the garden window. She stared out, a hand on top of her head.

"Happens sometimes, we've learned," Perry went on, speaking with authority. She brought the basket to a low table in the center of the room and neatly arranged a cloth and a carafe of what appeared to be milk. "Happened to my older sister, and that's how we knew about the spoon. What little milk Miss Tessa had? We allowed that to dry up and—"

"Perry, I beg you!" cried Tessa from the window. She pivoted. "I will take over from here. If you please."

"But it takes two people—"

"Mr. Chance will assist me," she said. "Go. When Joseph and I leave, you'll be glad to have had this respite."

Perry sighed dramatically and took her time arranging the milk, spoons, carafe, and teacup and saucer. Tessa loomed over her, arms crossed, breathing in and out. In Joseph's arms, Christian began to wiggle.

He managed, "Thank you again, Perry."

Perry bobbed a curtsy. "You're quite welcome, Mr. Chance. And if I might say, sir, that I always knew you would return home to London and be a gentleman about the baby and Miss Tessa and want—"

"*Good-bye, Perry,*" intoned Tessa, reaching for her son.

She settled on the sofa and positioned the baby on her lap with his back against her chest. Clearly accustomed to this position, the baby began an insistent sort of cooing whine and reached out with his thick, pink hands.

"That's right, Dollop," said Tessa. "Shall we show Pap— shall we show Joseph what a very good eater you are?"

With no warning, the words, *You may refer to me as Papa,* formed in Joseph's mind, but before he could say them, Tessa asked, "Can I impose on you to help? Perry is correct, it is a two-person job, I'm afraid." She nodded to the empty spot on the sofa beside her.

Joseph sat immediately. Tessa smiled but did not look at him, deftly taking one spoon and holding it out for Christian to grab.

"Does he feed himself?" Joseph asked.

Tessa chuckled. "No, but he is more able to sit still and makes fewer swipes for my spoon when he is holding his own spoon."

The baby extended his arm and opened chubby fingers like a fan, taking up the heavy silver. He brought the spoon immediately to his mouth and began to diligently gum the cool metal.

Next Tessa poured milk from the carafe into the teacup

and set it on a saucer. "If you don't mind," she said, "you will hold the cup of milk close, so that I may dip my spoon into it without risking spills. When the cup is on the table, half the milk ends up on the floor. Or on me."

"Right," said Joseph. He watched her spread a linen napkin over the baby and herself. Christian let out a long, impatient coo.

"Dollop," scolded Tessa gently, "can you show Joseph your very best manners?" She looked up and smiled, her blue eyes calm and clear and full of love. Joseph thought for a moment he'd forgotten how to breathe.

"Shall we?" She nodded to the teacup. Joseph offered the cup and she pooled a spoonful of milk and brought it to Christian's mouth. Like a baby bird, Christian opened wide and watched the spoon descend. She held it to his lips, and he slurped it up with a combination of gusty sucking and Tessa tipping the milk directly into his mouth.

When the spoon was empty, she scooped another draught. The baby sat still and silent, his mouth dutifully open, watching some combination of his mother's face and the spoon. His own decoy spoon was held tightly in his right fist like a scepter. At his side, his left hand curled tightly around Tessa's pointer finger.

Joseph felt every perforation in his heart bleed together until the organ itself was a levitating ball of light.

"That's right," whispered Tessa to her son. "My hungry Dollop." She glanced at Joseph. "It's not the most efficient way to feed a baby, but it gets the job done." She shook her head. "In the first days, when we could not sort out how to, er, get food to him . . ." She paused, looking thoughtful, the spoon halfway to the baby's mouth. "He screamed unrelentingly, so very hungry, while I wept. Perry was frantic. The Boyds, I'm sure, were regretting taking in their niece's pregnant friend. They sent for the doctor countless times, but his only advice was to keep trying. He felt the baby would sort out how to eat when he became hungry enough. If this did not happen, he told us we should seek out a wet nurse." Tessa bit her lip and her eyes went misty.

The baby squawked, impatient with the story. She shook her head and spooned the milk into his mouth.

"And did you locate a wet nurse?" Joseph asked.

Tessa shook her head. "I . . . It sounds foolish. Selfish and risky, especially since my baby needed nourishment, but the thought of another woman, someone more experienced at motherhood than I, living here with us and feeding my son in such an intimate way . . . ? I could not countenance it. I knew so very little about how to care for him, I worried that some other mother would, in a way, replace me. I'd already been through so much to have him and to have him properly. To be married, to give him a proper surname. I was determined to be his mother in every way."

Joseph considered this, considered what she had been through. Her family was lost to her, certainly. And her life as a carefree young belle was over. But did she also mean she'd had to give up Joseph?

He asked, "Who devised the spoon?"

"Perry's mother," she laughed. "Can you believe it? All the

way back in Surrey." She shook her head wistfully as if the story had happened to someone else.

"It is safe to say that I *cannot* believe it," Joseph said in a strangled voice. How had he not thought of her, struggling alone in London while he bemoaned his broken heart in Barbadoes?

Tessa went on. "Sabine set out for home on horseback. Don't worry, we sent her with two of the Boyds' grooms. She is an excellent rider and we felt she could make Surrey in a day."

"I've no doubt, but why seek help from so far away?"

Tessa shrugged. "Of course there were midwives throughout London who might advise us, but we didn't know who we could trust. God help us, we were so adrift, but Perry kept assuring us that her mam would know exactly what to do. It's one of those frantic moments where the most familiar way seems the best, even if it is more complicated."

Tessa sighed and sat back. "Perry's mother, thank heavens, sent Sabine back with instructions for exactly what to do. She described how her daughter's infants had been fed, first by sucking a cloth dipped in milk and then, when they can hold up their heads, with a spoon." She smiled down at Christian. "And that's what we did, isn't it, Dollop?"

The baby held open his tiny bird mouth for the next spoonful.

Joseph said nothing, making mental notes of all the people he would now compensate. A larger payment to the Boyds for the disruption of a newborn, some significant compensation to

Perry's mother in Surrey, money to the doctor. Stoker provided for Sabine and would not tolerate payment to her, but Joseph would make some gesture.

"Equal to the idea of the spoon," Tessa continued, "was Perry's mother's suggestion that we try goat's milk. Apparently, cow's milk can upset a newborn. She was correct, as you can see, he loves it. So I've actually splurged and bought a female goat."

Joseph blinked at her and she laughed.

"It's true. She lives in the mews with the Boyds' horses. Perry milks her every day. Or I do."

Joseph closed his eyes at the thought of his beautiful wife on a stool milking a goat to feed her baby. "I'm sorry, Tessa," he whispered. The words sounded insufficient, so woefully insufficient.

Tessa opened her mouth to speak but then closed it. She looked down at her son and then up at Joseph. She nodded. "I appreciate that, Joseph. Thank you for saying so." She took a deep breath and returned her attention to the baby. "We managed, didn't we, Dollop? The gift of a name and legitimacy is no small thing. Oh, and the money, of course."

Not nearly enough, Joseph thought. He opened his mouth to tell her this, but Christian suddenly let out an imperious squawk and turned his head to the side, refusing the next spoonful.

"And it seems luncheon has come to its rightful end," sighed Tessa. "All full up, are you, Dollop?" She dropped her spoon into the teacup with a smile and turned the baby onto her shoulder to pat his back. Within seconds, he released a healthy belch.

"Lovely, darling," Tessa encouraged.

Joseph chuckled, enjoying the sight of her with the fat, round baby on her shoulder. Suddenly, he felt an insistent urge to hold the baby.

"May I?" He set the cup aside.

Tessa could not hide her surprise, but she said nothing. She leaned forward to arrange the linen napkin on Joseph's shoulder and followed it with the drowsy baby.

"Give him a pat or two." She modeled how to burp him.

"What is his schedule after he eats?"

"Oh, Perry will put him down for a nap. And we may go, if you still—"

"May I?" Joseph asked.

"May you . . . ?"

"Put him down for his nap?"

Tessa blinked several times, almost as if she hadn't understood. "If you like." A little laugh. She leaned forward, and for a thrilling second, he thought she meant to kiss him. But she dropped a kiss on the baby's cheek. She was so close, Joseph could smell her familiar, soft floral scent. Joseph forced himself to sit perfectly still, if he moved—moved at all—the floodgates of self-control would snap, and he would tip forward and nuzzle her cheek.

When she moved away, his head felt light. He held on to the solid weight of the baby and cleared his throat. "Where do I . . . ?"

She was thoughtful for a moment, and then she said, "I will allow Perry to demonstrate naptime, if you don't mind."

He rose. "Alright. But if you would rather me not—?"

"I am pleased you want to do it, but I have a tendency to take over when I am in the room. If you really want to learn, I should remain back." She cleared her throat. "One of the lovely things about Perry is that she is never far. She has a tendency to be everywhere at once."

She looked at the door. "*Per—*"

The maid popped into the room. "Yes, miss?"

Tessa gave a knowing smile. "Perry, Mr. Chance would like to assist you in putting the baby down for his nap. Would you be so kind as to show him how it's done?"

The maid gave a gasp and clapped her hands together. "Oh, yes, Mr. Chance. It's only right through here, if you please. How masterfully you are holding him, if you don't mind me saying."

Joseph glanced back at Tessa, but she had turned away. She looked out the window, resting a pensive hand on her mouth.

Chapter Nineteen

The September wind blew from the north with the first hint of winter, and Tessa wished for her wool pelisse. Inconveniently, her winter cloaks were all made of bright fabric, sunny yellow and dusty purple and pearly ivory. She hadn't wanted to spend money to replace them when her wardrobe turned drab. The pregnancy had kept her confined most of the previous winter, but this year she would have to sort out some alternative. Today, she would shiver.

It hadn't occurred to her that Joseph would collect her in a phaeton, open to the cool air, nimble and quick. In truth, she hadn't thought much about how they would travel or even where they would go—she simply wanted to see him.

She'd heard nothing from him for a full day after Vauxhall, and the hours of silence had been agonizing. Despite the trauma of the night, Tessa had enjoyed the outing and felt closer to Joseph than she had since Berymede, and she missed him. She'd missed him when he was in Barbadoes, but this was a far more urgent, specific longing. She missed the smell of him, the sound of his voice, she missed telling him about Christian's antics of the day.

She'd passed the long day of missing him by scripting the perfect introduction to a conversation about leaving Belgravia, how and where and when. It pained her to address this, in theory and in earnest, but the longer she put off this discussion, the more it felt like the confession of her pregnancy all over again, this great secret she'd known all along but concealed.

Before Joseph had returned from Barbadoes, she'd worried the request would sound demanding and greedy. Now that he was back, she worried that her request would come off like a ploy to escape him.

Escaping him was the last thing she wished to do, but she could hardly invite herself and her baby to join his life in earnest. She wasn't even sure what he intended next for the guano venture. Here, too, she'd been too afraid to ask.

But no more. Tessa Chance did not enjoy the luxury of an uncertain future. She was a mother with an infant son, and they could not live with the Boyds forever. The topic must be raised. Today. On this very outing.

"Perry was thorough in teaching you how to put Christian down for his nap, I presume?" she asked Joseph as he steered the horses down Lower Belgrave Street.

"Thorough?" he repeated. The two horses were lively, probably more accustomed to open country roads than the crush of city streets. Reining them in took considerable concentration.

"Come now," she said. "Christian's naptime routine boasts no fewer than ten steps. And Perry is nothing if not precise. Surely you learned something."

He chuckled but did not smile. His eyes remained on the road. They rounded Hyde Park and took James Street in the direction of Westminster Bridge. They clipped along in an exhilarating mix of plodding slowness and bolting speed.

When a runaway horse darted into their path, Joseph reined in. Tessa saw it too late to steady herself, and she spilled against him. It was like colliding with a warm, muscled pillar in soft, wool clothing. His hands were occupied with the reigns and she splayed out, grabbing for any handhold—his thigh, the lapel of his jacket.

"Are you alright?" he asked, eyes on the road.

She nodded, picking her way back to her seat with the slowest, most lingering progress. She wasn't certain, but she thought she heard him clear his throat. Had he shifted in his seat? Did the proximity thrill him as it did her? Tessa considered this and was careful not to break her fall again. Each lurch bumped her against his shoulder and bicep, his muscled thigh. Her body pinged and sparked on impact, like a blacksmith's hammer connecting with the anvil.

Vauxhall had reunited her with the contained power of his body, although her desire to touch him had lingered since their time at Berymede. She'd washed nappies, knitted baby caps, and pushed the pram for miles, fantasizing about the feel of his strong hands kneading the knots from her shoulders, grazing her knuckles against her neck, tracing her chin, pulling her face to his.

And then he came back.

And it seemed they would never touch again.

But Vauxhall had disproved this in a way, and now she struggled to remember her prepared remarks about moving away. She watched the road instead, anticipating the sharp turn or erratic traffic that would spill her up against him.

"Tessa . . ." he began. Something about the way he said her name made her feel like she was on the swing at Berymede.

"Yes?"

"Are you aware how much I admire you for the life you have made for yourself and the baby? Everything you have achieved astounds me. The baby, the dockyard. *Admiration* is an insufficient word for what I feel."

"Admiration . . ." she repeated. Perhaps she had been the only one thinking about touching.

Traffic opened up, and they careened around the turn onto York Street. She held to his leg with both hands.

"That said," he went on, but his voice broke.

He feels it, she thought, and she couldn't resist giving the coiled muscle of his thigh a slight squeeze.

He cleared his throat and started again. "That said, I hate the thought of you living in the Boyds' cellar. Soon the mornings will bring the frost, after that comes the snow of winter. I lay awake last night, wondering if you were warm. If you had proper light. I . . . don't—"

He paused and lifted her gloved hand from his thigh and pressed it to his chest. Tessa stared at his hand over hers. She felt the beat of his heart, stronger and more rapid than the horse's hooves.

He began again. "I don't like you and the baby living in any cellar." He glanced at her, his blue eyes intent. "If I'm being honest, I don't like it at all."

Tessa's eyes sank closed. *Thank God.* She forced her brain to recall the details of her proposed move.

Joseph pressed on. "I am aware that I was selfishly ignorant of the arrangement while I was away, but now that I've seen it, I should like to discuss some . . . alternative."

Tessa paused, gathering her thoughts. What she said next was so very crucial. She curled her fingers around his hand and squeezed.

"Thank you, for your compliment," she began, but immediately regretted the formality. She bit her lip and continued, "I am gratified to hear it, because I have given the matter some thought. The Belgravia townhome has been a godsend, truly, and I will be forever grateful to Willow's aunt and uncle. But as you noticed, a mother and child . . . and a maid and our, er, goat . . . cannot impose on the Boyds' generosity indefinitely. Without being certain of *your* plans, I have taken it upon myself to conceive of some, er, solution. If you are amenable. Just to consider."

"Tessa," he sighed, "I am shocked that you have not fled the Boyds' cellar as fast as Christian's pram could carry him."

Before she could stop herself, she laughed. It was a sharp laugh, edged in bitterness. She slid her hand from beneath his.

"Yes," she said, "this would assume we had somewhere else to go, wouldn't it? I can hardly indulge in flight if I must provide for my infant first. And his maid and his goat."

"Of course," Joseph said. He sounded chastened, and Tessa swore in her head. The very last sentiment she wished to evoke was resentment. Or desperation. She wasn't resentful, and she wasn't desperate, not really. Not the way many lone mothers were desperate, not the way she would have been if Joseph had divorced her after her confession.

Still, the little jab was out before she could stop it, evidence of the occasional white-knuckled fear that seized her in the middle of the night. It was so very stressful, existing on the balance of his absent good graces and the kindness of Mary and Arthur Boyd. Daylight had a way of easing the anxiety, but managing a baby alone had left her with a truncated view of life. There was little room for fancifulness or hyperbole or the satisfying drama of stuffing Christian's pram with their possessions and fleeing the Boyds' cellar simply because it was small and windowless and had been originally designed for two servants.

She cleared her throat. "That is, the reality of our circumstances has forced me to be more pragmatic. And what I was trying to say is . . ."

They'd been idling at a slow amble, trapped behind a swaying coach overloaded with trunks. Joseph, impatient for progress, steered into the path of oncoming carriages to swerve around.

Tessa held on, refusing to allow the rough ride to silence her. "What I meant to say is, I feel the arrangements I made in the dockyard, however isolated, have given me some insight into a future sort of . . . occupation for myself, if you will. That is, a way to provide some small living for myself and Christian."

A cart swerved from their path and the horses surged again. Tessa spoke more loudly. "Obviously there is no real place for a woman working on the docks in London. The managers at St. Katharine have been very generous, especially because I made it very clear I came on behalf of my husband's business. But once the novelty has worn of, and if I were to do this kind of work on behalf of shippers who were not you, I'm doubtful they would be as welcoming. I'm doubtful that they would allow my presence at all.

"That said, I had the idea—and please understand, it is merely a thought—to seek out some other port, elsewhere in England . . . some smaller, less trafficked dockyard that receives fewer ships . . . that might be willing to employee me in some capacity—"

Joseph reined in the carriage so abruptly and steered from the road so sharply, she pitched forward. His arm shot out and caught her around the waist. Inertia slammed them back into the seat. Tessa let out a little yelp.

"Are you saying," Joseph began, "that you wish to join the staff in some port as a worker on the docks, Tessa?"

She smiled patiently, accommodatingly, the smile she gave Perry when she styled Sabine's hair. "No, actually. Although I can see how this could be misconstrued. I'm telling you that I wish to have some *role* in a dockyard. Not as a laborer, obviously, but possibly in the dock master's office, doing much the same work that I did for you at the St. Katharine Docks, merely in the capacity of clerk or other staff? Eventually possibly as manager or . . . something?"

Joseph opened his mouth to speak, but Tessa held up her hand. "Please, Joseph, allow me to finish."

She closed her eyes for a moment. This had spilled out all wrong. Her tone was meant to be thoughtful and aspirational, not frantic and naive. And she had not rehearsed how she might insert some possibility that he might wish to join them . . . to be a part of their lives when he was in the country . . . but she wanted very much to include it.

She licked her lips and looked around. They were parked on Bridge Road, not far from Westminster Bridge. Workers hammered scaffolding to railing. A farmer herded five plodding cows onto the ramp. To his credit, Joseph remained silent. He waited.

Tessa took a deep breath. "I've conducted some research around the notion of a small, local dockyard and discovered a village in the north of England that just might work. It's called Hartlepool. In County Durham."

There. She'd said it. She waited. Joseph blinked at her.

She added, "Do you know it?"

"No," he said. He had the voice of a man waiting for the doctor to read a terrible prognosis.

"Well, it's small—a village, as I've said. Very small compared to London. Only three hundred townspeople. However, the citizens of the town voted some years ago to create a working dock and a rail line that would connect the coal mines in Yorkshire to their small but workable stretch of North Sea coast. They've apparently worked very hard toward this goal, and their little dock opened this summer, just in July, and . . . and now they are making a go of exporting coal. Coal is quite different from importing or exporting goods, I am aware, but who knows what else they might eventually bring in? Even if it is only coal, they will require a staff to manage traffic to the docks.

"And I merely thought . . . I thought . . . perhaps if Christian and I were to relocate there, I could discover some way to earn a small living, as I've said, and we would be less of a burden to you. Unless of course you wished to . . . that is . . ."

She studied his face and lost heart. He looked confused and unnerved. He looked like a man who opened his front door to a raging storm.

Tessa abandoned any mention of his involvement and rushed to finish. "I haven't the money to purchase a house, of course." Now she looked away. The hardest bit was to baldly ask him to buy her a piece of property. And to ask it with no ploys or flirtations, as the Old Tessa might have done. She must simply state what she wished and ask him.

"For this," she continued, staring out at the bridge, "I am forced to rely on your generosity. We would not require much—just a small cottage. No more than two rooms. Eventually, Perry will want to return to Willow's service. Willow is a countess now and lives in a castle, as you know. Perry loves the baby, but I don't believe it was ever her goal to be a nursemaid. Her passions lie more to fashion, and she's quite talented." She shook her head. She was rambling.

"I know it is a very ambitious plan, not to mention wildly unorthodox. But I conceived it with no idea of what you intended for us. That is, after the guano, you've not said if you intend to settle in London or even in England. I was forced to think of some plan that would allow me to build on my new success at the dockyard, provide for the baby, and live a life that would give you freedom to . . . to do as you wished. To not worry with us. I had even thought, if you are willing to purchase some small cottage for me, eventually I might earn enough money in the dockyard to repay—"

"*Stop*," said Joseph. He held a hand like a conductor.

Tessa closed her mouth. Her stomach unspooled like the chain of an anchor as it plunged into the sea.

He said, "Forgive me. You have given me quite a—that is, I could not expect this. But that is the one constant with you, to be caught off guard." He glanced at her and then back at the horses. "That said, I can address the very last bit immediately. You will never, not ever, owe money to me, Tessa. You have already given me £15,000 in dowry. My partners and I have parlayed the dowries of the three brides into a windfall of nearly £1,000,000. And that is only with the first shipment. In fact, my bankers are preparing a withdrawal to return the dowry money into your safekeeping. Cassin and Stoker will do the same. We decided it was reasonable to view the dowries more like a loan than money we took outright. An investment, just like your original advertisement said."

"You earned that money, Joseph," she said softly.

He dropped his head back and stared at the sky. "I've done nothing but abandon you, Tessa."

"You married me," she said, but her stomach flipped and flipped and flipped. It wasn't even a declaration. There was no affection or feeling or intent. It was merely . . . an acknowledgment.

She hadn't allowed herself to feel abandoned, but it was true. She had been very much alone.

"And I will buy you a house," he went on, "if that's what you wish. I simply need . . ." He leveled his head and rolled his shoulders, looking at the bridge. "I need a moment. Please. You've just proposed the very last thing I had in mind."

"I am perfectly happy to negotiate or compromise—it is merely a place to start."

"I want to give you what you want," he sighed. He sounded . . . if not angry, more like frustrated. He was struggling to make himself clear.

I'm not challenging you, Tessa thought, but she said nothing. She sat very still and upright, staring patiently at his profile. Energy ricocheted through every limb of her body. She wanted to flap her hands and jump up and down like Perry.

"This is not what I had in mind," he repeated. He looked down at the reins in his hands.

"I am not surprised," she said.

"Do you mind if we ride on?"

She shook her head. "I never asked where you were taking us. To the office of your buyer, was it?"

"Eventually. I had another destination in mind but I've . . . changed my mind."

"Not on my account, I hope."

"I'm long overdue to call on old friends," he said.

The flipping in Tessa's stomach ceased. "We're making a social call?"

She'd not expected the world to stop when she finally spit out her request, but it seemed to warrant more consideration than a *social call*.

Furthermore, how would he portray their marriage to "old friends"? Or the baby? Would they blithely mention that while Joseph was in Barbadoes he became a father? They hadn't been able to stomach this discussion with the strange woman at Vauxhall Gardens, and now they would parade their odd circumstances in front of "old friends"?

Joseph made a clicking noise and reined the horses away from the bridge, turning back toward Mayfair. "Not a social call so much as . . . going home. To my family. Or, the closest thing I have to a family. The Earl and Countess Falcondale. In Henrietta Place."

Must we? thought Tessa, but she said, "Do they know about the baby? The earl and countess?"

"Probably."

"What will we say?"

"One of the many good things about calling upon the earl and his wife," he said, "is that we do not have to *plan out* what we will say."

Tessa considered this, an answer that was not really an answer. The earl had been Joseph's sponsor and mentor and his wife, Lady Piety, was held in the same esteem. Tessa had met them only once, at the wedding, and they had seemed lovely. Their affection for Joseph had been so very clear.

But to call upon them *now*? Is this what Tessa's request had driven Joseph to do?

But he does not seem outraged, she thought.

And he had not said *no*.

And it was no small thing to be taken, finally, to the home of the people he considered to be his family.

It was confusing, perhaps; but unless he intended for her to remain hidden in the phaeton while he went inside, it could mean . . . something positive?

She settled back in the seat. "Of course. An earl and his countess. 'Old friends.' Alright."

They drove along in silence for a moment, and Joseph said, "I'm not disregarding what you've asked, Tessa. Please. Just give me time."

Chapter Twenty

It had been careless and rude of Joseph not to have called on Trevor Rheese, the Earl of Falcondale, and his wife, Lady Piety, since his return from Barbadoes.

He'd been back in London for more than a week. His correspondence during his ten months away had been spotty. Worst of all, he'd left without saying a proper good-bye.

Joseph had told himself he'd been rushed, he'd been busy, but the real reason was that he cared about what Trevor and Piety thought of Tessa. Despite his own outrage at her duplicity, he would not have them dislike her. And they would have, immediately, if they had known what she had withheld from him. Their loyalty to Joseph was absolute, and they didn't know Tessa at all. His solution had been to keep away after the wedding.

Instead, he had scrawled a quick note before he'd sailed for Barbadoes. It said a hasty farewell and warned Trevor and Piety that his wife "wished for solitude in Belgravia" and please never to call. It had been cryptic and rude, behaviors that he deplored, especially where the earl and countess were concerned, but he had been reeling at the time. The rich gentleman's daughter who had fallen in love with him—with *him*, of all people—had in fact wanted only legitimacy for her bastard son. He'd not come so far up in the world after all. Even with all the money and support Trevor had given him.

Joseph had mailed the note, boarded a steam packet for Barbadoes, and he'd not seen them since the wedding.

Now, inexplicably, he found himself wanting nothing more than their warm, unconditional affection and embrace.

And besides, his plan to take Tessa on a tour of his house in Blackheath had been shot. Why take her to his house when what she really wanted was a cottage in bloody Hartlepool, wherever that was.

But more than anything, he was not ready to return her to Belgravia. The call would buy him time to think through his wife's very humble, incredibly unexpected request to relocate to the North Sea.

It was near twelve o'clock when they arrived at Trevor and Piety's townhome in Henrietta Place, and it occurred to Joseph that they might intrude on luncheon. He could but hope. Eating would give him more time to think, something he sorely needed, and less time for Trevor and Piety to ask pointed questions.

"You are joking," drawled Trevor Rheese, the Earl of Falcondale, when he came up behind his butler to see Joseph and Tessa on the stoop.

"Yes," said Joseph blandly. "I'm joking. It is not me. This

is not my wife. We are not standing in your doorway. I've engineered a mirage. Or could it be the result of old age on your eyesight?" At fifty, Trevor was still active and fit, but his encroaching decrepitude was a running joke.

Tessa laughed, and Joseph was surprised by the sound. She'd laughed at nearly everything he said at Berymede, but now their conversations were very Serious and Important. Had she laughed at him even once since his return? Had he been remotely clever?

No. I have not. He'd been suspicious and restrained and regretful. No wonder she wished to move to the North Sea.

But now Trevor was speaking to him in Greek, a long, profanity-laden jab under his breath, and bowing over Tessa's hand.

Joseph frowned. "Look at this princely greeting. When have I ever seen you bow over the hand of a lady?"

"Perhaps if you shared your wife on a more regular basis—or *at all*—you would enjoy my fine manners. But as it now st—"

"Oh!" gasped a voice from inside the house. "This wretched month has been saved!" Piety Rheese, the Countess Falcondale, shot out the door and leapt into his arms. "Joe, Joe, Joe! You've come home!"

Joseph caught her and spun, forcing Tessa to scramble back. He caught his wife's eye and winked. Lady Piety was only a few years older than Joseph, the mother of three boys, and still brightly beautiful. An American by birth, Piety greeted the world with an earnest enthusiasm rarely seen among reserved Britons.

"And you've brought your dear wife!" Piety said, wriggling free and spinning on Tessa.

Tessa was less prepared for Piety's voracious embrace, and the two women tipped back on the banister. Trevor and Joseph shouted in union and reached to upright them.

"But how long have you been back?" demanded Piety. "And you better say less than one day. I will accept no answer beyond, 'Piety, I've been back less than one day.'"

"Less than a day," said Joseph.

"You are lying to us—Trevor, he's *lying*—and thank God. Because if you have been in London for any time, any time at all, and you have *not* sent word, I shall never forgive you. But have you eaten?"

Joseph glanced at Tessa. She appeared a little stunned by the countess's reception, but she shrugged. "We have not eaten, but we could not impose."

"Stop, of course, you will take luncheon with us immediately."

"Don't you mean he will *serve* luncheon immediately?" asked Trevor, another long-standing joke.

Piety rolled her eyes and whispered to a maid. Within moments, they were seated around a massive table while footmen served cold meats and cheese, fresh bread, and quince. Bowls of parsnip soup steamed in the center of each plate. While they ate, Piety peppered Joseph with questions about Barbadoes, the journey, the guano. Every fourth or fifth question, she slipped in a domestic question pointed at Tessa. Nothing too specific, nothing that might press her to reveal more than she wished about her life.

Tessa was open and cheerful but kept her answers brief. All the while, the earl ate in thoughtful silence. Joseph could feel his old friend keenly studying the two of them.

"And how have you tolerated the London weather, Tessa?" asked Piety.

"Spring brought a bit more mud than I am accustomed to," Tessa said. "You will remember that the homes and roads of Belgravia are still being constructed. Very few streets have been bricked. We navigate less mud, I believe, in Surrey. But summer was lovely. We are so near the park."

Joseph cleared his throat. "Perhaps you have not heard . . ." He glanced around the table at the anticipatory expression on Piety's face. Trevor raised one eyebrow. "Or perhaps you *have*. Tessa gave birth to a baby in May. A boy. Christian. Christian Chance. My son."

Piety leapt from her chair so quickly the footman scrambled to catch it before it tipped backward.

"But this is what we heard . . ." now tears broke her voice ". . . but we couldn't be sure, and you sent no word, and we . . . we were desperate to be of some assistance and see the baby, but we . . . but we . . ." Now she brought a hand up over her mouth and looked to her husband.

The earl sighed and put his napkin beside his plate. "You'll have to forgive my wife, Mrs. Chance," he said. "Our sons are nearly grown—two of them left for school last week— and she has been driven mad by her limited access to infants. When she detects the presence of a relevant baby anywhere in her proximity, she runs mad. No child is safe, I'm afraid. It can't be helped. I'm sorry."

Joseph chuckled and glanced at Tessa. She was staring at her plate. He said, "Piety, I hope you will forgive our discretion about the baby. I promise, in time, to tell you all about him, and of course introduce you."

Piety retook her seat. "Honestly, I care less to *learn* about the baby and more about holding him in my arms. Will you say again what he's called? I was too excited to properly take it in."

"Christian," said Tessa. "He's called Christian. Christian Trevor Chance."

And now Piety was out of her chair again, the footman lunging. She rounded the table to embrace Joseph and then Tessa. Joseph caught his wife's eye as Piety clung to her.

Thank you, he mouthed. How had he not known the baby's full name? How had Tessa known the significance of naming him after Trevor?

Tessa smiled gently, but then Piety released her and held her at arm's length.

"Christian Trevor Chance," said Piety tearfully. "I love it." She hugged Tessa again. When she finally released her, Piety went to the earl instead of her own seat. Trevor pushed back and she settled in his lap.

"It's so very good to see you, Joseph," sighed Piety. "We think of you every day. Every single day. And, oh, how we have longed to see Tessa. Your wedding was the most beautiful, splendid affair. But there were so many guests, we only had the one brief opportunity to speak to you. I can honestly say it might have been the most lavish wedding I've ever had the fortune of attending. Your parents' estate must be one of the most beautiful in all of England."

Tessa smiled. "The wedding seems like a lifetime ago," she said.

Silence settled on the room, and Joseph thought about the wedding. It had cost him to keep his friends at bay all this time. He missed Piety's enthusiasm and Trevor's pragmatism. He missed their unconditional love. It had been a mistake, perhaps, to not confide in them.

"Piety?" he asked suddenly. "Could I impose on you to entertain Tessa for a quarter hour or so? I should like to speak alone with Trevor, if he has the time."

"Actually, I'm deuced busy today," drawled Trevor.

Joseph shook his head. "You are a man of leisure, as anyone who knows you is well aware. One of the many benefits of having a rich wife."

"I," countered Trevor, "am a very important architect." He tipped Piety from his lap. "World renowned. But I shall make time for you because you've finally shown your face after being back in London for . . . what was it, darling?"

"Less than one day," recited Piety, holding out her hand to usher Tessa from the room.

"Right," said Trevor sardonically. "Less than one day."

Joseph smiled and leaned back in his chair, considering all that he had, quite suddenly, decided to tell his friend.

When Piety and Tessa were gone and the footmen had been dismissed, he leaned forward and dropped his head in his hands. Speaking to the floor, he started from the beginning.

Chapter Twenty-One

The Earl and Countess of Falcondale were in possession of a beautiful pianoforte. A Stein in polished birch, imported from Germany in '26. Tessa barely grazed her fingers across the keys and they trilled to life.

Lady Piety had been leading her on a tour of their home, a magnificent townhome mansion that Piety had bought with a great inheritance years ago. Although Piety was gracious and the house really was a showplace, it was little distraction from Joseph's closed-door discussion downstairs with the earl.

It took no effort to guess what they discussed. Tessa wondered if Joseph had come here with a mind to unburden himself. An odd choice for their afternoon outing, she thought, but she understood the significance of a personal errand rather than some contrived diversion—tea in a café or a stroll through the zoo. It was no small thing to be introduced to the couple he described as "his family."

And maybe Joseph needed the advice of his old friend? Perhaps her request to leave London had driven him here?

Regardless, the earl would soon be told the truth about Tessa and their marriage and the baby. And soon after the earl knew, the countess would know. She glanced at Piety, so effusive and open and bright. She would have liked to have known the older woman, to count her as a friend the way Joseph did.

Now . . . ?

Tessa sighed. Each time she survived one moment of shame—the misery against the tree, that first missed monthly cycle, the confession to Joseph, her parents' rejection—she turned around to face yet another.

When she had been newly pregnant, she had distracted herself with hope in Joseph. After he sailed away, her solace was the baby. Today, however, staring down at the shiny pianoforte, she wondered if she could endure another rejection. Joseph's friends would surely discreetly, if not politely, turn her out when they knew.

Suddenly, Tessa wanted nothing more than to slide onto the piano seat and lose herself. Only at the piano could she forget, even for ten minutes, what she'd done and how she and the baby would survive. She couldn't control what Joseph discussed nor what the earl and countess would think of her. But just for a moment, Tessa might play.

"It's wasteful to have a proper music room when no one plays," Lady Piety was telling her. "I had high hopes that one of my boys might take up music as a hobby. But we've devoted so much of our lives to travel, it's not convenient to lug musical instruments on a ship." She laughed. "Trevor already believes me to be a champion over-packer."

"It is a beautiful instrument, a showpiece, even if no one plays," Tessa lied. Her fingers twitched to scramble over the keys. She heard music in her head. Her eyes returned again and again to the instrument, even while she trailed the countess around the room.

"Would you like to play, Tessa?" Lady Piety finally asked.

"Oh, I couldn't impose."

"Stop. I should love to hear it put to use. I adore music, but Trevor must be bribed to attend concerts."

Tessa chuckled at this, studying her hostess more closely. She was so endearingly . . . irreverent. Perhaps, Tessa thought, perhaps she and the earl would not lose faith in Joseph for marrying a desperate woman. Perhaps they would see his predicament in sympathetic shades of grey, rather than black and white.

Tessa drifted to the pianoforte, knowing she could not decline a second offer. She settled on the bench.

"There are sheets of music somewhere in this room, now let me think where I . . ."

Tessa barely heard. She dove softly into Mozart's "Piano Sonata No. 11," thrilling to the sensitive response of the keys. The brilliant simplicity of the notes dropped from each key and then swelled to fill the room. Her body responded immediately, eyes closing, heart steadying, shoulders rising and falling as she conjured magic from the keys.

Distantly, she was aware of Lady Piety sucking in a startled breath, of her settling into an adjacent chair. Between songs, the countess applauded. Did she speak? Tessa could not say, she allowed herself to be wholly taken in by the music, to sink beneath the surface of sound. She lost herself, trilling and pounding through her entire repertoire of favorites—popular jigs, classic sonatas, refrains from operas.

At last, when her neck ached and her fingers cramped, she took a deep, satisfied breath and sat up. She stretched her shoulders. The room had shrunk to the keys before her, and she blinked at the bright sunlight streaming through the windows.

Behind her came a slow, steady clap. She spun on the bench.

Joseph. He stood not far behind, his eyebrows and head cocked. *Look what you've found.*

Look, indeed, Tessa thought.

The countess had gone. Joseph stood alone in the room, so very tall and broad and handsome. Her stomach swooped at the sight of him. She'd thought he would never look more beautiful than he had with the milky cloth draped over his shoulder and Christian balanced on top of it. But now?

She felt tears well up in her eyes and she turned back to the keys.

He was never meant to be so handsome and measured and thoughtful. From the beginning, when Willow had placed the advertisement, he was only meant to be *some man,* some *anonymous* man. He was only meant to marry her, give her son a name, abscond with her dowry, and disappear. She was not to think of him again.

But he had never, not for a moment, been *some man.*

And when he had disappeared, Tessa had awakened every day wondering if today would be the day he might come back. And if there was some chance to salvage the unlikely strains of love they'd kindled in those weeks at Berymede.

Looking back, their early love seemed almost too easy, the expected combustion of young attractive people falling into lust. The feelings she held now for Joseph were combustible, yes, but they were a slow burn, built hour by hour, gesture by gesture, as each new intimacy was added to the fire.

The Old Tessa would not hesitate to say that she was *in love* with Joseph Chance. She'd loved him at Berymede, and she certainly loved him now. The New Tessa would concur, but she must force herself to proceed with thoughtful caution. Her regard for him now was part attraction, part kinship, part gratefulness, and part . . . something else. A magical, intangible wholeness that made her heart surge. Taken as a whole, her love for him now, the truest, purest love, had far more potential to crush her than the dazzling, playful love of before.

Although Tessa could admit that seeing him here now, with the music still echoing in her ears and the captivated look on his face, she felt the old stirrings of playfulness as she had not known since Berymede. She wanted to entertain him. She wanted him to sit beside her and gaze sideways at her bent profile, inching his hand closer and closer to her leg.

Joseph said, "It occurs to me that there's no pianoforte at the Boyds'."

She shook her head. "They are artists, not musicians, I'm afraid."

"You should have one. Actually, I am in possession of one. A pianoforte. It's at my home. If the Boyds will allow it, I shall have it sent over."

"You have a house?" she asked. Of course, the politer question would have been, *You have a pianoforte?* But good lord. *He has a house?*

"Indeed, I do," he said.

He gestured to the piano bench and raised his eyebrows. She scooted to the side to make room and he settled beside her. He smelled like brandy.

"The house is in Blackheath," he said. "A small Georgian mansionette, I believe it's called. Mostly empty, except for a bed and a card table. And a pianoforte."

"But you don't play," she said.

"No. I don't."

Before Tessa could stop herself, she said, "Is the pianoforte for me?"

"Yes."

She wanted to ask when he bought it. She wanted to ask when he bought the house, and did he love it, and did he love London?

Would he consider leaving the house or the city for a place like Hartlepool on the North Sea?

Was he aware that when she said she wanted to move to Hartlepool, what she really wanted was for him to move there with her, or somewhere else they chose together?

The questions piled, one on top of the other, like the rising notes of a sonata, and Tessa tried to sift through them, to light upon the most innocuous one, but each one seemed more pointed and telling and demanding than the last. And she was not ready to hear him say *no*.

Not yet, she thought.

And so she let the questions accumulate, let them build into a very high, teetering pile, and then she raised her hands to the keys, and she played them all away.

Joseph had left his discussion with Falcondale in curiously good spirits. He'd thought he might tell Trevor everything, consider the older man's opinion, and then try again to mesh his Plan for the Future with his ever-evolving knowledge of Tessa and Christian and their plans.

Instead, he'd told Trevor everything and walked away . . . invigorated. Propelled. Incited. Trevor had surprised him with advice that, only in hindsight, seemed predictable.

Stop playing the bloody coward, be a man, make some overture to her. A real overture. And suffer or enjoy the consequences, come what may.

"Don't take the tedious, unnecessary journey I took, Joe," Trevor had said. "Don't wait until she falls from a balcony and nearly *dies* to admit that you require her. You *do* require her, don't you? I've not misread your ravenous looks or generalized misery?"

Joseph had drummed his fingers on the table and not answered. "But Piety's affections for you were never in doubt," Joseph had countered. "Tessa has given me no certainty. She may want nothing from me—well, nothing save a cottage in County Durham."

Trevor had simply shaken his head. He waited.

Joseph had gone on, "It would be impossible to overstate my devastation when she confessed the reason for our marriage. All those weeks, I'd been completely taken in. Her affection had seemed as authentic as my regard for you, or your love for Piety. As a result, I can't trust any suggestion that she might still want me. And let's not forget that she's just asked me to move her to the bloody North Sea."

"*Coward*," Trevor had said. He'd raised his glass in a mock toast.

Joseph had rolled his eyes.

"So what if she might not still want you?" Trevor had sighed. "And by the way, if you go in seeking this milquetoast level of interest—'any suggestion,' for God's sake—I hope she rejects you on the spot. Bloody hell, Joe. Spare me the flaccid, head-bowed side shuffle. As if Piety and I have not been beating girls from your path since you were a boy. Rarely have I known you to be without some young woman swooning over you."

Joseph had considered this. Flaccid? Head-bowed side shuffle?

"Would you like to know what I think?" Trevor had asked.

"No, but I feel sure that you will tell me."

"I think you're suffering from your first-ever rejection. Or potential rejection. By a woman, that is. And not just any woman, a gentleman's daughter who you thought you didn't deserve from the start."

"Perhaps I do not deserve her."

"Likely you did not," Trevor had said. "But not for the reason you think. You see yourself as a servant and her as a lady, and you believe, 'She only chose me because she was disgraced.' The truth of it is, none of us deserves these women. Certainly, I don't deserve Piety, and I'm a bloody earl. And you don't deserve Tessa, despite being so much more than a servant. Please tell me the money and effort I've devoted to your education has earned this, at least. That you are fully aware that you are so much more."

Joseph had refused to comment. He'd taken a drink.

"Very good then," said Trevor. "Unless Tessa St. Croix harbors some predisposition for chronic lying—"

"It's not that," Joseph had said harshly, cutting him off. "It was never that."

The earl had leaned back in his chair, raised his eyebrow, and taken another slow sip. "Well, then. There's an inspired answer for you. If you believe this, then what in God's name are you waiting for?"

What are you waiting for? Joseph asked himself now as he watched Tessa lose herself in the swirling eddies of a Bach aria, eyes closed, shoulders drawn. She played like a woman walling herself in, note by note. It was beautiful, emotional, and moving, but different from the abandon with which she had played at Berymede.

He chuckled now, thinking of Trevor's view of his romantic exploits.

"Excuse me?"

The piano clunked to a halt, and Joseph and Tessa spun on the bench.

Piety stood in the doorway, tugging on leather gloves. Trevor leaned casually on the doorjamb beside her, tapping his hat in his hand.

"I hate to interrupt," called Piety, "but, Joseph, we've an appointment and must dash out, just for a bit. Beckett is with his French tutor, and we're meant to meet with the man at the end of the lesson. Another conflict of interest, I'm afraid."

Beckett Rheese was Piety and Trevor's third son, the wild one, the one with a heart for the open sea and little else.

Tessa rushed to stand, but Joseph grabbed her wrist and held her still. "Not old Monsieur Chapelle?" asked Joseph.

"Monsieur Chapelle has passed on, I'm afraid," said Trevor. "Done in by your refusal to memorize *Amphitryon* in the original French, no doubt."

"I beg you," said Piety, "please stay and enjoy the pianoforte. It is a thrill to hear music in the house. And when we return, we will take supper together. I insist. I shall send a note to Jocelyn and the duke to join us."

"We will," Joseph said, glancing at Tessa. She shrugged as if the decisions were his. He added, "If you really don't mind."

"Excellent," said Trevor, fitting his hat on his head. "It's all settled then. Make yourselves at home. I know Beckett will want to see you."

And then they were gone. Tessa and Joseph sat in tense silence, listening to Piety's voice trail down the landing and the stairwell. Seconds later, the front door opened and closed.

"We cannot simply loiter in their empty house when they've gone," Tessa whispered.

"Did you know, this was my house, too," he said. "Once upon a time."

She glanced around. "It was?"

He nodded. "Piety gave you the grand tour, I'm sure, but I'm doubtful she showed you my favorite room. Would you like to see it?"

She looked at the beautifully upholstered sofas, the vibrant rugs, the lonely harp. "Alright."

Joseph slid from the bench and held out his hand. She plunked out two or three more chords, like someone taking a few more bites before she left the table. She took his hand, her expression part anticipation and part hope—and ever so slightly shy. He felt a jolt of desire and possessiveness so strong, he almost pushed her back against the music room wall.

Instead, he cleared his throat and embarked on the long series of stairwells that led to the cellar kitchens.

"To properly introduce this favorite room, I must first tell you a story." He tucked her arm beneath his.

"I should like that," she said.

"I've told you that my mother was in the employ of the earl's late mother?"

She nodded, watching him with rapt attention.

"My mother," he went on, "was already a widow when I was a baby, and she raised me in the servants' quarters of the small manor house in which the earl—before he was made earl—lived with his mother, Lady Blanche.

"From the time I was old enough to work, I was also in service to the household. Trevor's father had been a second son, and his older brother held the title. Trevor's father died in a hunting accident when Trevor was young, and he was left alone with his mother, who was feeble and given to ill health. It's fair to say that sickly Lady Blanche and her son were largely forgotten in the hierarchy of the Falcondale earldom. We lived in a small manor house in the countryside. Trevor's education was paid for by his uncle and the household was given a small stipend, but that was all.

"The staff was small and informal, all Trevor could afford, but this suited his lifelong aversion to intrusiveness or fussing. He is private and largely self-sufficient. That said, my mother was instrumental in caring for his mother, and Trevor had a fondness for me. He eschewed the idea of a valet, but my mother did his washing and mending and I tended to his attire in as much as he required it. I kept his room tidy, I tended his fire, I cleaned his boots. He taught me to care for his horse and tack."

They reached the ground floor and Tessa looked around, expecting perhaps to be led through any number of wide, heavily molded doorways, but Joseph opened a small door and tugged her down a narrow set of stone steps.

"Trevor was not lying when he said he was an architect," Joseph went on. "He studied architecture in school, and before university, he spent hours in his library, pouring over books. When I showed an interest in his sketches, he began to teach me basic mathematics, world history, physics. By the time I was eight or nine, my life was divided evenly between working as Trevor's general manservant and learning as his pupil."

They reached a cramped landing, and two footmen crowded past, mumbling a respectful, "Hello, Mr. Chance," as they passed. Joseph crowded Tessa against the wall, making room. When the servants were gone, he took her hand and led her down a dim corridor.

"When I was ten or so, doctors advised Trevor to leave England and take his ailing mother to Greece because of the climate and sea air. Trevor had just finished university and was keen to travel, so he thought, why not? He moved us all to Athens."

He sighed heavily. "Our time in Greece is a whole different story, but in short, Trevor became the sort of . . . right-hand man to a fiefdom of unsavory characters, slumlords, men who owned tenement flats all over the city. He was originally hired to shore up the slums, but eventually he rose through the ranks and advised the chief slumlord in all of his various holdings and interests.

"And while Trevor served the slumlord, I served Trevor. This was a rather . . . dark period of our lives, the both of us. Trevor's mother was very ill, and he detested the work he did for this man, but we became too embroiled to see a clear way out.

"During the years in Athens, I was neither servant nor student. I was more like . . . steward, sword bearer—"

"Sword bearer?" said Tessa.

"Actually, Trevor prefers a matched pair of Scottish sgian-dubh daggers."

"You're joking."

"Joking? No. Showing off? Perhaps just a little." He

winked at her. "Athens is where I learned to fight, learned to speak Greek, learned all kinds of nefarious things that can still come in handy in dark pleasure gardens or far-flung ports to this day."

"But you did not stay there forever. You've said you attended university in England. When did you leave Greece?" Tessa asked, transfixed.

"We left when Trevor's uncle died unexpectedly and he was made earl. The slumlord was dazzled by the title and simply let us go. Lady Blanche was dead by this time, my mother too, and we made our way home. I was Trevor's only family and he was mine. He inherited the townhome next to this very house, and we moved in and plotted the next stage of our lives. Trevor was finally free of the burden of caring for Lady Blanche, and he wanted nothing more than to travel. I wanted to work as his servant and travel with him. But then . . ."

They came to a small room at the end of the corridor. There was a step. The wooden planks of the floor gave way to stone. A door to the garden glowed with daylight at the end of the little room, and heavy winter coats hung from hooks along both wall. Boots lined the floor. Joseph stepped down.

"But then what?" demanded Tessa.

"Then a certain American heiress moved next door, into this very house, and Trevor became . . . distracted. And he is still happily distracted to this day. But that, too, is a story for another time.

"By this time, my knowledge on many subjects had exceeded Trevor's and he had begun to hire tutors for me. Some met with me in Trevor's office, others I met in laboratories or libraries or museums. I was particularly interested in commerce and the economy of England, the way trade was managed between countries. Despite our joke about my French tutor, I had a proclivity for languages. I was a ravenous student. I relished learning. I knew the money Trevor spent on tutors was rare and indulgent, I knew my time away from household duties was unheard of, but I could not bring myself to refuse the next session or lesson or master. And that . . ."

He reached out and handed her into the small room. ". . . brings me to this. My favorite room in the house."

Tessa looked around, taking in the coats and the boots, the brushes, buckets, and umbrellas. "But isn't it a . . . boot room?"

"Yes," said Joseph, "the boot room. That door leads to the stables. Around the corner is the scullery. Just there are the kitchens."

He watched Tessa's face as she looked thoughtfully around the small room. Despite her own elevated upbringing, he doubted she would disparage the modesty of the room, but she was clearly confused.

He would tell her why—he'd brought her here for the sole purpose of telling her—but he was touched by her reticence. Since his return, she'd been so very careful about saying and doing everything right; she was determined to make no misstep. It endeared her to him. Everything about her felt so very dear.

A servant laughed in a distant corridor, and Joseph used

his foot to close the gallery door. They were alone in the small musky room.

"Am I . . . meant to ask?" she said finally, looking up. "Why is the boot room your favorite?"

"This is the room," Joseph said, "where I ceased being a servant and became a full-fledged, abovestairs member of this household." He glanced around. A pair of shiny black Hessians were propped neatly on an inverted shelf. Two muddy pairs of work boots sat beside it. There was a broom. Umbrellas. A stack of sodden broadsheets.

Tessa stared at the humble objects and waited.

Joseph took a deep breath. "One day, about a year after Piety and Trevor were married, Trevor and I returned from a session with my humanities tutor. It was spitting rain, one of those days when you can't distinguish the falling rain from the splashing mud. Trevor was out on an errand, so instead of my walking home, he came to fetch me in the carriage.

"My tutor, Mr. Coates, followed me out in the downpour to make sure Trevor was shown a short treatise I had written for an assignment. It was an editorial on the state of education in Britain at the time, and it drew on my research of state-provided schooling in countries around the world. It was very idealized, I'm sure, but Mr. Coates had liked it enough to submit it to some political journals he favored, and we'd heard that an editor or two were considering publication.

"As we rode home, Trevor read the piece, but he said nothing—which was not out of the ordinary. Unless the subject was architecture, Piety was more likely to take an interest in my studies than Trevor. He cared only that I convened my sessions and that I was prepared. In this instance, however, he read every word. The ensuing silence was . . . unnerving.

"He finished reading the piece, concealed it in its leather cover and retied the string. Then, silently, he turned to look out the window. I remember thinking, 'He hates it. It presumes too much. He finds me ungrateful because I propose schooling for all children, despite the effort he's made to have me tutored in private. He's bored. He thinks my writing is weak. He believes editorials are a waste of time.' Every defeatist thought entered my mind, and I was, quite literally, crushed.

"When finally we reached Henrietta Place, Trevor called for the carriage to bypass the front door in favor of the stable. We did this on rainy days if Piety was not with us, because it allowed us to enter the house by this room, rather than tracking mud in through the front door. So the carriage finally came to a stop just there . . ." Joseph pointed out the door window ". . . and we splashed through the alley.

"And I'll never forget, Trevor tucked the leather cover and my paper inside his greatcoat to protect it from the rain. And I thought, 'He wants it dry to throw it in the fire.'"

"So fatalistic," Tessa said.

Joseph raised his eyebrows. "I've developed a much thicker skin."

"Yes, I know all about your thick skin," said Tessa, and she raised an eyebrow.

For half a beat, Joseph lost track of the story. He cocked his head. The atmosphere in the room, the energy in the air, had changed. They hadn't touched, but something passed between them. A wave, a current. He longed to follow it with his hands.

"Right," he said slowly, eyeing her.

There was a high shelf lined with hats behind her head, and he leaned forward and grabbed it, propping himself over her. She looked up to see his face.

"We left the carriage," he repeated, "and stomped through the mud of the alley to this door. When we were inside, I shucked out of my outer coat and stooped immediately, down on one knee. My first duty in this room was always to pull Trevor's muddy boots from his feet. Later, I would return to clean the leather and polish them. He wouldn't wear them into the house until I had cared for them. I kept a clean pair here for that very purpose. I'd knelt at his feet and pried his filthy boots a thousand times.

"But this time," Joseph went on, his voice low, "Trevor said to me, 'We're all finished with that, Joe.'"

"He calls you Joe?" she asked.

"Yes."

"May I call you Joe?"

You may call me whatever you like, he thought, but he said, "Yes. Although I like the way you say 'Joseph.'"

She blushed. "But what did the earl mean?"

"Well, this is what I asked him. I can still hear my voice asking, 'What d'you mean?' And Trevor said, 'No more pulling my boots. No more cleaning my boots. No more service for you of any kind, ever again.'

"And I was devastated. I was only seventeen, but I struggled to rise from the floor like an old man. I actually thought I might bloody cry. I said, 'Are you sacking me, my lord?' Only very rarely did I invoke his title, and when I did then, my voice broke. I was ready to take my treatise and fling it into the mud outside."

"Oh, Joseph," Tessa whispered. She raised her small, perfect hand and rested it on his chest. Joseph stared at it. He wanted desperately to take it up and press it against his cheek, to nuzzle her palm, to kiss her fingertips. It had been years since he'd thought of this story, and he was surprised to feel a welling of emotion, almost as raw as that rainy afternoon, years ago.

"His opinion of me," Joseph said, trying to make her understand, "was so much more important than any other of my ambitions."

"And what happened?"

Joseph shrugged. "He told me he was terminating my employment. He said no boy with talent equal to mine should be wasted cleaning his boots. He told me Piety would hire someone else to look after him. And then, he told me I should clear out of my room in the servants' quarters and take a family room on the third floor. He said, 'You will devote yourself to your studies full time. You will be like a . . . like an annoying relative who freeloads off of my hospitality and will not leave. Only we both know you are not terribly annoying, and certainly you have earned your place in this house. You've been toiling here, largely unpaid, since you were a boy. And that says nothing of the great debt I owe your mother for her years of service to mine.'

"And then, as I was trying to sort through the magnitude of what he'd said, he added, 'In a year or two, we will send you off to university, so I might as well get used to someone else looking after me now. To break him in.'"

Tears welled in Tessa's eyes, and she blinked. "But what did you do?"

"I knew Trevor well enough to not belabor the point or overblow the gesture. I said something like, 'But surely I will pull your boots once more? Now? We're flooding the boot room. They're filthy, Trev.'

"And I'll never forget. He said, 'No, you won't. That part of your life is over. Take the paper you've written and show it to Piety. Tell her the changes she and I have been planning begin today. She will show you your new room. Supper is at eight o'clock.'

"And then he handed me the treatise and turned away. I did not argue. And I have not worked as a servant since that day."

Tessa breathed in a hitched breath and wiped a tear from her eye. The hand on his chest curled in slightly, her fingertips digging in to his lapel. He felt her touch all the way to his lungs. He looked from her hand to her.

"It's hard for me to envision you working as a valet," she said.

"I preferred 'man of all work' at the time, I believe," he joked.

Tessa held his gaze and then looked bashfully away. She saw a boiler hat hanging beside her on a peg, and she reached out and ran a finger along the smooth bill.

Joseph swallowed hard. He thought of kissing her then. Dipping down, lips on lips, just a taste. For now. Until . . . until he could do it properly. Until they weren't surrounded by boots and umbrellas. Until she was ready.

His brain scrambled for the next correct thing to say. "Being a servant, I'm guessing, is not so very different from being a mother."

She smiled at this, still studying the hat.

Joseph said, "For example, if it is a cold day, you must stand ready . . ." he plucked the hat from the peg ". . . with a hat. To keep bare heads warm."

Gently, he settled the hat on Tessa's head. She giggled but did not duck away. It was too large and dropped over one eye. She shoved it back.

"If a ride is in order, you are ready with gloves." He plucked a pair of fine leather gloves from the shelf and tucked them under his arm. He held out his hand. Smiling cautiously, Tessa reached out. Joseph took her hand and began to work the large, soft glove onto her fingers. She turned her hand, helping him slide it on. Her skin was soft and warm, her fingers nimble. The only sound in the room was the rustle of leather and the sound of their breathing.

When one glove was on, she was ready with the other hand immediately, holding it out. He slid the second glove in to place.

"And if it is very cold and wet," he said, taking a greatcoat from a hook, "you'll need this." They locked eyes again as he slid the heavy coat around her shoulders.

The coat enveloped her and he stepped closer. The heavy

wool would easy wrap around them both. She licked her lips, and Joseph felt his pulse all over his body.

Casting around for any excuse to touch her, he took up the lapels of the coat and joined the collar loosely beneath her chin. His hands brushed her face and she sucked in a little breath. She raised her face, smiling at him. He ran a thumb along her cheek a second time, never breaking her gaze. Her mouth was open, just a little. He tugged the collar, the slightest possible tug, and she stumbled closer still.

He scanned the walls; he was running out of garments in which to drape her. In the back of his mind, he thought, this was possibly the strangest seduction in the history of the world. He was putting clothes on her body instead of taking them off. They were in a bloody boot room, for God's sake. He almost laughed, almost gave up and laughed at his own feeble attempt, but before he could pull away—

She leapt up and kissed him.

One moment she was staring up at him, the next she was against him, her arms wrapped around his neck, her lips pressed against his.

The hat fell off, the coat dropped. Behind his neck he could feel her peeling off the gloves.

For the blink of an eye, Joseph froze, not believing. And then he growled and scooped her into his arms.

Chapter Twenty-Two

Tessa had kissed, perhaps, dozens of men in her lifetime.

Beaux and suitors, men she met at balls, men who had plied her with flowers and poetry and jewelry. Some she enjoyed, others were more like conquests.

But no kiss, not in all her twenty-three years of kissing, ever compared to the kiss that she . . . she . . . *seized* in the boot room of his earl's cellar.

And seized it, she had. She'd listened to his story, she had stood very still while he touched her fingers and her wrist and her face. She heard the rise and fall of his breath and the low, crackling register of his voice. She had witnessed his restraint.

Restraint was something about which she also had a fair amount of knowledge. Old Tessa or New Tessa or the Man in the Moon, she had always known when a man wanted to kiss her but held himself back. She'd known when they were too chivalrous or too afraid or when they simply did not know how to go about it.

Clearly, Joseph Chance knew how to do it.

Whether he was afraid or chivalrous or some other reason, Tessa could not say, she only knew that she wanted him, and he wasn't initiating, and this would be up to her.

"*Tessa*," he breathed when she dragged her mouth from his to suck in a breath.

She turned her face, offering her cheek, and he came down with a growl, dragging a raspy line of kisses along her jaw. The roughness of his whiskers and his labored breath, so very close to her ear, plunged her into a pool of sensation. She closed her eyes and dropped her head.

They had kissed at Berymede many times, and Tessa had enjoyed those kisses, but she had also kept herself just a little bit removed.

Well, her *mind* had been held back, even while she quite enjoyed being in his arms. Her mind hovered just north of the baby growing inside of her and just south of her ultimate goal of getting Joseph Chance into bed, the sooner, the better.

Any kiss had the potential to evolve into sex, and if she could possibly maneuver it, she had known every kiss must try. Most things she had done at Berymede had had some ulterior motive, kissing included. She hadn't been entirely sure what she'd done to spirit Captain Marking from kissing her to . . . what he did to her, but if she could possibly compel Joseph to repeat it, she had known she must.

In the last eleven months, as she'd lain awake missing Joseph, she wondered how, if he did come back—*really* back, all the way to her arms—how would she manage intimacy with him?

And now that it finally happened—well, now that kissing had happened—she felt tenuous . . . relief. She felt no fear, at least not of the kissing. And she wanted to continue kissing very, very much. When she thought about it (her brain was not entirely analytical in the moment), she would describe herself as *ravenous* to kiss and kiss and kiss.

When she'd launched herself at him, she'd cinched her arms around his neck—the fastest, surest way to catch him and hold him. Now, her hands roamed. She wanted his hair, his tousled, sun-streaked hair, and she dug her fingers in, sliding it between her fingers. His cravat was stiff and unyielding, ironed to parchment, and she crushed it, her fingers greedy.

He laughed against her mouth, seeking it out, kissing her again. She kissed him back, playing her fingers along his collar like she was unwrapping a gift, yanking at the unyielding cravat. After three tries, the stiff linen gave way and her fingers found bare neck. She opened her hand like a fan and reveled in the warm bronze skin.

"Tessa," he repeated.

He said her name like the word *yes*. An affirmation. An agreement. A pledge. He'd caught her around the waist, but now his hands inched slowly upward. He held her like she was a pillar, palms flat, fingers splayed, like he was carefully balancing her upright. When his hands were at her ribs, his fingertips grazed the sides of her breasts. When he moved up, the hollow of his palm slid perfectly over the curve of her breast. Here, he paused, allowing the warmth of his hands to seep through the wool of her dress. She fought for lucidity in the swirling sensation of the kiss, forcing herself to think about his hands on her body. She waited for the fear, and nothing happened—no recoil, no immobility, not even the slightest tremor of alarm. She felt only heat and closeness and the gentle strength of Joseph's large hands.

More, she thought—her pervading thought. She fell forward. More of him, closer, more of his hand on more of her body.

Finally, after what felt like months, when she was out of her mind with need, he ever so slowly contracted his fingers, testing the shape of her breast.

Tessa made a little whimper and bowed her body forward. Her hands dropped from his neck and clasped his shoulders. She dug in, feeling the rock-hard muscle beneath his coat. The fine wool was a frustration, thick and cool with heavy seams, a separation. She slid her hands beneath his lapels, roving over his chest and to the muscle-knotted trapezoid of his shoulders. She squeezed again, feeling the actual muscles. She sighed; he was so very strong and yet restrained. She delved deeper, reveling in the power that she knew he would never use against her.

"Tessa, you will be my undoing," he rasped, leaving her mouth to breathe, dragging his face across her cheek and ear and hair. He staggered, just a little, and pulled away to glance around. There was a bench against the wall and he stooped suddenly, lifted her, and pivoted the two of them. He fell onto the bench with an *oof* and pulled her in his lap. He dropped against the wall behind him, laying against a curtain of coats and scarves. His face was a mix of caution and hope and need.

Tessa laughed and fell against him, kissing his neck the way he had kissed hers, devouring the warm skin, rough with an emerging beard. Joseph groaned, and his hands went to her hair, holding her against him as she nuzzled and breathed him in, as she said his name into his ear.

The stiff fabric of her dress snagged against the buttons of his coat, and she never hated it more. It felt like a shroud. Her hair, so tightly constricted in the tight knot of a bun, began to slip free, and she was glad. His hands dug in to the loose waves.

"I hate this bun," he said. "I'm sorry, Tess, but I hate it so very much."

"I hate it too."

"May I . . . ?" His fingers began to work through her hair, massaging it free.

She didn't answer. Words left her. She could only kiss him. She slid into the swirl of sensation where there was no detested dress or bun, no Old Tessa or New Tessa.

Please, she thought hazily. *Please let me sit on your lap and be held and be desired and be close to you and to not be afraid, not of my future or my past.*

She slid her hands up his arms and clasped either side of his face, holding him in place. He chuckled and widened his legs. She slid lower into his lap, dropping into the notch formed by his legs. The proximity felt urgently right, her hips pressed against him, and she squirmed to nestle in. Joseph groaned. She'd jostled from his mouth and she rose up to recapture it. He groaned a second time and slid a large palm down her spine to cup her bottom. She gasped at the pleasure of the new closeness.

Her hair, now entirely free from the bun, fell over her shoulders and down her back. It tickled her cheek and stuck in her collar, a waterfall of blonde over the two of them. She shook her head, trying to toss it back. Joseph gathered it loosely, wrapping the thick weight of it around his hand and then gently propping it over a shoulder. It uncoiled, fanning out, and he strummed it through his fingers, following it to her waist. He toyed with the ends, and she loved the feel of his hand. He'd never seen her hair loose and down, not even at Berymede. Her hair had always been a vanity, and even as she transformed into the New Tessa, she couldn't bring herself to cut it. Now she reveled in the feel of Joseph bobbing his fingers against the ends.

When the last of it slid through his fingertips, his hand delved lower, feeling the roundness of her hip, then lower still to her thigh, hooked over his leg. She relished it all, kissing him with her mouth while her body burned beneath his touch. Her brain floated above them.

She was just about to slide her hands beneath his coat again, to peel it off perhaps, when Joseph's fingers skated down her leg and grazed the leather of her boot at the ankle.

It was a light touch, more pressure than a touch, but something about that contact caused her brain to hitch, then seize, then plummet from the misty heavens back to the dim, musty boot room on earth.

She went very still, sucking in a labored breath and holding it. She waited. The overloaded senses of touch and taste receded like a wave, while sound and sight crashed over her. His breathing was so loud. His hands were too big and too . . . everywhere. Clasping her bottom, wrapping around her ankle.

Before she could ask him to stop, he moved two fingers upward, the slightest graze, from the top of her boot to her stockinged ankle, just inches beneath the hem of her dress, and panic bolted through Tessa like a runaway horse.

"Wait . . ." she heard herself yelp, and then, "*No.*"

She pushed from his lap.

Joseph's hands flew back as if she'd combusted in his arms. His face was frozen in horror and guilt.

Tessa's panic flared, leaping inside her like a shooting flame, and then, almost as quickly, it dissipated. It sank slowly, deflated and powerless, like a limp sail. In its wake, the terrible feelings of regret and confusion and anger. Resentful, bitter anger. Captain Neil Marking had packed her with latent panic in the same way he packed a musket with powder. She'd been cocked to explode all along, sabotaged against loving touch.

"I'm sorry, I'm sorry, I'm sorry," she said breathlessly, clapping her hands over her face. "Don't stop. Please."

"Don't stop?" Joseph rasped.

She peeked at him.

He was sprawled on the bench as if he'd been blown there by a strong wind.

"You're standing across the room, Tessa," he panted. His voice was hoarse. "Granted, it is a small room. Hardly an

ideal room for a romantic encounter, but I was enjoying it."
He exhaled quickly, like he'd just cheated death. "I've . . . I've
overstepped, Tessa. Forgive me. Tell me how I've frightened
you."

"No," she said immediately. She thrust her hand out with
one finger raised like a governess. "No. It's not you. It was
never you."

Her brain thrummed with conflicting jolts of desire and
fear and frustration. She wanted to scream, but what did
screaming solve? She wanted to sob against his chest, but
she'd cried enough at Vauxhall. She'd needed tears that
night, but now crying seemed like a regression.

"Give me a moment, please." She turned away.

Tell him, tell him, she thought. *Tell him something, anything.*

She wanted to talk even less than she wanted to scream or
cry. She was loath to reveal a single, excruciating detail about
Captain Marking and the night that Christian had been conceived. But how much of her struggle with Joseph Chance
was because of what she did not say? She glanced over her
shoulder. He looked as if he was slowly dying of a gunshot.
He was owed some explanation.

And she had loved kissing him so very much. If ever they
were to kiss again, if ever she were able to muddle through
more than kissing, he must know of her . . . experience.

But how could she articulate what she did not understand herself? *Joseph, I enjoy kissing you and touching you but
there are certain ways that you might touch me that will send me
into hysterics.*

And I won't know these incendiary touches until we are upon them.

Good luck to us both.

She toyed with blurting out these precise things, but she bade herself pause, take a deep breath, think. She reached for practicality, which had been a mainstay of the New Tessa.

"Here," said Joseph gently, "Tessa, please will you sit, or let us go—"

"Yes," she said. Without really thinking, she sat down again, right in his lap. She sat squarely this time, facing away, her spine straight. They sat like children on a downhill sled.

When her bottom hit his thighs, Joseph went rigid. He made an odd sound, like someone had handed him a wet cat. He held his arms wide.

Tessa took a deep breath. She wanted the closeness of sitting with him without the intensity of looking *at* him. And she'd wanted to be still. Everything effective about the New Tessa had been still and deliberate, not hysterical and reactionary.

She raised her chin, examining the opposite wall. It was dotted with pegs on a grid, each peg hung with a man's hat.

"This family has a proliferation of hats," she said.

"Trevor doesn't like the sun in his eyes," Joseph answered cautiously. His voice was rough. "They travel much of the year."

"Resourceful," said Tessa.

"*Tessa?*" Joseph said. He sounded miserable. Slowly, he lowered his arms to his sides. He did not touch her. She reached on either side and gathered up his open hands. He clasped them, and she held on. He let out a fraught breath.

"Joseph," she began, "this has become so very strange, and I'm sorry."

"I was too aggressive," he offered.

Tessa shook her head at the hats. "No. No. I am determined to accept whatever amorous . . . er, tide you may wish to, er, be carried away upon. However—"

"*Accept my amorous tide?*" Joseph repeated. His voice was too loud in the small room.

"Yes," she vowed, trying to sound very open, "*however,* there is more to my experience with, er, kissing, than you and me. As you know. I hesitate to bring it up, but I worry there is no help for it—for me—if I do not. Can you tolerate it?"

"*Tessa,*" he breathed. "The only thing I can tolerate is not knowing what you want."

She sighed at this. Could she simply stop with this assurance? No, she thought, he deserved more. He deserved all of it. She forged ahead. "In the weeks before I met you, I endured an encounter with the man who fathered Christian . . ."

Tessa gritted her teeth. It was physically painful to form the words, as if she spoke around a horse's bit. Joseph fell silent, not a breath, not a shuffle. She had his full attention. She forced herself to start again.

"On the night Christian was conceived, the man who was Christian's natural father was rather . . . demanding. And he . . . he, well—"

Now she squeezed Joseph's hands tighter. She closed her eyes.

"What he did was," she said softly, "well, *one* of the first things he did was . . . to put his hand beneath my—" *Deep breath.* "That is, my skirt was lifted and his hand touched my ankle to begin, so . . ." She let the sentence trail off.

Flashes of memory rushed back from that night. The darkness of the trees at the edge of the clearing. Marking's face, lit by moonlight. The thin clouds sailing overhead, sailing smooth and fast, as if they couldn't be bothered to stop, even to block the light from the moon.

When she spoke again, her voice was dazed. "To be honest, I am shocked I reacted to you as I did, because you did not even touch my, er, ankle. Not really. I am wearing leather boots—I always wear sturdy leather now—but that night, of course I had worn silk slippers. I suppose it was the pressure of your hand and not that you actually took up my ankle, not that you . . . er, *shoved.*"

Tessa stopped talking after that. She'd forced out all she could say on the topic of Neil Marking and silk slippers and ankles. No one knew these fine details, not even Willow or Sabine. Tessa kept them locked so deep in her brain that she thought sometimes even she could not remember them herself. But then a word or a smell would trigger a memory so distinctive and clear, she was immobilized, and she was reminded that it was all there, trapped in her head, and the key was very handy, indeed. The key was, in fact, in the lock, and she need only to turn it to remember the horrible events inside.

Was it the wrong decision to share them, even a few of them, with Joseph? What husband, convenient or otherwise, wanted to hear the details of previous trysts, especially about a man who impregnated her? There was a reason she had not told him before the wedding, even with their entire lives at stake.

She could not say what was at stake now. It felt very much like the rest of her life all over again.

A fresh wave of despair floated up, and she stared at the Earl of Falcondale's hats, straining to hear her husband draw breath or clear his throat, straining for some indication that he would speak. That he would exonerate her.

Finally, after what felt like an eternity, after the circles of the earl's hats had seared into her vision, Joseph said, very lowly and with more steel than ever she had heard, "He was demanding in *what way*, Tessa?"

As much as Joseph did not wish to hear the details of his wife's previous affair, he could not let go of the extremely troubling words that had, haltingly, emerged from her memory.

Demanding, she'd said. *Took up my ankle*. And perhaps most disturbingly of all, the word *shove*. Added to that, she would not look at him. He was literally staring at the back of her head. And finally, terrifyingly, their kiss had ended because she'd leapt from his lap. She leapt like he'd jabbed a finger into a wound.

His wife, he realized—and he cursed himself for his slowness—had been coerced or strong-armed or, God forbid, *attacked*. By Christian's father. He was suddenly as sure of it as he was that she conquered motherhood alone or saved a dock slip for his bloody boat.

The idea of a man forcing himself on her spilled rage into his veins like scalding water. Through sheer force of will, he paused. He cleared his throat. He was careful about the tenor of his voice. He would not grab her up or demand that she reveal everything, *every detail*, and reveal it this instant.

She *was* talking. It was a private, halting, pained sort of talk. But it was progress.

He'd wondered if there was some ulterior motive behind the heavy, dour clothes and the minimalist hair. He hadn't asked what bothered her because he'd been too focused on what might please her. He'd thought mostly of the possibility of her feelings for him. Of a future. Hell, of a kiss.

And now they'd had that kiss, and not an everyday, neutral, accommodating kiss but a voracious, skin-searing, heart-exploding kiss that went so far beyond questions and answers.

But none of that mattered if she was being haunted by some incident or, God forbid, *incidents*. If she had been hurt in some way, emotionally or physically.

He rephrased his last question with forced calm. "Tessa, what do you mean when you say demanding?"

"Are you angry?" she whispered.

"No," he said gently. He wanted to shout the word. He continued, "I am curious. There is a reason that an otherwise . . . amorous—dare I say, enthusiastic—woman suddenly leaps from my arms like a frightened rabbit. I should like to learn what it is."

She said nothing.

He asked, "Is that reason me?"

She shook her head. "No. I've said no."

"Yes, you've said this. That means some other man has caused you to be afraid. I should like to know how and why."

"Oh, Joseph," she sighed, dropping her head in hands. She sounded exhausted. "Do you really?" A challenge, not a hope.

No, he thought, but he said, "Yes." He meant *yes*.

She looked at the ceiling and nodded. The beautiful curtain of her hair rippled between them. She sat up very straight, took a deep breath, and then—slumped. Slowly, very slowly, she settled back against him. The heat of his body segued with the heat of hers. He wanted to gather her up, but her hands burrowed again into his. He held on.

"It is unpleasant for me to discuss it," she said. "That's putting it very mildly. *Unpleasant*. But I will do it, if you are willing to hear it. And you believe it will be useful."

"The more we can tell each other, Tessa, the better off we will be," he said. "I believe. I hope."

She said nothing but squeezed his hands. She held his hands as if the grip kept her from falling from a great height.

When she kept silent, he said, "But perhaps this boot room has seen all the honest talk one corridor can expect for an afternoon. What do you think? Shall we seek out somewhere less muddy, with fewer of Trevor's sweaty hats?"

This felt like an unnecessary detour, honestly, and he wondered how he could endure the wait. But regardless of what she had or had not managed today, it would always be her choice what to say and when to say it. He could only wait.

It was the least he could do after not asking until now, after simply assuming. He'd assumed she'd had a youthful love affair. He'd assumed their passion was mutual. The alternative was unbearable to him, but he would wait to hear of it on her terms.

Except, God help him, for one detail that could not go unaddressed right here, right now.

"But Tessa," he said, "there is one thing I must say, even in the boot room. You mentioned something about . . . about accepting 'the rising tide of my passion,' and I want to be perfectly clear."

She went stiff in his arms, bracing herself, and he swore in his head. He would not make it worse. He forged ahead. "Any affection between you and I, Tessa, will be a mutual endeavor—something that we both experience. You are not beholden to the rising tide of—of any part of me. I've never compelled a woman to . . . want me in this way, and I'll be damned if I start now. Do you understand?"

Tessa considered this, nodding finally with an impatient sigh. She sounded a little weary of heartfelt lectures. Joseph had grown weary of them too. And he was so very weary of the bloody boot room.

"Right. Up you go," he said, hustling her up and shoving from the bench. "Let us find somewhere more comfortable in the house. After seeing the glories of the cellar, you'll not be surprised to learn that I know the perfect spot."

He tugged his demolished cravat from his neck. When he glanced at her, she was gathering up the long curtain of your hair.

"Your hair is glorious," he said. He could not stop. "I adore it." *I adore you,* he added in his head.

He looked again and saw her smile, a true smile, the first authentic gladness—delight for the sake of delight—since they'd entered the house.

I want to delight you, he thought. *I want the chance to make you smile every day.*

But first, I hear what I should have been told from the beginning.

First, I hear what terrible thing has been done to you.

CHAPTER TWENTY-THREE

Tessa allowed Joseph to lead her, first up a sweeping, curved staircase, and then up two more flights. At last, he drew her into a tiny attic corridor lined with servant's rooms.

"You're enjoying the behind-the-scenes service tour of this house, lucky girl," he joked. "Very exclusive. Given only to the most esteemed guests."

"Did you occupy one of these rooms, before the earl moved you to the family wing?"

"I did, in fact. And, let me guess—you wish to see." He winked at her. "I have noticed your keen interest in my days of service, by the way, so do not feign ambivalence. You aren't the first gentleman's daughter to have a taste for a strapping manservant like myself."

Tessa laughed. He was so very clever. He saw the irony and ridiculous in most things and didn't hesitate to name them. He teased but without meanness. She'd laughed more at his comments and observations than any man she'd known, and her brothers were prodigiously funny.

Joking aside, she knew the climb up four stairwells was designed as a distraction. He was calming her. He was allowing her to compose herself and the words she would say. He understood the challenge posed by telling him.

And the challenge for him to hear it? He didn't address this. Another man might threaten or demand, he might force her to report exactly what he wanted to know. Or he might lock it down, declare it in the past and forgotten.

Not Joseph Chance. She felt more in love with every step of the stairwell. She floated behind him.

"Are you certain we are welcome to prowl every level of the earl's home when they are away?"

"Quite certain," Joseph called over his shoulder. They'd come to a small rounded door at the end of the attic corridor, curved at the top like a mouse hole. He tested the knob, found it locked, and then felt around on the transom of an adjacent doorway. He came back with a key, unlocked the small door, and ushered her through.

She was immediately hit with the crisp, smoky air of London in September. Sunlight shone from an opening at the top of yet another small flight of stairs.

"The rooftop?" she laughed.

"Why not?" he said. "You've seen the cellar. Might as well see the other end."

He squeezed past her in the thin stairwell, pausing to steal a kiss, and she laughed again. She wanted to reach for him, to call him back. She wanted to say, *But let us not go out.*

Let us avoid the brightness and cold. Let's stay here, where it's safe and dark.

But he was already gone, pulling her toward the sunlight. She followed him onto a square widow's walk, large enough for only three or four people. The walk was lined with a high decorative border in shiny black iron.

All around them were rooftops and brick walls, church towers, and leafy squares of London. The city sky, so frequently shrouded by smoke and soot, shone blue today. The wind lifted Tessa's loose hair, and she turned her face into it and laughed.

"Are you frightened of heights?" Joseph asked, wrapping an arm around her waist. "I don't even know."

She shook her head and reached for the railing, soaking in the view. "It's wonderful," she whispered. Far more wonderful was the warm security of his large hands around her waist.

He came to stand behind her. "We can stay out here as long as you like. However long it takes."

She glanced back. His message was clear. The view was lovely, but they'd come to the top of the house for a reason.

"*Right,*" she said, but she made no move to begin

After a moment, Joseph said, "Should I . . . kiss you again?"

She craned around. "Kiss me *again*? You are aware that *I* kissed *you*?"

He laughed. "Rest assured that I will never forget that you kissed me. I shall never look at boot rooms the same way again."

She laughed and turned, burrowing against his chest. His arms closed around her like strong, safe ropes.

She thought of the Old Tessa, who had been carefully coached by her mother never to discuss the attentions of one man with a second man, unless it was to *ever so slightly* tease a healthy measure of jealousy.

She thought of the New Tessa, who avoided all men, and who thoughtfully and carefully said exactly what she meant to say with reason and calm. Emotionless and rational and businesslike.

Against his chest she said, "I don't want to tell you what happened the night that Christian was conceived, because it was horrible. It was the horrible culmination to a lifetime of flirtation and silliness and vanity, which I also have no wish to discuss. But I worry if I do not say it, I will fall from a very great height every time we endeavor to . . . to . . ."

She looked up. "I want a life with you, Joseph. If you can trust me to pursue one. If you . . . think of me in that way. And if you can accept my son. I want the life we dreamed of together at Berymede."

She paused, marveling that *this* had actually been easier to reveal than the events of the night with Captain Marking and the tree.

Joseph said nothing. He betrayed not even the slightest tenseness in his arms, not an intake of breath. She stole a look at his face. He stared down with a creased expression, like he'd wanted to speak but could not.

Tessa forged ahead. "I have vowed so many things since

you went away, but the most important vow was not to conceal anything from you. Not again."

"Tessa, I love you," Joseph said.

The wind blew in the moment, lifting her hair. Long swaths of blond literally stood on end—and it felt so very appropriate. Her whole body seemed to levitate. She stared, disbelieving, at Joseph's face. He looked almost as surprised as she was. He looked a little like he'd accidentally dropped someone's priceless heirloom dish.

"Before you declare that," Tessa said, "wait until you hear what I have to say." She could not bear to have him retract these words after she'd told him.

"I don't care what you have say," he said, but he released her and stepped back. Now he looked gravely serious. Now he looked determine to take every dish in the cupboard and throw it at the wall.

"Yes, well. Right then," she said. She felt cold without the circle of her arms, but she took her own step back. She turned and faced the skyline of London. She clasped the iron fencing.

She took a deep breath and the cold stung her throat. He had been right to bring her here. She could stare at the vastness of the city and feel small and inconsequential, but she could not get away.

"The man who is Christian's natural father is a captain in the Army," she began. "His regiment was garrisoned in Pixham last summer. During this time, there were a number of dashing officers at village assemblies or private parties.

This man and I, er, singled each other out as foils almost immediately. I flirted with him shamelessly. He was especially imperious and gallant, and he preened about with a manly sort of swagger whenever I was near. It was like a little game we played, one I'd played many times with many different beaux."

She glanced at Joseph. He'd crossed his arms over his chest. His face was patient, but he'd narrowed his eyes. Tessa had the thought, *There is listening, and then there is* listening.

Joseph, she thought, *is LISTENING.*

She looked away and bowed her head, staring at her hands on the railing. "It must be said—" She stopped and started again. "The story is not complete without acknowledging that my behavior before this time was . . . well, I suppose the best word might be coquettish? I laughed constantly, dressed colorfully, and danced with the energy of a playful kitten. I elicited, and gained, the adoring attention of most men. I loved the brotherly teasing of my family and the less-brotherly teasing of their friends. I relished my father's gifts and praise. I thrilled to the company of suitors and beaux and gentlemen callers."

She glanced at him, her face burning. Would her behavior seem ridiculous and vain to him, would what came next seem justified? His expression was placid.

She thought of those days, thought of the fun she had and the gowns she adored, the music, the gifts. Had she been ridiculous? She had been young and indulged, but she had never been cruel. Her friends would have admonished her if she had. Had her vanity been destructive? She'd had other pursuits—music and friendships and social errands on behalf of her mother.

She took a deep breath and continued, "For better or for worse, the role I played in our family felt very natural to me. It was not a contrivance. The Tessa St. Croix you met when you came upon me outside Gibson's Mercantile was very truly *me*. I did not contrive to dazzle you into some sort of web of calculated wiles in the weeks that followed."

"I accused you of this," he said softly. "After the wedding. I'm sorry."

She smiled at him gently. "I appreciate that. And I understand why. But please believe me. I like to think of that girl as the Old Tessa. Because of the baby, there is a chance that my personality was the slightest bit *concentrated*, boiled down to the most effective, but it was still truly me. And I did really enjoy you. I believed you to be so very handsome and fashionable and clever."

"And now you've learned that I contrive to impress girls in the boot room," he joked.

She shook her head and gave another small smile. "The captain called on me at Berymede several times, and my parents approved of him, in as much as they approved of any of my suitors. My mother's priority was my popularity. She wanted me to be the desire of a great many men. I believe the crowning glory in her own life was the great number of men she once held in thrall. A good match and marriage was important to her, yes, but once a girl is married, she counts her admirers as only one—her husband. His wealth and affections will sustain her through her life, but in my mother's view, I really believe there is no comparison to the great thrill of a *legion* of admirers."

Tessa pivoted and leaned back against the railing, staring east. "Aren't you glad to know you are married to the most prodigious flirt in Surrey?"

"I am glad to know I am married to you at all," he said. "It sounds as if I would have had trouble competing for your attentions if my chances had not been leveled by—"

"My desperation?" she provided.

She would not make him say it. She wanted to add, *I would have loved you regardless*, but she struggled, somehow, to go this far. It was like she could not confess this terrible circumstance with Captain Marking *and* profess her love for him in the same conversation. The exchange would overwhelm. A tower of fragile china too high to safely balance.

She went on, "At summer's end, the captain escorted me to an assembly in Pixham. And after we'd danced and laughed and had a generally wonderful time, he leaned in and asked me if I would honor him with a walk. Outside. In the night. Alone."

She took a deep breath, remembering his words. He'd whispered. His voice had been different, low and growly and suggestive. She'd been intrigued. Everything about his offer had felt reckless and provocative and exciting.

Tessa, who had grown weary of the dancing, had been flattered. Captain Marking had been so very dashing that night; breathtakingly adherent to her, possessive, dominating. He had made her feel like the only woman in the world who could satisfy some unnamed dark yearning.

"Because I was foolish and reckless," she went on, "I agreed. And when my parents had gone home and brothers were occupied, I allowed him to slip me out a rear door and lead me down a path into the forest. It was naughty and exciting, and I remember laughing as we ran down the path. It was all such a lark."

Stupid girl, she thought in her head. *Stupid, stupid girl*.

"Tessa?" Joseph called, and she looked up. His voice was cautious, like he was talking to a spooked horse.

"Will you take my coat?" he asked finally. "You are shivering."

"No," she said. She felt hot, so hot she thought she might incinerate. She *wanted* to incinerate, but she kept right on standing, telling this awful tale.

"We spilled into a clearing in the woods, and in the center was this massive tree. The trunk was as thick as the chimney in Berymede's great room, and he sort of backed me against it. I knew what was coming, of course, he had kissed me before, and I allowed it. I allowed all of it."

A deep breath.

The next bit gushed out like blood from a vein. "But then I wasn't simply against the tree, I was sort of locked there by his arms and the weight of him, and he started to kiss me, and it was fine, I suppose. The tree was hard and the night was colder than I'd realized, and he was quite heavy—he'd never pressed against me so firmly before—and the buttons of his uniform jabbed me through my dress. Very quickly, his kisses turned from familiar and nice to, well . . . sloppy and hard at the same time. I couldn't breathe, I felt choked. I tried to turn my head but he followed me—every way I turned, he followed me. And he was mumbling in my ear in a way that frightened me. I tried to call out, but every time he lifted his mouth, I had to gasp for breath. My voice wouldn't come. And his hands were everywhere. He was touching my body, containing me, preventing me from sliding right or left. And then . . ."

Another deep breath. She hesitated for a second before finishing. She'd already said far, far more than she'd wanted to say. The fine detail was entirely unnecessary. All Joseph really needed to know was that he had been aggressive and she had been afraid. But the moments had played in her head and she'd put words to them and out they came. She might as well say it all. She stared at her hands gripping the iron railing and rushed to finish.

"And then he held me by the neck with one hand and reached down to grab my ankle with the other. He forced my leg up and clawed beneath my skirt and ripped away my pantaloons. He unfastened his own breeches, and leaned in, told me what a good girl I was, over and over again. He . . . put—that is, he forced himself. And I . . . endured it."

She looked up. She blinked. She tried to unfurl her hands from the iron rail, but they wouldn't budge. Just as well; she did not trust her legs. And she did not trust her restraint; she wanted to fall into Joseph's arms. But would he receive her? She dared not look at him.

"Five weeks later," she went on, "when I told him I had conceived a child that night, he slammed the door in my face.

I told my friends I was in trouble, and they posted the advertisement. You answered it."

The end, she thought.

The wind blew, and her hair lifted from her shoulders and snapped and twirled. Her thoughts felt the same inside her head. She wanted more wind, stronger wind, she wanted it to lift her entire body and blow her away.

"Tessa?" Joseph said.

He'd not taken one step toward her. In her peripheral vision, she had not seen him move.

He went on, his voice very low and steely calm. "Tessa, what is the name of this person?"

She shook her head. "His name is not important. I'm not protecting him, I promise you, it's simply that I don't even like to say it—"

"I am not asking," Joseph said, "out of curiosity. I am asking because I will hunt this man down and kill him."

Tessa snapped her gaze to his. Her husband, so debonair and stylish, had transformed into a wild animal in a cage. His breath came in hard pants, his shoulders were tense, his hands were curled into fists, his face was a mask of rage.

"No, Joseph," she said and shook her head. Her voice tried for soothing calm. "No. It's not worth—"

"Why didn't your brothers call him out? Why didn't your father see that he was court-marshalled?"

She laughed a bitter laugh. "Why would they do that?"

"Because he *raped* an innocent girl. He attacked you, Tessa, just as surely as I will attack him. But I assure you, when I attack him, there will be amble opportunities for him to scream."

"Raped me?" she said, and she checked the street below, because she'd shouted it. "He didn't rape me, Joseph. I went with him willingly. I kissed him. I had done my level best to make him crazy with desire in the preceding weeks. My dress that night was—"

"*Stop*," Joseph gritted out, stepping to her.

He said, "No, *no man ever* lures a young woman into the forest, pins her against a bloody tree, and *forces* himself on her, except in the instance of *rape*. I don't care how much you flirted. I don't care if you were wearing the most beautiful gown in the world or your chemise. Unless you are fully willing, with total consent, no decent, honorable man has sex in this manner unless he is raping her, which is exactly what he did to you, and—forgive me—I am so filled with fury right now, I . . . I—" He stopped. "Tell me his name."

Tessa stared at him. "I will not."

Joseph jerked open the door to the rooftop. "You will."

"I will *not*," she repeated, louder.

He growled and began trudging down the stairs.

Tessa made a noise of shocked frustration and hurried after him.

"This is why you've taken to wearing the terrible dresses," he called over his shoulder.

Tessa swore, tripping to catch up with him. "Those dresses are modest! I am being modest."

"They are hideous. And you hate them. You look like

someone tossed a sack over your head and forced you to do penance. They conceal your personality." He ducked into the attic corridor and made for the next set of stairs.

Now I am chasing you? Tessa marveled. She quickened her step. "My personality could stand for some concealment."

"Never say that!" He vaulted down the stairs and made for the next set. "Your personality is as beautiful as your face. I want the dresses gone. I will burn them myself."

"You can't tell me what to wear!" She rounded the landing.

"Every time you wear a dress that you hate, you give him another piece of yourself. *Tell me his name!*"

"You sound like a madman," she shouted back.

"I am a madman! And I will kill him."

"You will not! You will stop sprinting down the stairs and come back right now and . . . *acknowledge* me." She stopped on the landing and breathed in and out, trying to stop herself from screaming.

He froze on the bottom step and looked back up at her. She held out her hands, palms up. *What are you doing!* She would not take another step. She sat down. The stairs were polished wood with a thick carpeted runner. She dropped her head into her hands.

Joseph forced himself to tap down his charged fury and take a deep breath.

"I'm sorry," he called. He was sorry, but his voice sounded indignant. He regretted his outburst, although not much.

He tried again. "I was prepared for every narrative but

this. I am never prepared for you, Tessa. My reactions are always just a little bit *off*. Or a lot."

His reaction to her story felt exactly perfectly right, but it served himself and not her.

She said, "If you are truly outraged on my behalf—"

"Let me be clear," he cut her off, climbing the stairs, "*outrage* is a generous word for what I feel."

"That's very . . . vanquishing of you," she said, "honestly. I feel safe . . . and vindicated. But I don't feel supported. If you truly want to help me, sit still. Please. *Be with me* in this moment. Let us both come to terms with this thing that I've never told anyone but you—"

"Your friends do not know?" This he could not believe.

"Joseph," she sighed, "I have been so ashamed." Her voice broke.

He swore in his head. He dropped beside her on the top step and pulled her against him.

She went on, "I will, perhaps, always struggle to see it as *you* see it—as an attack. I . . . I was raised by my mother to walk a very fine line between being so very pretty and yet also so very untouchable. The delicate balance of beauty and virtue was as important as the beauty alone or the virtue itself. I had to be pretty enough to drive a man to his knees but also stoic enough to fend off his lack of control."

Joseph growled. He wanted to vault up and down the stairs again, he wanted to punch the wall. He said tightly, "This is madness, Tessa. Pretty girls should not go through life with the underlying charge of fending off licentious men.

Your mother is mad. She has failed you, not the other way around. She has failed you in so many ways."

Tessa had no answer for this. She burrowed more closely against him.

He cleared his throat. "I want to support you, Tessa, honestly, but I am so very angry at this man. Worthless specimen of humanity."

"Please," she said, "do not pursue violence. Do not endeavor to learn who he is or where he is. To endanger yourself serves no purpose in our . . . future."

His stomach gave a little flip at the mention of *our future*, but he cocked an eyebrow at her. "Allow me to clarify," he said. "There are very few men who *pose danger* to me, Tessa. I learned to fight in an Ottoman-held Greek slum, and I've been in and out of scrapes in nearly every port in the world. If you prefer it, I will not seek him out. But if ever I encounter this person, he should be very afraid of me."

She smiled and he gathered her closer and kissed the top of her head, breathing her in. "Oh, God, Tessa, I'm so sorry. For all of it. Most of all, I'm sorry I left you alone in a fit of pique because I thought you . . ." He squeezed his eyes shut, hating himself. "I thought that you had seduced me and tricked me. I was focused only on my pride."

"I was afraid to tell you the full story," she said. "Fear kept me silent, not seduction and trickery. I've been afraid to tell you, even now. What if your generous view changes after you've had time to consider what you've learned?"

"It won't. And Tessa? No more fear." But he thought of her reaction to his hand on her ankle. He thought of her panicky leap from his lap. Their journey to no fear would be, perhaps, a long and arduous one.

But now he wanted only to love her, to calm her. "But perhaps we should take a step back," he ventured. "*Not* to lose our generous view, but simply to recover from the emotions of today. I feel like I've run to Windsor and back, and I've done nothing but listen. I can only imagine what you must feel." He looked around. "Clearly our stair climbing has scared away the staff, but they can be roused to bring tea. Are you hungry? What are your feelings about taking supper with Trevor and Piety?"

"To be honest," she began, "I'm not sure I can manage the social demands of a formal meal. I know the earl and countess are important to you, but . . ." She let the sentence trail off. "If you've run to Windsor, I've run to Scotland. Do you think I might decline just this once? Of course, you should remain."

Joseph made a dismissive noise and stood up. He held out his hand and pulled her to her feet. "Whatever you decide, we will do together."

"They made such a fuss about your visit. I couldn't pull you away."

"Of course you could," he sighed. "The truth is, I come and go from this house with feckless irregularity. It's rude and self-indulgent, but I do relish the homecoming I receive when I drop in after disappearing for weeks at the time. We will scribble a note and demand a future invitation."

"If you're certain . . ." she said.

"I hope the alternative is not to take you directly home." He held his breath.

"Well," she said shyly, "I did tell Perry I would be out all afternoon . . ."

"Brilliant," he said, trying not to think of all the satisfying ways he could carry on with his wife for the length of an afternoon. There would be, God willing, plenty of opportunities to cultivate that. Now she needed time and care and understanding. "I know a café around the corner that does a lovely cream tea."

Tessa made a face and shook her head.

"Right. I don't suppose you'd like to see my house in Blackheath?"

With no enthusiasm, she said, "Oh, yes, the Blackheath house . . ." Joseph was reminded of her request to move halfway across the country. Some of his hopefulness sagged. For this, he would require his own time and care and understanding.

He searched his mind for some innocuous, pleasant alternative. Something with no stake in their marriage that would offer some respite from the revelations of the afternoon. Suddenly, the answer occurred to him.

"I don't suppose you would consider," he began, "the originally stated purpose of this outing, which was to call on the guano buyers in their offices on Blair Street?"

Tessa's head shot up. Her eyes were filled with hopeful delight. "I *would* consider it," she enthused. "Oh, Joseph, truly?"

He chuckled. It was as if he'd suggested they call on the jewelers. "Truly," he continued.

She laughed—she actually laughed. "Do you find it suspect that this, of all things, should thrill me? No, don't answer that. I don't care. It's so very gratifying to be included in your work."

"Yes, well, I do aim to thrill. And now I see why you agreed to spend the afternoon with me. You came for the buyers."

"Don't be silly," she said, "I came for the boot room." And then she patted her hair, gave her bodice a tug, and clipped down the stairs.

CHAPTER TWENTY-FOUR

The phaeton ride to Blair Street required the same balance and white-knuckled grip as their journey to Henrietta Place, but Tessa needed no excuse to hold fast to her husband. She sat immediately beside him, one hand on his leg, the other on his bicep. He cleared his throat every time they made a turn, an intimate acknowledgment of her clenching hands, and Tessa smiled. She was so very happy. She never would have predicted that confessing (or, as Joseph viewed it, "revealing") the events of the night with Captain Marking would be so . . . liberating, so redemptive. She felt like she'd been trapped in a dark room for a year and someone had thrown open all the windows and unlocked the door.

When they cleared Whitehall, the traffic thinned considerably, and Tessa began to pepper Joseph with questions about the sale of the guano.

"Is the buyer an agricultural cooperative?"

He glanced at her. "Indeed, it is. A collective of landowning farmers throughout the country who have banded together. They buy fertilizer in large lots so they all benefit from lower costs. I sold them our entire first shipment before we'd even mined it."

"And they want more? You've said there is more guano to be had."

He grimaced. "Oh yes. There is more."

"What's wrong?" She laughed. "Are you not excited by the potential?"

"No, actually, that excites me very much. It's merely . . ." He steered around an overturned potato cart. "Stoker would call me out for laziness and affectation toward contrived poshness, but the guano mine is hardly my ideal place of employment." He rolled his neck.

"Like Vauxhall Gardens is not your ideal night out?" she surmised.

He harrumphed. "Vauxhall is a palace compared to the guano mine. The island is hot and desolate, and the mining is grueling. The food is terrible, we sleep in tents. The only diversion is reading by candlelight, but the winds preclude it. I dread going back, honestly. Originally, I saw no way around it, but now . . ." He let the sentence trail off.

"But now?" she prompted. She squeezed his thigh.

He made a growling noise and glanced at her hand. "But now," he repeated simply. They made the turn at Ross Street.

He started again. "I returned to England with what I thought of as my Plan for the Future. I was going to situate you and the baby with noble and stoic detachment—" She giggled and he said, "Clearly I've failed at this goal."

He went on, "I was going to return to Barbadoes and mine as much guano as I could and turn another profit. With that money, I was going to throw myself into local politics somewhere with potential for an eventual Parliamentary run. I still want those things, but my personal return to Barbadoes may not be, er, strictly necessary."

Tessa nodded, working to keep a reasonable smile on her face. She forced herself to raise her eyebrows in mild interest. She would not squeal. She would not clap her hands together. She would not throw herself across his lap and say, *Thank God, please never leave England again.*

"Stoker will certainly return to Barbadoes," he said. "Without a doubt. The mine suited him. He's good at managing sailors and miners and he's actually good at the physical work. He's a prodigiously good sea captain. But me . . . ?" He allowed the question to trail off.

She was just about to prompt him, *But you?* when he reined the horses and brought the phaeton to a stop in an alley. A boy darted from the shadows to mind the animals, and Joseph tossed him a coin.

"Is this Blair Street?" she asked. She reached out her hand to step down, but he grabbed her around the waist and lifted her to the ground. Her skirts whirled around her ankles, the heavy brown wool catching air like springtime cotton.

"Yes. Just around the corner." He held out his arm and led her across the bustling street. Tessa had become reasonably familiar with Blackwall that summer—the dock and warehouses, the searcher's office, and the waterfront—but she knew almost nothing of the crowded streets just two blocks north of the water. Up and down Blair Street, buyers, ship-builders, insurance brokers, booking agents, mariners, and investment firms catered to the busy shipping traffic of the River Thames.

She wished for her diary so she could take down the names and trades on the placards beside each door. Her future was still uncertain—hopeful, but uncertain—and she'd learned nothing this summer if not the value of expanding her knowledge, especially about an industry that so fascinated her.

"The buyers have summoned me only for signatures today, I'm afraid," Joseph told her. "But we can make an appointment to return, if it pleases you. You may learn the process of how cargo transfers to buyers and how the buyers distribute it to the customers."

"I should like that very much," Tessa said. He was just about to lead them around a crowd of sailors when the boy minding Joseph's horses gave a whistle.

"Oy! Gov'nor!" the boy called.

When they looked back, the boy was bent over the raised hoof of one of the horses. He waved them back with a wild hand. Joseph swore and turned them, but Tessa slipped her hand from his arm.

"Do you mind if I wait here while you go?" she asked. "I should like to take in the lay of the street. I've never ventured this far from the water."

"Right," sighed Joseph, squinting into the alley at his horse. "This shouldn't take long. I believe this enterprising young man has mistaken me for a patsy."

He tightened his gloves and stepped back into the alley. Tessa could not hide her smile as she enjoyed the sight of him walking away. Broad shoulders, long strides, no cravat at all, she'd seen to that. He propped a shoulder on the brick wall beside his rig, waiting for the boy to make his pitch.

Tessa turned away and ambled the length of two storefronts, reading signs and peering through windows. When a door opened on the third office she stopped and waited, craning her head to catch a glimpse of the office beyond the door.

"You'll not regret it, Simon!" bellowed a voice from inside. Tessa froze.

The voice went on, "I'll call again next week to compare the numbers. Mark my words. No regret!"

Her heart missed two beats.

Now a gloved hand extended beyond the open door, an ebony walking stick clutched just below its golden handle.

Tessa knew well the gloves and the stick. She knew the voice.

Her father, Wallace St. Croix, hovered in a doorway, right here, right now, a foot from her.

Every muscle in Tessa's body went tense, as if a thief had leapt from the alley to rob her.

Not a thief, she told herself—her father hadn't stolen from her, he had abandoned her. *Worse than a thief*, she thought, breathing hard. She felt like the marionette puppet that hung on the edge of Christian's crib. When she pulled its string, his arms and legs restricted wildly. Tessa felt wildly restricted. She felt like folding herself into a square of brown wool, doubling over until she was inside herself.

She looked frantically around, searching for a place to hide, but then her brother August emerged from the door, followed by her next brother, Lucas. They were putting on their hats, their faces were obscured, but of course she knew them. She had known them all—from the first note of her father's voice.

And now here was her father, stepping beyond the door, still calling to someone inside.

Her impulse to hide dissolved. The sight of him sent a surge of fresh anger straight to her heart. She would not run or play the victim. She would force him to see her.

"Hello," she said. Her voice was weaker than she preferred, but she forced the word out. It was something. It was more than the three of them managed. They stared at her as if she'd dropped from the sky.

She realized she'd not seen the boys in nearly a year, her father not in six months. And now her anger was mixed, inexplicably, with a shot of joy. Oh, how she'd missed them. The thick, athletic handsomeness of her brothers. The round, stooped stodginess of her father. The confident bellow of his voice. Her brothers trailed her father around like ladies in waiting. It was a sight she'd seen a million times, and a million times she'd regarded them with an affectionate shrug.

There they go. Smart and successful and adoring.

No longer.

Her joy evaporated when her brothers turned their faces away. Could they not even look at her? Meanwhile, her father's watery eyes narrowed and his mouth puckered like the pit of a plum.

Shame on you, she thought. *Shame on you for regarding me like a maid you fired for theft.*

Shame on you for bringing up the boys in the ways of business but teaching me nothing but how to flirt and look pretty and to entrap a man.

And most of all, most pitiful of all, shame on you for choosing not to know your grandson.

For how long they stood, staring at each other, Tessa could not say. Eventually, her brother August turned to her and half whispered, half called her name. He sounded as if he was embarrassed to say it out loud. He sounded as if they were meeting in an alley instead of a busy street. She raised her chin a notch.

"*Tessa,*" August hissed again.

"Hello, Gus," she said at full volume.

Her brothers had not been present when her parents had disowned her. Wallace and Isobel St. Croix had come to Belgravia alone. Even so, the boys had made no effort to contact her again. They'd disowned her without even looking her in the eye.

"Where," asked her father, "is the child?"

He appeared truly confused, as if he believed Christian would be forever attached to her, along with a sign the stated the date of her wedding and the date of his birth, a mere six months apart.

"My son's name is Christian," she said. "And he is at home. With his nursemaid."

Her father glared at her as if she was willfully lying. He looked right and left at the crush of businessmen and sailors maneuvering around them. A boy with a wooden placard and a tall stack of broadsheets had set up business nearby, and her father took her by the arm and pulled her behind his sign. Her brothers closed rank around them. She was walled in by disapproving St. Croix men and a broadsheet boasting the first weeks of the new king's reign.

"A nursemaid?" repeated her father. "And who pays for *this?*"

Tessa stared at him. Did he really believe her to be destitute? She knew her family wanted to detach from her, but had they also wanted her to suffer? Her churning stomach dropped.

She said, "My husband, Joseph Chance, provides for us."

"Chance remained married to you, did he?" her father asked.

"Yes," she said, "he remained." She tried to find words for how much more he had done, but Joseph's actions had been a stream of intangibles. Patience, curiosity, support, regret, and acceptance. Today—love.

"I see the wardrobe he provides," said Wallace. "Or perhaps he forces penance on you with this dress."

Tessa looked down at her brown wool dress. Of course her appearance would be her father's most relevant measure of her wellness. She had worked so hard to fix the parts of herself that had beguiled one man to impregnate her and another man marry her. In her father's view, the reform translated only to plainness. There was no redemption in his eyes.

She almost said this, but her father narrowed his eyes to accusing slits and said slowly, "Would you like to know of your mother?"

Tessa closed her mouth. She did not expect this. She had assumed that being disinherited precluded information about the state of her mother. The truth was, in spite of everything else, she had missed her Maman. She had called out for her during the agonizing hours of labor; and again, when Christian had been a ravenous newborn who would not suckle. She had seen a pretty purple hat and thought of her mother's love of violet, about their shared love of shops and pretty things and fashion.

But what of their shared love of each other?

Isobel's love of the family's reputation and her esteem in the eyes of society had been greater. Tessa had known this.

And still she asked, "Is . . . Maman well?" Concern edged out bitterness.

"No, she is not," her father boasted. His eyes bulged and he held his hands out. His expression said, *What did you expect?* "She is heartbroken," Wallace hissed. "Her only daughter is disgraced. Her son-in-law is a stranger, bribed with a dowry to give her child a name."

Tessa took a small step back. How foolish it had been to ask. Tears blurred her vision, she felt her throat begin to constrict. The bustle of the street felt deafening, while individual voices and horse hooves grew indistinct. She was underwater. She heard everything from the bottom of a miserable sea.

"But why are you in Blair Street?" her father went on. "This is rare form, indeed, Tessa."

"Joseph has business with a buyer. I've come to look on. I am learning the dockyard, if you can belie—"

Her father gave a snort of disgust. "*Looking on?* How can

your brothers go about their business in Blackwall if they are to fear colliding with you?" His pugnacious frown pulled his entire face downward, like wax on a candle.

Tessa tried to say she would not acknowledge her brothers in future.

She tried to say that their business and her business need never intersect.

She tried to say that, by the way, Christian superseded any disgrace that she had brought on the family—

But her voice had grown high and thin, her lip quivered. And she did not have the opportunity. Joseph appeared at her side.

One moment she had been alone with her scowling family, and then Joseph had been there, tucking a broadsheet beneath his arm.

"Ah, Wallace, imagine the odds. I can see your surprise, but never fear. We won't be in Blair Street long. Not today. And I wouldn't worry too much about future encounters. Tessa and the baby and I are looking at property in County Durham. On the North Sea. In Bartlepool."

"Hartlepool," Tessa corrected.

"That's what I meant," said Joseph. "Hartlepool."

His lips quirked up, betraying the slightest hint of a smile.

"Tessa has an interest in the new dockyard there," he said. "She's shown quite a capacity for importation. Entirely self-taught, obviously."

Tessa looked back at her father and brothers, at their stunned expressions, their distaste, their entire lack of control over anything she said or did. Her tears receded, and she felt a wave of fresh courage. "The future is at St. Katharine, by the way. The West India Docks is on the decline. You might look into it."

"Well said," cheered Joseph and took her by the arm.

"If we're all finished here," he told Wallace St. Croix and his sons, and he shouldered ahead, giving them little choice but to step aside. He steered Tessa into the street.

She did not look back. She stared down Blair Street, seeing nothing, hearing nothing, feeling shock and pride and gratification.

"Thank you," she said.

Joseph gave a weak smile, a smile that answers mundane comments about the weather.

"But you did not really mean what you said about Hartlepool?" she asked.

"Oh," he sighed, leading her around the corner to the buyer's office, "I'll need to own property somewhere in the bloody country in order to run for Parliament. County Durham sounds like as good a place as any. Why the hell not?"

Tessa stopped walking. He looked down at her. He'd said these words casually, agreeably, as if she'd suggested fish for dinner and he'd agreed.

"Why not?" she repeated softly, her heart in her throat. Truthfully, she felt her heart in her eyes, in the expression on her face. Her heart beamed from her chest.

Joseph winked at her and then led her into the buyer's shop.

Chapter Twenty-Five

It was decided that Tessa and the baby would travel to County Durham by private coach, along with Perry, a detachment of grooms, and a burly sailor named Benjamin who would manage the trunks and glare at anyone who dared give them a second look.

Joseph would remain in London for a fortnight, settle the most pressing of the guano business, and travel to County Durham by sea, reaching Hartlepool a day or two before Tessa and the baby.

Joseph hated to part ways with her again, but when she had recovered from the shock of his offer, her immediate priority became departing Belgravia as soon as possible. She was determined to relieve the Boyds.

Joseph was shamed by how uncomfortable she had been. Hartlepool might be a fool's errand, but he would do anything to make up for allowing her to live on the kindness of relative strangers these last eleven months. If Hartlepool turned out to be a terrible place, or the dockyard held no potential, if she hated it or the baby seemed unhappy, they would return to London and determine some other plan.

And there was the small matter of the boast Joseph had made to her father. He was determined to follow through. More important, Tessa had discovered the little town herself and she wanted it. Her reasons were plainly stated and made sense. Not an abundance of sense, Joseph noted, but she'd hedged no secrets and offered a line of logic they could both see. It was such a hopeful start.

And so Joseph had arranged for the coach, arranged for rooms along the journey, arranged for protection and every comfort he could predict. In a fortnight, they would rendezvous. In good weather, he'd need only four days to make the journey by sea, and he planned to leave in time to scout out County Durham for himself. She'd mentioned a "cottage," but in Joseph's view, his days of cottage life were long over.

He arrived early to Belgravia on the day she was scheduled to depart and went over the route and expectations with the coachman and grooms. Tessa and Perry soon convened in the doorway to oversee the loading of the trunks and make tearful good-byes to Sabine and the Boyds.

Tessa tried once again to convince Sabine to join her, but her friend declined. Everyone held the baby one last time. A debate ensued about the rightful owners of Tessa's goat. When, at last, the trunks had been secured and the baby had been fed and the goat had been given to the Boyds as a gift, Tessa sought out Joseph among the grooms.

"May we speak before I go?" she asked. She held the goat by a lead rope.

Joseph considered her. She'd worn a traveling suit that was not quite as heavy and oppressive as her usual drab shroud. The skirt and jacket were midnight blue. There was a matching hat. She looked elegant and beautiful and not entirely suited for minding a goat.

"I hoped that we would," he said.

She turned away, pulling the goat in the direction of the mews.

"I've charged Benjamin with locating a female goat in each town as soon as you reach the inn," Joseph said, rushing to take the animal.

"Yes, he's told me. We can manage with cow's milk if there is no goat," she said. "You've thought of everything."

"I've thought of you," he said. "Or I've endeavored to. There will be things I cannot anticipate."

"I've managed for months without you, Joseph. Perry and I will carry on as we have."

I don't want you to carry on as you have, he thought, but he would not detract from what she had achieved.

They neared the stable door and the goat picked up speed, anxious to be away from the humans and the carriage and an uncertain future. Tessa swung the gate and stepped inside.

He'd called on her frequently since the day at Trevor's house, the day they'd encountered her father in Blackwall. The plan to visit Hartlepool had come together very quickly, in less than a week, and it had required daily collaboration. Even so, the opportunity to be alone with her, truly alone, had not presented itself. Like a coward, he had not engineered one.

Trevor had accused him again of not being particularly attracted to his wife. It was an offhand jest, intended to spur him to action, but the claim made him almost angry. The desire he felt for Tessa had been so urgent and present for so long—nearly a year now, since they first met—that it felt almost like his shadow, a hulking reflection of himself that hounded his every step. But instead of weightless and easily ignored, his desire was a pressure that never let up, a pulsing, insistent burn.

Let it burn, Joseph had told himself. He would rather burn alive than relive the look of panic on her face when she leapt from his lap. And now that he knew why? He could not pursue her in the usual ways. He would wait and watch and proceed with extreme caution, his burning desire be damned.

In the stable, Tessa busied herself untying the goat and stringing the rope on a peg. "There is something I should like before I go, Joseph," she said, giving the animal a final pat.

"What have we forgotten?" he asked.

"A kiss." She left the animal and started to him.

"I beg your pardon?" he said stupidly, uselessly, the best he could do. His actual thought was *thank God*, which was surely the wrong reaction. His pulse leapt and his hands tingled, itching to scoop her up.

His distress must have been obvious, because she chuckled. Her blue eyes lit up the dim stable. She said, "And it's not because I am grateful that you have taken my idea of Hartlepool so very seriously." She stepped to him and placed her palms on his lapels. Joseph stared at her hands.

"I *am* grateful," she said. He had trouble focusing on her words. He stared at her mouth. She went on, whispering, "Even if the idea is utter folly—especially if it is folly—I am grateful. But I want to kiss you for no other reason than I enjoyed it so very much before." She paused, holding his gaze. Her speech felt a little prepared, but he didn't care. He would hear it again and again.

"I know my final reaction alarmed us both," she said softly, "but I want you to understand that my final reaction was not my only reaction. I have not stopped thinking about all the things I loved about that kiss."

And then the speech ended, and she raised her chin, and lifted onto her toes.

She looked so very earnest and excited and delicious, he'd almost been too enchanted to respond.

Almost.

Instinct prevailed, and he dropped his mouth onto hers. He had the fleeting thought, *This is actually happening*, and stifled a groan. He widened his stance and swept her against him, his hands surging up the curve of her back, kneading every vertebra of her spine. Restraint deserted him. When he reached her neck, he cradled her head.

She kissed like a woman, he thought, not a girl. He loved her proficiency, her confidence. Her anxiety aside, there was no shy, halting uncertainty in the way she kissed. She slid her hands from the rough wool of his lapels to the slick waistcoat beneath. Nuzzling close, she wrapped her arms around him beneath his jacket, sharing warmth, sharing a heartbeat.

He pulled away to trail kisses down her neck. "I should be going with you," he rasped against her skin.

"You should not," she sighed. "You should oversee delivery of your guano and sell the next lot. You should provision for the next expedition. Perry and I are accustomed to managing tight spaces and long stretches and babies. I am quite talented."

You are torture, he thought.

And *this* had been an ancillary reason he wouldn't travel with her. The thought of ten nights in ten inns seemed almost inhuman for him to endure. Not now. Not when there was so much to explore about their future.

The thought of exploring while also sharing a country inn suite with a chatty nursemaid? Thin walls and adjoining doorways and the four of them in a coach? It would require an amount of restraint and patience that he did not possess.

He'd been working beside her with maps and open trunks for a week and not touched her once, and now she was veritably climbing his body—and thank God for that. But when they finally, truly delved in to the topic of their life together, whatever it might be, and—hallelujah—when he could touch her all night long, he wanted to be in one location, and he wanted a locked bloody door.

"I pray God you are safe and comfortable," he said, and he scraped his stubble-rough face against her cheek.

"But we will miss you," she said. "And there is so much yet to say. And do."

He swiped his mouth across her lips and she strained to catch it.

"*Yes*," he rasped, burying his face in her neck. "So very much yet to do. In Hartlepool, whatever it turns out to be, we will take the time, however long. I can depend upon it, Tessa? Right?"

"Uh-hmmm," she agreed, searching for his mouth.

Joseph growled, swept away by her enthusiasm and the promise of more. He gathered her so close, he worried she couldn't draw breath, but then she was grabbing fistfuls of his shirt, wrestling him closer still. She met his passion kiss for kiss, deeper, more urgent.

Joseph swept his hands down her ribcage and beneath her bottom, pressing her to him. She made a whimpering nose and bowed in, swaying, clinging. He dragged his hands to her waist and lifted her, staggering to the stable wall. She released one hand and reached behind her, feeling for the smooth stones, but he pivoted and fell against it. Tessa collapsed against his chest with a sigh.

Joseph turned his head to break the kiss, gasping for air. "*Tessa*," he said, a plea, a prayer.

"You came every day," she panted, "but . . . never . . . once . . . kissed—"

He captured her mouth. "I didn't realize," he said, dropping his lips to her neck, "we could enjoy the privacy of the mews."

She laughed and arched her neck. "Boot rooms and stables," she said. "I'm beginning to doubt your affinity for the finer things."

"My affinity is for you, madam," he growled in her ear, "and there is no finer. Never has a woman excited me as you do."

"*Joseph*," she breathed, straining for his mouth.

"It will be my greatest pleasure to show you every finery."

"Your greatest pleasure?" she teased.

Joseph paused, reared back, and stared into her face. She looked at him from beneath lowered lashes, an expression of mischief and affection and need.

He made a strangled noise and descended on her mouth again. "Hartlepool cannot come soon enough," he said between kisses. "Not soon enough."

CHAPTER TWENTY-SIX

Tessa smelled Hartlepool before she saw it. The briny scent of cold sea and north wind hit her like a bracing slap to the face. Her eyes watered and her breath was carried away on the call of the gulls.

After ten days in a rocking coach with Perry and the baby, Tessa would be relieved to reach any destination, but she had prepared herself for the worst. Hartlepool, although not bustling or necessarily cheerful, seemed quaint and stalwart. The vast expanse of the roiling North Sea was its most distinguishing feature. Flat waves pulled back to reveal crescents of caramel-colored sand along the shore and then rushed forth to covered them up again. A thick seawall protected Hartlepool's easternmost street, and terraced lines of sturdy homes rose like inland jewels on a golden band. Tessa saw the small, tidy dockyard immediately in the center of town, its bright, unbarnacled quay walls strung with lines of loosely moored boats, mostly trawlers and schooners. Rising highest, taking up an entire jetty, was Stoker's brig.

"*He's come*," she whispered, mindful of the sleeping baby on her lap, and tears filled her eyes. Perry looked up from her book and then darted to the carriage window.

"He's come," Tessa repeated, clearing her throat. She had no idea why she was crying. She'd known all along that he would come.

"We're saved," said Perry, collapsing against the seat. Perry had not enjoyed seeing the countryside by coach and had even less interest in the seaside. "Thank God."

That from which they were "saved" was not named, but the maid seemed relieved they were able to decamp from the lurching carriage and spread across two rooms in a small but comfortable inn.

Mr. Chance, the innkeep informed them, had been a guest for two days already, although he was out when they checked in. Tessa was shown to his room by friendly staff, while Perry and Christian were settled in an adjoining room. A maid promised she would knock shortly with tea.

Tessa had not known how the rooms would be allotted when she and Joseph convened, and she tried very hard to be casual and breezy with the innkeeper, although the mere sight of Joseph's personal things—a row of coats and breeches in the wardrobe, a trunk of folded shirts and cravats, a tray of shaving articles—made Tessa's heart race. He would dress in this room. Undress. She would do the same. If she could manage it, they would have the wedding night that never happened.

She paced a small circle from a window to the large bed

and back again. She paused at a side table to examine a collection of cuff links and gloves and a stack of hatboxes. Joseph had never hidden his love of fine clothes, and he always looked so very posh and well turned out, but his wardrobe dwarfed her own. Well, it dwarfed the New Tessa's wardrobe. The Old Tessa could have happily gone toe-to-toe.

She looked down at her red velvet traveling suit. She had not burned her brown and grey dresses as he'd ordered, but she had slowly begun to bring out her old clothes. There had been little time to pack for this journey, and she'd asked Perry only to shake out four traveling suits and to pack a handful of old winter dresses still folded in parchment for storage.

She would test out the old dresses, she thought, in the same way she would test out her intimacy with Joseph. Cautiously. Hopefully. She wanted to feel safe wearing her beloved gowns, but that safe feeling wasn't guaranteed. She wanted a wedding night with Joseph—she wanted Joseph, plain and simple—but this, too, was not a certainty.

She was just about to unpin her hat and brush the creases from her hair when the door flew open and Joseph strode into the room. "*Tessa,*" he breathed.

His greatcoat swirled around his ankles, and he kicked the door shut with his boot. He looked even better than she remembered, better than he had when he'd first called on her in Berymede. She ran to him and he caught her with open arms and spun them both.

"I thought you'd never arrive," he said into her neck.

"It was an eternity. Perry threatened to resign every ten miles."

"Where is the baby?" he asked.

She pulled away and smiled. He had not said he would accept Christian as his son, not in as many words, but he was attentive and curious. It made her love him even more. "Your other room. That is, the room with the crib. He is napping, Perry is with him." She felt herself blush. She said, "The innkeep showed me to this room, and I just assumed that we would . . . I wasn't sure where you wanted each of us, but I thought—"

"I want you here with me," he growled, kissing her until her knees grew weak. "Christian can stay here or in the other room, or both. Perry should take the other room. Obviously."

Tessa laughed and drew herself closer, kissing him. They swayed together, devouring each other, hands roaming, barely remembering to breathe.

"Tessa, wait," Joseph said, breaking away. "I need to *pause*." He grabbed a handful of the bustle on her suit and squeezed. "I will require, I'm afraid, intermittent breaks."

"*No*—" she implored, clinging to him, and he laughed and staggered back. She went with him, refusing to let go. There was a chair nearby and he fell into it, taking her down with him.

"*Tessa*," he breathed, dropping his head on the back of the chair and staring at the ceiling. "I will perish from wanting you. Too late. I'm already deceased. You carry on with my ghost. But he cannot resist you either."

"You are very solid," she said. "For a ghost."

"'Solid' is putting it very mildly," he said. "But, Tessa? Neither of us should rush this. I'm determined. In this, we will require *pauses*."

Tessa studied him. He was joking, but his beautiful profile was strained.

"Did I . . . ? Have we—?" She didn't know what to ask. "Are you in pain?"

"Yes, I am in pain. But it is the most glorious pain imaginable, and I relish it. I simply need some respite on occasion. I won't toss you onto the bed and . . . frighten you."

Tessa considered the bed. She thought of being tossed. "That sounds exciting, actually," she said.

Joseph squeezed his eyes shut. "It is exciting, and we will get to that—but first, you and I will take things very slowly. We will *pause*, as I've just said, to make sure that I am always in control of my passion and that you feel very safe."

Now Tessa considered this. "And one day, I will say when we pause and when we are excited. One day, I shall be in control," she declared.

"God, I hope so," he sighed, and he kissed her again, and she realized with relish that the pause had ended, and she pounced on him.

After five minutes, when Joseph's cravat hung loose from the chair and Tessa's hair was a tangled blonde cape around them, they heard the distinctive sound of a baby's hungry cry.

"Christian excels at pauses," Tessa sighed, pressing her forehead to Joseph's.

"Well, that makes one of us."

CHAPTER TWENTY-SEVEN

Joseph helped Tessa feed the baby, and then he carried him downstairs and walked the grounds of the inn. Tessa remained inside, working with Perry to change from her traveling suit and repin her hair. Joseph had expected some challenge when he'd offered to take Christian, but both mother and maid had leapt at the offer.

To Joseph's delight, the baby seemed to recognize him from his days of calling to Belgrave Square. Tessa had pulled a woolen hat low over his head to protect him from the cold, and the infant clearly objected to this precaution. He scrunched up his eyes and swatted ineffectually at the tight, low cap with chubby fists.

"Agreed, mate," said Joseph when they were free from the women. "I avoid resemblance to a mushroom whenever I can," and he peeled the hat from the baby's head. Christian smiled at him, a genuine smile, with wet gums and eyes that were nearly pushed shut by the roundness of his cheeks. Joseph felt himself smile back.

The innkeep walked by in that moment and said, "That's a fine-looking son you've got there, Mr. Chance. Very fine, indeed. I knew when your wife arrived that it was the family you were expecting. I seen that baby, and I says to myself, 'That's the spitting image of Mr. Chance.'"

"Thank you," Joseph said, and he leaned down and kissed the top of the baby's warm, un-hatted head. Christian made his signature squawk and bobbed up and down. Something new and unfamiliar began to grow in Joseph. It took a moment for him to identify it, but as he walked away and his chest swelled and his shoulders straightened, Joseph identified it as . . . *pride*.

Christian was an alert and curious baby, eyes big on the horses in the stable, the yellow and red autumn leaves on the garden's lone tree, and most fascinatingly of all, a fat white cat with swishing tail who sat in a windowsill.

"You are smart, like your mother," Joseph told the baby as he circled back to the horses. He'd offered to have an open carriage hitched so that he and Tessa could tour the town, but Tessa had balked at the idea of riding again so soon and asked if they could walk instead. Joseph agreed and reserved a carriage for later in the week. He'd scouted a property for sale in the surrounding countryside and was anxious for Tessa to see it. He'd contacted the owners and scheduled a visit.

"There you are," called a voice from behind them.

The baby jerked around at the sound of his mother's voice.

"*Hello, Dollop,*" Tessa sang. "What have you seen with Papa?" She lifted Christian into her arms.

Joseph blinked at the intimate name, and he suddenly had trouble meeting Tessa's gaze. He had no idea how to be a father but he wanted, earnestly, to try. He cleared his throat, ready with a story about the cat, when he caught his first full view of the transformed appearance of his wife.

"Tessa," he said. It was all he could manage.

She wore a day dress in chalky blue, two shades lighter than her eyes. Her hair had been styled in two thick braids, coiled at her crown with a small blue hat perched at a jaunty angle. She wore an ivory shawl and an ivory silk pin in the shape of a gardenia on her lapel. Pearlescent leather gloves hugged her hands and disappeared into the sleeves of her dress. Tiny pearls traced her collar, sleeves, and hem. She looked like a sketch in one of Perry's fashion periodicals. In addition to the pretty dress, she seemed to step lighter, to speak with more lilt, to smile more easily. Joseph's thoughts rolled back to their first meeting on the street in Pixham. *No woman is lovelier.*

"You look refreshed," he said. Women grew weary of men who gushed. He allowed his eyes to do the gushing. He could not look away.

"Thank you," she said. "Perry is coming to take the baby. I trust he was well behaved. But where is his hat?"

"We grew weary of the hat." Joseph pulled it from his pocket in a wad. "He and I were discussing our impression of Hartlepool."

"And what conclusion did you reach?"

"We concluded," he said, "that we shall like it if *you* like it."

"This sounds suspiciously compliant."

"A father and son can comply without it being suspicious, can't we?"

Tessa went very still. She stared at Joseph.

"Does it distress you, Tessa, for me to call Christian my son?"

She shook her head. She seemed unable to speak.

"I cannot say what it's meant to feel like—when a man becomes a father. Trevor says it is a combination of worry and pride, hope and love. Exhaustion. Exhilaration. Protectiveness. And something more. Something beyond the realm of understanding."

"Yes," rasped Tessa. Tears choked her voice. "I would say this is accurate—about motherhood, at least."

"The affection I feel now for Christian seems like only the beginning of something that will grow to fill my life in ways I cannot imagine. It seems like a very large, very significant love that I find myself wanting, very much. If you wouldn't mind."

Again, she shook her head. She kissed the top of her son's hatless head. "It has been my greatest wish," she whispered. "Greater even that you would love me."

"Well, you shall have two wishes fulfilled, because I love you both. Oh, Tessa. I love you both." He bent to nuzzle her neck.

Tessa tucked herself against him and squeezed the baby. Christian made a squawking noise and began to kick. She burrowed deeper.

"By the way," Joseph said, speaking against her hair, "I've decided *not* to say those words again. *Not* until *you* say them. No more I-love-yous for you, my dear. I shall tell Christian, of course, because he cannot yet speak."

Tessa reared back. The baby grabbed the fat loop of one of her braids and she cocked her head, following the baby's firm grip. "But I do love you," she said.

"No," dismissed Joseph, working at the baby's clenched fist in her hair. "Unacceptable. Said under duress. Parroted back to me because we are discussing it."

"Stop, of course, I love you," she said, half laughing. "Christian, *ouch.* Let go."

"Perhaps you do and perhaps I do," Joseph said, finally disentangling the braid from the baby's fist. Christian wailed. "But you'll not hear *me* say it again until I hear an authentic I-love-you from you." He looked down at her and winked.

A gasp from behind them interrupted their conversation. "Why is the baby not wearing his hat?"

It was Perry, her youthful disapproval very clear. Joseph winked again and kissed both Tessa and Christian on the tops of their heads and handed the fussy baby to Perry. Tessa discussed meals and naps with the maid and then sent them on their way, but not before Perry reintroduced Christian to his hat. The baby's cries could be heard in Durham.

"The discussion of I-love-you is not over," Tessa said when she returned. "I am determined to be believed."

"Oh, I hope not," Joseph said, gesturing for her to proceed him on the sidewalk. "You must work to make up for lost time."

Tessa narrowed her eyes, studying him, and then looked toward the water. "Tell me more of what you and Christian made of the town on your walk?" she finally asked.

"He and I mostly made a circuit of the inn yard," Joseph said. "But we're told the town is grey and foggy, although the ocean views are splendid in the sun. You can expect fish at every meal, of course. Storms in November and February. *And* . . . there is a dockyard in search of a manifest clerk in their dock house."

"No!" Tessa spun to him.

Joseph clasped his hands behind his back and smiled. "Stoker, who is sulking around somewhere, by the way, learned this as soon as we'd made port and leased a slip. I checked around. There are several positions in the dock house, actually. It is not a busy port at the moment, but it holds potential, in my opinion. I will make no more presumptions or inquiries. I leave that up to you."

Tessa clasped her hands together. "Oh, I cannot wait to see it. But we should find the High Street first and get the lay of the town. Even if the dockyard holds potential, we cannot remain here if the people are miserable or the shops are depressing. What of your prospects in government?"

Joseph nodded and indicated a turn in the direction of Church Street, which was Hartlepool's main shopping street. "Could be worse, actually. The town counsel is particularly active—they are responsible for the new dock, as you reported—and several members are too old to run again. It is not out of the question. I would have to start very small since we are entirely unknown here. But that would be the case most anywhere."

"But look at the church," exclaimed Tessa when St. Hilda's came into view.

"Oh, yes, the town is in possession of an old Norman church. St. Hilda's. Built in the 1100s, or so I'm told. Hartlepool has a storied, almost ancient history with shipping, pirates, Vikings, all manner of sea farers. People here have been sending out and receiving ships for thousands of years. Well done, Tessa, if your aim was to find a spot to welcome the world to England and send England back out again. Well done."

Tessa stopped walking, shook her head, and placed a hand over her mouth. She looked so very happy. Joseph stepped back, allowing her this moment of delight; he soaked in his own pleasure, watching her beam.

After a deep breath, she took up his hand and they walked together, looking in on shops, asking questions of suspicious townspeople, and wandering through the knobby, bricked streets of the little town. They took lunch at a small café and devoted the afternoon to the dockyard.

Tessa introduced herself to a procession of stunned dockworkers, each more confused and spellbound by the beautiful inquirer than the next.

It was quickly obvious that the men endeavored to answer her questions *to Joseph* when he lurked about her, despite the fact that she made the inquiries. After the third answer was addressed to him, he excused himself and boarded Stoker's brig.

After an hour, Tessa had all of her questions answered and she and Joseph walked back to the inn. She chattered excitedly, relaying everything she had learned about ship traffic in the North Sea, the cargo and boats most commonly coming and going through Hartlepool, the usefulness of the nearby River Tees to the dockyard, and the weather in every season.

"But did you ask about employment?" he asked.

"No," she said, giving a little cringe. "I couldn't find the nerve. But I think they liked me. I believed they saw that I knew some small part of what I was asking about."

"I've no doubt they liked you very much," Joseph said.

And they've no idea that their lives are about to be forever changed, he added in his head.

And so, I hope, is mine.

Chapter Twenty-Eight

Perry insisted upon brushing out Tessa's hair and dressing her for bed like a proper lady's maid, and for once, Tessa did not resist.

For the night rail, Tessa wanted the right balance of special but not . . . overwhelming. The forthcoming evening felt overwhelming enough without a showy, provocative gown that promised something that Tessa, quite possibly, could not deliver. She finally agreed on a simple night rail in the softest pink and a burgundy dressing gown with matching pink trim. It was sweet but not girlish, fine without being overdone.

Be calm, be calm, be calm, Tessa chanted in her head as Perry brushed the creases from her long, unbound hair.

Calmness was the last thing Tessa felt. She was nervous and jittery and desperate to get her hands on Joseph. He'd been so helpful with the baby at dinner and Christian's bath. She laughed at the memory of the flowers and sweets and,

God forbid, original poetry that she'd once enjoyed as gifts from men. They now paled in comparison to Joseph holding the baby while Perry made up the crib and Tessa went to the other room to wash her hair.

Now the women had been on their own for more than an hour, and Tessa insisted on ten more minutes to rock the baby to sleep. When Christian's eyes finally slid closed, Tessa bid Perry a good-night and slipped from the room.

She paused before Joseph's door, wondering if she should knock. He'd said this was her room too. Was she meant to knock at her own door? What if Joseph was inside half-dressed? This possibility appealed to her and she reached for the door handle. In that same moment, the door whipped open. Tessa yelped and skittered back, and Joseph gave a shout.

"Bloody hell, you scared me," he breathed. "I was just coming for you." He looked right and left down the corridor. "Get inside," he breathed and scooped her from the corridor into the room.

"Sorry," she laughed, allowing herself to be scooped.

"This is why I didn't journey with you in the coach," he grumbled, locking the door. "I would expire with lust and jealousy if I had to watch you glide from room to room in your dressing gown for ten nights."

"Glide? I wasn't gliding. I don't glide."

"You were bloody floating. And your hair is glorious. You are . . . iridescent. You *radiate* in that thin silk and unbound hair and your . . . face. I've endured the tight bun and brown dresses for a month and now you're dressed like a goddess."

She laughed, looking down at herself. "You are . . . agitated."

"I am agitated," he agreed. "Excellent turn of phrase. And I need a drink." He went to a drinks trolley crowded with bottles. "One for you? Can't hurt."

He poured two glasses of amber liquid and held one out. She took a tentative sip, the liquor was warm and fiery. She considered him. He also wore an ivory dressing gown with gold brocade. It should have been lordly and stuffy but he looked very handsome. He still wore his buckskins beneath the dressing gown, but his feet were bare.

"Tessa," he began, downing his drink, "I've given a lot of thought to the way we should proceed. I want to embark on this in the most measured, cautious way. We should set out some boundaries, some *intervals*, so that we are careful to manage things slowly."

"And what if slowness only heightens my anxiety?"

"It's so very easy to leap ahead, trust me, but it can be more difficult to slow down."

"I'm not afraid of you," she said, and it was true, she wasn't afraid of him. She was afraid of spoiling this moment by discussing the life from it. She was afraid of having a cursory, diluted version of her wedding night because she'd panicked before.

But the panic had been *before*, when she'd not enjoyed the incredibly freeing experience of telling him what happened on the night with the tree. That was before he told her he loved her.

There was nothing cursory or diluted in the way she felt about Joseph.

He glanced at her, allowing his eyes to linger on the clingy silk of her gown, the loose fall of her hair over her shoulder. "There is pleasure in going slowly," he said. "We have a lifetime of pleasure at every pace."

"I'm not opposed to slowness," she ventured, wishing to sound agreeable. She wasn't fighting his technique, she was simply impatient with discussing it.

"For example," he began, "we might—"

Tessa cut him off by launching herself at him.

She'd not planned it—well, perhaps she'd planned a small part of it. It was one way, she thought, to redirect a thoughtful, long-winded prelude. She understood his desire to "pause" for her own good; but was there a less romantic phrase than "pause"? She couldn't bear to embark on lovemaking with the threat of *pausing*.

And so she had not.

She had thrown herself at him, a determined combination of the Old Tessa and the New Tessa and a Fourth or Fifth Tessa who had grown weary of talking and was so very much in love with him.

"*Tessa*," Joseph breathed, fighting for words between kisses. "This is not . . . part of . . . my plan. I'm so afraid of frightening you," he said.

"My only known fear at this moment is, 'a plan,'" she said and she jumped up, catching him around the haunches with her legs and wrapping her arms around his neck. He was given no choice but to gather her up, groaning as he pressed her to him.

"And now what am I meant to do?" he rasped.

She pulled back from the kiss. "But you don't *know*?"

He laughed, a low guttural sound, and it thrilled her. He staggered across the room, kissing her as he went. When they reached the bed, he tossed her. She landed in the center, gave a little yelp, and reached for him.

"You'll tell me," he warned, kneeling toward her, "if you need to pause?"

"Please don't ask that again."

"You will give me the time I require if *I* need to pause."

She sat up. "Why would *you* need to pause?"

"I don't," he said, and he shrugged off his dressing gown, revealing his bare, tanned, muscled chest and buckskins.

Tessa sucked in a breath.

He laughed. "But this will not be rushed, I swear to you, Tessa."

His oath was short lived. He dipped his head to capture her mouth; his body came down next, bare chest against the thin silk covering her breasts, his hip heavy against her thighs, his legs tangling with hers. The kiss grew deep and sensual very quickly, his tongue sweeping her mouth. Tessa reveled in the tingling sensation of all of his tanned muscle pressing against every soft, rounded part of her. He was so very substantial. And so very hard. Strength and beauty, sewn into a perfectly formed human male.

She was desperate to learn every part of him, and while they kissed, she set her hands to work on the planes of his back, the giant ball of his shoulders, his roped arms.

He stopped kissing her mouth and delved lower, kissing her neck, grazing her with his emerging beard, and then lower still. He used his nose to nudge open the edges of her dressing gown, laying a fiery trail of kisses as he went. He pulled back to stare down at her, and she felt the coolness of the room on her neck and shoulders.

"Alright?" he asked.

She nodded. "I want my dressing gown off." She sat up and he smoothed the burgundy silk from her shoulders, massaging her arms as it went. She shivered in her bare pink night rail and felt the instinct to cross her arms over her chest, but she resisted. She was brave, she wanted this. She had just leapt at him, she'd just explored his body with voracious hands. She wanted this.

He leaned on one elbow and propped over her. "I want to touch your—"

She cut him off. "I don't want to discuss each body part before it's called into question," she said.

"You're certain?"

She nodded her head.

"Right," he said, and while she watched, he dropped his gaze from her face and stared at the deep rise and fall of her chest. Slowly, ever so slowly, he raised his hand. She watched it hover above her breasts. And then he extended one finger to the thin silk between her breasts and traced a slow line in between.

Tessa sucked in a breath.

He drew the line back up, tickled beneath her chin, and traced it down again, lower this time. The third time, he traced the line with two fingers, grazing the sides of her breast when he passed between them. After tracing up and down with two fingers, he lifted his hand away.

Tessa gasped and looked at him. *Don't sto—?*

He smiled languidly and looked at her with half-lidded eyes. "Again?" he asked.

She nodded and reached for him. He allowed her to wrap her arms around his neck but he would not be pulled down. He remained above her on his side, slowly, deliberately, pressing two fingers to the pounding pulse beat between her breasts. Again, he began to trace a line between. This time, his finger circled beneath the swell of first one breast, and the other. Just the outline. A half moon that grazed the silk that contained her breast.

Tessa heard a moan and realized it was her own fevered response. Her body burned. Her breasts strained against the pink silk. Her world shrank to his hand and she felt herself bow up in the bed, rising to meet his finger. "*Please,*" she whimpered.

She thought she heard him mumble *thank God*, and he dropped his palm over her breast and descended on her mouth.

The kiss was secondary to the sensations swirling through her, and she fought the distance between them, struggling to pull him closer. He dropped from his side, rolling on top of her and rocked slightly. Tessa broke from the kiss and made a little gasp.

"Alright?" he panted, and she answered by repeating the same motion, rocking up to meet him. He groaned and returned to her mouth. She grabbed him by the face, slid her hands into his hair, holding him to her.

By some instinct, she pushed his head to her throat, and lower still, to her neck. He knew what she wanted and closed a mouth over her breasts through the silk. Tessa cried out with pleasure. Joseph moaned and worshiped her breasts with his tongue.

His hands circled her waist, traced her hips, and massaged the muscles of her thigh. Her left leg was pinned beneath him, but she drew up her right leg so he could trail the shape of it all the way to her curled toes. Joseph obliged, tickling the skin beneath her knee with the silk of her night rail. He hesitated when he reached the hem of her gown and then he traced one finger around the bone of ankle.

When Tessa felt the bare skin of his fingertip touch the bare skin of her leg, she froze.

Dark grey nighttime filled her vision.

A cold chill descended, submerging her in icy fear.

She tore her head to the side and gasped.

"Wait," she said in an airy, petrified voice.

Joseph froze.

Chapter Twenty-Nine

"Tessa?" Joseph said carefully. "Love? Tessa? You're alright. Breathe, Tessa, you're alright."

She rolled away from him and dropped her arm over her eyes. Her eyelids were squeezed shut but tears spilled out, streaking her cheeks. She held her breath until she felt light-headed and then gasped for a breath. She drew her legs up to her chest and pressed her face into the mattress. The residual desire strumming through her clashed with her panic, and she felt sick. She willed the nausea away and reached for the anger. The pity. The hate of Captain Neil Marking.

Anything but the panic. She'd promised Joseph she would not panic. She was not, by nature, someone who panicked.

Rage won out, and she gritted her teeth and squeezed herself more tightly into a ball. She would squeeze until she was a hard, impenetrable seed. She would bury herself deep in the earth this the cold autumn, incubate all winter, and then explode to life in the spring.

But who could wait until spring? Not Joseph? Not herself. She wanted to be sensual and affectionate and *herself*— her daring, reckless, carefree self—*right now*.

Oh, she was so very angry.

Angry at herself for succumbing to the fear, angry at Neil Marking, the bastard who had given her Christian but who had taken away parts of herself that she had liked very much. He'd distorted her love of beauty and poisoned her hope for sex.

"I'm sorry," she said softly, so softly she could barely hear it. The irony was that she sobbed so loudly in her brain.

"No," Joseph said carefully. "No apologies. We simply try again. When you are ready. We can have quite a lot of fun trying again."

Tessa considered this. The calm casualty of his tone called to her. She opened her eyes. She was buried beneath a tangle of her hair. She straightened one leg, and her gown rode up. She felt the cool air of the room on her exposed leg. Joseph would see that leg. Likely Joseph was staring at her leg right now. She considered this. It did not bother her. She quite liked her legs. She *wanted* him to see them. She wanted him to see all of her and for her to see all of him, but she could not predict when the panic would set in. She unfolded the other leg.

"Next time, however," Joseph went on, "we will do it *my* way."

"We will discuss," she said sourly.

"We will discuss, we will touch, we will taste, we will go in stages. And when we feel panicked, we will not allow it to undo us. Not me, or you. We will try again."

She rolled over and stared at him. He was lying flat on his back, his hands behind his head, lecturing to the ceiling.

He turned his head on the pillow and looked at her. "Remember when you revealed the details of the . . . attack, and I ran mad? Vaulting down the stairs and threatening murder?"

She nodded.

"*That* is my version of what you are doing now. I don't pretend to have suffered the same trauma that you did. You endured the attack and I merely heard you describe it. But madness carries us away in a manner that feels hopeless, and sometimes we require someone else to reel us in. To say, 'All hope is not lost.'"

"It might be lost," she said softly, but she thought *I love you*.

He said, "After you have experienced what I have in mind . . . after we have succeeded in this . . . you will not describe yourself or the process as lost for hope."

"You are too good to me."

"I love you," he said.

She sat up, smiling in spite of herself. "I love you, too," she tried.

He shook his head. "Nope. That was a reflex. You merely answered me. It doesn't count. This resets my vow not to say it again until you do."

She fell against this chest and held him. *I love you, I love you, I love you*, she cried in her head.

"But, Tessa?" Joseph mumbled, his lips against her hair, "now we should sleep." She had collapsed on his chest and he could feel the wetness of her tears on his skin. "We will try again tomorrow night. We will try again my way."

"No, we should try again now."

"Now we have taken ourselves too far, too quickly. I feel like an oaf and you are miserable. We will have another go in the morning."

She looked up. "In the morning?"

"Part of my nefarious plan is to leave you wanting more, anticipating the next bit, and you are not safe at any hour. My goal is to make you, er, *burn* so to speak. We want the burn to be hotter than the fear."

"It is," she insisted.

"Not yet. But it will be."

"And you?" she asked.

"Darling, I have already incinerated. I am the charred remains of a man who walks around in a whole man's clothes. Beneath them, I am smoldering, blue ash."

"I'm sorry," she whispered and Joseph swore in his head. He did not wish to make her feel blame.

"No apologies," he said. "This will be fun."

This will end me, he thought, but he kissed her and rolled her gently onto her back and gathered her in his arms and held her until she fell asleep.

Sleep, however, evaded Joseph. He thought of the so-called "captain" who attacked his wife, the worthless rotter, and what he would do to him should they ever have the misfortune of crossing paths. He thought of Tessa, how brave and enthusiastic she was, so gainfully willing to sort this out, despite her fears. A lesser woman might have sworn off sex forever. This made him think of sex forever with Tessa—and of the most fortuitous, positive way to bring it about.

He had passed the journey from London devising a series of lovemaking techniques that he would explore with her. The result, he hoped, would be either a breakthrough of her panic or his own expiration. The contemplation (alone) of the techniques had made the journey to Hartlepool the most sexually frustrating voyage he'd ever made, and he was bloody grateful it had only taken four days.

Then Tessa had arrived, and he'd known a new level of frustration as they toured the town and met with the dock-workers and waited for night to fall. When she'd finally come to him, he'd allowed her to distract from his slow, careful seduction because she'd wanted so earnestly to take the lead.

Chief among everything else were her consent and owner-ship of their intimacy, so he'd gone along.

Also, he could not resist her. He'd wanted it to work just as badly as she had.

But now they'd leapt too far ahead and returned right back to where they began.

This can be done, Joseph thought, finally drifting into a deep, dreamless sleep.

Tessa awakened some hours later, overwarm and tangled in her gown. She fumbled with the burgundy silk, desperate to be free. Joseph was stirred by her movement and slid, word-lessly, from the bed to shuck off his buckskins. When he climbed in beside her, long legs bare, Tessa swam through the bedsheets to latch onto his side, curling her legs around him, reveling in the access to him, *all* of him, warm and languid and heavy.

He turned to her, eyes still closed, and she swiped a kiss across his lips. He made a mumbling noise, and she kissed him again. And again. The fourth time, Joseph locked his arms around her and kissed her back, slowly, lazily. When he finally came up for air, he found her ear and whispered, "Tessa? I've a game for you. Do you like games?"

Immediately, her heart kicked into a sprint. She nodded.

"Lovely," he rumbled. "The game will start tonight, right now if you like, and it will continue for . . . as long as we like. Days, at least, perhaps longer."

His voice was low and gravelly, a sensual, sleep-ragged voice, and she felt his lips moving against her ear. Every cell in her body came urgently awake. She dug her fingers into his shoulders.

"The game is played when I designate one beautiful part of your body to touch, and if you allow it, and I am going to touch it, and only it, for five minutes, without stopping."

"Oh," she said against his throat. This sounded . . . promising.

"But please be aware," he went on, "I will not grope. I will not tussle or fondle or tease. It will simply be my hand. Gently there. The pressure. The warmth. The steadiness. It will be a slow and steady warming up."

"Will you touch me on the outside of my clothes? Or beneath?"

He considered this. "What do you think?"

"'Tis your game."

"Well, some parts that I have in mind are not obscured by clothing. Others are. Considering our ultimate goal and the reason we play the game—"

"My panic," she provided.

"Your *freedom*," he corrected. "I should think we will begin *outside* your clothes. But not your heavy winter coat. I mean more like this beautifully thin night rail." He grazed the silk on the curve of her hip with the back of his finger. "How does that sound.?"

Tessa thought about this. "Honestly? It sounds . . . boring. Not what I expected at all."

"Yes," he mumbled, nipping her bottom lip. "It will be ever so boring." He kissed her in earnest.

"You will simply touch me, unmoving, while I lay still for five minutes?"

"Well, if you are a very good girl, after *four* minutes, the steady touch may evolve into something like a caress. But this is not guaranteed. We will have to see."

"What if I say you may move? What if my mind has drifted, or I'm overwarm, or I have an itch?"

"Your *distress* is the only reason I will move away—which we both know to be a possibility. Less possible will be boredom or an itch. Heating up, I'll wager, is guaranteed."

"Oh, how very sure of yourself you are," she teased, but she would be lying if she said the notion of his game did not thrill her.

"Quite sure," he said. "And, after a time, likely when I

cannot endure a moment longer, I will slide my hand away. Only after these minutes of my touch, and only if you wish, may we revisit the area with any movement that might, er, interest you."

"And after that?" asked Tessa, her voice was a rasp.

"After that we shall go to sleep. Or we will carry on with our morning. Or our carriage ride. Until the next bit of your body is called into question."

"The *carriage*?" She raised her head.

"When we are alone, of course."

She thought about this. If she was excited by the prospect of making love in the bedroom, she was positively fascinated by the notion of a moving carriage. She glanced at Joseph. He was sprawled casually across the bed, playing with a lock of her hair. So very cool and collected. She narrowed her eyes suspiciously. Did she see a jumping pulse in his throat? Was he breathing heavily? She walked her fingers across his bare chest and flattened a palm over his heart. The beat *thundered*.

"Will we . . . kiss during this exercise?" she asked.

"If you like. But that is *all* we will do while I touch you. Or that is all *I* will do to you. You may do with me as you please. I invite you."

Now the game was taking shape in her mind. She thought of Joseph's large, calloused hand, the heat, the pressure. She thought of him working to hold very still—this had been his rule—while she kissed him. She smiled to herself and nuzzled her body against him.

"Alright," she said softly, swiping a kiss across his bicep.

He cleared his throat and shifted.

She pulled closer still, nuzzling again. "But shall we begin now?"

Another noise in his throat. "I thought you'd never ask."

Chapter Thirty

The hand-by-hand journey of Tessa's body began that night and extended four days. Taken as a whole (or in parts), it was an agonizingly delicious torture that Joseph had never known.

He began with her neck. He spread a gentle, cool hand from her jaw to her clavicle, and he kissed her. She laughed at first, she complained about ticklishness, but soon she was nuzzling in to his hand; a minute later, she was tugging at his wrist, willing him to do more. After four minutes, she was writhing beside him, begging him to engage his fingers, to caress, to touch her anywhere, everywhere.

He tried so very hard to be cool and languid and in control. Sensuality would be lost if he was cautious or trembly or behaved as if he had no idea what he was doing. Still, when four minutes had passed, and he could finally trace the line of her throat with this his fingertip, his hand shook. He was so very determined. He wanted to reclaim her neck, exactly the spot where that blackguard had pinned her to the tree. With determination and love, he seared a new, sensual, safe memory where a terrible one had been.

In the morning, he gave the same treatment to her bare breasts—one hand spread from the peak of one to the peak of the other. She was shouting his name and he was panting audibly before the minutes were up.

In the days that followed, in stolen moments when they were not exploring the town and County Durham, when they weren't laughing over meals or caring for the baby, he laid hands on the pulse point of her wrists, her raised knee on the outside of her gown; he touched the underside of the swell of her bottom while she lay on her stomach. And eventually, he touched the very center of her.

By design, he would save her ankle for last.

Through every other part of her body, never once did she panic, although she did moan in sensual frustration, she begged, she squirmed, she lifted off the bed. She loved and hated the sessions, and he regarded them with the same polar ferocity.

By the day they were meant to ride into the country to view a potential future house, they were both drunk with need. The dreaded, pre-lovemaking discussions had all but disappeared. They fell against each whenever they were alone, hands hungry, lips open, bodies surging.

As Joseph suggested, carriages were not exempt from this behavior. Carriages, in fact, were one of their favorite settings. Something about the light of day, the gentle sway of the vehicle; they were upright (or partly upright), he could reach all the way around her body, and there existed a new level of naughtiness. Tessa said this made her feel bolder, less like a pupil and more like an explorer.

By Joseph's calculation, they had "explored" every significant part of her body except her ankle. After that, he hoped she would be ready to endeavor the ultimate expedition of more traditional lovemaking. . . . possibly with some culminating end.

Joseph, honestly, had stopped thinking about when and how much and—and, well *when*. To think about it was to experience buckling knees, lost train of thought, and conversations paused in the middle. It did him no favors to think of how much would happen when.

Honestly, he couldn't believe that he still walked upright.

Instead, he explored his wife's body just as he promised, one beautiful, slowly awakening part at a time.

CHAPTER THIRTY-ONE

Tessa wore a dress the color of crushed violets for the carriage ride to the potential new house. Joseph had stopped dead when she'd bustled out in the ensemble, staring in open appreciation. She had smiled and glowed in satisfaction, discussing the care of the baby with Perry. It had felt so very gratifying to wear her old gowns and hats. She walked taller, she spoke in a voice that felt more like her own; and the appreciation in Joseph's eyes made her feel desired. The months in the drab browns and greys had made her feel as if she was slowly disappearing from view.

The decision had been made to leave the baby with Perry for their journey to see the potential new house. They'd brought him along on several of their previous rambles, but Joseph was so very excited to show her this mysterious property. Tessa looked forward to seeing it with no distractions.

"Is it far?" she asked, settling beside him on the carriage

seat. She would prefer their future home to be close to the dockyard.

"Not far. A twenty-minute ride. You can see the sea from the topmost room."

"Top room?" she asked. "Joseph, this doesn't sound like a cottage."

"'Tis a cottage. Says it, right in the name. Abbotsford Cottage."

"It has a *name?*" Tessa knew what to expect from houses with names. Berymede was a prime example, and one of the finest estates in Surrey.

"Of course it has a name, how else should we find it?"

"How *have* we found it?"

"We asked around about property for sale until we were tipped off to it. The sellers have a sentimental attachment to it and wish to meet prospective buyers in person. They were not available until today."

"And you've seen it?" she asked.

"From horseback," he said.

"What if the buyers don't care for us?"

"And what would they not love about the two of us?" he asked. "Beautiful wife, shipping-merchant husband with political aspirations. Adorable baby."

"What if they discern your sordid history?" she teased, snaking a hand around his arm. "What if they believe you to be an upstart former servant?"

"Then I shall say I am an upstart former servant and show them the size of my purse," he sighed, stretching out and tipping his hat. He closed his eyes. They were both exhausted.

Not-making-love took quite a bit of time they would have otherwise spent sleeping.

Tessa marveled at the patience and skill with which Joseph had approached her struggles to be intimate. Of course, she knew very little of the lovemaking habits of other couples, but in her mind, she thought she had possibly been shown the very worst of sex by Captain Marking and the most glorious by Joseph.

Still, there had been one thing he had not thought of that she thought might, possibly, make the enterprise more . . . Well, one thing that she hadn't been able to remove from her mind for many weeks.

"Joseph?" she asked when the carriage left the bricked streets of the town and bounced onto a tree-lined country lane. "May I tell you something that I like?"

He opened one, interested eye. "Yes," he said slowly, suggestively.

She narrowed her eyes. He would indulge her, she knew, whatever it was, but he would make her *say it*. So much of sex with him was *talking* about it.

"I like it . . ." she began, feeling herself blush. She couldn't look at him. She gazed out the window.

"Yes," he drawled, still reclining on the seat. He lazily closed his eyes.

Her heart was pounding, a reaction that he, undoubtedly, discerned. She cleared her throat. ". . . that is, I *liked* it when we were in Vauxhall Gardens, and you chased away those young men, and your accent—that is, the way you spoke— sort of . . . *changed*."

Joseph opened the lone eye again. "Changed *how?*" he asked.

But perhaps she could not *say it*. She made a noise of frustration. "Don't bait me, Joseph, you know I am damaged and fragile and just . . . er, learning."

"You are not damaged or fragile and you know more than most women who have been married all of their lives." Both eyes were open now, although he was staring at her with half-lidded casualness. "You're being shy on purpose, but if you want me a certain way, I should like to hear it."

She tipped forward and stared at her purple leather boots. "Your voice was, er, rough? It was, not the voice of a gentleman. That is, you spoke in a way that I'd never heard—from you." She could feel herself blush to the tips of her ears, but she pressed on. "It was as if . . . It was the way I assume you spoke before you were educated? Before you were a gentleman. When you were in Greece, perhaps, with Falcondale. When you were—" She lost heart and trailed off.

"Oh, *that* voice," he teased slowly, and then he sat up and snatched off his hat.

"I knew it," he drawled. "Trevor accused me of imagining it, but I've known it all along." He tossed his hat to the opposite seat and grabbed Tessa in the same movement. He pulled her into his lap, tickling and dipping her back. She yelped and then slapped a hand over her mouth, mindful of the driver.

Joseph kissed her hard—once, twice—and then dropped his lips to her ear. "I knew the gentleman's pretty daughter harbored some fantasy for the strapping servant from below-stairs."

Tessa laughed again, squirming in his lap. "It's not true," she said. "I'd not even heard your original accent until you fought off those men at Vauxhall Gardens." She broke free enough to kiss him, a quick buss of her lips, but he captured her mouth in a long, slow, languid kiss. She let out a little sigh, sinking in.

"I don't believe you," he declared when she finally broke away. "I saw a spark of interest in your eyes the very first time I mentioned the upstart story of my upstart life. On that first walk at Berymede. Admit it. It excites you." He dipped to nuzzle her ear, and she shivered.

"Well, perhaps it is a little true," she consented. "Did no small part of you fantasize about seducing the gentleman's daughter?"

"Believe me, love, there's a very large part of me that fantasized about it, and still does," he whispered in the other voice, the voice she'd heard only at Vauxhall. He surged against her, and she made a little whimpering noise.

"But is that what you want?" he growled into her ear. "Now? For our last beautiful bit of your beautiful body? In this carriage?"

She was breathing hard, her hands clinging to fistfuls of his jacket, but she shook her head. "You've said it's only a twenty-minute ride."

"Want the full hour, do you?" he asked again in his other voice.

She laughed and slid from his lap, straightening her dress. "If the cottage interests us, it will be very poor form to turn up with my hair undone and your cravat ruined. You've said the sellers are sentimental? Very poor form."

"Tonight then," he said. "*Love.*" And he retrieved his hat and rested it over his eyes, resuming his slouch.

Abbotsford Cottage was a fourteen-bedroom, Elizabethan-style manor house with ballroom, nursery, music room, detached servant's quarters, and walled garden with fountain. It had two high towers (no longer in use but architecturally striking), an arcade wall of arches, and a circle drive paved with crushed stone.

It was, in Joseph's view, as striking as Berymede, if not lovelier. This should not be a priority, he knew, but it was.

"Oh, Joseph," Tessa breathed as their carriage crunched up the drive. "Joseph, this is far, far too much." But her voice sounded awed and wistful and grateful. *This* had also been a priority. That Tessa would love it.

"Not bad for a stable boy, I submit," he teased.

"Stop, I wish I'd not said anything." Her eyes had not left the house.

"You will not wish that after tonight," he promised but she had slid the carriage glass to the side and leaned from the window, craning for a better view of the house.

They were greeted by the owners themselves, a shipbuilder with a shipyard in nearby Brancepeth. Sir Thomas Park and his wife Lady Winnifred were selling the house to relocate to London to be closer to their grown children. But they had devoted their marriage and child-rearing years in Abbotsford Cottage and could not bear to sell it to strangers who might allow it to fall in disrepair or build on in a way that jeopardized the historical integrity of the original structure.

After introductions and chitchat about the journey, Joseph allowed Tessa to take over. Her natural charm and vitality made every corner of the grand house seem like her new personal favorite. Her questions were thoughtful and flattering, her manner warm and well-bred. She behaved like the queen.

When Joseph asked for a few moments alone to discuss the property with his wife, Sir Thomas led them to the garden.

Staring down into the fountain, Tessa asked, "Joseph, be honest. How can we afford it? It's far too much. It's grander than Berymede. It's as grand as Willow's home, Leland Park."

"Do you like it?" he asked.

"Of course, I like it. But there is upkeep, there are servants—a veritable army of servants for a house of this size—there is fuel for fireplaces and lamps and candles. We had discussed a cottage."

"It's called Abbotsford Cottage."

"I am aware of the name. I'm also aware that I'm standing in the garden of a full-blown *estate*. Please tell me you would not bankrupt us to buy this because you think it will impress me."

"Are you impressed?" He put one shiny boot on the ledge of the fountain.

"Of course, I am impressed. But I was happy living in a cellar with two other women, a baby, and a goat. This is unnecessary. But I do love you for it."

"Nope," he said, "unacceptable expression of love. It rings false when you say it in response to this gift of a small castle. Keep trying."

She laughed and shook her head. "It *is* possible to hurt my feelings, you are aware? You can only toss this sentiment in my face so many times, before I will be forever wounded."

"What if I told you that I do believe that you love me?"

She looked at him thoughtfully. "I suppose I would ask you *why* you believe it."

"Well, perhaps there are many reasons, but chiefly, firstly, because I was terrible to you and despite that, you wanted me back in your life. After I abandoned you. Not only did you want me, you made it possible for our brig to make landfall. You tried to correct things. Why would you do this, if you did not love me?"

She smiled gently, a sweet, gratified smile not for him, just for herself. He watched her, enjoying her pleasure. He'd gotten it right, then. He wanted everything he did to be right for her. She stared into the gurgling fountain and he drifted beside her and put his hands on her waist.

"Joseph?" she asked softly. "Have I told you how very sorry I am—for the way I handled our days at Berymede? For the deception and the entrapment? I was desperate and afraid and I wanted you so very badly, but that's no excuse. I should have risked losing you by telling you the truth. That way, you would never doubt, even for a second, that I married you . . . for you."

His heart expanded, straining against the confines of his mortal body. He pulled her against him and nuzzled her neck. "I forgive you, Tessa. My dearest. And I *do* believe you love me, but I shall never, ever grow weary of hearing you try to say it."

"I'm not *trying* to say it. I *am* saying it. I've said it many times."

"Fine. Trying to say it exactly right."

"Oh, perhaps I should use a different accent? The poshest pout of a gentleman's daughter?"

"Now there's a promising notion," he said, trailing kisses along her jaw.

She sighed, by all signs enjoying his closeness, the texture of his lips and face, the smell of him; but then she glanced at the windows of the house and pushed him away.

"The sellers will toss us out if we are . . . inappropriate. But perhaps that's what you want. Perhaps my fears about this house are warranted. We've seen it, we've been naughty beside the fountain, and now we will be asked to leave—and what a lark it was. Is that what you intend?"

"What I intend," he said, "is to buy this house. Immediately. So I may carry on beside the fountain however I please. The money is not a concern, Tessa. You'll remember a small investment of £15,000 in dowry money? This is your net gain. And myself, of course."

He was about to tell her that he loved her, that there was

a part of him who relished the opportunity to buy an ostentatious house for his beautiful wife, but Sir Thomas and his wife bustled into the garden, leading a contingent of servants with tea trolley and trays of food.

"I hope you have time for tea," called Lady Winnifred, trapping them with the tea trolley and a scrum of servants who assembled a table and chairs.

"Oh, how lovely," Tessa trilled. "You are too kind."

"Sir Thomas and I have had a bit of a chat, and it's all decided," said Lady Winnifred, beginning to pour. "You *must* join us for dinner tomorrow and stay the night as our guests. We've dear friends visiting from Durham and a few other dignitaries from the county. Our cook is doing up a special meal. You'll be too full to trundle off back to Hartlepool after the fun, so you may stay as our guests. It will give you some idea of how the house entertains, and you may sleep beneath the roof, walk the halls, and learn its secrets. I know you must have grown weary of that cramped, musty inn in town. They do a passable venison stew, but I'll wager they've already run out of summer vegetables, and one does grow so very weary of turnip."

"Our friends are active in the Whig-party politics, Mr. Chance," said Sir Thomas, "one gentleman and his son in particular would be good men for you to know."

Joseph shot Tessa a look. *It's up to you.*

Tessa beamed at the couple. "We would be delighted," she said.

Chapter Thirty-Two

After much deliberation, Tessa consented to leave the baby with Perry at the inn for their night at Abbotsford Cottage. It would be her first night spent away from the baby since his birth. Perry had insisted that she and Christian were more comfortable at the inn. Certainly, there was far more room than the cellar in Belgravia. And Christian was deliriously in love with the innkeeper's cat.

"We must get a cat for Dollop when we settle down, wherever it may be."

"A cat and a goat," said Joseph. "And a horse. As soon as he is able to ride. I want all our children to ride."

Tessa loved hearing him talk about Christian as if he was his own son, but the mention of other children caused her to turn away. Even after a week alone together in an inn bedroom, after hours of intimate moments steeped in sensuality, her marriage to Joseph had still not been consummated.

The night before, she'd lain very still and quiet while he'd casually wrapped his large hand around her ankle. She had not cried out. She had not leapt from the bed. But, unlike all the other parts of her body, his touch on her ankle had been met with silence and stillness. She had been . . . stoic. It had taken all available strength not to cry out.

She had not been able to kiss him, she hadn't laughed, she hadn't explored his body. She hadn't burned with need for him and begged him to *do more—do anything more!*

She'd simply lain there, her heart pounding, her mind spinning, willing herself to carry on with four anxiety-ridden minutes of his warm, casual hand wrapped around her left ankle.

When Joseph saw her reaction, he had endeavored to withdraw. He'd never meant to experiment if she appeared unhappy or, God forbid, in distress.

But Tessa had felt the value of each of the other times he had touched her, and she saw the value especially his hand on her ankle. Joseph was slowly replacing the small ownership taken by Captain Marking and giving it back—first to her. Second, if she allowed it, she would share possession with Joseph, who, after he moved his hand, would return with tickles and tweaks and massages that drove her mad with desire.

All the while, she had been distracted by the joy of exploring his body, marking it and possessing the beautiful expanse of his muscle and heat, to call it her own.

"I believe my ankle is a problem," she'd told him, "because the moment the captain touched my ankle, I knew what was to come." She said the words into the darkness.

"I was finished," she went on. "Ruined. A rough kiss or even a tussle in the woods would have been unpleasant, but I could have recovered. When my ankle was under his control, when he bent my leg, I was powerless. It was the beginning of the end."

"We will get past it," Joseph had said against her hair.

But Tessa struggled to see how. The obstacle of the ankle was that it was the first thing Marking's hand found when he'd delved beneath her skirts. How could she ever forget the cold, terrifying realization that a man—this formerly dashing man—was clawing his way up her body from below?

"The beginning of the end," she had repeated and fallen asleep.

She'd awakened to Joseph whistling, fresh and hopeful; eager to see Abbotsford Cottage again. She could not remain downtrodden when he, denied so long, was cheerful and eager to spend a night in the beautiful home he wished to buy for her.

They arrived to Abbotsford Cottage in time to take another tour of the house and change for dinner before the other guests arrived. The house was as Tessa remembered it, grand but not opulent; a piece of history but also a home.

Ever aware that the sellers were auditioning them in the same way they considered the house, Tessa was generous with praise and open about the ways she might style the house if it became hers.

It was easy to be enthusiastic about the property—she had loved it at first sight—but even so, she struggled to focus. Her lack of attention felt like a betrayal of Joseph, who all but rubbed his hands together in anticipation over the library, the ballroom, the solarium. She wanted to enjoy it with him, but honestly, Joseph was the source of her distraction.

The longer the day wore on, the more determined she became that tonight their lovemaking *would* happen. Enough had been . . . well, *enough*. Her demons, surely, had been exorcized. She'd carried on, wounded and nervous, until she'd grown weary, even of herself.

It was fun (and useful) to enjoy Joseph claiming one part of her body at the time, but then they'd hit the barricade of her stupid ankle and Tessa wanted to rail at the sky. An ankle wasn't even one of her naughty bits. She refused to allow her anxiety to stand in their way another night.

She, Tessa St. Croix-Chance, once formerly the most notorious flirt in Surrey, *would* be bedded by her own husband. Tonight. In this beautiful home. With no baby in the next room. And no Perry to face in the morning. She would put the past to rest, satisfy Joseph (who had been so very patient), and satisfy herself.

The first step, she thought, was to look her very best. After the tour, Tessa reminded Lady Winnifred that she'd traveled to the house without a maid. The lady kindly provided a woman from her own staff and sent her up to assist.

The middle-aged maid arrived promptly and said almost nothing compared to Perry's constant chatter. She styled Tessa's hair simply, in a high, loose bun at the back of her head, with wisps of blonde dropping around her face. She was fastening Tessa into a cherry-red evening gown glittering with tiny iridescent crystal beads when Joseph let himself into the room.

"I'll finish," Joseph said to the maid. "Thank you, that will be all." The woman bobbed a curtsy and disappeared from the room.

"You look too good to leave this room," Joseph said, coming up behind Tessa. He dropped a kiss on her neck and she shivered.

"My mother adored this dress. It was never my favorite, it's stiff and uncomfortable, but it makes a statement." Tessa fidgeted, trying to find the most comfortable way to tolerate the sharp beads. She gave a kick of one leg, then the other, jostling the layers of petticoat that tangled around her legs. She caught sight of a red slipper beneath the hem, and she had the thought. An idea.

She slid her foot from beneath the hem again. She smiled. It was a simple idea, really; easy to carry out, pure in its own way.

While Joseph did up the buttons on the back of her dress, Tessa traced a half circle with the toe of her slipper on the carpet, like a ballerina. Crinoline scratched against the silk of her stockings. The beadwork cut into the skin beneath her arms. She had never once removed this dress without a network of tiny scrapes marring her skin from the embellishments.

Why hadn't she thought of this before?

The idea would have to wait until after dinner, of course, but she could whet his appetite. She could tease him, just a little, as he had done to her when he'd introduced his "game."

The idea of this thrilled her, and she was determined, suddenly, to bring her idea from theory to conjecture. She gave her skirts one final shake and reached for her ruby earbobs.

"Joseph?" she called casually. He'd drifted away to study the bookshelves.

"These novels are all about hauntings," he said. "Do you suppose we should take it as a bad sign?"

"Joseph, look at me."

He turned and blinked. "You are stunning. You are the most stunning creature I have ever seen."

Tears shot to her eyes. "Your compliments thrill me, I hope you know this. But I wanted your attention to tell you . . ." she crossed to him ". . . that I love you. *So* much." She raised up on her toes and kissed him softly on the lips.

"I love you too," he breathed. "But what prompted this declaration?"

He gathered her up. "You hate the house. Not large enough. Too large. No goats. No room for your parents and brothers."

"Tonight," she said, cutting him off, "we will make love. *Depend* on it." She wiggled free of his embrace.

He raised an eyebrow. "Do you mean . . . at dinner?"

She fastened her second earring. "*After dinner.*"

He paused. "Tessa."

She glanced at him.

He continued, "Do not pressure yourself into doing something for which you're not ready. It could set us back— and for no reason. Really, there is no rush."

"We've been married for nearly a year. It's hardly a rush to make love ten months on."

"You imagine the rush. We have a lifetime."

"We have tonight, and why shouldn't we? I am a prodigiously sensual woman. Or I used to be."

"*You are*—but sensuality was never the problem."

"I've grown weary of being a problem."

"That's not what I meant, and you know it."

"Know this," said Tessa, turning back, stalking to him. "I'm in love with you, I am undone with desire, and I am a woman who takes matters into her own hands."

"Oh, you are?" His eyebrows raised. He tugged on the lapels of his dinner jacket. He looked suddenly more interested.

"I am. When I wanted you for my husband and the father of my baby, I made it happen. When I wanted to kiss you, I did it. I kissed you in the boot room, and in the stable at Belgrave Square, and on our first night in the inn."

"I know that makes me sound suspiciously passive, but you realize how important it felt to allow you to initiate things," he said.

She waved this comment away. "Tonight, I want to consummate this marriage; and I shall make certain it happens. I am *initiating*. You've been warned."

She spun and stalked toward the door.

Joseph enjoyed Sir Thomas's dinner guests very much.

That is, he enjoyed them in as much as he could enjoy any strangers at any meal when he was preoccupied with the promise—threat? vow?—to expect sex with his wife.

And not just any promise/threat/vow. Tessa had come to

him with confidence and fire in her voice, with a spark in her eyes that lit the languishing fuse in his own. He tried to prepare himself for possible reconsideration, for a goodwill attempt that resulted with something less than sex, for fatigue, or missing the baby, for a stomachache.

And yet, he could not wipe the look in her eye or the mettle in her voice from his mind. It lodged in his chest and caused his loins to throb.

His wife hadn't asked, she hadn't hinted, she hadn't even *teased*. She'd informed him in no uncertain terms. Sex tonight, in the giant bed of the beautifully appointed guest suite.

Dinner, therefore, felt very secondary. He comprehended very little of the mealtime conversation. The guests were a father and son, Mr. and Mr. McMillan, and the son's wife. As Sir Thomas promised, both father and son were active in Whig politics in the area and informed him of men he should meet and lower offices that might, in coming years, be an easy win for a newcomer.

Excellent, good, what a lucky coincidence, he'd said again and again. Are we to pudding yet? Was it rude to encourage the men to forgo port and cigars?

Meanwhile, Tessa seemed unhurried and unfazed. She dazzled Sir Thomas, Mrs. McMillan, and Lady Winnifred with stories about Christian and, eventually, with her interest in the dockyard. Sir Thomas promised to introduce her to the Hartlepool dock master, a man he claimed to know well, and to recommend her if, as he put it, ". . . Joseph permitted Mrs. Chance to seek some role in the dockyard."

Joseph had been listening with one ear and he winked at his wife. It was a pity that such fortuitous news carried an addendum about Joseph's perceived "permission," but Tessa did not challenge him. She knew as well as Joseph that, if they smiled along, Sir Thomas would sell them his house, make the dockyard introductions, and then hie off to London, never to bother them again. Eventually, Tessa would show every man in town the role of Joseph's "permission" when it came to her employment.

After an exceedingly lengthy dinner, Lady Winnifred asked if Mrs. McMillan might play the pianoforte. The younger woman declined because she had suffered a burn to one of her fingers, and Joseph had never been more grateful.

He was just about to claim exhaustion and ask to be excused when Tessa asked if she might have a go.

Or not, Joseph thought, suddenly intrigued. He did love hearing his wife play.

Lady Winnifred accepted and Tessa hurried to the piano, settling her waterfall of fuchsia skirts over the small bench. Joseph lowered himself into a chair. He postponed his accelerated enthusiasm for *after*, and allowed himself to sink into the beauty of his wife at the keys of a piano. He narrowed his eyes. His gaze traced the curve of her waist and bottom. He promptly forgot the other guests, who sat primly around him, waiting for a minuet or waltz. He licked his lips and reveled in the next best thing to going to bed with his wife.

The composition that followed, a sonata, began with a soft prelude, like the first drops of rain. The notes rose, like a good, soaking shower. After that, she pounded a thunderous, drapery-trembling crescendo that threatened to shatter windows and take down beams. Her playing was like a storm, rolling through the cavernous house.

Joseph swallowed hard, aroused by the theatre of her playing and the drama of the sound. He watched the rise and fall of her shoulders, the sway of her body over the keys. Her delicate slipper on the pedal reminded him of a tongue darting out every fifth beat.

He shifted in his seat and glanced around the room. Maids and footmen had gathered just outside of doorways to listen. Sir Thomas and his wife and the elder Mr. McMillan stared at Tessa with disbelief and at the pianoforte with concern. The younger McMillans, Joseph was relieved to see, looked thoroughly entertained.

Bloody right you are entertained, he thought. When it was over, he clapped politely—clapped *ironically*, considering the insufficiency of the five other members of the audience. Their feeble clapping was laughable after the verbosity of her performance. Tessa, he saw, did not care. She rose from the bench, gave a little bow, and shot Joseph a flushed, hot look.

Joseph coughed, and then called out, "Well done, darling. *Well done.*"

After the performance, it was no surprise that their hosts began to suggest fatigue and ". . . overstimulation."

Well done again, Joseph thought.

The McMillans excused themselves and Joseph and Tessa soon followed, climbing the curved staircase to their appointed room in the guest wing.

Beyond pleasantries and praise for the meal to the hosts, Tessa had not spoken since her tumultuous recital. She rested a calm hand on Joseph's arm and allowed him to lead her.

His pulse, still elevated from her sonata, kicked up again. The same confidence he'd seen before the meal was also in the hand on his arm; it was in her enigmatic silence, her straight back and raised chin.

Excitement coursed through him, and he blew out a breath. He'd been in a near constant state of arousal since they'd convened at the inn in Hartlepool; and that said nothing of the previous eleven months, when he'd fallen in love with her twice but not taken her to bed once.

When they reached the bedroom door, she said, "May I have five minutes? Lady Winnifred is sending her maid to assist me."

"Right," he said, and he pretended to study a row of paintings down the corridor. When the maid arrived, his heartbeat kicked up yet again. Blood coursed through his veins at an invigorating, almost lightening rate. He heard his pulse in his ears.

When he heard the door gently click shut and he saw the maid descending the stairs, Joseph let out an audible breath. His loins grew heavy and tight. He rolled his neck and reminded himself that nothing was an inevitability. He would not perish if they tried, and tried, and tried again.

His hand shook as he knocked twice on the door. He tried to call out, but his voice broke like a youth. Swearing in his head, he pushed the door open and stepped inside.

The room was dim, lit only by the fire and a lone candle beside the bed. He squinted, his eyes adjusting to the darkness. He shut the door. He called out again. "Tessa?"

He scanned the room, giving full attention to the dark corners and curtained window seat. He squinted at the fire.

And then his body turned to stone.

Tessa stood beside the grate fully and completely unclothed.

CHAPTER THIRTY-THREE

Lady Winnifred's maid had not batted an eye when Tessa had told her she'd wanted unfastened from the red dress and stripped naked. Her host may have been shocked by Tessa's pianoforte concert but perhaps nudity in the guest suite of Abbotsford Cottage was not an uncommon thing.

A good omen, Tessa thought. Abbotsford Cottage would likely be her future home and she quite liked the idea. She couldn't believe they'd not thought of it sooner. If Tessa was unnerved by Joseph's hand rising in her skirts, why not simply remove the skirt? Why not remove it all?

She had barely positioned herself beside the warm glow of the fire when Joseph knocked twice and stepped into the room. She did not, thank God, have time to second-guess. She simply laced her hands behind her back—why play timid now?—raised her chin, and waited.

Joseph froze when he saw her. No metaphor could do justice to his expression. He looked exactly as if he'd opened the door onto an unexpectedly naked woman. Shock, then captivation, then enterprise. It was all chased with a very little bit of uncertainty, but enterprise prevailed. He *understood*. And he was immediately complicit. He paced three steps, stalking her, and then paced three back. He looked at her through narrowed eyes, he looked again and again, devouring the sight of her.

She allowed it. Her hands remained behind her back. She thrust out her breasts and he stopped walking.

"You're certain?" he asked.

"Certain," she said. "But I should like us both to be naked. Will you do it? So that we both—?"

"Yes."

He hopped on one foot and tugged off a boot. The other boot came next. After that, his jacket, cravat, waistcoat, shirt, undershirt, buckskins, drawers—all shed in a matter of seconds.

He stood tall and tan and muscled some five feet from her, his clothes in a heap on the floor. He was painfully aroused and Tessa allowed herself to study him in the way he had studied her—in the way he studied her still. She had touched every part of him during the past days, but she had not *seen* his body.

It was a work of art; the body of a Greek god.

The music she'd played after dinner, Chopin's "Nocturne Op. No. 2" in C sharp minor, rolled in her head, and she was emboldened to move first.

But he moved, too, they reached out in the same moment, and their bodies made impact like the sun meeting the horizon at dusk, smoothly, gracefully, unstopping.

Tessa felt warm, restricting muscle where she usually felt breeches or shirt; she felt his arousal against her belly without the barrier of her gown. She felt, and nuzzled, and kneaded. She rubbed against him like a cat. She raised her mouth across his skin and tasted.

Her senses were awash with him. The smell of his soap, the taste of skin, the sound of his breathing. She saw him only in flashes of the jumping firelight; his mouth descending, his hands brushing the hair from her shoulder.

Yes, she thought. *Yes.*

No talking, no stillness, no *caution*. No dancing around the edges. No *clothes*.

Why had they not done this sooner?

"It was a mistake," Joseph panted, "not to do this sooner."

"Everything has led to this," she soothed. "No mistakes."

He slid a hand down the dip of her waist and cupped her bottom, lifting her slightly and pressing her to him while he made one, delicious thrust of his hips.

Tessa's mind stopped. She'd felt precursors of this, moments of pressure that threatened to overwhelm her, to carry her away, but they had been mere flashes compared to the bright light of pleasure. She could only anticipate the *next* thrust. Surely there would be a next? She bowed her body, reaching . . . and there it was, he thrust again.

Tessa moaned into his mouth and he answered with her name.

When he pressed again, Tessa's knees threatened to give away. She wobbled, and Joseph lifted her and carried her to the bed. She felt his muscles strain as he endeavored to lower her down slowly, to bow her back like a tree branch, bent by a gentle wind.

But then she wrapped her legs around his haunches, and his strength failed him. He dropped her onto the bed and came down on top of her. The weight of him made her want to fall and fall and fall.

"Tessa?" he breathed, kissing her shoulder, her clavicle, her breast. "Alright?"

She nodded, pulling his lips back to her breast. He growled and kissed her again.

"You are more beautiful than I imagined," he said. "And I imagined your beauty quite a lot."

She should thank him, Tessa thought. She loved his compliments. She never felt more beautiful than when he told her she was a fantasy or a goddess or the prettiest woman he'd ever known, but she was rapidly losing her ability to follow simple thoughts. Speech in this moment seemed like a terrible use of her mouth and her brain. She wanted only to suck in breath, and feel, and press her mouth against any tanned or muscled (or tan *and* muscled) part of him that occasioned her lips.

Her body had begun to move of its own volition, to press up, to seek, and she was too lost to sensation to ask or consider or sort it out, she wanted only to let it go, to press and find what she sought.

"Tessa?" Joseph moaned. He sounded strangled. "Tessa?"

"Ye—?" So much talking, he was always talking.

"Tessa, love, you mustn't move like that. I won't be able to—*Tessa . . .*"

Oddly, *this*, her brain was able to follow. A plea. A *no-please-yes* from a man who was finally losing control. Was it unfair, she wondered, to agitate him, to entice and kindle and *move* when he'd been willfully touching her, bit by bit, until she was wild with desire for the last two weeks?

And furthermore, was it so very bad that it would be difficult for him to . . . ?

To . . .

Even in her fevered state, she knew the end of that sentence was *stop*. If she encouraged him, it would be difficult for him to stop.

"I don't want you to stop," she said. "Please, Joseph, don't stop. . . ."

"But we—" he panted, and then kissed her, the ultimate manifestation of "we," or rather the *prelude* to the ultimate "we."

"We've waited too long," she told him, turning her head to breathe. "We've teased and gone slowly and resisted and now we will lose control." She found his mouth and kissed him hard. "And we will revel in it."

Likely one earnest, restrictive moment had built on the next, and they had reached this point through days of smaller moments. But now they'd arrived, and she wanted nothing more than to thrust against him, and the more he tried to ask her to stop, the more she wanted to do it.

"Tessa, I'm serious," he rasped, and he tried to raise up from her.

She clawed him back, pulling his shoulder, his hair—an ear—whatever she could grab hold. She squeezed her legs around his haunches like a vice. He could not rise up without taking her with him.

"Tessa, are we—?" he gasped.

"Yes," she sighed.

"But are you . . . ?"

She opened one eye and stared up at him. His face was a mask of agonized restraint. And love. He looked down at her with such love. Her heart burst. "Please, Joseph," she said, tossing her head on the pillow. "Please now."

Joseph let out a curse, and he rolled them to the center of the bed.

"Loosen your legs," he said. His voice was low and rough.

"But I—"

"*Tessa*," he pleaded, and a heightened jolt of pleasure zinged through her. "I can't maneuver with your legs around me. Relax. Can you relax?"

Slowly, Tessa let her legs drop and untangle from his body. The new position felt open and vulnerable; the smallest current of unease snaked up her chest and into her throat.

No, she thought, it wasn't panic, it was simply the no-turning-back acknowledgment of what was about to happen. What she *willed* to happen. What she wanted.

Joseph detected her hesitation and leaned down. She raised her lips, thinking he would kiss her again, but he went straight for her ear and began to speak lowly, gravelly, in his other voice, the voice he'd had before he'd become a gentleman.

The words he said were inconsequential. Praise, encouragement, just a little goading, but the tenor of his familiar voice in the unfamiliar accent ignited her, and within moments, she was fighting for his mouth, begging for a kiss. Her body bowed up of its own volition, seeking, open and on fire.

When her breathing turned again to panting, when she strained against him and begged, he said an oath in a language she didn't understand and repositioned his legs. Tessa whimpered, resenting every time he pulled away, but then he was back, reaching between them. She felt his hand, felt his arousal, felt him pause . . .

She opened her eyes. He was poised above her, looking down, his eyes half-lidded but dilated to midnight.

"Do not ask," she said. "Do it. Please, Joseph, do it."

With an oath, he sank into her. Tessa made a little cry. The sound of that cry was different from her previous, lust-soaked cries, and the sound yanked her from him for the flash of a second. Her consciousness hovered somewhere between her daily life and this moment in time. On one side, she wore clothes, stood upright, thought logical thoughts; on the other, she was naked, prone, and in carnal throes with her husband.

If she tipped her thoughts toward everyday life, she would acknowledge some pain, she would realize considerable awkwardness, and she would possibly feel some panic.

However, if she tipped the other direction, she would ignore the pain, embrace the fullness and the weight and the union; and she would, possibly, maybe, perhaps, reach that very insistent . . . whatever-it-was that her body had been seeking so very hard. *For days.* But especially tonight. It was the urgency that kept her rising off the bed, an unattainable burn that needed just a bit more of . . . something.

Tessa tipped toward that something, her brain dropped back into the numbing sort of want that produced moans and sighs instead of questions and answers. She allowed every other thought to be chased away.

Above her, Joseph was very still and very breathless. He was so still and breathless, she thought he'd turned to stone.

Tessa opened her eyes to smile at him, to tell him she knew what came next, that she wasn't afraid, that he should *move*. But his eyes were closed. He wouldn't even look at her. He held his breath and squeezed his eyes shut and *endured*.

Tessa would have laughed except she'd made the conscious choice to not think too closely about it. Instead, *she* moved. Just a nudge. The movement felt fine . . . actually the movement felt rather promising and she moved again, more forcefully this time. More promise. She moved and she moved, and she watched Joseph's eyes spring open and lock with hers. And she raised her eyebrows—*this is a real thing that we are actually doing*—and he let out a guttural growl that sounded like the eleven months of pent-up desire being set free.

And then he took over. Tessa closed her eyes, lost to the rhythm and the sound of rushing blood and the burning rush coiling in her body.

And then the great coiling burn detonated within her, a spiral of sensation, every note on the piano played wildly and perfectly at the same time, and she lost herself for a moment, she went limp, she floated, she sank, she bobbed to the surface. Her body sang.

When she opened her eyes, Joseph had thrown his head back and cried out, another guttural release after months and months of separation and doubt and restraint. And then he called her name and collapsed on top of her, and she wasn't certain, but she thought there was a chance that he wept.

We've done it, she thought. She smiled at the ceiling of her new house. No other man entered her thoughts—no other time or place. Only her love for Joseph Chance and the strange journey that had brought them to this moment.

CHAPTER THIRTY-FOUR

Joseph awakened with only one thought on his mind. *Again.*

Again and again and again until I perish of making love to my wife.

It was a selfish thought, because he had no notion of how Tessa would feel about her boldness or his aggressiveness or any other part of their lovemaking, and one successful night did not mean they had solved her anxiety forever. He thought of the thing he had told her many times before.

We have a lifetime.

He was on the edge of the bed, his back to her, but could feel her warm and snug behind him. He rolled over, careful not to crush her, and watched her breathe in and out. Her hair was a long net of blonde over the half-moon crescent of her naked body.

"I can feel you watching me," she whispered without opening her eyes. She slid her leg to entangle with his.

"I will never grow tired of watching you," he said.

"What would you say if I said I want another go?" she said. She opened one eye.

His body, already aroused, surged. "Yes," he said, "I would say yes." He waited.

"With clothes."

"Alright," he said. He reached out and grabbed her wrist.

"And possibly . . . outside."

"You're joking," he said. He gave a tug, pulling her in for a kiss.

She laughed and shook her head. "I want to vanquish every demon. I want to make love upright. Outside."

He paused in his kiss. "Now you *are* joking. Hardly my style, Tessa. Although I shall happily take you on a guided tour of my style. Er, *styles*."

"Oh, I'm well aware of your styles. 'Pausing'—for one. Stationary hands on specific body parts . . ."

Now he growled and rolled over once, pinning her beneath him, and then rolling again and taking her with him. She yelped and flopped on top of him. He grabbed her hips and squared her over his arousal.

Her eyes went wide. He raised his knee and tipped her forward. Her hair rained down on him and her face hovered just above his.

"What'ya say, love? On top? Can you manage?" He used the voice of the Old Joseph, who was really the Young Joseph, the much younger man he used to be, the boy with whom he thought he'd been finished—and good riddance. Now, he was so very glad to have him on hand.

"Love?" he repeated. "How's about a kiss?"

Tessa made a delighted noise, a delighted hungry noise, and Joseph captured her mouth with a kiss and held her against him and thought there was never a man more fortunate than he.

Chapter Thirty-Five

Four months later. . . .

Tessa was alone on the day she reencountered Captain Neil Marking, except for Christian and his new nursemaid, Jeanie. They were in Hartlepool, walking from the dockyard to Church Street.

If the weather was fair, Tessa had Jeanie bring the baby into town by carriage to meet her at the dock master's office when her work was finished. The three of them would walk to a café and take tea and then travel home to Abbotsford Cottage before sunset.

It was a stretch, perhaps, to say the weather was fair that day. The cold of winter had settled in along the villages of the North Sea held them tightly in her icy grip. December had given way to the sleet and snowfall of January. But there was neither rain nor sleet today, merely cold sunshine, and Tessa bade Jeanie bundle herself and the baby and make the trip. Joseph also had business in Church Street that afternoon, and his partner Stoker was in town—he would sail back to Barbadoes with a hold full of coal Tessa had arranged herself. The baby would be asleep by the time dinner was served at Abbotsford, and she wished to show him off, despite Jon Stoker's alleged unease around babies.

Tessa snuggled more deeply into her fur-lined overcoat, bouncing Christian on her hip as she walked along Hartlepool's thick, barnacle-frothed seawall. Dollop remained a large baby, growing larger every day, but Tessa insisted on carrying him. They'd spent the day apart, after all, and Dollop thrilled to the sights and sounds of the ocean, which were much easier to see from his mother's arms than the deep bowl of his pram. Behind them, Jeanie pushed the empty baby carriage and hummed.

The red wool of an officer's coat was the first thing to catch Tessa's eye.

She'd never quite gotten over her visceral reaction to the bloodred coat of any soldier in the Royal Army. Long after every other anxiety had begun to fade away, Tessa still startled when she encountered a red-coated soldier. Her insides turned to ice, and she had to remind herself to breathe, to look away, to walk on.

But today, enjoying the rare full sun and the bracing sea wind, Tessa saw the crimson coat on a man in the distance and she did *not* look away.

Today when she spotted the red and gold, the braids and buttons, she looked harder. She stared and took a few more steps and stared more.

There was something about the line of his shoulders stretching the wool. Something more about the way the man in the jacket had propped his hand against the side of a distant building and loomed over someone, a girl—

Tessa took two more steps closer and squinted. Was it a girl? Did the soldier with the broad shoulders and the propped arm lean over a young, pretty girl with her face turned up and a bright, hopeful smile?

Fury and purpose spiked inside of Tessa like birds launching for the sky. She spun around and tucked Christian in the empty pram.

"Jeanie, will you locate Mr. Chance at the Mallet and Mole in Church Street and tell him to come here, to me, at the seawall? Tell him its urgent. And then please keep back. You and the baby remain far back. Do you understand?"

Jeanie, who was biddable but also smart, nodded and wheeled the pram around, hurrying away.

Tessa turned back and glared at the stain of the red coat against the grey bricks. She continued to walk. With every step, she thought about the months of shame she'd endured; about believing she'd invited the attack, that her own vanity had lured and teased and been impossible to resist.

She thought of the white-knuckle fear she suffered when she discovered she was with child, the guilt, the certainty that her parents would not recover from the shame.

And then she thought of Joseph, whom she'd almost lost because he'd believed she'd used him.

Her life had been saved, saved by her own ingenuity and the will to discover some other life for herself and the baby. And saved by Joseph, who forgave her, who insisted that there was nothing to forgive, who loved Christian as if he was his own son.

But this had all been chance and providence and the love

of two people with so very much love to give. Easily, so easily, her life could have taken another route. How many young women, she wondered, had been attacked and abandoned?

When she stepped close enough to hear the sound of his voice, his laugh, his signature low whistle, she *knew*. She would never forget the sound of his voice—or *voices*. He'd used one voice when he'd called on her and danced with her and walked her home from the village, but another voice to say sickly sweet, nonsense words in her ear while he attacked her. A third voice had been used to tell her she was a Very Bad Girl and to turn her away with a slammed door. She knew them all. For months, these voices had been phantoms howling in her nightmares.

Here today, Captain Neil Marking seemed to be employing his charming, conciliatory voice. His daytime voice. Tessa could just make out the young woman looking up, dazzled, of course, at his handsome face. Tessa continued to come.

As she approached, she prepared herself to see Christian's eyes, Christian's chin, Christian's smile. When she was close enough to make out the fine details of his face, he would be more than familiar, he would be features and mannerisms that made up her beloved son.

By luck, his head was turned, and his profile betrayed nothing. Black hair was the only sign that this had been the man who had, in his only generosity, given her Christian.

When she drew close, close enough to hear his ridiculous platitudes, to hear the reedy tenor of his voice, Tessa called out.

"Neil?" she said.

Had she ever referred to him as Neil when he had courted her? She'd employed the formal "Captain Marking" because it made her feel young and him feel important, and he'd never once offered for her to call him by his given name, even when he attacked her.

"*Neil?*" she called again.

He looked up. His first glance was general appreciation. A pretty blonde woman in a pretty blue coat had called his name. But then he realized that she didn't smile and her voice was hard and bored. And then he looked at her, really looked at her, and recognition dawned.

"Step away from that girl," Tessa said.

"I beg your pardon?" he laughed. He glanced down at the girl who leaned beneath him against the wall. He winked.

"Miss?" said Tessa. "I would warn you of this man. He is not what he seems."

She took another step and another. She bore down on them, and she wasn't even a little bit afraid.

Marking shoved off the wall and straightened to his full height. Tessa raised her chin. The fire inside her roared, fueled by indignation and purpose.

The girl was frowning at her and Tessa said, "Take heed. I know he is dashing and kitted out, but he is a liar and a betrayer, and he is very dangerous. Go home to your family."

"Dangerous?" said the girl. "But he is an officer in the Army. He is sworn to protect us."

"He is a predator," Tessa said. "And he protects no one but himself. You look like a bright girl—pretty, curious, clever. Take my advice, run far away from this one, as fast as you can. And warn your friends. He should be in prison, not the Army. There are other boys in your future; honorable, decent boys. This man has no honor. He is indecent."

The girl looked at the captain. His creamy skin had gone red and he bit off his gloves with terse, angry jerks. She looked back at Tessa, who did not flinch.

"Begging your pardon, sir," the girl said, bobbing a curtsy. She curtsied to Tessa, too, and fled.

"You are pathetic," said Tessa. "That girl is fourteen if she is a day."

"Perhaps I've grown weary of old bags like you," Marking said. He spat in the spot where the girl had been.

Tessa snickered. "If only you'd grow weary of every girl, so womankind would be free of your abuse."

"Oh *right*, I remember why your tail is so bent in a twist," Marking said, snapping his finger. "Tess. It's Tess, isn't it?"

She did not answer.

"You had a brat. The last time I saw you, you were crying on my doorstep, accusing me of getting you with a bastard. You, who'd been *asking for it* from the first moment I met you. You remember that, Tess? You remember the way you laughed at everything I said, the way you touched me *just so* when we danced? Do you remember *asking for it*?"

"What I *remember*," Tessa said, "is a man ten years my senior, who saw something pretty and happy and shiny and thought, 'I'd like to have that beauty and shine for my own.'"

"*Stop*," he drawled. "I gave you the thrill of your life, I'll wager. You don't look worse for the wear. Expensive coat. Nice boots. Fur hat. Feast for the eyes, actually. Figure's held up. I'd say whatever I gave you was good training. Not to mention, one of the best nights of your life."

"No," she said calmly, "you gave me fear, abandonment by my family, heartbreak, and an innocent soul for whom to provide. Would you like to know what I did with all of it?"

"No," he said, "but I've a suspicion you're going to tell me."

In the distance, Tessa heard a shout. Someone called her name. "Tessa!"

Joseph.

Tessa did not look. She held out a hand. *Not yet.*

She stepped closer to Marking. "What I did was, I released my family, I conquered my fear, I learned a trade that fulfills me, I found engaging employment in a new town that I adore, and I fell in love. I am happy. I am so deliriously happy. And I wanted you to know."

"Well," he said, "you're welcome. All because of me, is it?"

"In *spite of you*, you worthless snake. Keep away from that little girl. Do women of the world a favor and stay away from us all. You're small. You're pathetic. And you have terrible breath."

She had the small satisfaction of seeing a look of horror pass across his face. Likely the only barb to hit its mark, but she'd not approached him to make him come around. She'd approached him to take back the final piece of herself that he'd stolen the night against the tree.

She paused, staring into his pathetic face for a long moment, and then she turned and strode in the direction of Joseph's voice. Her husband hovered, along with Jon Stoker, some ten yards away. There was a loaded, coiled bent to his posture, the stance of an animal waiting for the unlocking of his cage. There was a wildness in his eyes, a look she'd rarely seen but she knew. God help Neil Marking because of that look. Joseph did not reach for her when she approached him, but she had known he would not.

She raised her eyes and gave one casual nod of the head.

Yes. That is him.

Without a word, Joseph began stalk across the road to the man in the red coat, Stoker jogging to keep up.

Jeanie stood on the sidewalk where the men had waited. The nursemaid watched their progress with a gloved hand shading large, fascinated eyes.

Tessa did not turn around. She looked at the young woman. "Don't be alarmed, Jeanie. The red-coated man is a criminal with an outstanding debt to Mr. Chance. Can you still see them?"

The nursemaid's face brightened with interest. "Oh yes, I can see them quite well."

Tessa leaned over the pram to fuss with the baby's hat. "Can you tell me what they are doing?"

"Oh yes," began Jeanie dramatically, "Mr. Chance has taken the man by one arm, and Mr. Chance's friend has taken him by the other, and they've dragged him around the wall, out of sight. And oh!" the nursemaid went on, titillated, "Mr. Chance has yanked off his cravat and tossed it in the sand."

Tessa nodded, taking up the handle of the pram and pushing toward Church Street. "Right," she said. "Some days, he does not require a cravat."

EPILOGUE

One year later. . . .

Living so close to the ocean was nothing like living near the River Thames and even less like living in Surrey.

The weather was unpredictable and dramatic, the smell of salt and brine was ever present, and there were boats—oh so very many boats. Brigs and schooners, steamboats and ferries.

The fledgling dockyard that Tessa discovered in Hartlepool was on the cusp. It needed only the demand of Yorkshire coal—which the railroad voraciously provided—and a smart, efficient dock master, which Tessa soon embodied. Under her unlikely management, Hartlepool became one of the busiest and most prosperous ports on Britain's east coast.

While some boats left, heavy laden with coal, others arrived with old friends. After the row with Captain Marking, Stoker set out for Barbadoes; he returned again the next summer with a third shipment of highly sought-after guano. In November, he set out again.

When Stoker had gone (and the dates of his departure triple-checked, as always), Sabine booked passage on a London steamship and visited Hartlepool. The Boyds had taken a holiday to Rome for the winter, and she planned to celebrate Christmas at Abbotsford Cottage with Tessa and her family.

Cassin and Willow visited often, although not by boat; the new railway from Yorkshire meant a journey of three hours. Cassin and Willow typically stayed only a day or so, but when Sabine came for the month, the earl and countess made a rare extended escape from their castle hotel so the ladies could enjoy a reunion. Sabine, Willow, and Tessa, the three Brides of Belgravia, together again.

"I've a letter for you, Sabine," Tessa said, reaching across her desk. "Before he sailed, Stoker asked me to give it to you."

The three women were gathered around the fire in the library that Tessa designated as her office at home. Outside the window, snow fell on the garden fountain, frosting it like a wedding cake.

"Oh, right. Thank you." Sabine snatched the letter and tucked it beneath her skirts. She took a prolonged sip of tea.

Tessa and Willow shared a look.

"You and Mr. Stoker seem to carry on quite a lively correspondence," suggested Tessa. She raised an eyebrow. "That is, for people who take such care never to interact in person."

Sabine looked out the window.

Willow said, "And for people who also happen to be *married*."

Sabine turned back, smiling. "Try if you must, but I'll not

be baited. We were meant to never see these men, remember?" She pointed a finger at Willow. "*You* promised. You said we would advertise for them and give them our dowries and then never bother with them again. I can't help if the two of you spoiled the plan by falling in love. Jon Stoker and I have simply done as you promised. *We're* going by the designated rules."

"*You*," said Willow, "are hiding."

Sabine shot her a look. "Yes, I am hiding. Hiding at a known address in a public city where I receive frequent mail from the man." She waved the letter in the air.

"But what does he write you?" asked Tessa.

"Oh, it's nothing personal, if that's what you think. He's being hounded by an old man in Mayfair who claims to be his long-lost father. When it is convenient, I run errands pertaining to this man's harassment and pass along information to Stoker."

Both of the women gasped. Willow said, "But I thought Stoker's father was a mystery, even to him. According to Cassin, he wears his illegitimacy like a badge of honor. Is he not thrilled? Is it *harassment* to be contacted by a long-lost father?"

Sabine tucked the letter away again. "The old man wants money, I believe. Likely he would never have sought him out if Stoker had not become a millionaire." She made an expression of distaste. "He's an impoverished aristocrat from what I gather." Another shrug. "The forgotten Duke of Something or Other."

"*A duke?*" asked Tessa and Willow in unison.

Sabine stared at her lap, refusing to say more.

Tessa and Willow shared another glance but decided not to press. When Sabine wished for them to know, she would tell them.

Suddenly, Sabine looked up. "You've been getting a significant amount of mail in Belgravia yourself, Tessa." She nodded toward the letters she'd stacked on the corner of Tessa's desk.

Tessa frowned. "Oh, yes. Those. I will read them eventually. I'll have to shore myself up before each one. They've sent as many to Joseph's address in London, and they are forwarded here. He reads them first to prepare me. I'm not sure why we bother, it's always more of the same."

Tessa's parents had learned of her lavish estate in County Durham and Joseph's wild success with the guano importation. Not long after, the letters began. In one note, her mother had even referenced Tessa's work in the thriving Hartlepool dockyard. They wrote, after all this time, to apologize and request a new peace. To meet the baby. To make amends.

"Because of the money—as with this man 'hounding' Stoker?" Willow asked.

Tessa shrugged. "Certainly the money and the house has not hurt." She stared into her teacup. "We did not hear from them before the house or the dockyard success."

"But will you see them?" asked Willow.

"I haven't decided," sighed Tessa. "So many of their values would have to be amended. I could not tolerate one ill word said against Christian—not one word of judgment, not even a sidelong glance. But they send gifts. Joseph has learned that they discuss me with their London friends as if there is no rift at all." She laughed without humor. "'Rift' is a generous word for what exists between us."

"If they mean only to exploit your success to impress their friends," said Sabine, "then why would you forgive them?"

Tessa nodded. "In the end, I'm less concerned with what they want or why and more about the effort it takes for me to remain angry. I am the one who suffers when I hold such bitter resentment so close to my heart. It takes work to polish and shine an old hurt all these years."

"What does Joseph say?" asked Willow.

A knock on the open door interrupted their conversation, and the women spun.

Joseph, holding Christian, and Cassin crowded the doorway.

"Joseph *says*," said Joseph, "let us eat and put this baby to bed. I've an important announcement to make, and it calls for food and wine and friends—and no babies."

"Yes, babies!" said Christian, throwing his hands in the air.

Tessa's friends looked to her, question in their eyes.

"Twenty more minutes, darling?" Tessa asked.

"Right," said Joseph. "Then you may enjoy Dollop for those last twenty minutes. Cassin and I will embark on the wine." He stooped to release Christian, and the toddler waddled to his mother and crawled in her lap.

Tessa kissed the top of his head and spun him to face her friends. "Go," she said, waving the men away. "Twenty minutes more. Will you send word to the kitchen?"

"Papa," Christian informed the two women smiling at him. He pointed at his retreating father.

"Quite so," said Sabine, grabbing his tiny foot. "And what great announcement does your Papa have for us tonight? Why such a fuss?" She glanced up at Tessa.

Tessa tried and failed to hide a smile. "Hold on to your purses, ladies. Mr. Joseph Chance is about to make a run for Parliament. But *shh*. Please don't let on that you know. He wished it to be a surprise."

"Tessa! How exciting," enthused Willow. "You'll not manage to keep your parents away now. A son-in-law in Parliament? But I'm glad you told us. Naturally I assumed you would announce another baby on the way. My confused stare would hardly be the reaction Joseph expected."

"Oh, well," rambled Tessa, blushing just a little. She squeezed Christian until he squawked. "There is *that* announcement as well, but even Joseph does not know it. I was going to tell him tonight. After he'd had his moment crowing about the campaign."

"*Tessa!*" said Sabine, leaping from her chair to hug her. Willow crowded in, forming a circle embrace of three laughing-crying women and a bucking toddler.

"But when will it come?" asked Sabine.

"Would you believe it? I know the answer this time," said Tessa. "In mid-May, just as Christian did. But we will do everything differently this time, won't we?" She kissed Christian's furry head. "Papa will be here, Mama will know what she's doing. And we'll have a big brother to help."

"Brother!" said Christian, and the women laughed. Tessa

clamped a hand over his mouth. "*Shh*, Dollop. But can you keep a secret until tomorrow?"

"Secret brother!" said Christian.

Sabine sat back in her chair, crossing her arms over her chest. "Right you are, Christian. I just love a secret baby, don't you?" She winked at her friend.

"Not as much as we love strangers who marry and part ways," said Tessa. She raised a brow. "Only to meet again."

Sabine narrowed her eyes.

"Meet again!" parroted Christian, hoping to elicit another laugh from his mother and her pretty friends.

Which they did.

All except for Sabine, who merely smiled and looked away, fingering the sealed letter tucked beneath her skirts.

Discover Sabine and Stoker's
road to love in

YOU MAY KISS THE DUKE

On Sale February 2019

ABOUT THE AUTHOR

USA Today bestselling author **CHARIS MICHAELS** believes a romance novel is a long, entertaining answer to the question, "So, how did you two meet?" and she loves making up new ways for fictional characters to almost not meet but live happily ever after instead. She was raised on a peach farm in Texas and gave tours at Disney World in college but now can be found raising her family and writing love stories from her screened-in porch in the mid-Atlantic.

Discover great authors, exclusive offers, and more at hc.com.